PRAISE FOR ROSE M. JONES

AN EXCITING, PASSIONATE, ENTHUSIASTIC author, Rose M. Jones writes with a unique personal style of conversation, using plain, simple language that is easy to read and understand. The author has an intimate feel for the characters of the story, enabling the reader to connect emotionally with each one. You laugh with them, cry with them, and experience each incident as if you were there with them. You will become a part of their lives.

A devoted author with an evolving writing career, Rose M. Jones is deeply committed, and she is one author to watch for in the future. Be sure to seek upcoming books by this author.

—JD La Bor,
Retired veteran teacher of thirty-one years

Mildred

The Bird Lady

Sean and Diane,
May you find your passion in life!
Rose M Jones

Mildred

The Bird Lady

ROSE M. JONES

Light Messages
Torchflame Books

Durham, NC

Copyright © 2021 Rose M. Jones

The Bird Lady
Rose M. Jones
rosejones.author@gmail.com

Published 2021, by Torchflame Books
an Imprint of Light Messages
www.lightmessages.com
Durham, NC 27713 USA
SAN: 920-9298

Paperback ISBN: 978-1-61153-403-0
E-book ISBN: 978-1-61153-404-7
Library of Congress Control Number: 2021909328

ALL RIGHTS RESERVED
No part of this publication may be reproduced, stored in a retrieval system, or transmitted in any form or by any means, electronic, mechanical, photocopying, recording, scanning, or otherwise, except as permitted under Section 107 or 108 of the 1976 International Copyright Act, without the prior written permission except in brief quotations embodied in critical articles and reviews.

Unless otherwise indicated, the names, characters, places, events and incidents in this book are the product of the author's imagination or are used in a fictitious manner. Any resemblance to persons, living or dead, or actual events is coincidental.

For Seby (Chip) B. Jones Jr.,
my husband, my friend, and my partner in crime.
Thank you.
The Journey begins with the first step.

AUTHOR'S NOTE

EVERY HUMAN BEING ON THE PLANET has three things in common: the date of their birth, the date of their death, and the dash between the two. The dash is what defines us, makes us unique, special, in our little quirky ways. It defines our character, our moral compass. It is the lasting mark we leave behind.

I began writing in religion class at Cape Fear Community College, which is located in Wilmington, North Carolina. I was told to write a short story to be published in the school-sponsored book. When I began to write, I found myself lost within my characters. My short story became so long that it was rejected. My professor, who happened to be a rabbi, told me that my writings were truly exceptional, and that I needed to keep going. Even though nothing came of that particular story, he planted the seed that eventually produced this book into existence.

A few classes later, I ran into another professor of biology, Daniel Norris. He was having an unveiling of his new novel. I was instantly inspired again to write. He told me that if I wanted it bad enough, it would happen. He gave me great tips on writing techniques and told me to visualize it being on TV. To write exactly what I saw. It gave me a new perspective to where I could see my words and feel my words as I was writing. It took me a few more years to grasp the information he bestowed upon me, and then it happened. I began to write again.

Then, at the University of North Carolina of Pembroke—studying for classes, writing papers, taking tests—my writing had to take a backstage to my degree. With every paper turned in, each professor said I should write a book because my writing was so unique. Again, inspiration struck, and so I wrote more. Before I knew it, the characters were coming to life, full of personalities. One of which is The Bird Lady herself.

I heard the voice of The Bird Lady through an eccentric lady that married me and my husband. Rev. May Craven, with her drawn-out Southern dialect, would captivate everyone in the room. I found that I yearned to hear her next words, which were most Godly and poetic in nature. I heard her say "Oh, child," with her slow Southern mannerisms, and my heart was instantly comforted. The Bird Lady was right in front of me. Her refined character and Southern voice that was most liquid and smooth, inspired the very essence of my main character, The Bird Lady. The book took off and became a life of its own.

The actual book took several years to write, because life happens when you least expect it. I found writing to be a luxury. Hurricanes and floods—most common with coastal North Carolina living—became challenging. With running a business and juggling school schedules to complete my degree, I found the writing this book was a much longer process than anticipated. With each keystroke, I found the characters were evolving, even if it was a painstaking process. I found myself meshed into their fictional life.

I believe God was a true inspiration and driving force behind this book. The book was written so others can find their own purpose—their dash, if you will. I had to find my own purpose. I wanted to leave my mark on the world to inspire others to do the same, but in their own way. Hopefully, when I am gone and my end date is written in stone, someone will pick up my book and read it. I pray it gives them motivation to pursue their dreams, and possibly alter their dash. With each life touched through the reading of this book, my dash will have even greater wealth. Thank you for reading my book. I hope it inspires you to make your dash count.

—Rose

ACKNOWLEDGMENTS

I THANK MY LOVING HUSBAND, Seby (Chip) Jones, for believing in me while I took the giant leap of faith to find my true passion in life. Through countless nights of my writing and doing schoolwork while running our family business, you stood by my side through the entire process, cheering me on so I could fulfill my dream, my dash.

Daniel Norris, novelist, publisher, and biology teacher at Cape Fear Community College, you inspired me to write. You told me that if I wanted it badly enough, it would happen.

Jim Burris, writer, illustrator, and all-around creative person, endless thanks for insisting that I not quit.

Judy La Bor, thank you for your mentoring and encouragement to publish this story. I appreciate you dearly.

Rev. May Craven, I love your charming Southern mannerisms. *Mildred The Bird Lady* was molded around your Southern whit and grace shared so freely in conversation. Thank you for being a true inspiration in my life.

Torchflame Books, your support and encouragement are truly appreciated. It is a delight to work with such a talented and dedicated group of professionals. A special shoutout is due to my editors, Elizabeth Turnbull, Mariah Jackson, and Ashley Conner for helping me shape my words to best express my thoughts and ideas with my readers.

CHAPTER 1

WHILE OPENING THE DOOR TO THE CORNER CAFÉ, I hear the bell above me chiming to announce my entrance. The chime isn't like a grocery store chime, or even a clang of a cowbell-sounding chime, like most stores. The sound is pleasant and inviting. It sounds like a bell that was rung by an angel—like the movie where the angel gets his wings in *The Christmas Story*—quaint and subtle.

Stepping inside, I glance around because this is a place I have never been before. I want somewhere quiet and quaint, but classy, to sit and just be by myself. Skeptical and picky, I find this café looks perfect for the order at hand. After a glance at the entrance, I notice the sign reads, *Please Seat Yourself*. So I do.

Carrying my satchel full of my drawing pad, a few pencils, and some other odds and ends on one shoulder, and my purse draped over my other, I choose a table close to a window in the front, so I can watch people as they saunter past. They act like the people sitting near the window are on display, like a distorted type of window shopping. It is as if the people sitting inside the café were for sale, like the latest handbag or designer coat. It feels a bit uncomfortable being on display for them to see, but the feeling soon passes.

While getting situated at my four-top table, so quaintly dressed in the finest decor, I can't help but notice the passersby outside the window once more. Some of the people that I think are gazing in at me, are actually looking at their own reflection in the window. The feeling of being on display is soon replaced with me watching them.

A woman dressed in a pretty, cream dress, complete with heels and stockings, is brushing back her hair with her fingertips as a makeshift comb, while checking that her makeup is just perfect. Paying careful attention to her lipstick, which she must have recently applied, she uses the tip of her pinky to ensure the lines are just so. Pulling downward on her dress, as to pull out the invisible wrinkles, she then sways side to side in judgment, appearing dissatisfied. She points her toe with her right foot, and then hikes her dress up to show her leg, ever so slightly.

Oblivious to her surroundings, she continues to pull up her dress while tugging on her stockings. My gaze is fixed upon her freshly manicured nails as she adjusts her stockings. She stares at herself for what seems to be several minutes, but in fact, is mere seconds. Her gaze meets the face of her own reflection, as if she is looking at her soul. If I wasn't paying enough attention, I would not have noticed the tear that began to form. With a glance side to side, down the pavement, she abruptly pushes it back for no one to see and begins to compose herself. It would have crushed her if she had seen me watching her from the other side of the window, which she saw as a mirror.

Her facial expression changes in an instant when she notices that this is not a mirror, but a window and a reflection instead. A window to where another woman is watching her. The other woman in judgment is, in fact, me. She is noticeably violated by my peering, but I get a glimpse of her eyes catching the reflection once more. I recapture her attention yet again. But this time, I give her a smile of approval, along with a quiet thumbs-up to show her that she is perfect. She stops, gives a puzzled gaze with a tilted head as to question my approval, but then the message sinks in. A little smile begins to lighten her somber face that once was close to tears. Her shoulders lift, and she takes a deep breath, as if she got my message and understands her importance in the world. We observe with each other and have our own little silent conversation. It is like we're old friends.

Before she turns to leave, with a renewed sparkle in her eye and a proud stature, she winks and says, with overexpressed words, "Thank You," even though I cannot hear her through the window. She, herself, is now accepting approval of her own reflection.

She soon fades away in the distance, no longer in my vision.

Adjusting my belongings that I took out of my bag; I peer at the window once more. I could sit here all day and notice the people and the happenings from this very place—exciting and entertaining, I must admit. What a beautiful afternoon.

After a while, a man dressed in a gray pinstriped suit is captured by the very mirror ... the window. The man staring back at him looks unfamiliar. The look upon his face reveals that he is not accustomed to seeing the man in the window as he appears. He is checking that his tie is on just right. He is quite careful not to look at the eyes of the man that stares at him from the other side.

His demeanor is different from the woman. His is hurried and nervous. A look of shame is in his eye as he, too, checks his appearance. It's like a man is not supposed to be checking his appearance in a mirror, and he is afraid to be noticed.

He is pulling and tugging to straighten the tie that is not visibly disturbed. All the while, examining his buttons to ensure he did not miss any. Did he get dressed so fast to think that he could have missed a button or two?

He gives a smirk of approval as he gazes up and down his form, which is quite becoming. He may work out in a gym. Quite suave, if I may say. Nonetheless, he is one that takes great care of himself. So why the uncertainty of his buttons? Who knows? He may have an important interview and is extremely nervous about his appearance. He certainly looks the part. Or he could be running late for an afternoon date. Maybe even an afternoon rendezvous with a lover, when he wants to look just perfect for his mistress. Oh, boy. He could have just left his lover and wants to make sure he is presentable to go back home to his loving wife and children. I suddenly feel an overwhelming sadness, if that is the case. Those poor children and that unsuspecting naïve wife.

I have to gather my thoughts. I have to stop sitting in quiet places while people watching. My mind tends to wander too much. Guess that's why I'm not married yet.

Others find their reflection to their liking, and just decide to simply adjust their clothing. I did see a few that totally disapproved of their reflection, and their faces were distorted in disgust. Some actually push their stomachs in, like the mirror window could somehow make the extra pounds disappear. Some are humorous, I must admit. I want badly to run out and tell them that they look perfect just as they are. But I don't dare show them that I am watching, as if I'm seeing them through a two-way mirror. I am sure the private grooming would not have been done if they knew someone was peering into their private lives on the other side. It's exciting and fun to watch others when they think they're alone. Private voyeurism, but not in secret.

My order, taken by a young man, is simple—coffee and a lemon pastry, which he advises to be the perfect choice. While waiting for my order, I can't help but notice a family peering in the window, trying to make up their minds if they are going to enter or not. Their kids are unruly, and the youngest of three is putting his tongue on the glass like a dog. The oldest one looks disgusted just to be with his parents, while pecking away at his cell phone. The middle child, standing off to the side, seems to be the tamest of them all. They must have decided on something else, because the mass moves onward down the street. I am relieved because I want a quiet afternoon without the laughter and nonsense of children. I just want to sit and draw. Not to mention, watch the entertainment outside the mirror.

Ah, my coffee and lemon pastry have arrived. Not paying too much attention because I'm trying to get situated, I find it placed appropriately upon plastic placemats that look as if they are made of lace. I must have said something under my breath about the children leaving, because the man smiles and says, "Me, too." He turns away before I can thank him properly for serving me.

While sitting at the street corner café, with my piping-hot black coffee, I reach for the spoon placed upon my napkin. I grasp a couple sugar packets and begin to flick the packets with my fingers to tear the top and not spill the sugar. I am able to empty the contents into my black coffee, making it more to my liking. I notice a multitude of creamers on the table and choose my favorite. It's the capful that is flavored with hazelnut. After emptying the creamer into the coffee cup, I tap my spoon delicately to slightly disturb the coffee and creamer. It begins to swirl, but not mix in color. Off-white hazelnut creamer dances around the deep, rich black coffee ... my own private ballet, right before my eyes.

Oh, if my cup could play music. I wonder what type of music it would be. Visions of a grand waltz playing in a ballroom full of men and women in gowns and tuxes, all spinning in time and in unison, just like in the movie *Pride and Prejudice*. Oh, wait. I know ... the tango! Yes! It has to be a tango, the dance of lovers, that takes over the entire floor, while others stand in amazement and dream that they, too, were that graceful and poised.

The coffee dances with the hazelnut creamer so gracefully and smoothly, it's almost erotic. The swirls are like arms holding its partner as they mold into one. Like dancers holding each other tight and moving across the floor with their feet barely touching the ground. I can almost hear the music in my mind and see the dance in my cup. I can feel my muscles tense up, as if I am the one dancing on the floor, holding my lover close. This is something that I love to do that just drives people crazy. But I can't help it. I see life in a much different light than most. I just don't see life, I live life. My mind wanders, and I dream life into existence.

I begin to stir my coffee until I feel it is perfect. I set the teaspoon down onto my napkin, watching the coffee swirl to a stop. I admire the changing color from jet black to a golden cream, which I must admit is much more appealing.

The tango is over, but now on to the aroma, which is delightful of rich hazelnut and coffee. I feel like a cartoon character floating in the air while seeking a scent that is all too tempting.

The ever so desired coffee finally makes it to my lips. I breathe in rich hazelnut and deep-roasted coffee that seems to reach my toes with excitement. Taking the first anticipated sip, to ensure that it is perfect, is the grand finale to the tango that I witnessed in my cup earlier. This day is beginning to look perfect for my inspirations.

I decide to pull out my sketch pad and my newly sharpened pencil and get to work. Flipping through the completed drawings so carefully, and not getting any of the powdered sugar on my pad, I begin to take reference to each one. Turning the pages slowly and recalling each drawing, as like a child, I come to a bright white virgin canvas just begging to be drawn upon. I pause, only to begin a distant stare out the window once again, my head perched upon my hand which is steadied from my elbow on the table. This is one thing my mother hated. But it seems to help me think.

A deep sigh comes up from the depth of my lungs.

"What shall I draw today?" I say, under my breath.

The flower outside the window in the hanging basket? How about the young girl sitting in the corner, reading the newspaper while waiting for a bus? Nah, something else.

My gaze fixes upon the coffee cup in my midst, where the dance—the tango—took place. I place my spoon closer to the cup and turn the cup just right, so it catches the sun beaming through the window before me. The sunlight brings the cup to life as it reveals all the flaws that it has acquired through its lifespan at the café. The flaws in the cup are what bring character to it. Just think of the age this cup has, what stories it could tell! This page can be practically anything that I feel. Today, this page belongs to this coffee cup and the story it may reveal. My pencil touches the paper, and inspiration comes.

I am an artist. Or so I think I am. I have always loved to draw and—what my mom called it—doodle, all day long. I don't like to draw anything like landscapes, or something with great distance. I like to focus on the tiny aspects in life. Not so much a person's full body, but the age of a woman's hands, or the wisdom deep within her eyes. Close, intimate details intrigue me.

Seeing the beauty in each stroke of the lead can bring life into any object. For example, the veins of a leaf on an ordinary house plant can be drawn in such detail that you can feel the life pulsing right on the canvas. Or the intimacies of a woman's eye that holds a tear getting ready to fall. It shows the raw emotion that could capture the glare of a reflection within her eye, revealing the feelings deep within her soul.

The art is in the pencil, touching the paper. The pressure of each stroke, or the angle of the lead can take you to any mindset and bring life to a canvas. Life that even the untrained eye can see and feel.

While most only see a forest, I see one particular tree, or the leaf, or even a bug perched upon the leaf. I would love to capture the morning dew droplet of that leaf, just as it is turning to fall. But somehow, I can't quite get my timing right. Just as I feel the moment, it's gone, and the droplet has plummeted to the ground.

Immersed in my drawing of the coffee cup handle on my canvas, I notice another cup of coffee is brought to my table. The waiter must have noticed that I was busy drawing the one I already had. He brought me another one because of this. I don't even touch it, let alone drink it.

For some reason, my eye is taken off my paper and then focused elsewhere. I'm not sure how long I've been focused on my drawing. No, it isn't the mirror-window this time. I can't help but notice an old woman sitting on the other side of the café, so quiet. I haven't noticed her, until now. She isn't dressed as you would see ordinarily. She has on a beautiful Southern belle hat, with a long gangly dress. The dress may have fit her years prior, but now she is much too frail. This woman, obviously, doesn't fit in the warm Chicago corner café, but nonetheless, she has charisma and a Southern charm that is welcoming to these bustling streets. It brings back haunting memories of a woman I once met as a child.

My pencil stops midline, and memories begin to flood my mind.

"Are you ready yet?" my mother yells down the hallway of our downtown apartment.

While grasping for the blanket to sit on, the cooler, and a bag full of goodies, she takes one last glance down the hallway for her daughter.

"Come on, Mary. Hurry up! Let's go play in the park." Her voice is anxious. "Come on, let's go!"

Mom is taking me to the park to play. She's waiting for me impatiently, but still waiting. Today, I am slower than she wants me to be. She is trying not to be harsh in

her words, but is also trying to push me along.

I get sidetracked a lot, and today my mind is distracted by what to wear. I've always had a lot of energy, and she likes to take me to the park to spend time with my Aunt Jackie and Travis. Not to mention, get rid of this energy.

A young girl about four years old comes around the corner with her own blankie. Yep, that's me! I peer up into my mother's eyes from down the hall, and she can't resist those big blue eyes piercing through that tussled curly red hair. How could you possibly be upset at a face like that?

I prance up the hallway, dragging my dirty blankie behind me. You can tell that I dressed myself today because I have on some mismatched outfit. But that doesn't matter to my mom, as long as I am happy and safe. That is all that she cares about.

Mom has taken care of me since my dad left a few years ago. Being strong is a trait that she has tried hard to instill in me.

"Come on, dear." Mom reaches for the blanket with one hand.

In her other arm, she's carrying all the goodies for the afternoon, and that old, ratted blanket is not on her list to take. But if it makes me happy, then it's coming.

"I'm coming, Mommy." I struggle with the heavy load in my arms. "Whew, that blanket is heavy," I say, as the load is shifted to my mother's arms. "I'm ready!" I bounce up and down, with my red curls following.

We both turn for the apartment door, and I stop in my tracks.

"Wait!" I yell out, as I run across the living room. "I want to take this!" I bend down to pick up the pretty red ball that matches my messy curly hair. "Can I, Mom? Can I take this?" I push the ball up near Mother's view to show her what I want to take, and whine, "Can I, Mom?"

"Certainly. But make sure you bring it back home with you."

We head out the apartment door and down the stairs to start our adventure. Mother is careful taking each step, trying not drop anything. I am carrying the heavy load of my pretty red ball, and that is just fine with my mom. I don't realize it, but my smile is infectious and keeps the mood bright, just as the sunny day.

We head across the street and down the road a piece to where we can cross the traffic to the park. The park is located all along the waterfront adjacent to many stores. There are shoe stores, clothing stores, and even a quaint country store where I can buy candy. But today it's a park day, and I am only focused on going to the park, not getting candy. But that may be in the back of my mind afterward. Until then, playing in the park is all I can think about. Can't put too much on a four-year-old's mind, anyway.

Just after we reach the park, mother notices that it is full of people. This is more than usual, but it's due to the change of seasons, and the sun shining on such a beautiful day. This sunny day is a welcome thing since the spring was such a dreary season.

It rained in the morning, but that didn't stop us. There are people playing with dogs in the dog park area. Kids playing with Frisbees, and some just hanging out on their blankets, reading a cool book. All the usual noises to match the sights: dogs barking, kids laughing, and the noticeable conversations between the parents. Even though it rained a lot during the night, the grass is inviting for whatever you want to do.

"Here." Mother grabs my arm to direct me. "Go over that way. We can stay there."

I head to the direction my mom is pointing. While dodging the other people, I notice an open area that is perfect for us.

"Right there, Mary."

My mom points out a beautiful green patch of grass that

looks like a shag carpet waiting to be laid upon. It's away from the other crowd of people, and in the shade, where we won't get burned from the piercing sun.

No one really thinks about getting sunburned in May in Chicago. But my mom is very careful, since she is an only parent, and it takes great responsibility to care for such an active four-year-old.

Once we reach the perfect spot on the grass, my mom begins unpacking the bundle that she carried. She starts with the blanket she brought. It's all in one piece, and it looks much cleaner than mine. She spreads out the blanket, starting with each corner, until it is fully extended, without a wrinkle. Then she puts my blanket on top in a bundle to allow me to curl up to it if I want to. The cooler is next to go on top of the blanket. The cooler isn't large, by any means, but it's big enough to hold a couple peanut butter sandwiches, some drink boxes, and a few cookies that my mom made the night before. My mouth begins to water.

"Are we going to eat now?" I jump up, clapping with joy.

"No, not yet, kiddo. We're going to have some fun first, then eat. Still too early to eat. It's only ten in the morning!" She giggles at my joy for life.

With my focus taken off the food, I grab my ball and begin to play. While I'm playing, Mom is fixing other items on the blanket, that she brought for her fun day. You know, things like books and games.

I focus on the other children playing in a small group just a bit away.

Feeling alone, I say, "Is Aunt Jackie coming, too?"

I am now bored and need some friends to play with. Aunt Jackie is Mother's sister. She lives in the same city but has to drive to get to the park when she's coming to see us. Aunt Jackie has a son that is close to my age, and we get to play together when they come over.

"I think so," Mom replies, and looks all around at the people in the park. "I don't see them yet, but they said they were coming to have a play day, too." She is facing out toward the street, searching for their car. "Oh, look!" She points toward the shoe store. "There they are!"

I saw Aunt Jackie's car pulling up against the curb and got so excited that I start to jump up like a new pony that doesn't understand the strength in his hind legs.

"Wait a minute, kiddo." Mother grabs me by the back of my shirt to pull me back down onto the blanket to keep me safe.

When my butt lands on the blanket, my curly hair bounces so hard it lands with a flip across my nose. With a wave of my hand, the curls are back where they belong. At least for a moment.

"They're coming. Just hang on."

I guess I look distraught but understand quickly that what Mother says is law. She sees them walking with what looks to be the same load of stuff that we brought from upstairs. They head this way, ever dodging the people, kids, and toys, but eventually get to us.

"Aunt Jackie!" I jump to my feet and almost knock her down.

I reach up as high as I can with my arms stretched outward and give her a huge hug with all my might. She smiles so big that the earth stops.

I step back from Aunt Jackie and notice Travis, who is a whole year older than I am. He's trying to look all grown up. He is already in school with the big kids, since he is five. He stands there with his plaid shirt and blue jeans with a torn knee. His blond hair is neatly combed to one side. One of his shoes is untied, I couldn't help but notice.

"Your shoe is untied." I point to his shoe. "I can tie it! Mommy showed me how."

I bend down to tie Travis's shoe, and he moves back out of my reach.

"I can do it," he says. "I learned how a long time ago."

When I stand back up, Travis bends down and begins to tie his shoe. He tied it much faster than I could, and it fascinates me, but I try not to show it. I want to be big like him.

"I start school soon, too," I say, to look big, too. "I get to go to kin-kin-kinderbardin."

"You mean *kindergarten*." Travis chuckles. "That's what I'm in now," he says, with a stance of ownership. "It's okay." He picks lint off his shoulder. "I have new friends there. But I'll be in first grade when you go to kindergarten."

"Will I get new friends?" I ask Travis, who seems to know everything, but not as much as my mom.

"Yeah, we all have new friends. You won't go to school until the end of the summer. Summer is just beginning."

I let out a sigh of relief because I got the news from a real person in school. Just then, I remember my new red ball.

"Wanna play?" I show Travis the new ball in my hand.

"Sure."

We both move away from the blanket and begin to play with the new red ball that I brought to the park.

Mom and Aunt Jackie begin to talk.

"I'm glad you came to the park today," Mom says.

You could see the hurt in her eyes that she tries so desperately to keep hidden from me. Her gaze becomes distant.

"What's up?" Jackie says.

"It's just hard with Mary's dad being gone." Mom's eyes begin to well-up, but not a tear would dare come out to be seen.

She turns her head to face the children as she watches them run off to play with the ball.

"Look at her." Her eyes lighten up with joy. "It's been so long that she doesn't even ask about him anymore."

She turns back to look at Jackie, and the joy soon turns to a distant wet stare.

"You are doing great with her!" Jackie says. "Look at that beautiful redhead. That girl is going to be just fine. You are going to be just fine. Hell, you are doing great!" She says, with power, as she points out the beautiful girl in the distance, playing with Travis. "You couldn't ask for a better kid. We have each other, too." She moves towards Mom and gives her a loving hug with both arms. "Since Mom and Dad died, sure, it's been tough. But we have each other and look at our kids." She points to the two of them playing with the ball.

Both of them smile and hold back the tears, and they know that the sisterly bond is not to be messed with. They sit in silence, enjoying their surroundings and the pleasant noise of the park. Both are lost in their own memories as time goes by, but only a few minutes have passed.

"Oh, you're right!" Mom jumps up and begins to wipe the tears that she's trying hard to hide.

Kind of hard to hide the tears from your sister.

She notices that Travis is coming back over to the blanket, but I'm not with him.

"Where is Mary?" she says, frantic.

"She's over there getting the ball and talking to that lady with the birds." Travis points toward the benches.

You see, the benches were just a little bit away from where Mom and Jackie were talking. But to a mother, the benches were miles away, and immediate danger was sensed.

My mom gets up and is on the move in one fell swoop, striding towards us. You know, the kind of walk where your mom is coming full steam ahead, with her hands clenched at her sides. Not to mention, her face is making an evil glare that says, *Don't mess with my kid.*

She notices I'm standing next to someone who looks to be a homeless lady, sitting on the bench, feeding the birds. I'm not in any danger, but this person is a stranger, and she looks homeless.

Just a few moments beforehand, my ball bounced over by the lady, and I went to go get it while Travis was going back to the blanket. All of the commotion must have disturbed the birds, because they began to fly around, causing much chaos, but not disturbing the lady on the bench. She almost seemed used to the birds flying around her.

"Hi," I say to the lady on the bench, my voice shy and child-like, but clear.

The lady doesn't respond to me, other than to give a glance in my direction. I notice she is dressed in a formal outfit that was fit for a queen but is dirty. She wears a big hat from church—a Southern-belle type. She has a brown paper bag sitting on the bench close to her that must have been full of bird food. She has a small amount of birdseed in her hand, along with the gloves that have the fingers cut out of them. The birds are flying around her while begging for more food, but they seem to know to stay away from me.

I decide to try again to get the old woman to respond.

"Hi, I'm Mary."

I'm not sure if she heard me.

The lady looks up with slow sad eyes that are full of tears. Trying to wipe away the tears with one hand, she holds out her other hand, which is full of birdseed. The rim of her hat shields me from the direct sight of her eyes.

"Do you want to feed my birds?" the lady says, in a calm, somber voice.

Her voice is different than I have ever heard, and she has a slowed nature.

"They seem to like you," she says.

Her speech was nothing like what I was used to with my mom or Aunt Jackie. She speaks extremely slow, while pulling her words. Not childlike, by any nature, but different.

I notice she's sizing me up. Starting at my feet, she notices that I'm wearing old tennis shoes with old, faded jeans and a green tutu-type dress on top of it. My shirt has some kind of writing on it, but the lady couldn't focus on anything to read it.

Unconsciously, we begin to size each other up. Her overcoat jacket is torn by the pocket, and the white stuffing is sticking out of it. Her dress is an old faded-blue lace dress.

Then our eyes meet for the first time. She catches a glimpse of my piercing blue eyes behind those curls of long red hair. It's as if the heavens opened and gave the lady an angel in her midst. I hold out my tiny hand and take a few pieces of bird feed that fill my palm. I toss it out onto the sidewalk, and the birds eat it all up in an instant. I am so mesmerized by the birds that I'm completely unaware of the tears coming from the lady's eyes.

"Wow," I say, under my breath, as the birds fly around me.

They are so close that I could touch them, but I think fear

keeps me from trying. Their wings are stretched out. I can see each feather as they take flight, flapping in the air, making a noise that I'm not accustomed to. I listen to their voices as they speak in their own special language.

I stretch out my hand once more, but this time I say, "Gimme some more," referring to the birdseed.

"Oh, chiiild." She shakes her head and purses her lips together, just as my mother did when I upset her.

She reaches into the bag and puts a very small amount of birdseed into my hand once more. My hands are too little to hold the amount of feed she held.

"Manners, my chiiild," she says, under her breath.

I am too busy to pay attention to her speaking to me. I am so excited to be feeding these wonderful creatures. The birds are coming in from all directions by now, since they know I was now feeding them. Their wings were flapping so close to me, that if I'd wanted to, I could have touched them. But I was way too scared.

"See, I told you that they liked you. These birds won't hurt you. My husband … would come here every day … and take care of them."

Her voice cracks with every word she speaks. You could tell she didn't make a habit of speaking.

I watch the lady feed and care for the birds, just as her husband did for many years. Her brief smile turns to sorrow, and the tears begin again. The dirt on her face isn't dirt at all. It is her make-up that has smeared down to her chin from crying silent tears of pain.

I would later learn that the loss of her husband earlier that week had taken a huge toll on her. She buried her husband earlier that day, and just needed to take care of his birds, just as he did for many years. They depended upon him to come and spend time with them, feeding them. She knew these birds meant the world to her husband, and she wanted to make sure to carry on the task. It was her job now. It was just so terribly hard to tell the birds that he was not coming back.

Somehow, she felt that they understood this. Her husband

was sick, and the birds gave him strength every day. Even though he was a wealthy man and from prominence, his death went unnoticed. No one knew who he really was, nor her. She was just a lady on a park bench, feeding the birds, in what looked to be a homeless person's overcoat.

The woman had mud on her knees where she prayed to God to keep her late husband safe in the heavens above. The dirt upon her face was indeed her makeup from crying tears of silent pain. Her shoes were no longer pristine to match her blue lace dress, but brown from the dirt where she walked in the graveyard an hour or so beforehand. Her hat ... oh, the hat. That hat set her apart from all the women I have ever met. The hat was large and full of life, as if it came straight out of the South or the Kentucky Derby. Or possibly belonged to the Southern belles of Wilmington, North Carolina, during the Azalea Festival.

The hat was full of white and blue lace, with flowers intertwined, trying to match the lace dress she wore to bury her husband. The torn overcoat belonged to her late husband, so it was large and not fit for a woman. But she wanted to keep him close to her, and it was raining the night before, so it seemed fitting to wear it that morning.

While I am noticing her clothing, I see the woman hold onto a necklace that seems dear to her heart. She holds onto it with a tight grip, but tenderly in grace. Then she tucks it deep within her dress while closing her eyes, as if she is saying a silent prayer.

Out of nowhere, I feel my arm jerk back like it was being pulled out of its socket. I look back to see the source of my pain, and it is my mother.

"Mary!" she yells.

I am startled by the tug on my arm.

"You come back here, young lady!" She pulls me close to her side for safety. "You stay away from that homeless lady."

Mother's stern voice is instruction that I'm not going to ignore. I know my mother doesn't mean any harm with the harsh words about the homeless lady, but she is in fear for my safety.

"But she's nice," I plead, while being dragged off back inside the park. "Look, Mommy, birdies." I point to the birds flying around our heads.

"I meant the chiiild …" the woman turns her head to try to see my mom, " … no harm." The woman keeps her head low, not to gain eye contact with my mother. "She was just … feeding the birds and getting her red ball." The lady is still not making any eye contact.

Instead, she shrugs deep within her overcoat, as to hide from the world. Being invisible seems to be the best place for her at this time. Crying in peace was where she wanted to be. Taking care of her husband's birds by herself, and crying, by herself, all alone.

She musters up the energy and the will to lift her head and eyes, only to see the two of us leave. I am being led away by my mother's gripping hand. It's too late to make my case to my mother. We are already gone.

I turn to get a glimpse of the lady once more, only to notice the big beautifully placed hat upon her head. I notice the lady begins to turn to me as well, but before we can see each other, my mother's grip strengthens around my arm. The lady seemed to be upset at me being carted away in such a manor, but somehow, I think she understood why.

"I told you not to talk to strangers!" Mom heads back to the blanket.

Each step feels wrong. I know I did nothing wrong. My mother is scolding me in a way that I haven't known before. Her grip on my arm is so tight that I am literally being carried while my feet are dangling in the air below. My toes only graze the earth as she drags me off and back to our blanket.

With each step toward our blanket, try to plead with my mother.

"But Mom—"

"No!" She pulls me closer to her. "That old woman does not want to be bothered by a young girl like you."

What did that mean? A young girl like *me*.

I begin to feel the warm tears fall onto my cheeks. My bright-blue eyes are no longer blue, but red from crying. Did that lady not want to talk to me? Did I do something wrong? Questions flood my young brain, and tears begin to fall even harder.

Our brisk pace is halted.

"Now stop that!" She gives a quick little shake of my arm.

The sea of people begins to look at us, which makes my mother even angrier. Everyone in the park is focused on my mother's stern voice and my wailing cries. My tears turn into a full-on bawl. I just don't understand. She turns and begins the arm pull again. I try to get my mom to explain once more.

"But!" I yell.

We stop dead in our tracks once more. My mother flips me around, so we end up face to face, eye to eye. Oh, boy, this just got serious.

"But nothing! I told you not to talk to strangers." She shakes my arm with every word she speaks to add emphasis to what she's saying. "She looks like an old homeless woman sitting there on a park bench, feeding the birds like some ... bird lady."

Making a statement like that is unheard of. My mother isn't like this. My mother never passes judgment on anyone. But she wants to keep me safe, I suppose. Safe from what? I still didn't understand. People are kind. Why aren't I supposed to talk to The Bird Lady?

"When you get older and have a little girl, you will understand. But until then, I said no!"

My mother's finger comes out and points right at my chest. Her nail jabs into my shirt, which brings a quick pain to my skin. This time, mother's voice means business, and what is being said is the end.

After what seems to be a long, tearful, scolding walk, we arrive back at the blanket and begin to eat the lunch that Aunt Jackie is pulling out of the cooler for everyone. Once the peanut butter and jelly sandwiches hit the blanket, nothing else matters. Tears are subsiding, and the sniffles are soon gone as well. I am hungry from playing.

With peanut butter on my cheeks, and jelly on my chin, I am

happy again. That is, until I see The Bird Lady out of the corner of my eye. She is sitting there all alone.

I notice one thing that isn't quite right. I am careful to make sure my mom doesn't know that I'm watching her. The Bird Lady is wiping her eyes. It's hard to tell, seeing her only from the back. Is she crying? I want to go back over to her, but Mom forbade me from doing so. What's wrong? Did I upset her? Her bag of bird food is obviously empty, and she is watching the birds leave, one by one. Some stay behind, as if they are trying to console her. With the passersby making noise, the few birds lingering soon depart as well. The Bird Lady is alone.

With the last few bites of the sandwich, I glance up and realize she is gone. The bench is empty. No birds, no Bird Lady. Looking for her in all directions, I cannot find her. Soon afterwards, the park bench is filled with another family playing in the sunlight. Even though the park is full of boisterous families, dogs, and laughter, it feels empty now, but I'm not sure why.

My mom puts a piece of paper in front of me, and a pencil for me to draw. She wants to keep me busy, so I won't get away from her again. Even though The Bird Lady was long gone, my mom knows my attention span is short. I begin to draw, and time goes by before I know it.

"Look!" Aunt Jackie points to my piece of paper. "Look at that!" She moves closer to get a better look, while reaching for my mom's attention.

She captures my attention and motions to reach for my paper. I easily give it up. Aunt Jackie picks up the paper and examines the picture I'm working on. It seems as if she actually likes my drawing. She tilts the paper to my mom's view, with her eyes wide open and her mouth to match.

"Do you see this?"

My mother grabs the picture and takes a long gazing look at it.

"Hmm," she says, with approval.

After all, she still hasn't settled down from the commotion of earlier.

I notice a faint smile coming from my mother's lips.

"Let me see!" Travis tries to grasp it out of my mother's hand. "What is it? Is it a dog? Or a stick figure?"

"Stop it, Travis!" yells Aunt Jackie.

She wasn't happy with Travis's actions, and had to stop him before he ripped the picture.

"Check that out!" Aunt Jackie is amazed, and I am, too.

She turns to me with an inquisitive look I have not seen before.

"Where ... where did you learn to draw like this?"

"I dunno."

What other answer did she expect from a four-year-old?

Aunt Jackie begins to look around the immediate area to see if I was drawing something close, or something from memory. And there it was. The very flower that is on my paper.

"Is that what you are drawing?" she says.

"Uh-huh!"

"Look at this. See that flower?" She points to the flower just off the blanket.

It's a weed, after all, but still a flower in the midst of the clover. She fingers the detail, even though drawn by a four-year-old. The details are particular. It has some distortion regarding the scale, but it is spot-on from a young girl's point of view.

"This girl has talent," she says to my mother.

She gives me my picture back and provides me an affirmation of a pat on my head.

"Pretty good, kid!"

Travis, feeling left out, begins to act up to get attention, instead of me getting all the praise. He grabs for my picture again, only to be stopped by his mom.

"Stop it, Travis!"

He plops down on the blanket, face red with anger.

My mother puts her arm around me and smiles. "It's beautiful."

I lift my blue eyes off the picture and gaze up at my mother. I made her happy, after all that. She is no longer angry with me.

I can't help it, but a big yawn comes from deep in my lungs. Tired from the excitement of the day, I ask to go home, and we do so.

As the weather grows warmer and the summer begins to take full shape, my mom and I frequent the park, along with Travis and Aunt Jackie. I see The Bird Lady, day after day, sitting on the same park bench. I don't dare approach her, due to my mother's stern directions. But something about her always seems to catch my eye to watch her every move. Someday, I will speak to her again ... someday.

"Ma'am," says a distant voice, out of nowhere. "Ma'am." I hear it again.

"What," I say, as if I were in a distant trance and just awakened from a vivid dream. "Oh, I'm sorry. Were you talking to me?"

Feeling a bit awkward, I notice a man standing next to me, with a coffee pot in his hand. This is odd. I'm shaken, being brought back from my memory. The waiter that I had a few hours ago wasn't the same person. Did my waiter go home?

"Would you care for more coffee?" he says again.

Unclear just how long he was actually standing there, I gaze into his midst as if I were deep in thought. I appear embarrassed due to my ignorance of him being there.

"Yes, please." I push my cup toward him, away from my drawings. "I'm sorry. I was deep in thought, I guess."

He must have been watching me because he knew not to touch the cup of coffee that I was drawing, nor the spoon placed next to it.

"It's okay. I knew you were working on your artwork, and I didn't want to disturb you. That's why I brought you the other cup of coffee. One to drink, and one to draw." He is pointing at my canvas.

He pours the coffee carefully, as if to preserve my work of art—a simple coffee cup handle, and the beginnings of the coffee cup itself.

"That's nice." He tries to see my work a bit better. "Such detail. I never really saw my coffee cups like that, but after looking at it ... I mean, really looking at it, I can see so much more." A second pause. "At first, I just thought it was a cup," he says, with a tone of arrogance, "but you brought my cup into a new light."

I gaze upon him, since no one has ever spoken to me like that.

"Thank you for your compliments." I give a half-witted smile.

"So why didn't you draw the whole cup? Why just the handle and the side of my cup?"

My gaze focuses upon the drawing.

"It's the details that make you see the entire cup," I reply, "even though you can't really see it. Your mind begins to fill in the blanks when you see the other parts in great details. I will draw more of the cup as I go, but not all of it."

I point out the various details of the sketch. I can see him following my hand as I am describing the drawing. It's almost like he's admiring my hand and not the drawing.

"If you draw the whole cup, you can put the name of the café on it." He points to the sign. "May I have your drawing when you're finished? I would like to frame it and put it up in my café." He points to the wall.

"Your café?"

"Yes, I take care of all my customers. I'm not only your waiter," he glances around the room, "I'm the owner, too!" He stands proudly, grabbing his apron.

By him standing up beside me, I'm then able to see the edge of his chin and the charisma of his smile. One man, obviously proud of his life's accomplishments. His tousled black hair is a feature that catches my eye.

"I come out front from time to time to meet my customers. What is your name?" He sits in the chair beside me.

I'm not used to waiters being so forward, but this one, I must admit, I don't mind.

"Umm, Mary." I fidget with my pencil and do a once-over to make sure I don't have any powdered sugar on my blouse or pants.

Oh my gosh. My face! I hope I don't have any powdered sugar on my face.

"My name is Mary." My voice cracks because he notices me.

And not just me, but my artwork, too!

"I'm Charlie. Got it—Charlie's Café?" He points to the sign just in view outside the front window.

He puts the coffee pot down and offers his hand. I grasp it and shake carefully, not to look too forward, and not to look too eager. His handshake is firm, but not tough. His hands are smooth, not like a working man's hand, but one that could be a business owner.

"I can also cook a wonderful Italian dinner or a nice steak for you, if you'd like sometime. I have a wonderful dinner menu if you stay."

"Oh, thank you. But I believe I may just finish my coffee and draw a bit more, if that's okay."

Oh, how I wanted to stay and stare into his dreamy eyes and watch his black hair as he tossed it off his forehead.

I pull my canvas back over in front of me and pick up the pencil as if I am ready to go back to work.

"Okay, well, I would like to see the finished cup sketch, and if I may, frame it for my café. I would very much like to hang it on my wall. Could you put my café name on it, too?" He points to the sign out front.

"We'll see how it turns out, Charlie," I say, with a shy voice.

"Well, I see that you want to get back to drawing. So, Mary ..."

He bends down slowly while he grabs my hand, pulling it close to his mouth. He gently kisses the back of my hand. His kiss is warm and inviting, sincere—slow with respect, not like a quick peck. He lifts his eyes ahead of his body movement. I am in shock of the gentleman and his grace standing before me.

" ... until we meet again."

Did this just really happen? Did he just kiss my hand, and I turned to mush, really?

I blush and turn my head like a schoolgirl. Me? Shy? I'm

strong and courageous, just as my mother always taught me when I was young.

While my head is turned, I notice the old woman again, with the big hat. He notices I am looking at her.

"That is my mother," he whispers to me. "She likes to sit here with me and see people. She keeps to herself, though." He looks at her, and then back to me. "It's okay. She is very lonely, and it's good for her to be here."

You could feel the closeness as he speaks of his mother.

After looking closely at her, you could see the illness that has befallen her. She gazes into the distance, as if to be lost in an unfamiliar place, but familiar enough not be scared. Possibly Alzheimer's? Not sure, and too afraid to ask.

He stands to his feet, picks up his coffee pot, and heads off to another table, where a couple snuck in and is sitting. I watch him only for a few minutes, not to be too noticeable. His charm follows him, table to table. I find myself taking his inventory: personable, charismatic, educated. Oh, those eyes. And that hair, so dark like a haunting forest. Under his apron, which was tied behind his back, his form-fitting trousers.

Oh my gosh. What am I doing? How can a man have such an effect on me? Too good to be true, for sure.

Once he fills their coffee cups, he glances back at me and smiles. He sees me watching him! I turn back to my drawing, trying not to be so noticeable, but it is way too late. I smile back. I can't help it!

I brush back my curly red hair, darkened from age, dangling in front of me, and begin to work again on my drawing. Charlie goes behind the wall, not to be seen again.

With my pencil in hand, I start to sketch in the name of the café: Charlie's Café. I put details in to make it look authentic to his sign. My hands sketch the C with such caress, as if I am touching him. The same feeling is present with each passing letter in his name. I am oh-so-careful to make his name appear on the coffee cup in my drawing, just as it is on the sign in the front window. For some reason, this is extremely important. I find myself paying more attention to the sketch of the name, instead of the cup itself. Although, the sketch of the cup is authentic, I must admit.

As time has passes by, I glance up outside the window of the café, not to focus on anything, but to give my eyes a break. I gaze outside and think of what a wonderful day this has been. The ever-inviting memory of The Bird Lady, and a new acquaintance—Charlie.

After stowing my sketchbook and pencil in the bag, I pause for a moment. I pull out my sketchbook once more and thumb to the page I was just working on. I give a glance around the room and begin to tear the page out of my book carefully, to not hurt the page's integrity. I leave the café without a goodbye. But I did leave a big part of me behind. The sketch of the coffee cup and handle that had *Charlie's Café* was still on the table, along with my signature.

Oh! My signature. I almost forgot.

I pull out my pencil and begin to sign my name to my beautiful page of art, making the *M* large and full of life, with swirls and character. Followed by *a,* then the *r*, and lastly the *y*. All of which do not outdo the large *M*. Next, is my last name, which is done the same, with the first letter big and full of character, and the rest of the letters smaller. There, *Mary Parker*. I swipe the page over my name with my little finger, as if I am putting on the finishing touch.

Whether he would really frame it or not isn't the question. The question is ... does he really like my artwork? I guess I'll never know.

As I leave the café, I glance back at my table, where I was most of the afternoon—a gesture that I do to ensure that I haven't forgotten anything. I view, once more, the sketch of my coffee cup on the table, with the name of the café beautifully placed upon it like an etching on a glass window.

It's odd to me to leave a sketch behind. It is as if I am leaving an old friend.

Next to the sketch is a napkin that I left as well.

I hope you enjoy your coffee cup!

Thank you,

—Mary

I thought about putting my phone number on it, but that would seem too forward. Besides, what could he possibly see in me?

I turn and continue out the door, which has the old-fashioned bell at the top, ringing my every entrance and departure. I don't see Charlie, but he's standing beside the wall, watching my every move as I exit the café.

The bell chimes once more, and I am gone.

CHAPTER 2

SOME WEEKS HAVE PASSED since that day in the café. Work is hard and being here seems to be such a chore. Oh, how I just want to draw myself out of this office.

"Want to get lunch?" says a faint voice, from the cubical next to mine.

My life is in a cubical. I work here every day. I wish I didn't, but my mother told me long ago that my doodling would never pay the bills.

"In a minute," I reply. "I have one more email that I need to get out before I can leave."

My fingers are dancing on the keyboard. I work in an office, with many others. My friend, Lilly, sits next to me. We help each other get through every day without stress.

"Come on!" she says. "You can't stay here through your lunch again. You need to get outside more."

She's right. I spend too much time sitting at this desk, trying to make a measly living. I could be a great artist.

Yeah, right! I sell insurance over the phone, making appointments, and trying to earn enough so I can get out of here someday. I've said that for hmm … three years now, I think. But today, Lilly is right. I need to get up and get outside.

"Okay, I'm ready." I grab my purse and stand as if my body weighs a thousand pounds. "You're right. I need to get out of here." I peek around the cubical wall. "Now, where to?"

"I don't know," Lilly says. "How 'bout the café down the street that you mentioned? It's close, and as usual, you wasted some of our lunchtime to sit and send stupid emails to people who don't want our business."

"The café?"

I have been trying to put the café out of my mind, to no avail. I couldn't. Charlie ... oh, I can't. Why not?

"You know, the one that Prince Charming owns?" Lilly says, with a blushing laughter.

"He probably isn't there, anyway," I say, with a hint of hope.

I haven't seen him or even thought of him for days. Well, at least, I won't admit to thinking of him.

"So, let's get going!" Lilly grabs my arm and pulls me towards the elevator. "Lunchtime doesn't last all day, you know."

We look like two schoolgirls going to meet a young football player. Or giddy roadies chasing a rock band that has just landed in our city. Two women in corporate dresses, running down the office hallway, was quite a site for many to see.

We make our way to the elevator and out the building, pushing our way through the hustling crowd, all fighting for space in the street. The café is just two blocks away and is in good walking distance from work.

We get to the café, and I hear that all-familiar chime of the bell on the door. Looking around, I do not see Charlie, but I do notice the old woman in the corner, with her big-rimmed hat: his mother. He has to be here, if she is here.

The feeling of excitement is deep within me. A feeling that I cannot dare show Lilly. She would play off that all month long, making jokes and teasing me. I haven't dated seriously in quite some time. Well, actually ... never, really. I am a career woman, working, paying bills. You know, the one that doesn't have time to have fun. The one that stays home to feed her cat. Well, I guess I'm not that bad. Though I do have a cat.

But then there's Lilly. She is full of life. She has long, jet-black skinny braids that go down to her waist and match her deep brown, dewy skin. She has dark seductive eyes that usually catch all the guys' attention. She's the kind of girl everyone like— you know the ones—the lighthearted, let's-go-have-fun ones.

Her frame is so thin and perfect. I guess we make a great pair as friends. I keep her grounded, and she keeps me from growing moss as I sit in this earthy doom. God, I'm glad I'm out of the office.

"Here. Let's sit here, if that's okay." Lilly puts her purse down and pulls the chair out to sit.

She sits quickly and flings her braids around her shoulders to keep them in submission.

Out of nowhere, he appears.

"Here, let me get that for you."

My chair is being pulled out by none other than a perfect gentleman—Charlie. He is here! His black unkept hair glistens from the afternoon sunlight, and a dash of powdered sugar is on his cheek. I look like a schoolgirl. Or at least, I feel as if I am, for a moment.

My gaze meets his. Peering at him through my red curls once again, I feel the connection that we made once before. I feel like I never left from the first time we met.

Trying to look composed, I reach for my chair. He pushes it gently into my legs as I sit in it. It's as if he did this for every woman he met. Oh, what am I thinking? He does do this for everyone. He is the owner.

"It is very nice to see you again, Mary."

He remembers my name!

"Thank you, Charlie."

I begin to bite my lip, as if I were twelve, seeing the love of my entire life for the first time. Blushing childlike features begin to consume me. Oh my gosh! Get composed. Get it together, girl.

"Coffee?" He looks at me once again.

"Yes, please," I say, under my breath, like I was Marilyn Monroe. "Umm, I'm sorry." I clear my throat. "Yes, please." This time, my voice is clear.

His focus goes to Lilly. "And for you, ma'am?"

See, I told you! He is this charming to all the people that come into this café. Not just me. I am no one special to Charlie. No one at all.

Her eyes are wide open, and her mouth looks like she's at the dentist. She blinks to snap herself out of it.

"Coffee for me as well." She gazes into his eyes.

Oh, crap. Lilly is lost to his charms, too. Oh, great! Lilly ... she is so eternally beautiful that no man can resist her. How could I even think of bringing her here?

Charlie sets down the cups and begins to pour the piping-hot coffee into each one. Then he places each cup on a saucer next to the fixed silverware, quaintly arranged upon the elegant napkins. After he's finished, he gazes up at both of us.

"Very well. I will come back for your orders."

He turns from our table to disappear behind the wall.

Lilly is still staring at Charlie as he walks away. He holds her attention like a kid in a candy shop. She's almost drooling!

Lilly looks at me with her mouth so wide you could drive a Mack truck into it.

"That was, umm, Charlie?" She makes a point to emphasize each word.

"Umm, yes." A little school-girl smile comes out, along with a hint of blush under my freckles.

"Damn, he's cute!" Lilly sits back in her seat, disappointed that I met him first.

She begins to look around the café, making comments about how pretty and quaint it is. Then she gasps. Her hand stretches out, with her manicured finger pointing to the wall.

"Is that one of your drawings?"

Lilly has known me for quite some time, and she knows that I have a passion for drawing. She could spot one of my drawings a mile away. I almost think she is my best critic, since she *is* my best friend. She has a few of my drawings in her apartment.

I turn my head to the corner, just above where his mother is sitting. And there it is! That is my drawing of my coffee cup, with the name *Charlie's Café* on it. In disbelief, I gaze at the signature on the bottom right corner. That's my name! My artwork is framed. And it's here. Here! For everyone to see.

"Yes, it is!" I beam with excitement. "That's the one I drew a few weeks ago. He wanted it. I didn't actually think he would frame it."

We're both staring at the artwork as if it were from one of the great artists.

"Why not?" Charlie walks up behind us.

Once again, I'm startled by his unannounced presence. We are so mesmerized by the drawing being framed and in the public's eye.

He comes to the table and puts down our hazelnut creamers. He remembered the creamers, and me.

"I told you I would," he says to me.

"Yeah, but … I didn't really think you would hang it here." All of a sudden, I become shy.

"But your work is so complex and real." He looks back at the picture. "I didn't realize it, but you even drew the hairline cracks and the chip in the rim. The drip that is getting ready to run down the side of the cup. And the spoon with coffee residue that is lying on the napkin next to the cup. The detail is impeccable!"

He studied my drawing. He saw the detail and understood the effort it took me to create it.

"Maybe someone will come into my café and notice your masterpiece."

Lilly is lost in translation. She looks at me, and then at Charlie. She can see how smitten Charlie is with me. As he describes the drawing with such care and detail, she sees the words as they fall out of Charlie's mouth and onto the table. Each word spoken is as if he were making love to me through my drawing, and it gives insight to his soul. Seeing this, she realizes Charlie is off the market, and so am I. I just didn't know it yet.

"Can I offer you the special today?" He points to the sign near the door.

We both focus our attention to the sign, and in unison, agree. Charlie writes it down and soon disappears behind the wall again. His black disheveled locks of hair are gone from sight.

"Oh, honey," Lilly says, like she just learned some good secret. "He's got it bad for you."

She folds her arms and purses her lips while she sits back against her chair like she is the only one in the room who knows this good secret.

"No, he doesn't." I smirk. "Why do you say that?"

She leans forward. "Really? You have to ask that?"

My smirk gets even more noticeable.

She brushes her braids off her shoulder. Her eyebrows bow up, as if to say, *How can you not know this secret exists?*

"You think he's interested in me?" I reply, in total disagreement. "I just drew him a picture, and he framed it for his café. He was merely showing his appreciation."

I sip my coffee, as if I don't want to explain myself anymore.

"You are so blind, Mary!" Lilly picks up her coffee cup and takes a sip, then places it back onto the table.

"Blind? Blind about what?" There he is again.

Charlie brings out two specials and places them in front of us.

"Blind about what?" he says again, as if we didn't hear him the first time.

He gives an expression of waiting for an answer.

"Nothing," I say.

"Enjoy the specials. And Mary, I hope to see you again." He turns to help another customer.

"See." Lilly wears an I-told-you-so smirk. "Do you see it now?"

I take a bite of my special. "Don't be silly."

I begin to brush off the invisible crumbs on my lap. It kept me busy, and it gave Lilly the message that I was not going to talk about this.

"Hmm. We'll see." Lilly picks up her fork and begins to eat.

We both dig in, racing the clock for our lunch break.

As we head back to the office, Lilly wants to talk about Charlie the whole walk, but I try to divert her attention to other things, such as window shopping. I just don't want to talk about Charlie anymore. Actually, I want to talk about him all the time, but I want his thoughts all to myself. I don't want to share my private thoughts with her.

Charlie is special to me in my own mind. I just don't think he feels the same. He was being nice to his customers, and I was a customer—one that drew him a sketch of his cup. I'm just an insurance saleswoman who drew him a sketch that he framed for his café. A starving artist, with my first sketch showing in a public café.

I pick up my phone and place my hands on the keyboard once again. Ugh. Work again.

I hear a voice coming from the cubical wall.

"Lunch again, tomorrow?" Lilly says.

You could hear her fishing for going back to see Prince Charming.

"No," I say.

"Why not?" she says, with disappointment. "Don't tell me you're going to bring something from home again."

I pause because I really want to say yes, so I can see him once more.

"Because tomorrow is Saturday." I smirk.

"Oh, yeah. Wow, today is Friday!" Her energy level just spiked.

"Get back to work," I whisper. "You're going to get us in trouble."

We both get back to working and make those dreaded phone calls for sales. The day is almost over. We can endure a few more hours.

I find myself staring at the walls of my cubicle instead of making phone calls. My cubicle is filled with drawings of things such as flowers, an eye with a distant stare that reveals a tear drop forming, and a park bench with a woman feeding the birds. I don't have pictures of children or husbands, like most of the people here. Someday I will, but not now. My thoughts melt into my drawings, remembering the time I drew them and what they meant to me.

The one of The Bird Lady catches my mind today. It is crude because I have learned a lot since then. But the meaning of the drawing still conjures kind moments, as well as pain.

I remember when I drew it, like it was yesterday. My mind slips back to that time.

※

I find my mind back as a child sitting on a park bench during a class field trip. I feel those all too familiar feelings of shame and awkwardness.

"Look!" says the boy sitting next me. "Look what Mary is drawing!" he yells, to get the attention of the other kids in the class. "Mary's drawing that homeless woman over there!" He points to The Bird Lady, with laughter in his voice.

He is making fun not only of my drawing, but of the lady on the park bench as well. I try to shield my drawing from the other kids, as they are laughing all in unison now. I glance up and see their faces as they laugh at my choice of subjects for the assignment. Why are kids so cruel?

We are in art class and on a field trip. The field trip brought us to the park that is close to where my mother and I live. We come to this part of the park often to play with Aunt Jackie and Travis. This is where I met The Bird Lady when I was four. I am now twelve—an awkward age, at best. Our art class takes us to places where we can find subjects for drawing. I particularly like going to this park because I take a small flower and draw it in great detail when other students draw larger scale subjects—kids on a swing set, or dogs playing.

It was in this class that I found my passion for art, and how to draw the details of life. For example, I see the woman on the park bench, feeding the birds. I don't usually draw something of this size. It's usually a single flower, or even the hand of the woman, but I can't get that close to her to get that detail. So this scale will be just fine for my assignment.

I move closer to her, but not to catch her eye. I recognize the woman from years past, but I don't think she recognizes me. She is facing the water, but still on the same park bench. It's as if time has stood still for her. Her clothing is the same. And yes, she is still wearing the same wide-brimmed hat. She is unaffected by the kids laughing.

We have been there drawing for quite a while. With my drawing close to being finished, I think I will go up to her and apologize for them being so rude. I have always wanted to speak to her, after all these years. I just want to tell her that I'm that little redhead that had the ball when I was young.

I begin to walk towards her, when I hear my mother's voice in my head telling me that I shouldn't talk to her, The Bird Lady, the homeless lady. But why? Why would it be wrong for me to say hello to her and apologize for them being so rude? It is the right thing to do, so I begin to walk again towards her and her flock of birds, regardless of my mother's voice inside my head.

With my pad and pencil in one hand, and my jacket in the other, I go up to the lady on the park bench. Once I approach the bench, I see the wide-laced brim of her hat tip up, and the lady's eyes meet mine. While standing next to her, I see her eyes lighting with joy with each passing second. A smile begins to warm her face, and her eyes squint from the smile. You know, the smiles that show not only in the face, but within the eyes as well. It is genuine and welcoming.

"Hi, I'm—"

"Yes, chiiild." The slow, Southern drawl of charm comes to light. "I remember." A pause that seems forever. "You are ..." she looks to the sky, as if to tap into her memory of people, " ... you are Mary, right?" She points to me with her crooked old finger, aged like a fine wine, and colored worn fingernails.

I am shocked to hear my name come from her lips.

"Yes, I am." I slowly sit next to her, while trying not to disturb her flock of birds. "How did you know this?"

"I remember your bright red, curly hair from way back."

By this time, I'm sitting next to her on the park bench, within reach. Her hands go up to my hair, and she puts her fingers in my long red ringlets, although not quite as brilliant in color.

"When I first saw you, your curls came across your face and down your nose, and you tried to cover your bright blue eyes, but they just couldn't be hidden. It is a dead giveaway." She glances over in the distance. "You live close, with your mom, right?"

Her words are chosen carefully and spoken with a sense of poise and clarity. Her Southern charm permeates my ears with a caressing ease.

"Yes, I do," I reply, with hesitation.

"Oh, don't worry, chiiild." She leans back against the park bench in a relaxed stature. "I met you on a day that I will never, ever," she grabs the necklace around her neck, "ever, forget." Her voice begins to fade, as if she were deep in thought.

Her Southern drawl is lengthening each word with emphasis that is much different for this Chicago city.

"But I was only four years old, if I remember right."

How could she possibly remember such a day?

"I met you on a day I will never forget. Moments after I buried my best friend, my husband." A long pause as she regains her composure. "I came to talk to the birds." She points to the birds.

Time begins to take on a different scale. Each second seems to last forever, but I don't mind the time being slowed. I invite the change.

"You see," she picks up the brown bag of birdseed next to her, "I had to come tell the birds that he wasn't coming back to feed them anymore." She pauses between each sentence, and sometimes each word, and places emphasis on certain words. "But that I would take care of his birds from that day on." She tosses a handful of seed onto the ground, and the birds scurry around, grabbing every desired piece.

"What do you mean, his birds?" I look at the flock.

The birds belonged to no one. They were free to fly where they wanted.

"Well, you see, child." She takes a deep breath, as if to open the door to her soul and reveal her thoughts. After mustering up the courage to speak of the past, she begins. "He would come down here and feed the birds every day. Even though he was so sick and didn't feel good enough to come, he still took care of his birds," she says, with great sadness, then puts her hand on the park bench and begins to caress the bench where he sat before her. "When you came up to me on that day, I wasn't sure how to tell them." A tiny tear broke free. "But then you ..." slowly, she lifts her head and her eyes, and she points to me. The brim of her hat is fully lifted. " ... you came up and told me your name." Her head and eyes look up to the sky above, and she begins to speak, almost as if the words were made for a song. "You looked like an angel with the sunlight and your bright red curls, tight ringlets hanging in your eyes. Such innocence." Her eyes fall, but only for an instant. "You gave me the strength." She raises her eyes once again to meet mine.

"I did that?" I say.

How could that be? I was only four.

"Yes, chiiild, you did."

A tiny smile comes from her that brightens her demeanor. Her eyes and face pull back, as if a dog was being praised for a job well-done.

"You were my saving grace, and when you came to me, it was as if my husband was telling me that everything was going to be okay."

I have never thought of myself as an angel, but if that's how she sees me, then I guess I am.

"Your mother was so angry with you for talking to me then." The pain re-enters her voice. "I looked homeless." Her smile turns into sadness once more. She attempts to press the wrinkles out of her dress. "I was just dirty from burying my husband. The cemetery was very muddy, and I had to take care of his birds and tell them that he wasn't coming back." She throws another handful of seeds on the ground. "It hurt. It did, indeed. But chiiild, I understood ... why your mom told you ... not to talk to me." She lifts her hand up to meet mine, and her tiny frail fingers grab onto mine. "You were quite young to be out on your own." Our hands are interlocked, as to console each other. "How old were you then?"

She didn't catch my age the first time.

"I think I was four, not quite five. I'm twelve now." My chest lifts with expression of age.

"Yes, chiiild, your mother had a right to be quite upset with you." She attempts to console me from that day. "After all, I was a complete stranger to her, and you. I see that you have listened to her." She touches my arm so slightly. "I see you from time to time, along with your family, here in the park." She pauses once more. "So ... well, then, why the change?"

"I came over here because those kids were being so mean to you." I point to the kids still laughing at me for talking to her. "They aren't my friends. They're in my class."

"It's actually quite okay. I am used to people laughing at me. I am here," she looks toward the birds once more, "taking care of my husband's birds. They only see what they want to see." She pauses to find the right words. "Since I am here every day, they all think that I am homeless and have no other place to be." Her words become distant.

I could see that every word hurt.

I look over toward the kids once again. They're all gawking and laughing for us to hear. How can they be so cruel? I don't understand.

I notice she is now focused upon my sketchbook.

"May I see?" she says, with excitement, her hand reaching out to mine.

"But it's really not that good. That's my art class." I point once again to the kids making jokes and laughing.

She pulls my sketchbook out of my grasp, and I let go unwillingly. Only my teachers have really seen my work. And my mom.

"But it's really—"

"Really, what!" She let out a loud, "Oh, chiiild! This is really, really good!"

As she thumbs through the pages, she finds the page that I didn't want her to see. Her gaze becomes a humble stare of approval and reflection.

"And this is me and my husband's birds?" She runs her fingers over the picture, as if she is talking to her husband through the picture.

You can see the joy radiate from her eyes as she touches each bird individually. She pauses with a great breath of air.

"And this is how you see me?" She runs her fingers over herself in the drawing.

"Umm ... yes," I say, under my breath.

What if she hates it! What if she's disappointed in my vision of her?

She caresses the strokes of my pencil. "Such character and grace in this woman in the drawing."

She speaks as if the person in the drawing is not her, but a woman from a distant time. Her hands are still caressing the drawing.

"Look at her hands, as she holds the bird food. Look at the way she stretches out to feed them."

Her fingers continue to caress the picture. She speaks so eloquently of the lady in the picture, as if she were not herself. But then she is brought back to the realization that it is indeed her.

"You caught my soul as no one else has ever." A tear falls to the page. "Oh, goodness, I'm sorry." She tries to capture the tear in midair, but to her dismay, it still plummets to the paper below her.

She tries to wipe the tear off, but only smudges the spot where it once was.

Oh, my drawing! My schoolwork that I have to turn in is smudged.

I want to scream, but instead I say, in an unusual calm, "It's okay. It adds character." I giggle, trying to show that I am not upset my drawing has been ruined.

Or was it?

"Oh, chiiild." she purses her lips. "You didn't sign it."

"But it's just my drawing." I lift it up to show her once more that it was my drawing.

I must admit it was a drawing that I was proud of, but it was done by me.

"Oh, chiiild." She takes the drawing from my grasp and holds it in front of me to ensure she has my full attention. "Your drawing is a work of art. Your drawing is special. Do you know why?" She runs her fingers across the drawing, as if she were touching herself.

"Umm, no," I say.

"Because chiiild." She lifts her eyes to ensure that I am looking at her.

I wasn't, of course, but her long pause instructs me to pay attention to her. So I lift my eyes to meet hers. She has an endearing smile. Her eyes are warm and inviting.

"Because it could have only been drawn," she lifts her hand and touches my nose, "by you."

When she said that, I instantly felt the value of my drawing.

"So do I just sign my name?"

"Oh, no, chiiild." She focuses on the drawing once more. "Your signature is as special as well." She points down in the lower right corner of the page. "This is where you put your mark."

"Umm, my mark?"

"Yes, your mark. You know, your own special way of signing your name." She reaches for a piece of paper to demonstrate. "See this?"

She begins to write my name in a beautiful script with a huge letter *M*, and then each subsequent letter smaller than the *M*. And then she begins with my last name.

"Do you see how important this part is?" she says.

"Umm, I guess so." I still wondered why signing my name was so important.

"You guess so?" Her posture becomes rigid, her face wrought with disgust. "Chiiild, this is just as important as the drawing itself." She emphasizes each word. "This is how the world will know that *this*," she shakes the drawing at me, "was drawn by no one else but, *you*."

"Oh, I see."

"This is part of your dash in life."

"My dash?" Now I'm confused.

"Yes, chiiild." She puts the drawing onto her lap and begins to explain. "Life is made up of three very important dates."

I look puzzled. But I'm still listening.

"First, you have your birth date." She motions out the number one with her finger. "The date that you take your first breath in this world."

"Okay," I reply.

"But at the end, you have your death date."

Now I am really confused.

"Okay." I'm trying to follow along.

"And chiiild, what you do with your life is your dash between those two dates." She leans back against the bench. "What you do with your dash ..." an awkward pause only makes me yearn for her words, " ... defines you as a person."

"Okay." I'm getting closer.

"So this drawing here," she lifts up the drawing once more, "is a very important part of your dash." She smiles to show that my drawing is an important part of not only to my dash, but her dash as well, because it was of her. "Putting your especial signature on everything you draw adds to your dash."

"Oh, I understand."

Again, the drawing is even more valuable.

"So next time you do a drawing, leave your special mark to show that it belongs to you." She smiles again. "And you only."

"Okay." I smile to match hers.

"Even if you give it away someday, it will still have your special mark on it." She points down in the lower right-hand corner of the drawing. "Okay?"

"Yes, ma'am. I understand."

Off in the distance, my teacher is calling for the class to come back together. I hear them call my name between the giggles from the children.

"I need to go. And I'm sorry for them being so mean to you." I begin to grab for my book.

"Truly beautiful! I must say. It's okay, dear." She hands back the book. "A true artist with true talent."

The teacher calls once again, this time with a whistle added.

"Thank you. I have to get back to class." I turn and run back across the park to my group gathering together to get back onto the bus.

"I will stop again if I see you," I yell, waving while running towards the bus.

My teacher is motioning me to move faster, and the other children are steadily laughing, making comments, and chirping like a bird.

"I hope so." She waves and smiles.

She turns back to her birds and says, under her breath, "I hope so." She settles back into her bench. "I do hope so, chiiild."

Even though her spirits were noticeably lifted, the somber quietness overcomes her. Alone on the bench with her husband's birds, she finds solace once again.

Standing in line to get on the bus, the kids all begin to laugh and make fun.

"I can't believe you were talking to that *homeless* lady over there." One boy points at her.

He makes sure to emphasis the word *homeless*, to ensure everyone hears him, so they, too, could get in on the joke.

One guy grabs my sketchbook and holds it up for all to see. "And look, she even drew her!"

The crowd begins to laugh at me. All the kids were passing my sketchbook around as if it were a prize of their own. Each one in my class takes their turn laughing as they grab my prize drawing.

My book! That's my book!

I try to grab my book away, only to have it held higher out of my reach. I'm the same age, but \ shorter.

"Stop it!" I scream. Fearful my book was ruined; I reach for it once more. "Stop it!" My hands make contact with my book, and I pull it close to me for security. "And she is not homeless!" I yell.

I pull my sketchbook toward me to protect my most prize possession. These are my thoughts and feelings put into drawings that can only come from me.

I check the sketchbook for pages that could have been torn or damaged by the kids playing and making fun of me. I turn the pages back to where the sketchbook cover is now protecting my artwork. Some of the pages got creased and folded when it was being thrown around outside the bus door. I want to cry because I feel like my heart was just thrown upon the sidewalk and stepped on.

Something makes me look at The Bird Lady, and I notice she is watching the whole thing. She saw me as they took my book and laughed at me for my drawing. It was on top. You could see the hurt and dismay in her demeanor, but I was too far away to see her face.

She notices all has calmed down, and she turns around to sit back on the bench. Some of the kids notice she is watching the whole thing. They aren't sure if they're in trouble or not. The look on their faces turns to guilt. But not all are so somber. Some are still laughing.

Being next to get on the bus, I turn. "Now, leave me alone!"

I take the first step onto the bus. I find my seat and stay to myself, with my book in my lap. I open the book to look down at my drawing of The Bird Lady and run my finger over where the tear had fallen minutes before. The tear drop has dried but left its mark. I can't help but look back at that very park bench to get one last glimpse of her. She sits motionlessly as we pull away.

With my hand still upon the drawing, I am pulled closer into the moment. The tear ... that tear was given to me from her heart, which was in so much pain, even I could feel it.

I rub my finger upon it once more. It had dried, but left a smudge on the drawing, next to her shoulder. That smudge burned a lasting memory into my mind.

I take my pencil out to put the final touch on my drawing. Following the Bird Lady's instruction, I put my mark on it. I begin to draw it in my mind, and then it just happens. My drawing is now complete with my mark, my special mark. *Mary Parker* is sketched on the bottom right corner, for all to see.

⸎

Back at work, the memory of that day in the park, while in class, was filed deep within my brain. I take the picture off the cubicle wall and hold it as if it were made of a delicate paper that could fall apart at any moment. After all, it is now old. I drew it at twelve.

Looking at the details of The Bird Lady and her flock of birds, I see the carefully placed lines upon her face, around her eyes. That smear from the fallen tear, after all these years, is still there. But it looks a bit different now. I'm not sure how, but different.

Oh, how I wish I could see her once more.

CHAPTER 3

IT'S THE END OF THE SCHOOL YEAR, and exams are being given. I find myself, once again, in art class, the only class I seem to love. Sure, other classes are interesting. But in art, I can express myself in ways that words cannot.

Today is much different than most. Even though this is still art class, it's more advanced, and I am now in eighth grade. I'm fourteen. Our teacher loads us on a bus again to go to a destination that we know not where. The usual kids are yelling and making fun of people as we drive down the busy streets. I just sit quietly by the window, watching the world pass by. The telephone poles are whisking by, along with the cars that are parked on the sidewalks. Each different in color and size, but when I find myself staring at the images, they all seem to blend together as one long car.

"Where are we going?" I ask the teacher who is sitting in the seat on the other side of the aisle, but in the same row.

"We are going back to the park where we were at the beginning of the semester." My teacher looks through some papers in his briefcase. "I want to see if your perceptions have changed from the beginning of the school year."

This teacher is different than others I've had. He actually examines the drawings, the details, the talent. He sees progress, so I can't help but ask him questions.

"The park by the water?" I say.

"Yes, Mary," he replies.

He has something on his mind, but I'm not old enough to know.

I peer out the window in expectation of seeing the park once more. Just a couple more blocks and I can visit with The Bird Lady once again. Because I live so close to this park, I feel as if I am going home.

The bus comes to a stop, with the brakes squealing. The driver gives his instruction on how to exit the bus and where to stand for attendance. No one is listening to the directions. All the class just stands up and begins to move to the front of the bus. Each one of us is bumping into another while pushing to get off the bus.

One by one, the class exits the bus while the teacher is trying to take attendance and is giving further instructions on where in the park we are to be. Meanwhile, I'm stretching my neck to see if The Bird Lady is at her park bench. I can't see her for all the people in the park, so I look even harder. I just want to talk to her once more. It has been a few months since I spoke to her.

All I see is an empty park bench. How could this be? She is always here feeding the birds.

I decide to walk over to the park bench and sit, in hopes that she would appear. It seemed empty without her. I waited for a few moments, but there was no Bird Lady.

I had to draw something from the park for my final assignment for the year, so I look around. Easily distracted, I am looking for The Bird Lady, but I stop at the sight of the birds. They would be a good subject to draw, so I begin.

Sitting on the park bench with my pencil in hand, I begin to examine the birds and their movements, their every detail—the shape of their wings, their feet, and their faces. They look the same if you just glance at them. But if you really look at them, they are all different. Some have all-white feathers, while some have black speckled feathers as well. I notice one bird has an unhealed broken leg, but it is still here with the flock. It's missing a few toes, and he doesn't use it like the other birds. He hops more than walks—an injury that must have been from long ago. They all look at me, as if to know me. Could they really remember me from all this time? Nah, how could they?

I choose to draw the bird with the broken leg, since he seems to be the slowest in the bunch. I am able to study him and then take my time drawing his every detail. The feathers are the hardest, since each quill has to be drawn. He is different, as are all of them. But he has a black tip on his one wing. Unclear if it is dirt, or meant to be, I draw it as I see it.

His broken leg is shorter than the other. A birth defect, possibly? It doesn't seem to hurt him, but it did look off. I wonder how he broke it. Or if someone broke it for him. I feel anger when that thought comes to mind. I have to stay focused on my drawing, and I push the anger away.

Next, I draw his eyes, his beak, and his nose. Yes, these birds have noses. Well, at least, holes where they breathe from. I am careful to include all the details that I can possibly see.

When the light hits the bird's eye just right, you can see the brown in it, and then the black. He's focusing on me. It's like we're communicating. He knows I need him to stay still so I complete my portrait of him. Trying to catch his very personality in this drawing almost seems easy. The bird has his head cocked to one side, as if he is posing for his portrait of distinction.

An hour or so has passed, and I feel a presence over my shoulder. I am just about finished. I look up. Thinking I'm going to see my teacher standing over me, or another student waiting to poke fun at me once again, I hear a familiar voice come from behind.

Standing over my shoulder, my drawing is very easy to see.

"Isn't he beautiful?" The Bird Lady whispers, as not to disturb the moment.

I examine my work. "Yes, he is."

At that moment, I begin to understand the very essence of her being here to take care of the birds. The connection I found with the bird is enough for me to understand the dedication with her and her husband's birds.

"He was my husband's favorite." She comes to sit beside me, ever so carefully.

Her voice is warm and inviting. She tugs at her dress to straighten it just so.

"You know, he named them all, but I could not remember them." She smiles. "He loved them like they were his children. So he named them and talked to them as if they were his children." She grabs for that necklace, just as she did several years ago when I first met her. "My husband would come down here for hours and talk to the birds and feed them. We had a daughter at home, but—" The words stop just as fast as they started.

She found the strength to finish. "She died very early in her life." She turns and points to the corner five-and-ten store behind us. "He would get his feed from that store every day, and they would put it in a brown paper bag for him to feed them."

"From that store?" I turn to see where she is pointing.

"Yes," she replies.

"That store has been here for years. I think it's as old as I am." I chuckle.

"Actually, that store is much older than you. It was here before a lot of these other stores came in. But that store has always stayed a five and ten, and I am glad that it has."

She turns back around to face the birds once more. Her words are again drawn out and elegant.

"I believe he came down here to deal with her death." A long pause. "And then it was as if he talked to her through the birds."

"That is kind of sad," I say.

We sit in silence for a few moments.

"I can't help but notice ... I love your accent," I say.

"Oh, chiiild, I am really from the south." She reaches for her hat. "I grew up in Charleston, South Carolina, and moved here with my family." She smiles. "I guess that's why I sound so different from you."

"Well, I like it." I can't help but smile. "I like it a lot."

"May I see your drawing?" She holds her hand out for permission.

"Sure." I hand my drawing pad over to her.

This time, I am much more forthcoming with my drawing

than last time. My masterpiece is now in her hands for her admiration.

"You capture him well, I must say. I am sure my husband would be pleased as well." She turns the sketch at different angles to see even more detail. "And to see his old boy looking so fine." She wears a smile of pleasure.

Turning it once more, a much more pleasing smile comes from her aged eyes.

"Yes, he would be very pleased, indeed."

"This is my final drawing for class for the year." I point over to the area of the class. "We have to come here again to draw another picture to see what we have learned this year. It's a different class, with a different teacher."

"Oh, dear, it looks magnificent."

Her words of wisdom and encouragement bring comfort.

She notices the bottom of the drawing once more. "Remember your mark?"

"Oh, yes, thank you!" I reply.

Her attention is taken back to the area where the class is.

"I see your class is gathering up to get on the bus. You better get back over to them." She points to the bus and the teacher.

After carefully closing my sketch pad, she hands it back to me.

"Oh, gosh, thank you. I wouldn't want to miss my bus." I get up with a swift motion, grabbing all my items. "I love talking to you. School will be out for the summer, and I would love to come sit with you more if I can."

"As long as it is okay with your mother." She purses her lips, as if there is a possibility it wouldn't be okay with her.

"It's okay. I will see you again soon." I run toward the bus, waving goodbye to The Bird Lady.

You know, I still don't even know her name. So for now, she will still be The Bird Lady to me.

Reaching the bus in time, I get in line to get on behind my class. We all file onto the bus and back to our seats.

"You talking to that bird lady again?" I hear from a boy's voice in the not so distance.

"Yeah. And she's actually really nice!" I say.

"Sure she is. She's just an old bag lady that plays with birds," the voice says.

Laughter fills the bus from the other kids chiming in with the remarks.

"Shut up!" I yell. "You don't know her!"

"Now, kids, stop it right now!" the teacher yells, from the front of the bus.

I hear the boys chirping like a bird and saying *bird lady* under their breath so the teacher can't hear them.

"Bird lady, *chirp, chirp, chirp*. Bird lady ..." they chant.

"Stop it!" the teacher yells again.

The troublemakers are made to stay quiet, thanks to the teacher. But I don't think that'll be the end of their harassment.

I can't help but smile, even though they are being so mean to me. I have a new friend, The Bird Lady. I sit quietly the whole way back to school, while they try to taunt me with their antics. It isn't going to get to me anymore. I will see my friend again soon.

My focus goes back to my drawing, and to put the final touch on it—my special mark. I make sure I do it just like I did the last one. That way, they are all the same.

We make it back to our classroom, and the teacher instructs us to bring up our artwork for grading. I am next to last in line, and I can hear his comments to each of them as they turn their work in. Then it is soon my turn, and I reluctantly hand the teacher my sketch. Most others handed in drawings of dogs, kids playing, and even a water fountain. But my drawing is of a bird. A bird with a broken leg.

My teacher holds the sketch up close to examine the technique. He takes his glasses off, but not totally, gazing over top of the frames. Then he takes his glasses totally off and uses them like a magnifying glass, close up to the picture. He bites his lip as if he is trying to see even closer.

He looks at me, and then back at my drawing. I can see the

amazement in his eyes with each cast of stares.

"This bird has a broken leg." He points out the broken leg in my artwork.

I wondered if he was asking or telling me about the broken leg. He acts like I didn't know it was broken.

"His quills are drawn with such perfection to see each individual feather. The detail is rich beyond your years." Now, he is becoming excited. "Where did you learn to draw like this?"

"I don't know." I glance up at the rest of the class, in hopes no one is listening to the teacher critique my artwork. "I practice a lot."

How could I possibly say that he taught me when he didn't.

"I draw what's in my heart, and what I see."

"The detail." He is holding his glasses up to the drawing once more, as if to examine each individual line. "This is exquisite! You can almost feel the bird and see its emotion while it is looking back at you." His voice becomes louder.

"It's because he *is* looking at me."

I can see the other students starting to look at me, getting angry because they didn't get the response from him that they wished.

"I don't know. I just drew the bird the way I saw it." I try to play off the meticulously drawn artwork.

"And you signed it?" he says.

"Yes. I was told that an artist always puts her special mark on every drawing."

I hear the students roar with laughter. Even hear some of them say things like, "She thinks she's an artist." But it was unclear where it came from. I am too focused on what the teacher is going to grade.

"You may be the next artist." He hands the sketchbook back to me.

"Thank you, sir." I grasp the paper in my hand, while hiding my glee deep within me.

I head back to my seat, waiting for the bell to ring to go home. I can't help but notice the boys that were making fun of me are fuming from anger and envy.

One of the boys whispers, "Did you put your mark on it like a dog marks his territory?"

Laughter rings out.

"Here, let me find you a fire hydrant to mark."

Laughter fills the room, but I just keep on walking back to my desk.

One of the boys get out of his chair and pretends to pee on my desk by lifting his leg.

"Look, everyone. I'm leaving my mark!"

"Take notice, students," the teacher says. "You will see this girl's name someday."

They aren't laughing anymore. They don't dare say anything about my drawing, because the teacher is watching their every move.

The bell rings, and I'm out the door, heading home, for the school year is over. High school is next on my list, but summertime is more important now.

<hr />

The sunlight is glaring into my room as I try to lay in bed. It is the first day of summer, and I don't have to go to school today.

"Ah," I whisper to myself. "Summer is finally here." I peek up at the window with the half-closed curtain to take inventory of the amount of light shining through the window. "Yep, it's summer all right," I whisper again.

"Honey." Mom pokes her head into my room. "I know you don't have school today, but can you get up so I can talk to you before I go to work?"

She hurries down the hallway, to the kitchen, where I imagine she is going to be making me my favorite breakfast.

I get out of bed ever so slowly because I have nothing to do this morning. Pushing the covers off my body, I swing my legs onto the floor. It's still chilly in the morning, but I know that the heat of the day will soon be near.

After pulling on some clothes, I head down to the bathroom and then on to meet my mother in the kitchen. She is sitting in a chair at the table, sipping her coffee, and I notice that there isn't any breakfast on the table for me.

"Honey, I want to talk to you before I go to work."

Oh, boy. Here it comes. She is going to tell me about the babysitter for the summer, and the rules that haven't changed in years. You know, the usual things. But this morning feels different. There isn't a babysitter here to be introduced.

I sit with her and begin to listen to my usual summer speech. I reach for the orange juice carton on the table and pour myself a small glass as she begins to speak.

"Honey, I've been thinking."

Oh, great. Here it comes.

"As you know, summer vacation starts for you, but it doesn't start for me. I have to work every day so we can afford to live here."

I'm sipping my glass of juice, waiting for the shoe to drop.

"I'm going to try something different this summer."

That sparks my interest.

"You are almost fifteen, and I think this summer, I am not going to hire a babysitter for you. You have proven to be adult enough to stay home by yourself this summer. But here again, there are going to be rules. If you can't follow them, I will hire a babysitter."

She takes a final sip of her coffee, and then begins to rinse her cup out with water.

Did I just hear this right? She is not going to hire a babysitter for me?

Stunned with the recent freedom that I've just acquired, I try not to look too excited, and respond in a normal tone.

"Thank you, Mom. I won't let you down."

She hands me a piece of paper with a list of rules on it that look pretty normal from the past years. Things like, no boys, no riding the train … you know, normal stuff. I'm not going to jeopardize this. She finally trusts me to do this on my own. My mother has always taught me right from wrong and how to be independent.

While my mother is grabbing for her purse, she takes one look back at me as she hikes it over her shoulder. In one fell swoop, she grabs her car keys in the other hand.

"So we have a deal?" Waiting for the answer, and to see my demeanor, she stands in the doorway to our apartment.

"Yes, Mom, I will be fine." I take another sip of my juice. "Besides, I want to draw some today."

"You mean, doodle?" She giggles.

"Yes, Mom, doodle." I snicker.

I hate when she mocks my drawings.

"My teacher said I am going to be a great artist someday."

"You know, someday you will need to get a real job and pay for your own apartment. Your doodling will not pay your bills," she says, as she is walking out the door to her real job that has put food on the table for us and a roof over our heads.

You know, she is probably right. My doodling may not ever pay the bills. But for now, it is what I love to do. Someday, I want to be a great artist, or even work for a company that I can draw illustrations for. I love to draw.

The door begins to close, but only after a little squeak that it's had for years. I lock the door behind her, just as she instructed, and begin my day. But first, I turn around and back up to the door and ponder what to do. No babysitter, no one to tell me to make my bed or clean my room. I'm here all alone, for what seems to be the very first time. Am I a grown-up?

After my chores, I decide to put on a pair of shorts and a tank top since it is June and the sun is shining bright through the half-pulled curtains in the living room. I run to my room and grab a pair of socks and my tennis shoes so I can go outside. After tying my shoes, I grab my sketchpad and a few pencils, and shove them into my book bag. Yes, I decided to go to the park today to see if The Bird Lady is there.

Giving a once-more glance around our apartment to make sure I covered everything so I could leave, I throw the book bag straps over my shoulders and go on my way out the door. Checking the watch my mom gave me, I notice that it's afternoon, and that I have plenty of time before she is to come home. After locking the door with my new key, and taking a deep breath of freedom, I am on my way. No babysitter. I can do this.

Getting to the park is no issue at all. I know exactly where to go because I was there for, like, only a thousand times before. But this time, I'm almost fifteen, and all by myself for the first time. While standing at the edge of the park, I notice the usual groups of people playing games, reading, and throwing balls for their dogs. I notice the sunbathers in their scandalous bathing suits that I wasn't allowed to wear yet. Yeah, better not even try that one yet on Mom.

I weave through the different groups of people, dogs and toys. I end up next to the water, where the park benches are located. Then I see her. The Bird Lady is here, and I feel like my day is complete. Now, carrying my book bag in my arms, I walk close to the park bench.

"Hi," I say, my breath heavy. "See, I told you I would come back to see you." My smile is beaming with accomplishment.

My hair is blowing softly in the gentle wind coming off the waterfront. My eyes are begging for her to look up, and she does.

"Oh, hello, chiiild." Wrinkles on her cheeks succumb to a smile as bright as her eyes.

She pulls her bag of birdseed out of the way and close to her leg to make room for me to sit next to her.

"Here, sit down, my chiiild." She pats the park bench like its soft cushion, or like she's instructing a puppy dog to come up and sit with her.

Nonetheless, she is inviting me to be with her, and I am pleased for the invitation.

I plop down while still holding my book bag close to my heart with both arms.

"Thank you," I reply. "I'm glad you are here today."

I brush back my curls to get a better look at her and then the birds. Some birds are flying about. Some are standing before us, waiting for their prize. But the one with the broken leg is standing off a bit, gazing at me.

"How are the birds today? I say.

"They are quite hungry today." She throws a handful of food out toward the water. "I think they could eat forever if I kept feeding them." She chuckles. "Here." She reaches into the bag, only to pull it out with a rich bounty of birdseed.

She places her hand in mine and deposits the birdseed for me to give to the birds. Closing my hand carefully, not to spill too much, I thrust my hand out, while my fingers open to give freely what is in my hands. The birdseed spills to the sidewalk. Just as it scatters in every direction, so do the birds. I feel the appreciation from the birds as they eat to their content.

Sitting on the park bench, I find myself nervously swinging my feet, which do not touch the pavement below. My tennis shoes are dirty and well-worn. Sometimes my legs swing in unison, and sometimes alternating, but I find myself at a loss for words.

"What's wrong, my chiiild?"

The Bird Lady notices I am fidgety today, and honestly, I don't know why.

"I don't know your name," I reply, under my breath.

See, I wasn't sure if she told me, and I just forgot. But nonetheless, I am afraid to ask again, even if for the first time. My legs begin to swing faster due to the anxiety I'm feeling.

"Oh, honey, is that what's bothering you?" She giggles, and as if her dress was newly wrinkled, she presses it down to straighten it. "My name, child, is Mildred. Mildred Whitefield."

She extends her hand out toward mine. I feel weird because I've known her almost my whole life, but it seems as if I'm meeting her for the first time. I extend my hand out to meet hers and grasp her hand to shake it. Her hand is so much older than mine. The wisdom in her hand portrays the years, just like a tree shows its rings. Each age mark, each freckle, each wrinkle placed just perfectly upon her skin. Only one ring, and that ring must have been her wedding ring. But wait, she said her husband died when we first met. Did she remarry? I do not remember her saying anything about being remarried. Actually, she spoke fondly of her husband, as if he were here with us today.

"It is a pleasure ... to meet you, my dear Mary." She gives a smile of approval.

Our hands are still intertwined.

"Thank you." I smile in return.

Our hands slowly part.

I see her grasp onto the necklace that she holds so dear to heart.

"Your necklace is pretty."

She pulls it out from her dress neckline to show the prized heirloom.

The necklace is a locket placed on a chain made of a tightly woven white gold. The locket itself is that of beautifully etched white gold, with a large script *M* on it. It looks to be a custom piece. Nothing that I have ever seen.

"That is very pretty." I gasp with amazement as she shows me the face of the locket. "Look! It has an M on it, like my name, Mary!" I say, not thinking that she just told me her name started with an M, too.

"That is the letter in my name, too. Mildred, M."

"Oh, yeah, I get it," I say, feeling stupid.

"You know ..." She lifts the necklace up so I can get a better look.

Her hands are shaky from age, but steady enough to hold the necklace for me to see the details. Her nails show her polish is worn and needs to be redone. The color of her polish is dull from age. Nothing bright colored like the kids my age wear. But here again, I am a teenager.

"My husband gave me this when we first started dating." Her fingers caress the M on the front of it.

I can see her mind wander off into distant memories. She turns the locket over and shows off the back of the necklace, where an inscription has been placed. It is good that the actual chain of the necklace is long, so she didn't have to unclasp the hook on it.

Her fingers caress the back, just as she did the front.

"What does it say?"

I can see that she is deep in memories, but my curiosity has taken me back in time with her. I lean closer to see the locket.

"My husband had this engraved just for me." Her fingers are then moved aside for the inscription to be seen.

"It's beautiful," I say.

"*For the love of my life. Love, Harold.*" She reads the inscription out loud, but her voice has a crackle to it.

"His name was Harold?" I am begging for more information.

"Yes, it was, chiiild. And he was the love of my life as well. He gave this to me before he went off to the war. He wanted to make sure I would wait for him."

I've never met anyone that went off to war. I only heard about it in school.

"How old was he?" I say.

"He was nineteen." She gazes at the locket. "I was seventeen when he left."

"Wow. Were you scared?"

"Yes, but I knew that this very locket was important. It was a promise ..." she pauses to ponder the memory of that day. " ... that he was coming back for me." She holds it tight in her hands once more. "Oh, I almost forgot." Her voice raises with excitement.

She grasps onto the locket with both hands, holding it within her fingers. She takes her thumbnail and begins to pry the locket apart. I hear a faint snap, and the locket opens, bearing gifts inside like a time capsule.

"I have not," she fumbles to hold the precious locket, "opened this in years." She reveals the contents of the time capsule for me to see.

I peer down at the locket and see two black and white photos of young lovers. One photo is of a young woman with curls pinned up under a hat, much like the one she is wearing at the moment. The other photo is of a serviceman in his uniform. He looks much too young to serve. I couldn't help but notice the acne from his young age. His eyes are young and look scared, yet proud to serve his county. His hair is cut short—you know, military style.

"He gave this to me," she fumbles the locket, "along with a promise that he was coming back to me," she touches her heart when she says *me*, "after the war was over." She gazes at the photos that she hasn't seen in quite some time. "Shortly afterwards, he fulfilled his promise and came back home to me." Her face lightens up with an endearing smile. "He then went to my father and asked him for his blessing."

"Blessing? What does that mean?"

"In my time, child, men had to ask the girl's father for their hand in marriage. It is called a blessing."

"Oh, so that's what a blessing is," I say, with amazement. "So did he get it? You know, the blessing thing."

"Why, yes, he did. That is how we became husband and wife." She chuckles.

"Oh, yeah. I knew that," I say, feeling stupid.

"It's okay, chiiild. I know you kids do things differently now."

"So how long did it take for you to get married?"

"Soon afterwards. Our families came together, and we went to be married in the local church." Her face softens. "It was a beautiful, but very small ceremony. Just our families coming together. Nothing like you kids do it nowadays. You know, with that," her face begins to contort, "booming music and big fancy cakes that cost an arm and a leg."

"I don't know much about that, but my cousin got married and the cake was really big, and we danced all night to the band she hired."

Hmm, I guess she is right.

"That's what I mean, chiiild. My mother cooked dinner where all the neighbors brought some good southern cooking, and we played music on whatever we had, and knew how to play." She pauses. "Nothing like those big TV weddings that the rich people have to show off."

What she wasn't telling me is that her husband was from old money. His family was well-off, but they didn't flaunt it like the people on TV do.

"We were very, very traditional."

She begins to close the locket, but only after she takes yet another long gaze into her nineteen-year-old husband's photo. A love so precious, and so long ago. Her face lit up as if the photo was taken just yesterday.

Upon closing the locket, the snap makes a loud *pop*, as if it were closing the memory deep within the confines of the locket. A precious memory kept safe for time to come.

"It's really neat that you still have it after all these years," I say, trying to console her aching heart.

"Yes, chiiild, I have kept it safe," she still holds the locket close to her heart, "for many years." She gazes down to her left hand, where her wedding band is. "And I still wear my wedding band, too. Even though," pain fills her eyes, but there is an aura of relief that he is with God, "he left me," she points to the heavens above, "to go home, years ago."

Her right hand is fingering her wedding band, turning it around and around upon her frail finger.

Then I realize that it was about 11 years ago that I first met her on this very park bench.

While admiring her wedding band, I say, "It sure is beautiful."

I now have a new understanding of what the wedding band on her frail finger means to her. I didn't really understand that, until now.

You see celebrities getting married and flaunting their wedding rings on TV, and then on the next show, they're displaying the divorce. In those cases, their wedding bands didn't mean anything, except probably to get people to notice them, or to sell another movie. But this ... this is different. The ring that is still on her hand after all these years proves that love is real. The love between them will last forever, even if they are not alive.

This is the love I hope I can find someday.

But what do I know about love? I'm still too young to even have my first kiss.

"You," she points her finger into my chest to make the point, "make sure that if you meet a nice man, one that will love you like my husband does ..." the pause takes her breath away, " ... I mean, did ..."

Oh, that was painful to see and hear come from the depth of her heart.

"... that he takes the time to ask your father for your hand in marriage." She pauses to gather her thoughts. "And that your father gives his blessing."

I notice that a Southern woman speaks in phrases, not whole sentences. But with her talking to me like this, it makes more sense. It is spoken with love and sincerity, but also in a directive that cannot be mistaken. My mother speaks like a machine gun—quick and to the point. She gets the message across in mere seconds, where The Bird Lady speaks eloquently, but direct.

"Umm," I look to the birds, "that may not happen for me." My face and mood become sad yet withholding.

"But why, chiiild? He must be a gentleman to deserve to be married to you. He *must*, get your father's approval beforehand. None of this," her face becomes distorted with disgust, "shotgun, quickie marriage stuff." She flicks her arm to show how disgusted she is with the marriages nowadays.

"Well ..." I pause, afraid to answer, " ... a guy can't ask my dad to marry me."

"Well, why not, chiiild? If he is a gentleman, he will."

"I don't talk about it much. Actually, I can't remember when I talked about this with my mom, but ..." I gather my thoughts on how to actually say this, " ... my dad is gone." My voice cracks.

Speaking about this hurts. How could I have just blurted it out like that? My own mom won't even talk about it.

"What do you mean, gone? Is your mom a single parent?"

Since this is the time of on-again-off-again marriages, she thinks that this is what has to be happening here. The Bird Lady wants to know more but is cautious now in her questioning.

"Well, I guess you can say that." My voice gets quieter.

My body begins to turn inward. My legs begin to swing once more. This time, the birds are beneath me, and they scatter with each swing.

"Careful, chiiild." She puts her hand on my knee to instruct me to stop swinging while the birds are in harm's way. "Are your parents divorced? There are a lot of single households in this world," she says, as to judge the world that did not follow the gentlemen's code of honor.

She knows that she is putting the stick into the bee's nest, as they use to say in her time.

"No, they aren't divorced. Not really." I take a breath. "My dad is …" The incorrigible pause once more. Oh, here it goes. "He's just gone."

"Chiiild, gone as in *gone*?" she says, in a secret code kind of way, the ache of losing her husband felt once more.

"Umm, yeah. He died a long time ago, before I met you."

There! I said it out loud.

"My dad is dead! He's gone! Just gone!"

My voice is childishly loud and obviously irritated because I am revealing a part of me that has not been talked about ever.

"Oh, chiiild. I am so sorry, chiiild." She tries to comfort my pain.

"It's okay. It happened so long ago that I haven't thought of it much. Sure, I see kids with their moms and dads, but my mom keeps me so busy that I just don't think about it anymore."

"What happened?" she says.

"Not really sure." My legs begin to swing again from the anxiety brewing within.

I quickly get ahold of the anxiety and stop my legs from swinging, so I don't dare hurt my newfound friends, the birds.

"I was really little, and one day he just never came home."

A tear formed in my eye, but I wasn't accustomed to showing it fall. I haven't cried over my dad in so long that he is a distant memory in my mind.

"My mom sure cried a lot, and I remember her telling Aunt Jackie that she wasn't sure how we were going to make it." I pause to gather my thoughts. "I never really understood what that meant back then."

I look over the water, out past the birds. I see the ripples in the water that are being made by the softly blowing wind. Sparkles are forming on the water from the sun catching its essence. The sparkles are dancing with each passing ripple.

"My mom has always taught me to be self-sufficient. Work hard for what I want. You know, study hard in school. Never expect a handout."

I remember my mother's speeches to me throughout the years of my childhood. The conversation got really raw for a teenager. She could see that I have aged beyond my years.

"We never talked about him, and I never asked either," I say.

"Did you go to the funeral?"

"Nope. If I remember right, there wasn't a funeral. Nothing. He was just gone, and there were a lot of sleepless nights, with my mom crying at night."

The painful memories are vivid, but I tried to obscure them. I remember lying in bed late at night, hearing my mom sob in the other room. I tried to comfort her a few times, but I think I made it worse. I reminded her of him.

"I'm sorry, chiiild." She puts her arms around me.

Oh my God. She hugged me! What just happened? The Bird Lady opened her heart to me and gave me a hug. A real hug! The hug is so inviting and feels like a warm summer day was injected into my heart.

And the smell ... oh, she has on a perfume that I have never smelled before. It hits my nose with a sweet exhilaration of flowers. These flowers are not overpowering, by any means. But much more like an inviting summer day that comes in the wind as you drive your bike down a country road. I haven't smelled anything like that in a very long time.

I remember that smell when I went to visit my cousins in North Carolina. I think they called it jasmine. That is probably why her hat is so special to me. I saw those hats in North Carolina when I was visiting. We went to the Azalea Festival and saw all the Azalea Belles in their long, beautiful gowns. Belles of all ages were in the parade, and they were treated like royalty. The parade was long, with marching bands, horses, clowns, and fire trucks. The mansions were adorned in their flowers. Now, I understand why I love her Southern charm so much.

Feeling awkward, I look down at my book bag, which I never even opened.

"I really better be getting back home before my mother gets there."

The timing is all off, and I bet it sounds cheesy, but I really do have to go.

"Okay, then." She backs up, as to get the clue that things are getting too intense.

After all, we did spend the entire afternoon just sitting and talking. Just me and my new friend, Mildred. Otherwise known as The Bird Lady. The lady with the Southern drawn-out wisdom under that big, beautiful, tattered, Azalea Belle hat. The lady with the funny way of talking, with her broken words and awkward pauses. I have my first real friend. Not a friend from school, but a *real* friend.

I get up and reposition my book bag on my shoulder and turn to head back home.

"Thank you for today!" I meant it.

I am so happy to have an adult talk to me like I'm not a kid. I think this responsibility thing with Mom is going to work out just fine.

With a big smile, she says, "It was a pleasure, my chiiild."

Her eyes soften, along with her voice. You could see she needed to talk to someone, too. We both, in a sense, saved each other from this loneliness that surrounds us.

"Can I come see you again soon?"

"Why, sure you can, chiiild. I would love to talk to you again. It was indeed a pleasure." Once again, she speaks with her Southern charm and hospitality. "Just look for me and my birds.

I am usually here." She waves her hand to point out her flock of birds.

"Okay. Thank you." I turn to leave through the park to get home but turn around again and wave. "See you soon."

"See you soon, chiiild."

She turns to the birds to give them the last few morsels of seed. When they are finished, she crumbles up the bag and tosses it in the trash can close to where we were sitting.

The walk home is uneventful. You know, when your mom fills your head with all this bad stuff in the world that could and would happen to me if I were to walk alone, or even talk to a stranger. It just doesn't seem to happen. Some of our neighbors and shop owners say hello to me as I walk by and instruct me to tell my mom this or that. But they usually just say hello.

My walk is different. I feel different. I stand up a bit taller and feel older somehow.

I get upstairs to our apartment before my mom makes it back from work. This is a good thing, especially on the first day of being on my own without a babysitter. While sitting on my bed, I hear the fumbling of the door lock, and then the all too familiar squeak of the door as it opens. My mother's voice appears before she enters the doorway.

"Mary?" My mother bustles in the door, carrying bags of groceries.

The bags are making a lot of welcomed noise.

"Coming." I head into the kitchen to help.

Mom bought the normal groceries, but this time she has a frozen pizza. We don't normally eat frozen pizza.

"You did well on your first time without a babysitter. Thought we would have a treat tonight," she says, looking for approval.

"Cool." I giggle.

"So," my mom says, "what did you do all day?"

She scans the apartment to see if movement of things is apparent, or if the TV is on a particular movie channel. But she finds none of that.

Gathering up my book bag off the kitchen table, I hesitate to answer, but what could it hurt?

"I went down to the park today." I lift my gaze to see her reaction. "You know, to find things to draw," I say, to reassure her.

But no response comes.

I decide to sit in the chair and talk to my mom like an adult, instead of running off into my room like a spoiled child.

"I saw Mildred there."

"Oh, wow, is this a girl from school?" She is opening the pizza box.

"Umm, no." I pause, getting ready for the shoe to drop. "It is the lady that feeds the birds." I'm anxious for a response. "You know, the lady you call The Bird Lady."

My mom is still fumbling with the pizza, getting it into the oven.

"Uh-huh," she says, under her breath.

She is waiting for the rest of the story before giving her reaction.

"It is really neat talking to her." My voice begins to get excited as I tell her about my day. "We talked about how she and her husband ... well, he died ... how they were young war-torn lovers, and how their love is timeless. She even showed me a picture of him in a really cool locket that she wears around her neck. You know, she even still wears her wedding ring!" With each passing word, the feeling of warmth spills from my mouth.

"Well ..."

Oh, great. Here it comes.

"Sounds like a bunch of malarkey to me."

Mom gets cold when I begin to speak about love. Me, a fifteen-year-old. What do I know about love, anyway?

"We also talked about how her husband asked her dad for a blessing to marry her. Isn't that funny? He had to get permission." I chuckle, as if I just got the joke. "She told me that when I want to get married, my boyfriend has to ask my dad for his blessing, too." My excitement of the day is changed. "I told her that is not going to happen with me."

"You spoke about your dad?" My mom is now engaged in the conversation.

"Yeah, I did." I reach for a glass to get something to drink. "So …"

Oh, God, I want to ask so badly, but I'm afraid to. Oh, crap, here it goes.

"So what happened? You know, to Dad?"

Whew! There it is. The question that has been on my mind, but I was so afraid to even think about.

My mom slowly sits in the chair on the other side of the table. Her face is flat from emotion, and she almost seems lost. She opens her mouth, but nothing comes out. She gazes at the ceiling, as if there is someone writing the words for her. She squints, trying to read the words that aren't there for her to see. Mom then runs her hand across the table like there are crumbs from the last meal.

"Your father was gone a very, very long time ago. He was in the service somewhere." Her voice begins to change in pitch. "I have no idea where."

Her eyes meet mine. She seems different at that moment. She is such a strong woman. This person that is sitting before me doesn't look like my mom at all. Sure, she has the same facial features, but it's as if a door in her personality was just opened, and she became a different, calmer, almost lost person.

"I wasn't allowed to know where he was. Something to do with secret stuff." She scratched her head, as if talking about this hurt.

A tear forms, and her face gets tight. Wrinkles form above her eyes. Her nose and mouth clench together. The tears fall, but in silence.

Oh my God, I remember those tears. They fell when I was a child, lying in bed awake at night, listening to her cry about my dad.

I did it. I hurt my mom. I opened a door that was locked away in her heart for a long time. If I had any idea this was going to happen, I would have never asked. But I had to. I needed to know.

"Your father never came home. We never had the chance to get married. He was just gone."

Her tearful eyes reach for mine. You can see that she wants to run over to me and put her arms around me, but she never does. Her motherly composure takes over once again, and she wipes the tears off her face. She stands erectly to show me just how strong she is supposed to be for me.

Then it hits me. The love of her life may have made the same promise as Herold did. You know, the one to come back and then get married. I guess he never came back. That's why they never got married.

"But—"

"There is no *but*."

She was getting angry now because she feels the pain that was pushed down inside her heart for only her to know.

"I'm sorry."

I feel responsible for the pain I just caused her, but I did get some information. He was in the military.

The oven buzzer goes off and breaks the ominous feeling in the apartment. Pizza comes out of the oven, and we sit down at the kitchen table to eat. Yes, my mother and I always eat at the kitchen table together. My mom calls it tradition, and it is a family value to sit and talk together. Since it's just the two of us, we need to stay connected.

She cuts the pizza in equal pieces and places it upon the cutting board in the center of the table. She hands me a paper towel and a fork. Even though it's pizza, we try to eat civilized, with a fork.

Only a few moments pass, and it seems like the hurtful conversation was that of days past. No more words are spoken for a few minutes, and then she changes the subject, like it never happened.

"So what else did you do today?"

While in mid-bite, she catches me with my mouth full. That just isn't fair. Sort of like when a waitress comes to a table to ask if there is anything else she can do for us, and we all have food in our mouths. We all just have to nod, as if we love our food and nothing is wrong. You know, that kind of unfair.

I swallow my food. "I did my chores on the list."

I notice my mom glancing around the house to inspect my work. She seems pleased.

"I went for a walk to the park, with my drawing book."

She tilts her head.

"What else did you do at the park?" Her question matches her face, serious and concerned.

Notice, no boys were mentioned in my lack of response.

"Did you doodle today?" She clears her throat. "Sorry, draw. Did you draw today? Did you meet any boys?"

Oh my gosh, I actually did not draw anything today! I just spent the whole day talking to Mildred and feeding the birds. Will Mom get mad if I didn't actually draw?

I can't help but laugh. "Noooo."

"I ..." I have to pause before I speak to her.

My mother has always taught me to think before I speak. It is a sign of wisdom.

"Mom, this lady is a very nice Southern lady, and she is not homeless at all. She takes care of the birds because they were her husband's, and he died."

When I finish the sentence with *he died*, my voice changes. Empathy begins to pour out because I feel the loss of my dad. And I think my mother sees the connection. This is the first time I even talked, or have shown any kind of emotion, about my dad being gone. I don't even remember him.

When my mother sees the emotion that is finally being shown about my dad—or so she thought—she sees something that she couldn't take away. She wants so desperately to keep her daughter, me, away from the homeless lady. But this is different. I am different.

Oh, here it comes again.

My mom turns into a volcano, and words erupt like molten hot lava burning their point into my ears.

"I want you to stay away from that homeless Bird Lady!" She

picks up her plate with a half-eaten piece of pizza on it and slams it on the counter.

"But Mom! She's a really nice lady!" I stand.

"I see I will have to get a babysitter again this year. Filling your mind with all this love stuff."

"No, Mom, you don't have to do that. I will be good. I don't need a babysitter. Even though Chicago is a huge city full of bad things, I can handle this. Mom, please give me another chance! No babysitter." My voice softens.

"Okay, one more chance. No more homeless people. And no more Bird Lady!"

"But she's nice!"

"I said no!" Her voice is just like it was when I was four and being scolded in the park.

I run to my bedroom like any fourteen-year-old would and close my door. I want to slam it, but that would only make my mom order a babysitter, for sure. So I carefully close it. But in my mind, I'm slamming it so hard the house shakes off the foundation.

I hear my mom cleaning the kitchen, and I just stay in my room. I hear the sniffles, but I'm not sure if she's crying or not, so I go to my bed. I feel a tear on my nose as I lay on down. Why am I crying? Is it because I can't go see her anymore? Am I crying because Mildred's husband died? Oh, wait, am I crying about my dad? I saw my mom start to get upset when I mentioned Mildred's husband dying. Was mom upset about Dad, too?

After an hour or so, both of us calm down. I decide to come out of my room and go into Mom's bedroom, where she is up reading a book. I sit down cautiously, just in case she is still on a rampage.

"I'm sorry, Mom."

I couldn't have my mom mad at me. We are all we have.

My mom raises her arm up so I can curl into her side with my head on her shoulder, facing the book, along with her.

A deep sigh comes from my mom, and her chest raises up and down. My head goes up and down, since I'm lying on her. It's kind of funny to ride the sigh with her. As she exhales, she blows my hair onto my face. She takes her glasses off and puts them on the book.

"I'm sorry, too. I'm not getting a babysitter." She puts her hand across my forehead to push back my curls to see my bright freckled face.

I turn my head so my eyes meet hers, and I can see she was crying earlier. I think she notices that I was crying earlier, too.

"We need to stick together. If anything happened to you, I would be lost," she says, with a soft, crackly voice.

She touches the tip of my nose with her finger to get her point into my head.

"I know, Mom."

A half-cocked smile is all she can muster.

"Go to bed. It's late."

I get up and go to my bedroom so we both can lick our wounds from the argument. Nothing is broken, but the wounds are still there.

A week has passed, and I'm feeling cooped up in our little apartment. My mother and I are sitting at the kitchen table, watching TV, and eating dinner. This is something that is important to my mother. And well, I guess I kind of like doing it, too.

The news is on TV, and we notice that a homeless woman was beaten in the park yesterday. My mother is too busy to notice, but my heart sinks. Well, it actually doesn't sink. It's in my throat, and I feel like throwing up. The newscaster doesn't say the lady's name, but it has to be her.

Oh God, I'm not going to see her ever again. She was my friend. My only friend.

As I am lying in bed, trying to sleep, I can't help but toss and turn. The only thing I can think of is my friend, The Bird Lady, in the park. Why would anyone want to hurt her? She was so sweet, and she took such good care of the birds, her husband's birds. Maybe it wasn't her. Maybe it is another homeless lady in the park that got hurt. I have to find out. Tomorrow, I will go to the park, even though my mom won't let me. I have to go. I just have to.

Morning comes, and my mom knocks on my door. She notices I'm already up. This is different. It is summer, and I can sleep in. But today is different. I couldn't sleep last night. To be awake when my mom is getting up for work? Yep, today is different.

"You're awake already," she says.

"Yeah, I couldn't sleep at all," I say, my voice groggy.

"Why?"

I can't tell her why. I don't want her to know what I am going to do today. I'm afraid that I'm going to have a babysitter walk through the door at any time.

"I don't know. Just couldn't sleep, I guess." I try to sound convincing.

But I don't think she's buying it.

I fumble for something to wear to head down to the kitchen to get some cereal. As I'm pouring the milk onto my cereal, my mother comes back into the room with her keys in her hands.

"Are you sure you're okay?"

"Yeah, I'm fine." I take a spoonful of cereal in my mouth.

My mother is standing there, not convinced.

"I'm fine, really." With my mouthful of cereal, it doesn't quite come out like that.

"Honey, don't talk with your mouth full."

I shake my head to show I understand her.

With my mouth full, it takes me out of the conversation, and she is free to leave for work.

"Bye, honey. See you later." She heads out the door.

I wave to her, since I can't speak. The door closes, and the lock turns. I am alone. Now, if I wait a few minutes for her to leave, I can head to the park.

With the coast clear, I can get dressed and head out the door. I feel like I can't get there fast enough. Down the stairs and down the street to get to the park seems like such a long walk.

There it is. The park. Now, where is she? I feel my heart begin to race, like a panic.

I go to the park bench where she's normally feeding the birds. She isn't here. My heart sinks like the Titanic, with the orchestra playing on the deck, soothing the doom bestowed upon the crew and passengers. I take a good, hard panoramic look around the entire park area, praying to find her.

I run over to the park bench, pleading with the birds to talk to me. Where is she? The birds are flying around, just as they always do, begging for their birdseed. The park seems scarce this morning due to the news, but still some people brave the unseen dangers. This park is extremely long, so who knows, it could have been a homeless lady blocks from here. But I have to know. All I know is that my only friend, Mildred, isn't here.

I sit on the bench in silence, gazing out over the water, pleading for answers. The water glistens, as always. The birds fly around, as usual. All the normal noises are emulating from the people in the park. Doesn't anyone care about the lady who was just hurt here?

Suddenly, I get it. Being seen as a homeless lady, you inevitably become invisible to most people. It's like a homeless man sitting on the side of the street, holding a sign asking for food. Almost everyone walks past him, as if he is invisible. No one wants to stop and even give him a few dollars to help him, or even his family that could be left in a street alley. No one speaks to people of the street. They don't even say, *Hello*, or *Have a good day*. How could they have a good day? They are society's throwaway people, sleeping in the corners of the night, just waiting to commit a crime. Or worse, a crime committed upon them.

But wait, is Mildred invisible? How can she be? My heart begins to hurt so bad that I can't help but cry. I find myself crying for a lady who no one cares about.

"Why the tears, chiiild?"

The voice of a Southern angel rings out from behind me. She comes around the park bench, only to be met by an overexcited girl who has sprung to her feet.

The tears of pain are now tears of joy that I cannot control. Why am I crying so hard? Before I can control myself, my arms fly around her, and I sob like a child. She puts her bag of birdseed down on the park bench. Stunned by the sight of me crying so hard, she begins to slowly wrap her arms around me. It's like she's hugging a caged big cat, waiting for the final scratch to happen. Before I realize it, she hugs me with both arms to comfort my wailing soul. I have never felt this type of warmth from a hug—an endearing deep hug that is protective and caring.

"Chiiild, what on earth is wrong?"

I can barely get a word out between the gasping breaths. Oh, how I want to stay in her arms forever. The sweet smell of her perfume and the safety I feel against her chest. I find myself thinking of my mother and how I wanted to be held like this last night. Why can't my mother hold me like this?

I get control of my breath to breathe words in and out.

"I..."

Oh crap, here they come again. Those tears just won't stop.

"... I saw the news last night."

We're finally able to part enough for her to look at my swollen red face. She brushes back the dampened strands of hair away from my face to get a better look at my bright blue eyes that are now more prevalent since my face is deep red.

"What, chiiild?"

I realize that she doesn't even understand why I'm so upset. She must not have seen the news last night.

"The lady ..." my face begins to distort once more as tears begin to well up within my eyes, "... the homeless lady last night that was hurt in the park."

My pain is real, and she now understands the source.

"They said that a homeless lady was hurt in the park last night, and ..."

I feel a twinge of shame. I said *homeless*, and I am now referring to her as being homeless again.

"... and, I couldn't see if it was you."

She now has the whole truth. Here I am. A little, but grown-up teenage girl pained by the mere thought of her friend being hurt in the park last night. The importance of her presence in the park comes to light.

"But chiiild, I told you. I'm not homeless." She tries to reassure me with her Southern charm and sincerity. "I'm quite all right, chiiild."

She lifts my head by placing her hand on my chin, bringing my attention up to hers. She directs me to sit on the park bench by holding my hand and pulling me downward. We sit in unison, side by side.

"I was afraid."

I'm finally able to talk in a normal speech, since the tears are subsiding, and my breathing is back to normal.

"I heard something this morning. It never occurred that you would think it was me."

I'm not sure if she thinks of it as a slanderous thought, being just like everyone else. Most people see her as being homeless, a kind of menace to society. But I see her as a valued friend that could have been in danger. Either way, my pain is still real, regarding the admiration we have for each other. In both of our eyes, we have been long-time friends. She has watched me grow up in this park as time has passed.

"I am so happy you are here today," I blurt out, with anxiety.

"I'm happy you are here as well."

My words are met with an endearing smile.

"I told my mom that I came to see you," I say, to show her that I'm not hiding from my mom.

"Oh, chiiild. And was she angry?" She purses her lips with each word.

"Well ..." I want to be truthful with her, but I cannot be fully. " ... she didn't believe the part about the timeless love between you and your husband. I told her about your locket and his picture, about how he went into the military and gave you the locket to promise his return."

I begin to slow in my words. Oh, crap, I opened the door to my own stuff about my dad.

"I told her that we were talking about my dad." My face drops.

"And did you talk to each other?"

"Well, he was in the military, too." I give a smile of accomplishment about getting information. "He didn't come home." The accomplishment turns into sorrow.

"Was he killed in action, chiiild?"

"I don't know."

"What do you mean, chiiild?"

"My mom told me that she wasn't allowed to know where he was, and that he did secret things. So he kinda died in secret as well. He just didn't come home.

"I also told her that you still wore your ring and talked about him all the time."

My words force her to finger her ring and twirl it around in memory.

I chuckle. "And she asked me about boys."

"Boys?"

"Yeah, she asked me if I talked to any boys." My voice is crackling with giggles.

"Well, chiiild, there is enough time for all that. You are still young."

"But I'm almost fifteen."

I plead my case, but I'm not sure why. I don't have a boyfriend.

"You were young when your husband gave you your locket."

She grasps her shirt where the locket is beneath it.

"Yes, but things are much different now."

"I just wish I could have the kind of love that you had with your husband—umm, I mean, *have*."

"Oh, chiiild, you will." She seems unbothered by the thought of him being gone.

I get restless and jump up to go back home. Even though it's early in the day, I know my mother would be angry at me if she found out I was in the park with The Bird Lady.

"I have to go home." I turn to leave. "My mom doesn't really want me here today."

I have to tell her the truth. After all, she is now my friend. I'm not going to lie to her.

"Don't get into trouble, chiiild." She motions for me to go. "Better get home."

I feel like a puppy being told to go home. But she is right. I have to go home. I don't want to upset my mother any more than she already is. I don't want a babysitter for the rest of the summer—what's left of it.

CHAPTER 4

THE SCHOOL YEAR HAS BEGUN ONCE AGAIN. I have the usual classes, but I want to make sure I have some type of art class as well. My mother isn't very happy about it, but as long as I take other classes that she wants, then it is okay. She doesn't want me to be an artist. She thinks that doodling is just a hobby. No one can really make money from doodling. Sure, she sees the talent that I have, and my drawings are good, according to Aunt Jackie.

We don't see them hardly at all. Travis is working at a skate shop and is either there or in school. He mostly hangs out with his friends. He doesn't even like talking to me in school. But that's okay. I don't really like him either.

There is this one boy in my English class that is pretty cute. His name is Jake. We sit in the back. He sits behind me, and is mostly looking over my shoulder, checking out my latest drawings. I wonder why he doesn't take art class, if he likes art so much. Maybe he can't draw, and just likes mine. That's okay—he's still cute.

I know it's English class, but the teacher is really boring. I sit there and draw my way out of the classroom with my thoughts, while trying to understand what he's teaching.

The bell rings, and everyone jumps up to leave the classroom. While gathering my books and my drawing, the unthinkable happens. The cute boy speaks to me.

"You know, your picture is really pretty." He pushes past me.

Stunned by the mere fact that he spoke to me leaves me

speechless and standing there like a stupid schoolgirl mute from anxiety.

A small smile comes up from the depths of my soul. I can't dare let him know just how excited I am that he is talking to me. He speaks to me with kindness. Not like all the other kids that make fun of my drawings. He likes them.

Before I can find my tongue to speak, he's gone. He files out of the room with everyone else. I miss my moment. I am a total jerk! Good thing it's Friday and I don't have to face him again until Monday.

I leave the room, checking around each corner of the doorway, just in case he's there waiting to talk to me once more. Saddened by the passing of the moment, I immerse myself in the crowd, the hustle and bustle of high school. The waves of people trying to get to their classes swallow me whole. I am a mere drop of water in this big tidal wave. A spot on the wall, like the homeless woman. I'm invisible.

It's now Tuesday, and I'm trying to get my locker open. Since it's a new locker, I'm having problems. I see a girl standing close to me on my left, and I set my books down to see what she wants.

"Hi," I say to the girl who looks preppy, with her plaid miniskirt and her freshly ironed, white button-down shirt.

She looks like a girl who normally wouldn't talk to me, but who knows, this is a new year.

"Hey, I haven't seen you around here before," she says. "A few of the girls are meeting after school, and I thought you might like to come hang with us."

My stomach feels nervous, and I usually listen to my gut. But what the hell.

"Umm, sure. Right after school?" I'm happy to just be accepted.

"Yeah, out by the old tree in the back of the school. We all meet there."

"Yeah, sure." I figure I may as well meet some new people.

I never even caught her name before she left around the corner. I guess I can ask her when I see her next.

The school day goes by slowly, but I am excited to meet new friends. I can't believe they're talking to me. When the last bell rings, I hurry to my locker to get my books for homework and put the book away that I don't need to take home. I make my way out to the tree where the girls are going to meet me. I notice that no one is there yet. I guess I'm the first one there. So I sit on the stone wall next to the tree.

Looking around at the other kids walking by, I don't see anyone I recognize. I don't see the girl who asked me to come. I decide to wait a few more minutes ... and wait and wait. With each passing minute, and no one coming, I feel my heart hurt a little bit more. It's obvious that she played a trick on me. Figures. I guess this is one reason why I don't have any friends.

I can't help but notice a flock of girls walking past, all holding their mouths, laughing in my direction. Some of the guys that are with them are hanging onto the girls like they're property, to show that they have arm candy. I never saw the girl who asked me to the tree, but it's apparent that I'm the joke. I tuck my tail between my legs and have to walk home since I missed the bus. High school sucks.

⁂

It's finally Saturday, and I can't wait to see Mildred. I grab my drawing pad and pencil and push it in my bag, trying to hurry out the door. My mom isn't used to me going to the park alone, but I'm older now and she can't keep me inside.

I get to the park on the cool autumn day, and the leaves are swirling in the wind after blowing in off the water. The trees are bare, but there are a few leaves hanging on for the very last day. As I walk across the grass, the leaves crackle beneath my shoes, giving Mildred announcement of my arrival. She is seated on the same bench as always. I am so excited to talk to her that I disturb the birds when I storm up to her.

I plop down on the seat next to her, like an elephant, and begin to tell her the great news. I'm in my usual seated position, with my legs pulled up against me, and my arms wrapped around them to hold them up on the bench. I sit like this to contain my swings.

"You won't believe what happened at school yesterday!" I say.

"Oh, chiiild, calm down and tell me."

"He talked to me!" I can hardly get a word out because I have a hard time breathing from running to the park.

"Who, chiiild? Who?"

"Jake," I say, as if I am demanding her to be a mind reader.

"Who?"

"Jake! You know, the guy that sits behind me in English class?" She doesn't remember the name.

I have never been interested in boys before. I'm so nervous from the thought of Jake liking me, my legs fall off the bench and I begin a nervous swing back and forth, like a silly schoolgirl does sitting in the principal's office.

I grab my pad and hold it up not far off my lap.

"He likes my drawings!"

"So did you get to talk to him?"

"Well, no." My face goes flat.

"Chiiild, what do you mean, no?"

"Well ... I got so nervous that I couldn't talk. I wanted to talk to him, but the bell rang, and he left."

"What do you mean, left?"

"We had to change classes. He left."

I act like she understands how high school works. But I guess things were different when she went to school.

"Oh, I see, chiiild." She throws another handful of birdseed onto the ground, just as another flock of birds fly in for their morning brunch. "Maybe you can talk to him on Monday."

My legs begin to swing again. The Bird Lady puts her hand ever so slightly upon my knee to remind me that the birds are below me. I get the message and stop the swinging. My mind begins to wander as I gaze out over the water.

"I hope so," I say, under my breath. "Something else happened, too."

"Well, what, chiiild."

"A girl played a trick on me. But it's okay." I begin to fidget with my hands.

"What kind of trick?".

"Well, this girl asked me to meet some other girls after school at the big tree, and no one showed up." I gaze out over the water.

"Well, that wasn't nice." She sighs.

"Nope," I mumble, and bite my bottom lip.

"Some people aren't really friends. You, chiiild, have to figure out who is a good person. Or a person who ... well, isn't."

I can see that she wants to add more to that, but she is trying to be nice.

"I understand." I flash a little smile.

What she doesn't know is that I understand all too well about people being mean to me. It's hard for me to find a nice person because they are usually all making fun of me. But I'm so busy thinking about Jake that it really doesn't matter.

❦

Monday comes slower than usual. Oddly enough, I really want to be in school today. I can't help but think of Jake all the time. I have never felt like this before, but I want more.

Walking to English class, I hear a group of girls giggling. And guess who comes up to talk to me? The girl who played the trick on me.

"Hey, I'm sorry," she says, still giggling. "My friends changed their minds on meeting." She motions back to the giggling crowd.

"Oh, it's okay, really," I say, trying not to show that it made me mad. "I love having friends like you." I smirk. "Makes me understand what it's like to have sincere friends, which you, clearly are not."

I turn around. Going to see Jake is much more important than dealing with these fake people.

English class comes, and I'm sitting in my normal assigned seat. The bell rings, and he is not in class. I look all around to see if maybe he's late to class. My heart sinks as time passes. I just want to talk to him. I want him to look at more of my drawings. I really just want to look at him. Maybe tomorrow.

School ends, and I find myself doing my homework, distracted. I sit on my bed with my headphones on, homework on my lap, and one thing on my mind. No, it's not my homework. It's Jake. What has he done to me?

In art class, we have another field trip. I need the distraction. We all load up on the bus, and I just assume that we are heading back to the park. The teacher seems to like the park for us to get subjects to draw, but we aren't going that direction.

"Where are we headed this time?" I ask the teacher.

"This is a special treat today." He seems excited.

"Oh, really?"

"Yes. We are going to the Museum of Art."

I am excited that we are heading somewhere different, but disappointed because I was getting used to going to see Mildred and having a subject to draw that I love.

We pull up in front of the museum, and everyone gets up all at once. The teacher yells at us to sit down. He gives us directions on what we can and cannot do. We cannot touch anything. We cannot run. We cannot yell.

Once we get to the door with our tickets, and wristbands are purchased, we filter into the museum, one by one. Some go off into their own groups, and others hover around the teacher. I find a hallway that is intriguing. I wanted to go to the drawn art section. I really want to see the art that another artist is displaying.

As I'm walking down the hallway to the art section that displays pencil and other mediums, I notice a hallway that goes off to the right. There are people standing around, looking at photos. It gets my attention, so I meander down that hallway first.

I see the section of dance. There are beautiful dancers posing in various forms, all to accentuate their body forms. They look so skinny, so perfect. Their bodies are picturesque and porcelain.

Their skin is white and fragile. Their arms are long, and their legs look like they could scale a high-rise building. So beautiful, I can almost hear the music in each photo.

I look in the display cabinets and see the shoes that they wore on stage and wonder how their toes fit in there. I wonder how they could walk in them. Oh, the pain they must have felt on stage to do what they love.

I decide to go to the hallway for the pencil drawings. As I get there, I notice several different formats—some of landscapes, some of people's faces, some of flowers, and some of close-ups. The close-up drawings are what I like to do. I can see me having my drawings in here someday. I would like to be famous for my artwork, but I don't think I'm good enough. That doesn't stop me from dreaming.

I don't realize it, but I spend my whole field trip time in these two displays. I missed so much, but I saw what I wanted to see.

The class meets in the lobby to get on the bus. While the teacher is trying to get everyone together, I can't help but walk around and look at the plaques on the wall. I notice that the museum was founded by a husband and wife. It tells of their story and how they built the building that houses all the art of the community. It was originally named The Whitefield Art Museum. I'm not sure why the name on the front of the building just says *Art Museum*, in funky letters. It doesn't matter. We're heading home for the day. Our trip is over.

Jake didn't come back to school until Thursday. As I sit in class, I can't help but feel him staring at the back of my head. Oh, how I long for that feeling. It's like his breath is caressing my neck while I long for his touch and for him to kiss me. His eyes are piercing the back of my neck. At times, I feel my hair stand up. These are feelings that I am unaccustomed to feeling.

Then it happens.

He touches my shoulder with his finger to get my attention while the teacher is facing the blackboard. I'm nervous to turn around because I'm going to get caught. But I can't help it. I lean back in my seat and try to look at him from the back of my head—a feat that I must say is not feasible.

He leans forward to whisper in my ear. Jake speaks to me with such grace.

"What are you doing on Friday?"

I hear a few girls that are sitting in the next row giggle, like they just told each other a joke. I glance over, and I see all of them looking at me. I guess they're laughing because he's talking to me. Either that, or I'm the joke.

What? He's asking me what I'm doing on Friday. Why would he be asking me?

"Nothing, why?" I have to ask.

"It's Homecoming," he says.

Oh my God! It's Homecoming! Is he going to ask me? Why would he ask me? Everyone makes fun of me.

"Umm, I know," I say, trying not to look too excited.

"Would you go to the football game with me, and then the dance?"

He just blurts out the question I want to hear so badly. The girls let out yet another cackle.

"Girls, knock it off!" the teacher yells.

She took reference of where the talking is coming from, sneers, and then turns to write more on the board.

"Look at the geek," one of them says, looking at me. "She thinks she's actually going on a date with Jake." She smirks.

Trying not to look stupid, I calmly pull myself together.

"I have to ask my mom first. But yes!"

I want to jump up and down and scream at the top of my lungs, *Yes!* But I have to ask my mom first. Oh, I can't wait to get home!

Class ends, and the bustle is louder than usual. The crowd of girls is huddling and laughing, and it seems like they are laughing at me, but this is normal.

I want to go ask my mom permission to go to the dance, but I have to go to the park first to see if Mildred is there. I want to tell her the great news that he asked me out on a date. A real date!

I get to the park with my book bag from school, which is

unusual. I always go home, then visit Mildred on the weekends. But this is different. I notice she is on the park bench, like usual, so I run over to her, since my time is limited to get home.

Before I even reach the bench, I blurt out, "He talked to me!"

All excited and full of energy, I plop down next to her, and my book bag flies to the ground beside me.

"Who, chiiild?"

"Jake! You know, the guy in my English class." I attempt to force the information into her mind. "The guy that sits behind me, Jake."

"Oh, chiiild, yes," she says, with a big smile of approval.

She does indeed remember.

"What did he say?"

I can't help my legs from swinging in excitement because I feel like I'm going to explode.

"He asked me to a dance."

"Oh, my." She pauses. "Did you ask your mother?"

"Not yet. I'm going home to ask her now, but I just had to tell you!"

The excitement is so overbearing that it doesn't matter that I haven't asked my mother yet. I was asked out on my first date, and I am going to go.

"Do you think your mom will allow you to go on a date already?" She is peering into my eyes, looking for a truthful answer.

"Well ..." I want to believe that she will. But in reality, probably not. "It can't hurt to ask."

"Well, chiiild," she sits upright, pressing her dress with her hands, "if you are going to dance, you have to know how to act appropriately."

Huh? What does that mean? I am just a girl going to a dance. It's not a formal ballroom dance.

"What do you mean?"

"Have you ever worn a dress?"

"Uh-huh."

"When?"

"Umm ..." I have to think for a minute, " ... well ..."

I can't answer her. I know I had one from Easter, but it was a couple years ago, and I think I am a little bigger now.

"Well, you don't know how to sit wearing a dress, then."

She begins to instruct me. Her posture becomes stiffer, and her head is lifted. Wow, she looks so beautiful. I see her beauty hidden deep within. Even though her clothing is bulky for the weather, I see a beautiful young, vibrant woman in an old woman's frame.

"Do you see how I am sitting?" She runs her hand from the top of her head down to the tip of her toes.

She is instructing me to look like she's a game show host showing off the merchandise. I can't help but notice her hands are stretched out, with her thumb and first finger stretched the furthest. Her next fingers, all the way to the last one, are curved in slightly. Oh, such grace radiating from her frail fingers. I also notice her legs are elegantly crossed.

"Why are your legs like that?" I point to her legs. "Aren't you supposed to cross them like this?" I hike one of my legs over the other, like I am a clumsy elephant.

"Oh, goodness no, chiiild!" She puts her hand on my knee. "A proper lady never crosses her legs at her knee." She then provides the correct pose with her legs, but in slow motion. "See."

She puts one leg down to the pavement, with her foot flat on the ground, but at a slight angle. She then crosses her other leg at the ankle, not the knee.

"This is the proper way to cross your legs." She demonstrates once more.

If I'm sure, I think her toes point just a bit, like she was a dancer.

"And then you fold your hands in your lap like this." She places one hand inside the other, and in the most elegant form, elongates her neck and turns slowly towards me. "Knees together."

"That looks pretty," I say.

"Now, if you have a cover."

"A cover?"

"Yes, chiiild. Like a pretty cover-up that goes over your shoulders when you get chilled at night."

"Oh, I get it," I say, like I really understand what she means.

"You take your cover and drape it over like this." She has the imaginary cover-up and drapes it over her knees. "And this is to hide your knees."

"My knees?" I tuck up my legs to reveal my dirty knees. "Why hide my knees?"

"Because, chiiild, it is just the proper thing to do."

That makes so much sense now! Mildred must have been a dancer. Her body is so erect and upright, with such grace and elegance. Her toes point subtly. Her head is held high, elongating her frame, like a dancer would as the curtain was called for her to perform.

"Are …" I am embarrassed to ask because of how old she is.

"Oh, chiiild, just ask," she whispers, with an essence of the wind.

"Were you a dancer when you were young?"

A great sigh comes from the depth of her lungs. She smiles with a deep remembrance of being on the center of the stage.

"Oh, yes, chiiild. I used to dance on the stage, under the lights, where I was able to express anything I wanted."

She puts her hands on my cheek, and her face glows with a youthful shimmer.

Then she jumps to her feet. "Now, you need to learn how to walk in a dress and stand in a dress."

I have no idea that I need to know how to walk and stand in a dress. I just thought I was going to … well, you know, walk and, umm, stand. I was wrong.

She saunters back and forth, with her head held high and her chin up.

"Now, you try," she says.

I get up and walk back and forth for her approval. She giggles under her breath because it isn't nice to make fun of anyone.

"Oh, chiiild, you walk like a boy."

A boy? But I am a girl!

She demonstrates once more. I try once more to copy her. Each time, I feel myself getting better and better. Confidence is building.

"Much better, chiiild." Her face is beaming with approval. "Much better. Now, sit down, but in a dress."

I sit down hard, like I always do. Realizing that I made a huge mistake, I hop back up and sit down again. This time, I pretend like I'm at the dance. I pretend that I'm a beautiful young lady in a beautiful gown, sitting down to meet my lover. I cross my legs, but only at the ankles. I smile because I know I just learned how to be a lady. It's like I took a crash course in finishing school. I just hope Jake notices.

"Oh, chiiild, you are so beautiful. I could only wish ..." she pauses for a long moment, " ... I could see you." She sits back on the bench to tend to her birds once more.

Realizing that I'm running later than planned, I have to get my book bag and run home. But not until I thank Mildred properly by giving her a big hug. Then I run off to get home before my mom does.

It seems like it takes forever to get home, but I get there before my mom, as usual. I want to go to the dance so badly, and I'm afraid my mom is going to tell me no. I decide to start cleaning the kitchen in hopes of getting her in a good mood.

I hear the key enter the door lock, and then the familiar squeak of the door as it opens. My mom enters the apartment and puts her groceries down on the counter. Her purse falls to the floor, and her keys quickly follow. My mom grunts as she bends down to pick everything up.

Oh, this isn't going too well. She seems agitated.

I wait for dinner to be over, but we're still at the table. My mom is quiet during dinner, and I ask her what's wrong. I thought I did something wrong.

"No, honey, it was just a rough day."

I feel a little bit relieved, so I take a deep breath and go for it.

"Mom, can I go to the school Homecoming dance tomorrow

night after the football game?"

Whew, I did it. I said it. I asked to go on my first date. Well, I think it's a date. It's with a boy, so it has to be date.

Mom is noticeably lost in her thoughts. I guess she didn't really hear me.

"Mom?"

"Hmm?" She puts her fork down and looks up at me. "Oh, honey, I'm sorry. What did you say?"

Oh crap, I have to get up the nerve to ask again. Well, here it goes.

"Can I go to the Homecoming dance after the football game?"

"A dance? Huh? And this is at the school?"

"Yes, in the gym, after the game."

"And is there a boy that you will be going with?"

Oh, there it is. The reason for me not to be able to go to the Homecoming dance.

"Umm, yes. His name is Jake, and he is in my English class."

I have never even spoken of Jake to my mom. I have only told Mildred. Wow, I think I'm closer to Mildred than I am to my own mom.

"Well, since it is a school function ..."

I wait impatiently for her answer.

" ... I will drive you there and pick you up."

"But Mom, Jake asked me to go with him. The whole school will be there with us."

"Well, if you go with him, you will be home right afterwards. Like eleven o'clock, and not a minute later."

"I promise."

I go calmly into my bedroom. But as soon as the door closes, my heart screams with joy. I'm careful not to allow any words of joy come from my mouth. I have to call Jake and tell him that I can go. Oh, what to wear? I have a pretty Easter dress that will have to do.

Friday is here in no time. I walk the halls in a complete daze. School is not on my mind at all. Thank God, because if I had a test, I couldn't even remember my name at this point. English class is next, and I anticipate seeing him before our big date. Wow, I'm going on my first date!

I walk into the English class to see that Jake is already here. He is sitting in his seat, and I can't keep my face from smiling as I walk down the aisle to my seat. I put my books on my desk and turn around to talk to him. My face is beaming at the mere sight of him.

"Hi, Jake."

"Hey, there," he says, looking at the group of girls gathered around the other desk.

They all seemed interested in our conversation. I just pretend not to notice them, or Jake paying attention to them. He's getting ready for the class.

He then turns his head and looks at me with those dreamy eyes.

"What time can I come get you?" he says, to seal the deal on our date.

The girls burst out in laughter once again. Why are they laughing?

I'm so focused on Jake that I don't pay much attention to them.

We agreed on six o'clock, so we could make it on time to the game.

The teacher comes into the room, and I have to turn around. With the starting of the class, my mind begins to wander. How am I going to do my hair? Is my dress pretty enough? It doesn't matter. My mother would never get me a dress for a date.

This class can't end fast enough. I want to go home and start getting ready.

After school, I go home and start my primping. After a shower and blow drying my hair, I begin to rummage through the closet to find my dress. Where is my dress? Beginning to panic, I run to my mom's room and look in her closet for my dress. That's when

I see it. A dark blue dress that my mom has. I have never seen her in it. I pull it out of her closet and proceed to put it on.

The dress is beautiful, and it looks like it was made just for me. It has thin straps that go across my shoulders, but the straps are also across my back in a crisscross pattern. The dress is sleek and silky, shiny, and soft. The hemline is perfect because it isn't a hemline that I saw before. It is jagged on the bottom, with points and pleats. I absolutely love this dress!

I notice my mom standing in the doorway, with tears in her eyes.

"You look beautiful!" she says, in a soft motherly voice.

Her little girl has grown up before her eyes. I am embarrassed, but proud, so I stand tall with grace. My mom rushes into her closet and pulls out the shoes that go to the dress.

"Here. Try these on." She pushes them to me with excitement.

I pull the shoes out of the box and slip them onto my feet. They fit! Wow, I'm not a little girl anymore. My mom sits me down in front of her mirror and begins to brush my hair. It isn't easy brushing my curly, now auburn hair that once was bright red. But she tries not to cause too much pain while she does it.

She pulls my hair to the side and puts a few pins in to hold it in place. All the while, she leaves wisps of ringlet curls draped over my shoulder. With a dash of hairspray, I look totally different. That was fast.

Next, makeup. Mom applies a tiny bit of makeup to finish off the final touches. A small strand of pearls to offset the dark blue, and hair spray again to hold the look into place. I smile because the young girl in the mirror is now a beautiful young lady. That's me!

I stand to my feet and twirl around for my mom to examine my final look. I notice she is taken aback by the vision before her.

"You are going to be the most beautiful young lady there!" she says, with a smile.

My mom is proud of me. Fighting back tears, she holds my hand with might.

"Oh, one last thing." She reaches for the bottle of her finest perfume and tells me to close my eyes.

I do as she requests, and I feel a gentle mist being sprayed upon my face and arms. Oh, the smell of the heavens pours down on me. I hope Jake likes it. Oh, Jake! He is going to be here any minute.

Mom walks around the chair that I am sitting on while she is doting over me. All of a sudden, she becomes serious. The look of joy is no longer on her face, and I can see that she means business.

"Now, this is technically a date, right?"

"I dunno. I guess so."

Of course it's a date! I didn't want her to think it's a date. I'm going to the dance with the entire school. How could that be a date? We aren't going alone.

"Now, no funny business!"

Funny business? Really? My mom calls it funny business?

"You know what I mean, young lady!" The stern voice of reason is right in front of me.

"Oh, Mom!"

How can she think I'm going to get into funny business? "Ewe! That stuff is gross. I'll be lucky if I get kissed."

The teenager is front and center. Oh, great! Now I act like a child. I guess I'm just embarrassed to talk about this stuff in front of my mom.

"Now, Mary, I mean it!"

A knock on our apartment door comes from down the hall. Mom walks with me to open the door for his arrival.

She opens the door to be greeted by a suave, elegantly dressed man in a tuxedo. You know Mom had to get a look at him first to see if he fit the bill or not.

She lets him inside the apartment. You can see that she is smitten by his appearance. I guess she approves, because all of sudden, her voice is no longer stern, and her demeanor is inviting.

He has a box in his hand.

"This is for you." His voice is like an angel.

It is filled with words properly spoken. He seems to be refined, which is very different from how he acts in school.

He opens the clear carton and pulls out the white carnation that is woven between fresh greenery. It has a band on the back of it so I can wear it on my wrist. I raise my left arm out for him to slip in on, while my mom is busy taking photos. One after another, I keep hearing the clicking of the camera. Oh, how embarrassing.

"Now, I need one of you two together." She pushes us together.

Did you hear that? Together. We are together.

The camera clicks over and over again. And the smiles begin to be painful.

"Here." I hand her my phone. "Take one on my phone." Getting fidgety, I say, "Mom," in a pleading tone.

You know, the tone that tells your mom in a secret code that everyone knows how embarrassed and tired you are, and that you really want to run away from her right now before she embarrasses you even more.

"We need to go so we are on time." He touches my elbow to direct me to the car.

We turn to leave our apartment, and I hear my mom give those directions that I do not want to hear.

"Now, make sure she is home before twelve."

I feel like a kid again.

"I will, ma'am."

Wow, he calls her ma'am. That is gentlemanly.

"Mom, the dance is after the football game. Can it be more like one or two? I think the dance actually ends at twelve."

"Well, I guess so."

You can see that she is remembering when she went to dances and leaving early from them wasn't fun.

We turn to leave, and the door closes behind us.

Outside of the apartment building is an unfamiliar car parked. He holds my hand and directs me to the really cool car.

"This is your car?"

I can't help but notice that we don't have a parent driving us. OMG, he is actually going to drive us to the football game, and then to the Homecoming dance.

As we got closer to the car, I feel myself bite my lower lip because I am so nervous. I cautiously turn around and notice my mom peering out the window of her bedroom, which faces the parking lot. Is my mom going to be angry with me? I don't think either one of us thought of how I'm going to get to the football game and then back. I think we both just assumed his mother was going to be driving us.

I notice his car isn't anything like a family would drive, so it obviously isn't his parents' car. It looks like a sports car. It has two doors, it's low to the ground, and is jet black. The windows are slightly darker than cars I have been in before. The hood of the car is long and seems to go on for miles.

He reaches for the door handle on my side with his free hand and opens it for me. He still has my hand in his and guides me into the car. I am beaming with a smile from ear to ear, but not too much to look cheesy. He is being such a gentleman, and my mom is watching his every move.

I wiggle my way into the car, making sure my dress looks perfect. I carefully put my feet inside, careful not to scuff up my mom's shoes. Once inside, the car door closes, and he moves toward his side of the car. Staring at the dashboard, I admire how it looks like the cockpit of an aircraft. Oh, how I want to learn to drive.

I make sure my mom notices that I put on my seat belt, to reassure her that I am going to be taken care of. We drive off slowly out of the parking lot while I watch my mom gaze out the window. A little wave is given by my mom as she realizes her little girl isn't so little anymore.

We get to the football game, which is not too much fun for me. I'm more interested in watching people stare at me sitting next to Jake and wondering why I am even there. I'm not in the *in-crowd*. I'm the girl that everyone makes fun of. But I look absolutely amazing! I feel like a million dollars, and this night belongs to me. Well, Jake and me, that is.

After the game, everyone is heading over to the gym for the dance. Some decide to go out to a nice dinner. I have no idea that I'm going as well. Although, my nice dinner turns out to be the local pizza parlor. I don't care—I am with Jake.

We eat our pizza and then go back over to the school for the dance. Excitement fills the room as we walk into the gym. Balloons and streamers line the room. Tables and chairs are set up, but no dinner is being served. On the far end of the gym is the stage, where bright flashing lights are in accompaniment with the bass of the music being played. There is a group on the stage playing upbeat music that I haven't heard before. The lights are low.

We find a table with a group of people I have never seen before. I can tell they are football jocks and cheerleaders. None of them are in the group of people that I hang with. Of course, I don't hang with anyone, until now.

I sit carefully in my chair. My back is elongated, my chin tucked in, with my head held high. My legs are crossed at the ankles, just the way Mildred taught me. I try to look ladylike and proper.

While sitting at the table, some of Jake's friends come over with their girlfriends, and he introduces them to me. He says I am his date. I didn't hear the word *girlfriend*, but that's just fine by me. I'm happy with the word *date* because it is the first time I was on one.

I look around the gym to see the decorations, and I notice a small group of girls, five or six of them, standing in a huddle to my right. They all have on long evening gowns with flashy sequins. I guess their parents make a lot of money to get them dresses like that. I glance down at my dress, and sure, it's plain, but I look perfect to me. Besides, I have on my mother's pearls, and I sure don't see any of those girls wearing their mother's pearls.

One of the girls leans over to another and puts her hand to her face like she is telling her a secret. But the music is too loud for a secret, so she has to repeat it to her a little louder.

"Look at Mary," she says. "She acts like Jake really likes her or something, huh."

And the group of girls all cackle like a bunch of geese. I try to ignore them because no one is going to ruin this night for me. No one. I keep looking around like I don't hear them, and like that doesn't bother me.

"Hey, Mary," one of the girls yells at me. "Hey, watch this." She turns back to the group of girls once more.

Another girl yells louder, "Hey, you!"

And this time, they're all watching me. I motion my hand to my chest to ask if they are calling me.

"Yeah, you," she says.

I look around for Jake, and I notice he is with his usual group of guys, hanging out. While he's talking to his friends, the group of girls want to dance and leave their boyfriends behind. I can't believe it, but they ask me to dance with them. My face becomes red, but I accept. I notice that some of the girls in the group are those in our English class. They keep to themselves pretty much, but still ask me to dance in their vicinity. Am I becoming part of the *in-crowd*?

What no one knows is that I dance in my bedroom to the radio, and to music videos on TV. I wanted to learn the latest dances for this very night. I am finally able to dance out in public.

We dance a few dances, just the girls. I think I did okay. I copy a lot of what the other girls are doing so I don't look stupid. Dancing is much different with high heels on. Plus, they dance way cooler than I do. Then a slow song comes on.

Oh boy, a slow song!

The boys break up their man-fest on the sidelines and come over to their partners. Jake comes to me and I suddenly feel awkward. I didn't practice how to dance a slow dance. I'm not sure how to do this. I look up from the ground and watch the other girls. And so I begin to copy them again.

I put my arms up over his shoulders, and then it happens. He puts his hands on my hips. The way he holds me is endearing. He pulls me close, and I put my head on his shoulder, but not really. He is much taller than I am.

We sway to the music, and I am totally lost in my own little world. Suddenly, everyone else on the planet is nonexistent. It's like the band is playing our own little love song, and we are the only ones dancing. No one around to see us or judge us. The dance feels like it is an eternity. My heart belongs to him. I feel as if I am melting into him when I look into his eyes.

So this is what love feels like.

After the slow dance, I notice some of the group decides to leave. What? I don't want to go home yet. He asks me if I want to get out of there. I'm not quite sure what he means by that, but I don't want to be the outcast. So I agree.

We all run out to our cars. I stand waiting next to the car door, but Jake is already sitting behind the wheel. I thought he was supposed to open the door for me. I guess I am wrong. I open the door for myself and sit inside the car. We race out of the school parking lot, one by one, like the green light turned red at a racetrack. Several sports cars squeal their tires, all racing for an invisible finish line. No more gentlemanly gestures. No more opening of the door. It seems as if it was all a show for my mom. But that's okay.

"Where are we going?" I say, as we file out of the parking lot behind each other.

My seat belt is all that is holding me in the seat as he whizzes around the corners.

"We're going to the after-party." He smirks as he squeals his tires.

Oh, my! My mom is going to kill me. I didn't know anything about an after-party.

"That's cool! I just have to be home on time."

I'm scared of what's coming next, but I'm excited as well.

We all pull into the local hotel. I'm not sure why we're here, other than it has a really nice restaurant downstairs. Can't see us going there because we just ate pizza.

"Why are we here?" I say.

"This is where it's happening. The after-party!" He flings open the door and starts to skip away, with me closely behind him.

I have a really bad feeling about this. The girls are hanging on to each other, whispering and giggling, and the guys are all rough housing in the parking lot while racing to the glass doors.

The closer to the door, the more settled Jake becomes. And then the gentlemanly gestures begin once again. I guess it's the sight of the bellman that makes him change.

We all come in together and proceed to the elevator. With about ten of us in the elevator, one of the guys presses 7, and the elevator moves.

The elevator door opens, and the party is noticeably down the hall. We all gather at the door to the room, and it opens to let us in. The room is already full of people, so there are about fifteen or so in there with us. This room is nice. It has two bedrooms, and then a suite where the party is. There is a hot tub in the corner, with a couple girls in it, and they look naked. They are under the water enough not to be sure. Besides, the bubbles are hiding the rest of what the water was attempting to hide.

Music is playing, and the dancing is pumping. I notice something right off. There is a ton of alcohol, and everyone is drinking. I find a glass being shoved in my face by Jake, and I take it because that is what I'm expected to do. I take a sip, and the drink is very sweet. Hmm. So this is what alcohol tastes like. I think I like this, and it goes down easily. The party is beginning.

By this time, I begin to loosen up and start dancing. The room is spinning, and I like it. I suddenly don't have any anxieties about being in front of people I don't know, and I feel like I fit in. My shoes are off, and I am still in my dress, with the shoulder strap off my arm. My hair is no longer the way my mom fixed it.

I feel myself being lifted up by my waist and onto the coffee table.

"Your turn."

The room roars with cheers.

OMG! I'm on the coffee table, and they want me to dance for

them. The more they cheer, the more I dance. I don't care if I can dance or not. I'm just happy being part of the crowd.

I begin dancing like I'm on stage, begging for dollars. Flipping my hair, feeling my body, becoming erotic. My body is numb from the alcohol, I guess. I'm fitting in. They treat me like I'm one of them.

I start to feel weird—you know, kinda dizzy, confused. The music doesn't sound like music anymore. The sounds are resonating like some tribal beat that I haven't heard before. With all the laughter in the room and the beating of the drums in the music, I feel like I'm having a sensory overload. The room suddenly feels like it's getting smaller. I am having too much fun to care. My eyes don't want to focus well, either. So I get off the coffee table to let another girl dance on it. I feel Jake's hand, and I am trying to get off the table. I fall into his arms, and I kiss him. It just happens, and before I know it, he is kissing me. I feel his tongue in my mouth, so I copy him. I am not very good at it, but I do what they did on TV. He then leads me to the bedroom.

We get to the bedroom, where another one of the couples is making out on the bed. He sits on the other side of the bed and pulls me toward him. My feet weigh a thousand pounds, and I end up tripping and falling right onto the bedside. I begin to giggle like I meant to do that.

I am able to get my feet underneath me as I stand by the bed where he sits. Before I know it, he lifts my dress over my head. My body won't stop wiggling, like I am still on the coffee table. I look over at the other couple, and Jake just put his finger over his mouth, like I am to be quiet, so I don't disturb them. How could I not disturb them? We just fell into the room like a herd of elephants. The other couple is so busy, they don't even notice we're there.

Next, he reaches behind me and unclasps my bra. It falls to the ground. I wrap my arms around myself in embarrassment. No one has ever seen me like this! I am so shy, even my mom hasn't seen me totally naked since I was a baby. But he reassures me that it's okay. He is in total control. He stands up and lays me on the bed next to the other couple.

"Awee rrrrrrel lee caaaannnnnt dis," I try to speak.

Nothing is coming out of my mouth that is in my head. I want to tell him that I can't do this, but my mouth won't say it. He just puts his finger over his mouth once more, and then he puts his hand over my mouth to ensure I keep quiet.

Then he begins to take off his clothes—all of them. Right there in front of me is a naked boy. Oh my God, he's naked! His penis is so big and hard. It's the first one I've seen up close. I feel a strange tingling between my legs. I don't know what's going on. The room is spinning. This must have been what my mom was talking about. I feel like I am in trouble, but I can't stop.

With my underwear still on, he lies upon me, kissing every inch of my neck. My body begins to react to his caress. I find myself getting lost in the feelings, or the alcohol, feelings, alcohol—I'm not sure which one it is, since both are new to me. I want him, I think, but I'm not really sure I want to be doing *this* with him, *here*.

I remember seeing in movies that the girls moan a lot when they were doing this, so I try to. I just sound like a sick cow. I'm not sure if I'm moaning loud, or actually trying to scream. I can't help but think of how he knows just what to do. He seems so experienced.

I feel something strange upon the side of my leg as he is kissing me. I think it's Jake, but it's the guy next to me. With Jake on top of me, kissing my neck and rubbing into me, the guy next to me is rubbing my leg, while his girlfriend is sucking on his privates. All I see is her blonde hair bouncing up and down, and I just assume that's what she is doing.

I can't stop. I want it. By this time, whatever was in my drink has taken full affect. I didn't know alcohol could make you feel like this. My eyes are rolling in the back of head, and my neck is being forced to hold up a thousand-pound head. What is going on with me? I feel myself in and out of consciousness. I'm not sure, but I think someone is holding my head up for me.

Just then, Jake moves my panties to one side. I feel myself

slipping away. Before I know it, he thrusts his penis inside me. Oh, the pain rushes my body. This pain brings my body astir. I don't think he knows I was a virgin. The key word—*was*. I think I passed out.

"Mary!" I hear in the faint distance. "Mary! Wake up!"

I feel a hand grabbing my arm and shaking me to wake up. I think it's my mom.

I am groggy but starting to come around. My eyes are not opening, but I'm hearing other girls giggling.

"Is she dead?" and "Geeze, Jake, what did you do to her?"

The giggles keep ringing in my ears, and my eyes begin to open. I notice several people are in the room. Some are naked, but most are getting dressed to leave.

Even though I am really out of it, I hear one of the girls yell, "Jake! How much did you give her?"

Give me what? What was she talking about? I drank one drink, that I knew of.

I feel my arm being shaken so hard I thought it was going to break.

"Wake up, Mary! Get up!"

And then one of the girls slaps me across the face.

"Wake up!"

"OMG!" I say. "What time is it?"

I can't find my phone or my clothes. Or anything, for that matter.

The laughter rings out. Everyone is happy I'm awake and somewhat okay.

Then from the back of the room, I hear, "Damn, girl, you were getting it on tonight! Here we thought you were a nerd."

I look up. "What? What do you mean?"

I try to sit up and push back my tousled hair that my mom had beautifully styled for the dance.

Jake says, "We had no idea you are as wild as we are."

The laughter commences once again. I am fumbling for my clothes to cover myself up out of embarrassment.

"Oh, don't worry," another guy says. "We all have seen you

now. You really are a wild child."

I don't know what they're talking about. I can't remember what happened. My head is still foggy, and the room is still spinning.

I don't want to look like an outcast, so I just giggle along with them. But on the inside, I am screaming for help. Did I have fun? I can't really remember much. I remember I just want to cry, but I don't dare.

Pulling myself together as we're leaving the hotel room, I feel like a complete mess. What the hell did I just do? I manage to get all of my belongings and get dressed as quickly as I can. Oh, my pearls! I reach for the pearls that my mother put on my neck, and thank God, they are still there. I guess the other girls just thought that they were dime store costume jewelry. They are my mom's pride and joy, and I was only entrusted to borrow them, along with the dress and shoes.

We get back into the car and head to my apartment. I am so ashamed I don't say hardly anything on the drive home. I feel like I'm sitting in the fetal position, but upright. I begin checking the rearview mirror, making sure my hair is like it was when I left, and my makeup isn't all smudged. But it's no use. I look like I feel—used. I couldn't help but notice the pain coming from my ... OMG, why does it hurt so bad?

As we pull into the parking lot of the apartment building, I notice the time on my phone.

"I am late!" I yell to Jake.

His driving becomes more respectable and slower. He pulls up to the curb instead of a parking spot, just to let me out.

"Oh, who cares," he says, with a calm voice. "Just tell your mom that it's all my fault, and you will just get grounded."

Sounds like he did this all the time with other girls. But I'm supposed to be his girlfriend.

Before I know it, he runs over to my side of the car and opens the door once again, just as he did when we left. The show is back on for my mom because she's still waiting in the window, where I left her hours before. He walks me to the door to greet my mother. A total gentleman on the outside, but a monster, a true monster, in private.

My mother swings the door open, with a stern look. "You are late, young lady!"

"It is all my fault, ma'am. My mom and dad took us out for ice cream after the dance."

His voice is so convincing and calm. It's as if he were a professional liar. I keep my mouth shut and do not breathe a word. I'm not sure if I'm more afraid of my mother or Jake.

Not sure if she should believe him, she doesn't say another word, and motions me to come inside. Even though I'm not late by much, I'm still late. And to my mom, that is enough.

I walk down the hallway to my bedroom to get undressed and get into bed. I stand in front of my full-length mirror, totally ashamed of my behavior. I begin to rub my mouth to get the lipstick off, when I'm actually trying to get the taste of him off my lips. But it is no use. My lips, my body, my soul are stained with him.

I take my underwear and throw them in the garbage pail in my room. They have blood on them. I'm not sure if this is what it's supposed to feel like after having sex for the first time. I thought it was supposed to be a magical moment, like on TV. Nothing about this felt magical.

I'm afraid to talk to my mom about the night. But I think she knows something is wrong. I am different.

My bedroom door opens, and the light behind my mom illuminates her aura.

"Are you okay?"

I want to cry and tell her the truth, but I can't.

"Yeah, Mom. His mom and dad are really nice, and we were having so much fun that we lost track of time. I'm sorry."

She comes in and sits on my bed. The light is still behind her.

She smells the essence in the air. "Have you been smoking?" Oh, shit! I must smell like smoke, with all of the other people smoking in the hotel room.

"Ewe, no!" I snap. "His dad smokes."

"Hmm." You can see she isn't buying the story, but Jake did say that we were with his mom and dad.

At least all the smoke smell covers up the alcohol smell on my breath. I don't allow her to get that close to smell my breath. I would be dead, for sure!

My mother looks down and sees the garbage pail with my underwear in there.

"Why did you throw these away?" She points at them.

"Eewwe. I started my period, and they got ruined."

It was kind of a relief because I guess if she thought I was on my period, then I didn't have any kind of sex. Little does she know.

"Are you okay now?" she says, with a different tone.

"Yeah," I reply, not to start up a conversation with her.

"Anyway, was the dance nice?"

I really don't want to talk, but I have to keep the conversation light, so she doesn't ask about Jake.

"Yeah, it was fun, and I'm tired from dancing nonstop."

"Well, since you were late, you are grounded, at least. Oh, and I don't think that you being in Jake's car is a good idea either. Do you understand me?"

"Yes, ma'am."

I know that I'm in trouble, but Jake was right. I did only get grounded.

"That means to school and right back home!" A pause. "Got it?"

I hear the anger swelling up from within.

"Yes, ma'am."

The conversation is over. Well, it wasn't really a conversation at all. It was her orders, and I will follow them.

My mother's figure fades in the hallway light behind her and the door closes. She's gone, and the interrogation is over.

I pull the covers over my head and proceed to cry as quietly as I can.

Monday comes, and I am leaving a long weekend of being stuck in the house. After all, it is getting colder and it's raining, so it isn't so bad to be stuck inside.

I feel people looking at me differently today. I hear them giggling as I walk down the hall. I notice a group of girls that I have never seen before standing next to the lockers. As I walk by, they are whispering to each other. They're holding what looks to be papers, or printed pictures. They are turning them upside down and then right side up, while what looks to be them sizing me up.

As I walk past them, I hear one girl say, "Is that the girl?" She is pointing to me.

"Yeah, that's her. What a slut."

Then I realize they are all talking about me. I am the only other girl in the hallway with them. The once small group of girls quickly turns into a crowd.

I hear a few of them saying things like, "Hey, here she is," and "Quick! Come here to see her."

They are laughing out loud now. The hallway fills quickly with swarms of people all looking at me. It's like I'm the main attraction for some freak show.

The main group of girls is fueling the laughter. All of the commotion causes the pictures to fall to the hallway floor. I can't help but look at them. I bend down to get a closer look.

I am in total disbelief. My stomach sinks like the Titanic. The initial shock of the ship sinking was hard enough to handle, but the aftermath of the slow death is sure to come. The pictures are of me—dancing, kissing Jake, naked. That is me! I want to throw up. How could this have happened to me? I was on my very first date with a guy I thought liked me.

By this time, the hallway is filled with what appears to be the entire school. People are gathering around to see what's going on. Some are grabbing the pictures off the floor as fast as they fall. It's impossible to get all of them. I find myself crawling on the floor, trying to grab the pictures from their view. I grab as many of the pictures that I can so no one else can see them, but I guess

I'm too late. They are all over the school, and everyone knows what happened. I notice a lot of them are grabbing their phones and bursting out with laughter. I am now on social media. I am the scandal of the high school.

"Look! The slut is ashamed of them now," says one of the girls in the crowd.

"Is that really her?" says another girl.

"Let me see!" Another guy runs through the crowd, reaching for the photos. "Do you think Jake will share?"

A burst of energy comes up from the depths, like an explosion.

"Stop!" I scream. "Leave me alone!" Yet another plead for my sanity.

"Look at the slut trying to save her precious pictures!" yells one of the girls.

While crawling on the floor, grasping for the photos between and around the sea of legs, I glance up and notice that it is one of the girls from the party. I'm not positive it's her because I was drunk that night, but I'm pretty sure.

"Not so pretty today, are ya!" she yells, once more.

Tears fill my eyes as I meet face to face with the girl making fun of me. I want to disappear into the woodwork, where I was used to being. But now I am the center of attention.

"Why are you doing this?" I scream at her.

I don't know who she is. I only saw her at the party. But she is one of the girls that was drinking and dancing, too. I vaguely remember her dancing on the coffee table after me.

Then she notices I recognize her. Her eyes become wide with fear, and she begins to hide her face in the crowd.

"You!" I scream. "You were there!" I fling my hand and point at her. "You were laughing at me at the party, too, and you didn't even try to help me!" My voice begins to crack from the intense emotional pain. "How come you aren't in these photos? You were there, too!"

I have never yelled like that before. I am ready to fight. But to fight for what? I already ruined my reputation, and thanks to everyone in the hallway, they've all seen me naked.

"You talking to me, slut?" she says, playing up to the crowd.

Her smug, mean-girl attitude is making the crowd join in with her.

"You must have me confused with someone else." She glances around the crowd of onlookers to make sure that they're believing her. "Besides, you were too drunk to notice, right?"

"Huh! See, you were there! You lied. You were at the party."

I did see her at the party in the hotel.

"Why didn't you help me?"

I begin to remember pieces, but only a few, and I'm not sure if they were true memories or not. But I do remember this girl is in my English class, along with Jake. She seems so quiet in class, and she doesn't take notice of Jake at all. Or at least, I didn't see her doing so. I always thought she was just one of those really smart kids who didn't want anything to do with me.

"You talking to me, slut?" Now she's acting all tough and bully-like.

She puffs up her chest like a prize fighter, while pulling her book bag off her shoulder.

"Why didn't you help me?" And then, my voice softens. "I was obviously passed out and look what they did to me!"

I find myself so defeated that I throw the handful of pictures right in her face. The pictures hit her and reflect off like a summer thunderstorm as they crash to the floor. They are all over the floor once more, just begging to be picked up by the onlookers. All they do is stare, laugh, mock, and bully me.

"You knew I was being hurt! Why didn't you stop it?" I feel hate and shame at the same time.

She is a horrible person, allowing such a terrible thing to take place. My soul was ripped out of me not only once in the hotel room, but again here in the school hallway, next to the lockers.

"You looked like you wanted it! You were having too much fun. Why would I stop that?" She is smug, and with her interjection, proves to the onlookers that I am a slut.

"They hurt me! They took pictures of me while ..." my voice

cracks from holding back the tears of anger, and I have to pause to catch my breath, " ... while I was passed out!"

My voice becomes louder and louder from the anger building from within me. I am hyperventilating from all the attention.

"Is this a game that you jerks play? Is this a game?"

The truth that I don't want anyone to know just comes out of nowhere. Something reaches down to my lungs and pulls it out like a secret being held under lock and key.

"But I was a virgin!"

OMG! I said it. Now the whole school knows it.

"I was a virgin. I didn't want any of this."

She smirks and tosses her curly blonde hair back like a Barbie doll.

"Yeah, sure, you *were* a virgin." She laughs out loud and glances around the hallway, looking for backup from all the other kids in the school.

And that's all it took.

"You bitch!"

A burst of energy comes up from the bottom of my toes, like someone behind just shoved me hard. You know, the kind of push that happens at a subway stop to an unsuspecting passenger who falls to his death.

I take a leap of towards her. I lunge at her so fast, that when I hit her, she flies back against the locker with a *thud!* Her book bag breaks, and all of the contents spew over the hallway. The crowd bursts into screams and laughter. It happens so fast that all I see is blonde hair against the lockers, then books flying through the air in slow motion.

I don't even know most of the people in the hallway making fun of me. I am no longer the shy girl with her drawing pad, hiding in the corner. I have now become the biggest fool in school. I am the most popular topic. I'm waiting for the news crew to come and interview the new slut in school! I can just hear it now: *Disgraced Girl Becomes Sex Toy. News at 11.*

While she is sitting against the lockers in total shock of what just happened, I try to grab as many photos as I can. I dash to the bathroom. I run around the wall to safety and slam the stall door. I'm not sure if I am going to throw up or scream. I am in the bathroom stall, and I can't help but bawl. I don't care who is in the bathroom to hear. I lost my soul. I want to die. I guess being grounded is actually okay, because I just want to hide in this bathroom forever. I hate school! I hate trying to be popular! I hate life!

I am sitting in one of the stalls, sobbing. The tears are coming so fast and so hard that I can't stop them. I find myself gasping for air just to breathe, but what's the use now?

It's one of the ugly cries. You know, the ones where your face gets beet-red, your mucus runs down your chin, and the mascara makes you look like a rabid raccoon.

I'm staying in this bathroom until school is out and everyone goes home. I need Mildred!

A faint voice comes from the bathroom, outside the stall door.

"Are you okay?"

The bathroom is empty, so her voice sounds hollow, bouncing off the porcelain wall tiles. But it isn't a match for my bawling.

I keep crying. I think I'm crying so hard that I don't realize someone is talking to me.

I hear it once more. "Are you okay?"

I sniffle, trying to get the snot from running down my nose.

I reply, in my slobbery voice, "Huh?"

I glance up to peek out of the crack in the door, only to notice a pair of old, worn tennis shoes that look like hand-me-downs. The color is faded, and it looks like the sides are drawn on by a marker, in hopes of making them look new again.

"Are you okay?" she asks once more; her voice sweet and calming.

"Why do you care?" I snap. Why would anyone care?

I don't hear anything for a few seconds. The shoes are no longer where I can see them. She must have left, but I didn't hear the door open.

"Those girls are so mean to you," she says, in a soft voice.

I think she wants to talk to me, but she is afraid that if someone comes in, they will find out. Her voice is faint, not to be noticed by anyone outside the door or in the hallway.

Pulling the toilet paper off the roll, I blow my nose and attempt to gain some composure. I grab what pictures I was able to get from the hallway and reach for the door lock slider.

Am I really hearing a voice of someone nice out there? Or is it one of those girls pretending to be nice, so when I open the door, they are going to make fun of me some more?

I open the stall door with caution to peek out into the bathroom, though I'm ready to fight again.

At first, I don't see anyone. I look around the room where the sinks are, and still don't see anyone. I guess she left. As I'm washing my hands, I look up at the mirror, and there she is. I close my eyes in disbelief that someone is being nice to me. I don't want to talk or see anyone. I want to be left alone.

When I finish washing my hands and splashing water on my face, I turn around to see if she's still there. I see a plain girl in jeans and a frilly shirt. Her hair is messy. She wears glasses and has freckles. Her shoes are obviously hand-me-downs. It is her. The tennis shoes match the ones I saw from the stall.

She leans against the bathroom wall, holding her books in one arm and more photos in the other. She extends her hand with the photos toward me. And then she pushes her glasses up on her nose. Her glasses are so thick that they don't sit on her nose right.

"Here. I tried to grab as many as I can." She hands me the photos.

I look at her with disbelief. She wagers a half-smile, anticipating my reaction.

"Those girls," she motions with her head and eyes towards the doorway of the bathroom, "are really mean to you."

I guess this is real. She is trying to be nice to me.

I take the photos from her and try to speak, but my voice chokes. I have to clear my throat to speak.

"Thank you."

As the photos are placed in my hand, I feel the tears come racing back again because of the sheer shame of what I did.

"Was that really you?" she says.

Duh. Yes, you stupid girl! How stupid can you be to ask that?

But I answer with a slight nod of my head. The tears are coming back again, and once more, I can't talk. My face squints from holding back the tears.

"My name is Sandra." She smiles.

Her meek hand is extended, while holding her books close to her.

"I'm Mary," I say, with my voice still not to full potential.

"I actually like Sandy, but my mom calls me Sandra." She pushes her glasses up on her nose.

I reach out my hand to shake hers, and our hands come together. I couldn't help it, but those stupid tears come rolling down my face again. Oh, my head is pounding from crying so hard.

Sandy turns around and gets more toilet paper for me.

"The paper towels are too stiff and will hurt your nose."

Why would she know that?

"They make fun of me, too. I have some experience with crying in the bathroom."

Funny, but I never noticed her in the bathroom before.

"They make fun of you, too?" I say.

"Yeah." She puts her head down.

She reaches up and pushes her glasses up on her nose once more, while crossing the toes of her shoes over each other to hide the marker stripes on the tips.

"Did you do something like—"

"Umm, no. Not quite that bad. I can't help it, but I have to wear these big stupid glasses." She pushes them up on her nose again.

After looking at them, they are thick, and they make her eyes appear much bigger than they are.

"I can't wear those contacts like all the popular girls do." She turns to look at herself in the mirror to see if she looks okay. "So they call me names like four-eyes and Coke-bottle eyes, and try to knock me down in the hallway, or knock my books out of my hands."

"I'm sorry," I say. "I would never make fun of your glasses."

"Well, I saw what they were doing in the hallway, and I felt bad, so I followed you in here."

I blow my nose with the toilet paper that she hands me, and I make a funny honking noise. Our eyes meet, and then a big burst of laughter comes from both of us.

"That sounded like an old goose!" She laughs.

"Yeah, it did!" I chuckle.

Oh, it feels nice to laugh with someone and not be laughed at.

With another piece of toilet paper, she turns on the water and dampens the corner of it. She reaches over to me and begins trying to help me get the makeup off my face. With a little work, I begin to see a difference.

"Look!" She turns to look in the mirror. "Turn around. Look, we both have freckles." She points to the mirror, like she is pointing to me directly.

Funny, but it kind of evens out the playing field with us.

"Yeah, we both do, don't we?" I reply.

The bond between us is growing as we console each other.

The bell rings for class. We're both late, since we were talking in the bathroom, but that doesn't matter much. I don't think either one of us really wants to be in school.

She grabs her books and starts to head out of the bathroom, but not without first turning around to write on a piece of paper. She hands me the paper, and I look down. It's her name and phone number.

"It was nice to meet you ..." She looks puzzled for a minute.

"It's Mary."

"Oh, yeah. I'm sorry. It was nice to meet you, Mary." And she smiles.

"Thank you for talking to me." I return the smile.

I decide to write my name and phone number down for her as well. I hand it to her, and we head out of the bathroom, but not without great caution. Are they still out there? Waiting for the next opportunity to attack me once more?

We turn the corner to go into the hallway, and it's empty.

Whew! Thank God.

We both look at each other in relief and laugh. Oh, it feels so good to finally have a friend. I think she feels the same. Or at least, I hope so.

CHAPTER 5

A WEEK GOES BY, AND IT IS PURE HELL. Some of the girls are still trying to poke fun at me, as well as some of the guys, too. I try to suck it up. I go to school every day, not to tip my mom off. But I keep to myself, in hopes that all the commotion will die off.

It does. And it seems that the mass of partygoers are now focused on their next victim. I feel so sorry for the next person. I hate Jake. I hate all the boys here at this school. I hate all the girls that were making fun of me.

I get to see Sandy a few times during the week. We don't have the same classes, but we make sure we pass in the hallway just to get a glimpse of each other and make funny faces at each other. Since I'm grounded, I can't call her. But I will when I can next week. Until then, I will have to be happy seeing her in the hallway between classes.

⁕

It's finally Friday, and my grounding has ended. I so want to go to the park and talk to Mildred. I can't go until Saturday, so I just have to wait. I called Sandy, but she was at piano practice. Her mom told me that she is going to be practicing the piano for a while and can't talk to me until tomorrow. I am happy with just knowing I can use the phone again, and that she will know that I tried to call her.

Saturday morning comes, and I am free to go to the park. It's cooler yet again today, so a jacket is in order. Halloween is

MILDRED THE BIRD LADY

coming soon. The cool Chicago air is blowing in, but I still want to go see Mildred. So off to the park I go.

I head to the park with my headphones on, listening to the latest music on my phone. The park is almost empty, but Mildred is there faithfully feeding her flock. I walk up to the bench with the announcement of leaves beneath my feet.

"Well, hello, chiiild. Why are you dragging your feet?"

"Huh?" I take the headphones off.

I know that what I just did to Mildred is rude. She has taught me to respect people as they talk to me. Saying *huh* to her is disrespectful.

Noticeably irritated by the headphones, Mildred says, "A lady never drags her feet when she walks."

I am careful to sit beside her, not to disturb the flock of birds eating at her feet. My heart is heavy, and she quickly takes notice. I am holding everything in, and I'm about to burst. I need to talk to her so bad.

After wrapping up my headphones and putting them in my pocket, I begin to fidget.

"I have not seen you in days, chiiild. What happened?"

I can't help but to start crying. I am so ashamed to tell her, but I think she is the only one who will understand me. Sure, I talked a little bit with Sandy, but she only saw the pictures. I never really told her what happened. I have to tell Mildred. And so I begin.

"The guy, Jake, that was supposed to be my date for Homecoming dance?" I pause to see if she remembers, and she nods. "Well," the tears come down in waves, "he's a jerk!" My words are filled with blubbering idiocy.

"Oh, chiiild, what happened?" Her voice is soothing, with concern.

She is expecting me to say something childlike. For example, he likes someone else, or he never showed up. I don't think she is ready for this.

I reach for my phone to show her the picture of how pretty I was. The photo is also of Jake standing beside me with his arm around me like I was a trophy.

"See how pretty I was?"

"Oh, chiiild, you look beautiful." Mildred's eyes are beaming. "Magnificent! So, what happened, chiiild?"

"I got drunk." I look into her eyes to see if she is going to yell at me, and she doesn't.

I'm not sure if she didn't hear it, or if it just didn't sink in.

"We ..." I was afraid to finish the sentence, " ... did it."

I gaze off into the water as to imagine myself drowning. I think that could be a much better option at this point.

"What do you mean, chiiild—*did it?*"

Oh, God! And the words fly out of my mouth like a shotgun.

"He got me drunk, and then did it to me. You know, sex."

Whew! I said it out loud. Feels like a load has been taken off me.

"Hmm. I don't recall a wedding happening last week. Or even an engagement, for that fact."

The tears come again. "And," now the hard part, "they took pictures and gave them to everyone at school."

The shame pours from my soul.

"Oh, chiiild."

The look on her face is one that my mother had when she was so upset with me that she was going to burst.

Mildred puts her arm around me and pulls me in close to her. A hug isn't going to make this go away.

"Was ... was this your first time?"

OMG! Yes! I was a virgin. How could she ask me that?

I look up at her, with my legs just swinging hard as they could.

"Uh-huh." My face is distorted by crying the ugly tears.

"And Jake did this to you? Did you want him to?"

"Of course not!"

"Did you tell him no?"

I wanted to yell, but I was speaking calmly. "Umm, I'm not sure. I mean, I think so. I tried. But there must have been something else in that drink he gave me. I was so messed up.

Oh God, I don't know. I hate him!" I could no longer hold my emotions.

"Don't hate him." She looks at the water. "Hate is a very strong word, chiiild."

"What? Why not?"

How can she say not to hate him for hurting me?

"Hate will hurt you more than it will hurt him. I'm so sorry this happened to you. Of course you're angry. You should be! This is not how a man is supposed to treat you. My husband, when we met, he was such a gentleman. A true man in uniform." She pauses in remembrance. "He was even afraid to hold my hand." She rubs her hand as if he were holding it then. "He took me to dances, long walks, and even out for ice cream." She is still rubbing her hand. "And he never even tried to kiss me. He was a perfect, perfect gentleman in every way. He knew that my momma would hit him," she balls up her hand as if she were holding something, "with her rolling pin, and then bury him in the swamp if he tried anything at all with me! He respected my momma, and because of this, he respected me."

I am so confused, but I listen intently.

She turns her body towards me, instead of the water. She lifts her hand and points to herself.

"When you demand respect and give respect, you provide a message." She pauses. "And the message ..." she pauses once more and looks out over the water, "is no one should *ever* disrespect you! Let me be clear" she points to my chest, "You did not deserve for this to happen to you. You are not at fault. But you did make choices that led you into a dangerous situation. You are responsible for your own choices. But Jake is responsible for his actions—and so are all the other kids who've hurt you." I can hear the anger building in her voice. "Listen up! No boy deserves anything from you that you don't want to give him. You owe nothing to no one. What happened to you was wrong. It was rape. And it makes me so angry for you." She purses her lips.

My eyes catch hers, and I feel so stupid because I understand what she is saying.

"Wow, I never thought of it that way," I say.

If I demand respect, then they must respect me? What if they don't?

"I guess I didn't think about respect with Jake. I just wanted him to like me."

It's like a light went on inside me.

"Jake had ulterior motives with you. And the all-co-holll, missy."

Oh God, here it comes.

"No more, Mary! You are far too young to handle such a grown-up poison. You got it, Mary? You must learn the word *no*! And mean it. If you say it, and they don't hear it, then say it louder. No means no."

Her Southern dialect and slowed nature are now sterner and more pointed.

"Yes, ma'am."

I mean it. I am no longer going to mess with alcohol or guys. Even though I'm fifteen, I am not ready yet. I guess I learned my lesson. It was hard.

"As soon as he handed you alcohol, you should have said no!"

"Yes, ma'am," I say, with my tail between my legs and my ears pinned back like a dog that was just scolded.

"So I expect you are in trouble with your mother?" She looks up at me, demanding the truth. "Did you even tell your mother?"

"Yes, ma'am. I got grounded. But I didn't tell her everything. I was grounded for being late for my curfew."

Shame overcame me for not telling my mom the truth.

"You should be! Now quit your bellyaching, chiiild, and stop feeling sorry for yourself." She sits ridged on the bench. "Pull yourself up! And learn," she puts emphasis on the words, "from your mistakes. What happened, happened." She gathers her thoughts. "Now deal with it." I find her gathering her thoughts once more while peering at the water. "Remember, you must learn that very important word: n-o." Her eyes demand my attention once more.

"I will."

"The word *no*! The word *no* demands them to stop. The word *no*, chiiild, is a complete sentence." Her face becomes distorted with confusion. "Did you not think of saying no?"

I just sit there looking like a fool. I can't say anything that will make it right. I become a teenager again.

"I tried to tell him that I couldn't do it, but all my words were jumbled up. I'm not sure if it was the alcohol. I've never had alcohol before." I wanted her to know that all of this was really my first time. "And I wanted him to like me."

"Like you? How absurd!" Her voice is much higher. "Did you feel like it was wrong?"

"Umm, yeah. I guess so."

Oh, I should have just kept my mouth shut.

"You guess so? Let me be clear: it was wrong. You did not deserve to be hurt like that. What Jake did to you was criminal."

Her words began to sting with each syllable.

I just hang my head low and shake it because I know she is right. Feeling defeated, I cannot even muster any response.

"Well, you," she points her finger in my chest once more, "must learn how to say no!"

"Yes, ma'am."

I want to run away and yell that she doesn't know anything, but she is right. I should have said no louder, and I should have stopped it.

"And Missy, you need to tell your mother!"

An unnerving quiet time bestows us as she begins to feed the birds again. My legs are no longer swinging but are still. I feel empty in shame, but full of wisdom. I dare not cry in front of her.

Then I feel the familiar feeling of her arms wrap around me. The smell of her perfume is inviting. She holds me close until the tears leave. I so wish this conversation would have happened with my mom, but I feel closer to Mildred now. She knows everything about me. My secrets, my dreams. She even knows about my dad. Well, kind of.

The tears stop, and I take a handful of birdseed and begin to feed the birds. They, too, know my secrets. Somehow, I think I am safe with them, too.

I feel a drizzle in the air, and I decide to head back home, as Mildred decides to do the same. We part and go our separate ways through the park. I did notice that she is much slower these days.

◈

Sunday comes, and I decide to call Sandy. Her mom answers and tells me that she is getting ready for church. She instructs me to call back afterwards. I never knew anyone who went to church, so this is unfamiliar to me.

I do what she instructs, after noon, and I finally get to talk to Sandy. We speak on the phone, and she tells me that she is practicing for her piano recital. I am intrigued. I've heard piano music on the radio, but not in person. I ask if I can come listen to her at her house, but her mom says no. She is in competition, and she needs to focus. I am disappointed but understanding.

Monday comes, and I notice Sandy in the hallway at her locker. I didn't realize, but it's right down from mine. I wonder why we never ran into each other at the lockers, and then I realize that we did. It was when I was berated by the masses with photos and jokes. I guess I didn't notice her because she is invisible, too, just like me.

I walk over to her locker.

"Hey," I say, with a big smile on my face, freckles and all.

Sandy looks up from her pile of books and responds with a familiar smile that I once saw in the bathroom a week ago.

"Oh, hey."

My day becomes brighter seeing her. I don't have any friends here, since I am so quiet and drawing most of the time. But this lifts my mood.

"I tried to call you this weekend," I say, "and your mom said you were busy."

"Yeah, I am really busy all the time," she reaches for another book, "with piano lessons and this recital coming. She has me practicing all day long." She gives a huge sigh to show just how tired she is. "Not to mention all the homework I have in my English lit class. I want to scream!" She gives me a forced smile.

I have regular English class with Jake. She must be in a more advanced English lit class.

I hold my books close to protect them from the passersby.

"Yeah, I draw a lot, but I don't get into competitions," I say.

"Did you hear about that guy, Jake?" she says.

"No. I have English with him later today. What happened?"

I hope the world dropped on him. Maybe he fell off the face of earth. Or better yet, got run over by a bus.

"Someone from the school board called because they heard about the Homecoming dance after-party. He got expelled!" she whispers because people are coming down the hallway.

My stomach drops. Who else knows about the after-party? I only told Sandy and Mildred. OMG! Who else knows about the alcohol, the sex, and the photos?

"There are a whole bunch of people who got expelled," she continues. "I even heard the police were here. But I didn't see them. I heard they were all taken away."

I was at the after-party, and I didn't get expelled. I wonder how they got in trouble, and I didn't? What did she mean, taken away? Did they all get busted?

The bell rings, and the entire hallway rushes to get to each classroom. I turn to walk to class, and realize Sandy is going in the opposite direction.

"Hey! Call me after school," I yell, as I wade through the sea of students.

She turns around, and someone slams their hand on her books, and they plummet to the ground. Books are scattered out on the floor, and what looks to be pieces of paper with lines and dots are floating in the air. The laughter rings out.

"Hey, four-eyes! You dropped your books again," one of the girls says.

Really! This can't be happening to her. I feel myself getting mad. Actually, livid.

I turn around and head right for the girl who started it. I don't know her, but all I see is her fluffy blonde curly hair. I catch up to her and reach out for her. All I can reach is her hair, and I end up getting a handful of it in my grasp. I yank down, and the girl flips backward, falling onto the floor. Her cute little miniskirt is too short to cover her white underwear while she is holding her knees up to her chest. Her pressed white school-girl shirt to go with the miniskirt is no longer cute, but now a mess. Her books are also scattered about the hallway.

By this time, I am right in front of her. It's her! It's the blonde that made fun of me. But this time, I'm the one in control and demanding respect. Oh, it feels so good to be the one standing, with her sitting on the floor, in complete shock.

The crowd bursts into chant. "Fight! Fight!"

I can't help but look around for where the fight is. What I realize is that they are chanting for me to fight her.

With her on the floor, and me standing over her, I begin to yell. This is my chance!

"Stop being a bully!" I scream.

I look back at my new friend to see that she is crying in shame while picking up her glasses and attempting to put them back together with the same tape as last go around. She is trying to straighten up her homework, and then I notice it. It's her music. Her music is all over the floor, and everyone is stepping on it.

What if that was my artwork on the floor, and everyone was stepping on it? It made me even madder.

She picks up her music and tries to see if all of it is there. It's the music for her recital. These pages of music are like gold to her, and this blonde girl is treating it like toilet paper.

The crowd is pulling in closer and closer, trying to get a front row seat h.

The blonde girl jumps to her feet, flips her curls back into submission, and yells, "How dare you touch me! You slut," while egging on the onlookers.

Oh, here we go again. The slut thing once more. Now, that word doesn't hurt me anymore. It's just a word.

Remembering the conversation that I had with Mildred, I am going to put my foot down and start demanding respect. So here it goes.

"Sure, something really wrong happened last week." I take a breath to hit her again. "And, as I remember, you were there as well!"

I point my finger into her chest as she is forced to take a step backwards, which makes her flop back on the floor. Her legs are pulled up against her chest, and her little cheerleader miniskirt is revealing her underwear again. I didn't think she cared, though. She is sitting like a child waiting for her scolding.

"I was forced to drink alcohol that I have never had before, and then ... I was *raped!*"

The whole school hears me, and the sound of people gasping is deafening.

"You should know—you were there laughing as it was happening." I bend down over her to demand her attention. "Yes, I realize that I was raped. But this isn't about me! What you just did to her ..." I point up the hallway to my friend, while looking at her crying, then turn back to see the blonde cheerleader in total awe, " ... that was wrong! She has to wear those big glasses because she has to see. And she is probably a better student because of those big glasses. Her glasses make her look beautiful!" I turn around to give my new friend a wink.

With a quick snap of my head, my focus is back on the bleach blonde.

"Your blonde hair comes from a bottle, and that makes you fake. You are a bully." I bend down even closer. "And no one deserves to be treated like this from anyone!" I yell, as I glance around the hallway to see who is listening.

The blonde tries to get up, and I push her back once more.

"So stop it! Stop being a bully. We are all tired of being bullied by you and your little cheerleader bleach-blonde friends."

The crowd cheers. The hallway is filled with yells and students that should be in their classes. The blonde is no longer in control. I am! I demand respect, and I am going to get it. My new friend deserves respect. And from now on, she is going to get it, too.

The crowd gasps. I glance up again, only to find the principal standing behind me. She looks at me with eyes I have not seen before. She is neither angry nor disappointed, but shocked that I am the one in control of the fight.

The principal looks down at the blonde girl and the theatrics are on. Tears are rolling down her face in hopes of getting me into trouble, when I was standing up for my rights, as well as the rights of my friend. I am standing up for the rights of all the girls she bullies.

"You, young lady." The principal points at me. "My office, now!"

She throws her arm back and points toward the hallway where her office is.

The blonde girl begins to smile, as if she has just won the prize fight. What she doesn't know is that she is being directed to the office as well. Her victory is short-lived and inconclusive.

She arises from the hallway floor and wipes her face off while she picks up her books.

"But I didn't—"

"Go!" the principal yells.

The crowd begins to dissipate as they go to their classes.

The principal then focuses on Sandy and asks her to come as well, after asking her for her name. By this time, Sandy has repaired her glasses as best as she could and has located all the pages to her recital. Her face is still wet from crying, though.

We all arrive in the principal's office and are sitting in the chairs against the wall, waiting to be called into the office to hear our fate. Sandy is the first to be called in. The blonde cheerleader and I sit, waiting. We don't dare speak to each other or look in each other's direction.

After what seems like forever, the door opens, with Sandy coming out in tears.

Oh crap, why is she crying? She didn't have anything to do with the actual fight.

Then the principal comes around the doorway and asks for the blonde cheerleader, who rises and goes into the room. The door closes behind her.

A long while goes by, and I hear a lot of *buts*, and *I didn't do anything*. You know, the usual things that people say when they're in trouble.

The blond cheerleader comes out of the room, in tears as well. She turns me and mouths *Bitch*.

I think the real justice is going to happen after this office visit. I am afraid to go into the room. I have never been in trouble before.

It is my turn, and I stand up and try to be brave. I enter the room and notice a big desk with pictures. There are a lot of bookcases lining the walls, with tons of books that look important. I also notice several frames with certificates in them. They all have her full name on them, from different colleges.

I feel nervous. Yep, I think I'm dead.

Then I notice pictures on the desk of what appears to be the principal's family. I can get closer now to see that they are, indeed, her family. She has a daughter, too. Younger, I think. I did notice a picture of a baby that looks to be a boy, because it has blue on. Nowadays, blue clothing doesn't really mean that it's a boy, but I'm guessing it is.

I choose the big brown leather chair next to the door. It looks comfortable. Plus, it is close to the door for easy escape.

Then the principal has me get up and change chairs. I am now seated right in front of her desk, in a chair that is fitting for an office, not the comfy brown leather one.

She sits behind her desk with a stern look on her face. She gathers papers that were once scattered about her desk. They are probably of the other two students' records. She then gets up, goes to the file cabinet, and rummages through the folders.

"Hmm, let's see," she mutters.

I am just sitting there quietly while I examine the pictures on her wall. They are nicely arranged. Oddly enough, I notice artwork that was drawn by who I believed to be her daughter. It catches my eye. Sure, the picture is more childlike than the ones I draw, but she has talent. It is cute and full of color. It looks like a tree, and a swing set next to it. Nowhere near scale, but it is cute. It has a stick figure family. I find myself lost in the picture as I am trying to figure out who is who.

The principal says, "And your last name is?" She pauses for an answer.

No answer comes from me. I am too busy admiring the artwork that bestows her walls.

I can't help but feel the awful heaviness of the room, with her stare toward me. It forces me to take my gaze away from the artwork that is captivating my attention.

"Oh, huh?" I say.

She glares down from her glasses. "What is your last name?"

I have to clear my throat because I'm so nervous.

"Mary," I say.

"Your last name?"

"Oh, I'm sorry. Parker. It's Mary Parker."

She digs through the records and finally comes to mine.

"Hmm. Here it is." She pulls the file out and tosses in on her desk as she pulls the chair out to sit.

She opens the file and seems disappointed by the expression on her face.

"Is there something wrong with my file?" I say.

"No, you are a very good student with no infractions whatsoever." She wears a half-cocked smile. "So why don't you tell me what happened." She sits back in her chair and folds her arms across her chest like a detective.

With her closed-off demeanor, I don't really think she is going to listen. But I decide to respond anyway.

"She pushed my friend's books." I gesture the push. "Like this. And her books fell to the floor."

"You mean Sandy's books?"

"Yes. Then she called her four-eyes."

"Who did?"

"I don't know her name, but she is the blonde cheerleader." I motion outside in the lobby.

"Oh, you mean Angel?" the principal says.

"Angel? Is that her real name?" I chuckle.

"Yes, Angelica is her real name. But you don't know her?"

I want to tell her about the last week, but I can't.

"No, I just know her from school. But I didn't know her name until now."

I actually know her from dancing on the coffee table while drinking and making out with all the guys.

"So what else happened?" The principal is writing down the details.

"Well, it made me mad. That girl—"

"You mean Angel."

"Yes, that girl Angel bullies everyone!" I feel an urge to sit up on my chair because I feel like I am being charged by a court.

All of a sudden, I feel as if I need to act as Mildred taught me. To be a lady, and not a frumpy teenager.

"She does?" the principal replies.

"Yes, she does!"

"How so?"

"My friend is always bullied by her. She is always hitting her books to the floor and calling her names because she wears thick glasses. It's not her fault she can't wear contacts. She is really nice. She came up and helped me when ..."

I have to stop because the stuff about me is about to come out. I don't want her to know anything about it.

"When, what?" she says.

I can't tell her. But I have to. She needs to know what kind of girl this Angel is. She isn't any Angel in my book. She is a bully!

"I can't tell you."

"Now, Mary, you are in my office for fighting, and you could be suspended. You better tell me what is going on, or I will have to call your parents."

"You can't call my parents. My dad is gone."

Then, before I know it, my face is getting wet. Oh, crap, I can't stop the tears.

"Well, I'm sorry, but I will have to call your mom, then." She reaches for the phone.

"No! Please don't."

"Well ..." She picks up her pen and lifts her gaze in anticipation of my next sentence.

"It started with a guy in my English class. Jake. He asked me to the Homecoming dance."

I glance up at her, and she is writing.

"Uh-huh." Her gaze meets mine.

I could tell she already knew the story. She just wanted to hear my version. After all, everyone else was suspended or expelled. Oddly enough, Angel was still here in school. I guess she talked her way out of it, or her parents gave a lot of money.

"Please don't write this down," I say. "I want to tell you, but you can't write it down."

She puts the pen down and begins to listen. She sits back in her chair and folds her arms once more.

"Well, Jake took me to the dance, and I did some stupid things. He kissed me, and I think this Angel girl got jealous." I pause to catch my breath.

Oh, God, I can't breathe. But I have to at least tell her what happened today.

"I know of Angel, but I don't really know her. She isn't a very nice person. She was in on all the stuff that happened to me. I mean ..."

Oh crap, I hope she didn't catch that, so I try to continue without missing a beat.

" ... that happened. The next Monday after the dance, here at school, she made posters of me and told everyone that I was a slut." My voice becomes shattered. "I'm not a slut!"

I feel the words bunch up in my throat like a Black Friday sale at Walmart, with the doors getting ready to open.

"I was a virgin."

"Oh, are you the one that all the commotion was about? I didn't see the pictures, but I heard they were bad."

Oh, great! She knows all about it.

"As a matter of fact, I got a phone call from a board member about the whole thing." She sits back in the chair and purses her lips in total disapproval that I was involved. "The lady from the school board demanded that Jake be expelled, as well as everyone involved with that dance. Or should I say, after-party."

I look up and shake my head in shame. "So why am I not expelled? I was there, too. It's pretty obvious! The photos were of me."

"I can't reveal who called, only that she is on the school board, and somehow she knows all about that night." The principal again purses her lips.

Confused, I just shake my head in acceptance.

"So what happened today?" she says.

"That day, Sandy told me she was being bullied by Angel, too. So when she started bullying her today, I couldn't take it any longer. I stopped it." I pull my sweater close to me. "I didn't mean to hit her or push her down. But someone had to demand respect from her."

"And that's why you were yelling about her being a bully?"

"Yes, that's why."

The principal picks up her pen and begins to write once again. She is writing so fast I begin to get nervous.

"Oh, please don't tell my mom about the dance."

The principal arises from her chair and grabs a form off her table. She sets it down and begins to write again.

"I am not concerned with the dance, or the jealously of another student. I've already taken care of the students who were mentioned in the phone call."

She missed a few students, but Jake is gone, and that is the most important thing to me.

It takes her several seconds to gather her thoughts.

"However, I am concerned with the bullying in this school."

She looks perplexed as to how to reprimand me. After all, I am the one who stood up to the bullying and stopped it.

The principal comes out of her chair and moves to the one next to mine, in front of her desk. It seems to put us on an equal playing field. She is no longer the one in charge, but now talking to me like an equal. Weird feeling.

The tears are beginning to well-up because I think I'm in deep trouble, and she is coming around to soften the blow.

"Mary, what you did today was very courageous." She gives a small approving smile. "However, you can't fight violence with violence."

Tears are right on the edge of falling once more.

"I do understand why you did what you did. You were protecting your friend from being bullied ... and it is a commendable thing to do. I heard you speak about respect to her, and demanding respect as well."

"What?" I sniffle. "You were there? You saw what happened?"

She leans back in her chair. "I heard what happened, and I saw what happened as well.

I just wanted to see if you were going to tell me the truth."

Oh, no! She heard me when I said about the party and the alcohol. I wonder if she heard about the rape.

I begin to get a sick feeling about what is going to happen next. I just look up at her with confusion, in hopes the punishment isn't going to be too awful. Besides, what could be worse than what I've been through the past few days?

"I saw how you spoke to her in anger, but you didn't hurt her in anger. You pushed her down so she would listen to you, and you stopped the riot in the hallway. But how you did it was a violation of school policy."

My heart sinks. I know that I am in deep trouble.

"You also spoke of being raped." She pauses. "Is this true?" She puts her hand on my shoulder to talk to me. "Are you the girl in the pictures?"

"I don't know what you're talking about."

"Well, if you are, you can always come to me, and we can talk about it. Having a boyfriend isn't easy at your age—"

"He's not my boyfriend! He is a jerk!"

She tries to console me. "I can't make a report until you report it to me."

Whew! I am not speaking of this to her at all. She knows too much.

"Please don't call my mom."

"I have to because of what happened today. And I have to give you a detention for one day for fighting," she says, her tone reluctant.

"Did that Angel girl get into trouble, too?" I say.

"Yes, she has a week suspension. I have seen her in school. She is being watched for bullying other students. Thanks to Sandy, she told me what happened today."

"But Sandy was crying, too, when she left your office."

"Well, she was embarrassed about what happened."

The principal completes the paperwork and hands me a copy after I sign it. I turn to leave her office, and she stops me.

"Mary."

"Yes, ma'am."

"If you need to talk, I am here." She motions to her office. "I can help you through this," She smiles, then hands me a business card with a phone number on it.

It is a card for a rape crisis hotline.

"Yes, ma'am." I turn to leave her office with my tail between my legs.

There are other students in the office waiting area, trying to see what is going on. They all know that I was just in a fight, and they want to know what I got for punishment. It's none of their business. I look them all in the eyes and proceed out into the hallway, where more students are looking at me. I think that they're completely surprised that I am the one in trouble. I'm a quiet little art student who finally stood up for my rights. A real shock for most. Most of all, me.

After leaving the principal's office, I begin to walk back to my locker before class. I notice Sandy is there as well. With everything that just happened, I missed my class and need my books for the next class. As I'm standing next to my locker, I begin to turn the lock combination. The lock is open, and so is the door. I sit my book bag on the floor to pull the books out from the class that I missed and begin to reach for the books that I need for the last part of the day. I can't help but reach for my sketch pad. As I touch it, I feel this presence behind be. I'm afraid to turn around because I feel it is the blonde cheerleader, Angel.

I take a chance on it and turn around. It's Sandy. She is still upset.

"Hey." I close my locker.

"Hi." She pulls her book bag over her shoulder.

"Are you okay?"

"Yeah. I'm glad you helped me, but how much trouble did you get into?"

"I'm good." I readjust my book bag. "She said that she was glad that I stood up to a bully, but the way I did it was not correct. So I got a one-day detention. How about you? Are you okay?"

"Yeah, I guess." She hangs her head down and pushes her glasses back against her face with her entire palm, in total defeat.

"What's wrong?"

She should be happy that the situation was handled.

"Well ... what's going to happen when she comes back to school?" Sandy looks up at me with worry. "She is only suspended for, what, a week?"

"Well ... now she knows that we won't stand to be treated like this. I push my chest out and lift my chin, as if I just won a battle.

"Yeah, but ..."

"But what? We stood up to her! We told her, no more. And the principal knows, too. A good friend of mine told me that if I want respect, I must demand respect and act respectful."

Sandy giggles as she looks up from her glasses, which are always down on her nose.

"Hmm. Yeah, I guess I need to work on that one, huh?" she says.

And we giggled together with our little inside joke.

"Well, okay," Sandy says, trying to convince herself.

She has always lived in a life of fear. Fear of what Angel was going to do next. To some degree, I have, too. Angel turned my life upside down in the past week. But things are different now.

I am stronger, and Mildred taught me how to accomplish that.

"Call me after school." I begin to run off to class.

"Okay, but I have to practice tonight."

"Okay, later," I yell.

After school is out for the day, I am quick to call Sandy. I have to know if she is feeling better after class.

She answers the phone.

"Hey, Sandy, it's Mary."

"Oh, hey!"

"So how are you doing since school?"

"Good. But I can't talk long. I have to practice before my dad comes home from work."

"All right, I just wanted to make sure that you were okay after what happened in school."

I hadn't realized it sooner, but my Mom is standing behind me in the kitchen.

"I'm fine. But I have to practice piano now."

"Okay, can I come listen to you play sometime?"

"Yeah, yeah. I gotta go." She rushes off the phone and hangs up.

"So what happened in school today, sweetie?" my mom says.

"Umm ..." Oh, I don't want to tell her, but I have to. "I will be late coming home from school tomorrow."

"What's up?" This time, she stops what she is doing and looks right at me.

"Well, I kind of got detention today," I murmur, under my breath.

"What?"

Oh, damn, here it comes.

"But wait, Mom. I got detention for sticking up for one of my friends."

"Detention? You got detention?" Disappointment is oozing from her eyes. "I got a call from the principal, but I couldn't answer it. She just told me that I need to call her back." She throws her dish towel on the counter with a big sigh.

"Mom, it's not like that."

"So tell me, why is sticking up for one of your friends so important that it got you in trouble? You are never in trouble."

"Sandy was being bullied, and I stood up for her."

"So how did that get you detention?"

"Well, I kinda pushed the girl down in the hallway," I say, under my breath.

"Mary! You were in a fight at school?"

"Not really. She was hurting Sandy, and I couldn't allow it anymore." I stand up on my feet.

"Really?" she yells.

"Mom!" I realize I just raised my voice, and I have to calm down so that I don't get into a fight with my mom. "I went to the principal's office, and she told me that Angel has been bullying people, and they have been watching her. I am just the one who stood up to her. I only got a one-day detention, but Angel got a week suspension."

"And this is acceptable?"

"Umm, no. But she was bullying other girls, and someone had to stand up to her to show her that she was wrong." I have to pause to gather my thoughts. "Mom, I was taught that if you want respect, you have to demand respect." I look her right in the eye.

My mom is thrown off by my convictions.

"Well, that is true." Her facial expression is that of defeat.

I could see my mom wonders who taught me this.

"So when I saw Angel hurting Sandy, I had to help her. She couldn't help herself. So I had to help her." I wear a tiny smirk because I know I'm showing my mom that I am growing up.

"And you have to get detention for this?"

"Well, yeah. I did something right, but I did it in the wrong way, and I have to go to detention for it. But it's okay."

"Hmm ... really?" She looks up with her eyes full of nothing but questions.

"I not only helped Sandy, but I helped other girls, too."

"I see. Who were you talking to?"

"That was Sandy."

"Oh, the girl from school?"

"Yeah." I gaze off into a magazine I grabbed from the pile of mail my mom brought in.

"What do you mean that you want to listen to her?"

"Oh," I put my magazine down, "she plays piano, and she is practicing."

I'm confused because she is interested in my friends.

"That's nice," she says.

Mom continues doing what she was doing, and I go off into my bedroom. I feel like I passed a huge milestone with my mom today. We talked like adults. A real adult conversation with my mom!

The next school day goes by quickly. I do notice that some of the students are looking at me differently now. It's like I am stronger and a force to be reckoned with.

I have to spend the time in detention after school, and I stop by my locker to get my sketchbook, so I have something to do. I find a seat by myself at a large table so I can place my sketch pad out with my pencils. I draw the hour away. I don't focus on anything in particular. I draw things like piano keys and notes that are on a sheet of music. I think it would be neat to give to Sandy. You know, to try to cheer her up.

The next day at school, I meet Sandy at our lockers again. I give her the picture of the piano and the notes that I drew in detention the day before. She totally loves it! She then gives me a note. But it isn't just any note. It is an envelope with an invitation inside.

"What's this?" I say.

"It's my piano recital." She has a bounce in her step and voice. "It's this weekend, and I want you to come. It's actually Friday. Well, tonight."

"Can I? Am I allowed to go? Really?"

Now, I am really excited. I have never gone to see a friend in anything. I have never heard a piano up close.

"Yeah," she replies, with a beaming smile.

Her glasses are slightly out of place, but with a quick wisp of her index finger, they are right where they belong, on top of her freckled nose.

"There is another ticket in there for your mom, too."

"Oh, wow! Thanks!" I turn to go to class.

I call my mom from school to ask her if I can go to the piano recital, and if she wants to go with me. She says she has to work. So I have this extra ticket, and I don't have anyone to go with me. My mom says she would drive me, but she can't stay. I guess I'm okay with that.

I go directly home from school and am trying to get ready for the piano recital.

"Mom, will you help me decide what to wear?" I say, while going through my closet.

"You can wear a nice dress." She pulls out a cute dress from my closet. "Here, try this."

I slip the dress on. It is perfect for the recital. Even though, I'm not sure what perfect is. I just know that it isn't as formal as the Homecoming dance, but nice enough.

My mom drops me off at the front door of the Art Museum, where the concert is being performed. After making sure I have my ticket in hand, I go about finding my seat.

Let's see, the aisles are in letters, and the seats are all numbered. I find my seat letter and number and sit down carefully while placing my ankle over the other, just as Mildred told me to do. It's ladylike to sit proper when in a dress. My back is rigid, as if I am going to eat a proper meal. But I quickly realize that I need to sit back into the seat. The seat beside me is empty because my mom couldn't come, but I'm too excited to be upset. I am going to see Sandy play.

I can't help but look around the seats to see who's here, as if I would really recognize anyone. The people are all wearing dresses and suites.

A short time passes, the lights go dim, and the announcer comes out onto the stage with a spotlight focused on him. He welcomes us to the piano recital and introduces the players. Then he says it. He says her name, Sandra. I think I clapped so hard my hands went numb. She is second to perform.

The curtain goes up, and there it is, a beautiful huge black piano. It glistens in the bright lights that are high above. It's as big as a car! Then a young man comes out onto the stage. He dons a black tuxedo with tails that look as long as he is tall. He sits and plays something I have never heard before. It is classical music. I try to understand it, but I am too excited waiting for Sandy.

His recital is over, and then it's time for Sandy. I sit on the edge of my seat with anticipation for her to come onto the stage. She comes out wearing a long red dress and she looks absolutely elegant. Her dress flows with each step she takes.

I have never seen her like this before. She is so homely in school, where she wears mismatched clothes and hand-me-down shoes. How can she possibly be dressed in this beautiful evening gown?

Her gown is deep red, with sparkly sequins made of gold that shimmer in the lights as she moves. Her hair is styled high on her head, with curls beautifully draped over one shoulder. I think she has gold in her hair that sparkles as well. The only way I recognize her are her glasses.

After maneuvering with her unusually high-heeled shoes, she stands in front of the crowd with pure confidence. Who is this girl? She's living a double life. She has such charisma and poise. She looks like a professional performer. She is ... beautiful!

She sits upon the long bench in front of the bright black and white keys just begging to be touched. Her hands are stretched out over the keys, and then it happens. Enchanting music rings out from the heavens as her fingers run up and down the keyboard. She sways to the rhythm, as if the music is coming out of her soul. Her hair swings as the music fills the room. Everyone is in awe of her recital. With each note she presses upon, the pristine ivory keys reveal a little more of her. A lively rendition with soulful grace encompasses the room that is filled with parents and guests. She loses all sense of insecurity; she becomes her music.

Her choice of music is exquisite. I listen with such intensity that I almost forget it is Sandy. I find myself swaying, trying to get a better view of her instead of the lady in front of me with the big hair that smells of Aqua Net hair spray.

I am so impressed. I now understand why she guarded her sheet music with such intent. It is her life, her heartbeat. Much like what my drawings mean to me.

Sandy pours her heart out to the audience. They can't help but get caught up in the emotion of the sounds. At the end, everyone rises to their feet and provides Sandy with a round of applause that seems to last forever. I can see the embarrassment on her face as she gazes upon the audience. I, too, rise to my feet. Once again, my hands hurt from clapping. I am so proud of her.

Sandy leaves the stage and allows the next player to enter. I was too interested in Sandy that I think I totally missed the next player, and maybe the next afterwards as well.

When the recital is over, all the players are gathered in the back room of the hall. Sandy invites me to meet her mother. I go back to the room, and there she is.

Sandy is standing in her beautiful long evening gown. She is so graceful, and I don't recognize this Sandy at all. At school, she is awkward. She is shy and afraid to speak up. But behind a piano, she becomes a person in control, pounding out her emotions and feeding the souls of those who listen to her.

Sandy is standing there with a bundle of flowers that her mother brought for her.

"Look," she becomes a little schoolgirl once more, "my mom brought me flowers!" She pushes them into my view.

I smell the sweet aroma of the flowers as they pass my way.

"It is customary for the concertos to get flowers after the concert."

"They are really pretty!" I say.

"Mom, this is Mary. My friend from school." She directs her mother's attention to me.

"Oh, hello, Mary." Her mother puts her hand out for me to shake so graciously.

It isn't like a real shake. Her mom's hand is actually palm

down, like she is expecting me to kiss her hand. I just grab it and put it up right so I can shake it properly.

"Hello." I can't help but smile at Sandy.

"How did you like it?" she asks me.

"I totally loved it! I had no idea you were so good."

"She practices every day for things like this," her mom says.

"Well, she is very good."

"Thank you, Mary," Sandy says. "Where is your mom?"

"She had to work. She dropped me off."

"So you need a ride home?" Sandy turns to her mom. "Mom, can we take her home?"

"Sure."

"Oh, you don't have to do that. My mom will come back for me."

"Call your mom. I will take you home."

"Yes, ma'am, I will." And I call as instructed.

The drive is short, and the conversation is entertaining. I learned so much about Sandy and her love for music. I ask her where she got her beautiful dress, and I am surprised to find out that it's a rental. I had no idea you could rent such a beautiful dress. I found out that her mom and dad are divorced, but she sees him often. I told them that my dad isn't here either.

Conversation is so easy with them. It is like we have been best friends for years.

CHAPTER 6

WHILE SITTING IN THE KITCHEN with Mom on a bright summer day, she is opening the mail, and I can see that she has something on her mind.

"What's up, Mom?"

"Oh, nothing."

"Come on, Mom, really, what's up?"

"Well, your senior year is almost here." Her voice cracks. "And I'm wondering what you are planning afterwards. If anything."

"Hmm. Haven't really thought about it." I take a bite from my sandwich.

"College?"

"I thought about a school for the arts." I cringe.

"Now, you know how I feel about your doodling." She turns to use the trash can.

"Mom! It's not doodling," I yell.

"I didn't mean that. You are really good. You really are. But artwork does not pay the bills. And you know that."

Feeling sorry that I got into this conversation to begin with, I try not to get angry with her. She is right. Unless I'm someone prominent, most likely a dead artist, I won't be famous at all. Most artists don't become famous until they die. Kind of sad, but true.

"I don't know," I say. "I will look some options over."

The conversation stops, and she goes back to what she was doing. I decide to go to the park, my favorite place. I grab my book bag and head out the door. She knows where I'm going. I always go there.

I get to the park to talk to Mildred. This time, I am sitting on the park bench before her. Since she isn't there yet, I decide to take out my pad and begin to draw.

In the midst of a drawing, I hear her approach with her slow gate. She grabs for the bench to steady herself. She moves herself around the bench to get a better position in the front to sit. I look up and see her melt into the bench.

With a deep sigh she says, "Whew, chiiild. I'm afraid I am getting old." She situates her dress and pulls out the bag of bird food.

The birds are flying in from all locations, with the usual chirps and squawks to greet her. She lets out another big sigh, and finally catches her breath. She gazes at my drawing with admiration.

"Oh, chiiild ..." the pause gives way to her endearing words, " ... that is really good!"

Her pauses between words and thoughts have become more frequent, and apparently more painful.

"Thank you," I say, but it isn't the usual upbeat response that she is accustomed to.

"What's wrong, chiiild?" She throws the first of many handfuls of birdseed to the ground.

The birds burst with excitement, and their wings are hitting our heads as they are all fighting for position.

"You know, I'm entering senior year of school. My mom wants me to plan for my future and what college I am going to be attending."

"Well, chiiild, that is an important decision to make. Do you have any ideas?"

"Well, I really want to draw." I lift up my sketchbook into her view. "But no one becomes successful at art until they're dead. Then their artwork is worth millions."

"And, what is wrong with studying art? That is your passion? Your heart?"

"I know it is. But ..."

"But what, chiiild?"

"My mom says I can't pay my bills with my art. I have to actually make money to pay to live and doodle. That's what my mom calls it, as a hobby."

"So find a school that you can study to get a career, and ... study art at the same time. You are really good! I mean, really good!"

Blushing, I can't help but feel that she is right. I am really good. All of my teachers keep telling me I am so good that I will become famous someday. Oh, how I want to believe everyone.

"I will look," I say.

Later that day, I decide to look for a school that will make both my mom and me happy. I find one, but it isn't here. It's far away. Could I possibly go to college in another state?

Well, I first have to graduate high school, then worry about college.

With tons of applications in for college, I don't think about it much. I am spending a lot of time with Sandy and working at the five and dime. The summer and school year go by so fast that it seems like yesterday when I was looking at colleges. Mom helps me choose my college, but what she doesn't realize is that she is also helping me decide where I am going to learn about art. As long as I can do both, I am happy with that.

Right now, I am getting my finals done, and then I will be walking the stage for my diploma. But first, I need to find my inspiration to complete my final drawing. I need to go see Mildred.

She is sitting on her bench and feeding her husband's birds, like always. I plop down beside her with an important question. I grab my pencil and begin to draw. Mildred is accustomed to sitting next to me while I draw. She usually just keeps on feeding the birds, and never pays any attention to my drawing.

My pencil graces the page with direction not given by my hand, but by my heart. I know every inch of Mildred and can draw her by heart, with my eyes closed. But I pay close attention to the details of her every wrinkle, given not by age, but by wisdom.

Her hands are stretched out before her, and the birdseed is

falling to the ground. I am able to draw the action of the seed falling from her hand, and the birds before her begging for food. I am able to capture the essence of her knee that is showing, as her dress is hiked up from sitting on the park bench. The lace around her wrist is delicate, displaying the hands of love. Her nails are long, but unpolished. They are still taken care of, but not finished.

I find myself so engulfed in her image that I flip the page and begin a new drawing. I have to sit back from her to get this drawing's perspective, though. I capture the image of the brim of her Southern belle hat that surrounds her face. I capture her every freckle and age spot upon her cheek and nose. Her eyelashes are short but yield eyes of great wisdom and care.

With each stretch of her hand out to the birds, her eyes open wide to see if they are getting fed enough. I am able to capture the wetness of her eye as it glistens from the water in front of us. It isn't a true side view or portrait, but a view that reveals both eyes, her full mouth, and nose. Her hat obscures the rest of her face, but the design on the hat makes up for what is missing.

I become lost in my drawing as the time passes. She, too, does not realize the passing time. The closeness we share is speechless and endearing.

After stepping back from this image, and not in such close-up detail, I am able to capture one of the birds as he reaches for the seeds. It is like he's photo bombing the shot of a camera. I am eager to put him in the drawing. He belongs there.

Time has passed, but I came here for two important reasons. One is to draw, and two is to ask her my important question. She is special to me, and even though my mom is going to my graduation, I really want Mildred there, too.

"Will you come to my graduation?"

"Is it that time already, chiiild?"

"Yes, Mildred! You know I have been studying all week to graduate. I have one more test to take, and then I'm finished."

"What class, chiiild?"

"I have to turn in my art project, but you know I always get A's."

"Have you been working on it? Is it finished?"

"Well ..." I add the final touches to it, " ... yes, it is!"

"What is your final drawing?"

I turn slowly and give a half-cocked smile.

"You!"

"What do you mean? Me?"

"My drawing is of you."

I notice a tear in her eye.

"You drew me?" She wears a grateful smile. "Can I see it?"

"After my grade comes in, for sure!" I say, with a slight hop on the bench.

I get up and pull myself together because I need to get home. But first, I have to turn around because I realize that she didn't answer me.

"Well?"

"Well, what, chiiild?" I can tell she is goofing around this time.

"Can you come to my graduation?"

"I will try, chiiild. I am very tired." She turns to look down. "But I will try."

Her frame is beginning to match her frail fingers.

"Okay, see you there!" I start to run home.

I jump in the air like a basketball player reaching for the hoop.

With me running off into the distance, she mutters, "You have no idea how tired ..." she takes a deep breath, " ... I am. I will hope to go."

I have no idea her health is fading, but she is a strong Southern woman.

⁂

Today is the big day! I find myself standing in front of my closet, wondering just what to wear.

I begin pulling out a few dresses, but something isn't quite right. Then my mom comes into my room with a dress from her closet. Oh, no! That is the dress that I wore on Homecoming night!

"Mom, I can't wear that!"

"But you wore it to prom, right?"

"No, I wore it to Homecoming, my junior year."

"Well, you can wear it now, too, right?"

"Hmm." I can't let her see my displeasure. "I would rather wear this one." I pull another dress out of the closet.

I cannot tell her that this dress is the one I was raped in. I hear that he moved away with his family, so I will never run into him again. I'm not sure if it has something to do with the photos or not, but he is gone. And I am happy about it.

I pick out the plain black dress with short sleeves. I put it on, and my mom gasps.

"Oh, honey, that looks great on you!"

"It is perfect for graduation," I say, while primping.

I'm finished with my hair and nails, and ready to put on my high heels. One last check in the mirror, and off to the living room to get my cap and gown in the bag.

"Oh, Mom."

Mom is putting things into her purse that she is going to need. You know, the important things like, camera, tissue, and parking directions.

"Yeah, what's up?" she replies.

"I asked someone to meet us at graduation."

"Oh, yeah? Who?" Mom stuffs even more things into her purse.

I pick up my cap and gown bag and am checking to ensure everything is there.

"I asked Mildred."

"You mean," she wrinkles her nose, "The Bird Lady? The homeless lady that feeds the birds in the park, right?"

"Mom, she is not homeless!"

"But Mary, she is always sitting in the park, feeding the birds.

Doesn't she have a home? Have you seen it?"

"Well, no."

"So you are going to have a homeless ...

"She's not homeless!"

"Okay, not homeless Bird Lady."

"Mom, her name is Mildred. She has a name. It's Mildred, Mom."

"Okay, Mildred. So she is coming to your graduation?"

"Yes, Mildred is coming to my graduation."

"Well, then, I can meet her."

"Cool! I want you to meet her. She is a really nice Southern lady."

My mom has never heard me talk about a person like I talk about her. Southern? Lady? Yes! Mildred is most definitely a Southern lady with charm and grace. She is also a little edgy, but full of knowledge about the world. I love that about her.

This is going to be really weird having my mom and Mildred together. It is like my two worlds colliding in midflight. Mildred knows so much more about me on a relatable level, where I can tell her anything. My mom is the authoritative director who I respect as my elder. My mother is, well, my mother. Mildred is my friend.

Standing in line to graduate, I almost break my neck trying to see where my mom is seated and looking for Mildred in the audience as well. I wish they could sit together, but Mom still doesn't approve of me talking to her. She still believes that she is a homeless woman. Every now and then, she still calls her The Bird Lady. But that's okay. I know who she is. She is my first real friend.

It's my turn to walk the stage. I am careful not to trip, but I'm still trying to see if Mildred is there. It's impossible to see her. I can't even find my own mom in this crowd.

I reach the principal, and she hands me my diploma in a pretty vinyl book. I am directed to smile for the camera, and then I hear it.

"Mary!" my mom yells, from the sea of people.

Startled, I turn to see my mom is standing on her chair, with a camera to her face. Oh my gosh, how embarrassing! The crowd laughs and claps because of my mom's determination to get my photo. I just laugh and join in.

"That's my mom," I say to the principal.

"She's proud of you." She smiles.

"Yeah, I guess so," I say, still embarrassed by her actions.

I take my diploma and walk off the stage to let the next student come to the principal. I move down the stairway, behind the girl in front of me, and follow her back around to our seats.

"Was that your mom?" she says.

"Yea, it was."

She smiles. "I wish my mom was that proud of me graduating ..."

"I'm sure she is. My mom is just embarrassing." I giggle.

We laugh together and watch the ceremony. Then I hear a familiar name being called. It's Sandy!

I jump to my feet and give a "Whoot! Whoot!" waving my fist in the air like I am at a football game, to show her that I am so proud of her.

I sit back down in my assigned seat, and the girl next to me is full of laughter.

"Like mother, like daughter," she says.

"Ha. I guess you are right." My face is warm. "That's my best friend!" I wear a beaming smile.

"Yep, I guessed it."

And the laughter begins once more.

We quiet down because we are going to get into trouble. We anticipate the end of the ceremony. Even though we're happy everyone is graduating, it seems to last forever, and it's hard to sit there.

Graduation is finally over, and I still do not see Mildred. I look and look, so I guess she didn't come. Disappointed, I find myself settling for Mom and Aunt Jackie. Travis graduated a year before me, so he isn't here.

Mom and Aunt Jackie take pictures of me everywhere. It

is so many pictures that I begin to tire of smiling so much. My face hurts, and my feet hurt in these shoes, too. I'm ready to go home, but Mom and Aunt Jackie are celebrating by going out to dinner. There are many parties going on, but my mom wants me to celebrate with them since I am going to college soon. I remind her that I have to work the next day, so we don't stay out late.

Before work, I decide to go to the park to see Mildred. She said that she was just too tired to go to my graduation. I could never be upset with her. It was disappointing, but not upsetting.

I have to go to work now, so our meeting is short. As I'm leaving, I notice a lady sitting on a park bench near us, but down the way. She gets up and sits next to Mildred. I am late and cannot go back to see who she is.

The summer seems to go by quickly. I find myself packing for school, and I decide to visit Mildred before I move away. I have been dreading this day. I am leaving my dear friend.

I drive to the park and stop by the street. I pull out my sketchbook, as I always do, but this time it wasn't to draw. It's to show Mildred my final drawing. You see, I haven't seen her all summer. The realization saddens me.

I walk up to the park bench where Mildred is sitting and find that woman with her again. Feeling jealous, I cautiously approach. Mildred slowly lifts her head, and beneath her big hat reveals her endearing eyes. A relieved smile glistens in her eyes. She still speaks in that Southern drawl, but now much slower, and harder to understand.

"Oh, looky here. My chiiild, Mary, has come back ... to see me and the birds." She gives a warming smile.

"Yes, ma'am," I say, in a soft tone.

"Have you met Mary?" she whispers, as she turns to the lady next to her.

"Why, no I have not." The lady speaks in a Northern, quicker tone.

She turns her head to meet my attention and extends her hand.

"Hello, I'm Antoinette."

I try so hard not to take her inventory, but I haven't met anyone that even spoke to Mildred. Who is she? Why is she sitting next to my friend? I haven't been here all summer. Has Mildred replaced me?

"Hello." I grasp Antoinette's hand. "Is this your daughter?" I ask Mildred.

Antoinette chuckles and then turns away not to be noticed. But it's too late.

"Antoinette is my new caretaker," Mildred whispers, as she lifts her hand, now much frailer than the last time I saw it. "I don't know if I ever told you, but I lost my daughter long, long ago."

I feel utterly stupid for even asking.

"My daughter was taken from me at her birth because she was born still."

I didn't dare ask what that meant.

But wait, "Caretaker?"

"Why, yes, chiiild. I'm tired. Antoinette," she turns toward her with a smile, "helps me."

"What she is trying to say is that I help her around the house. And I also help her get to her birds."

I begin to look at Antoinette as a person who I feel like I should be. I know Mildred doesn't have any family to take care of her, and I never really thought of her as being too old to take care of herself. I know her to be strong and self-sufficient.

Mildred then leans over to talk directly to Antoinette.

"Deary, would you mind if we speak in private?"

Antoinette arises. "Yes, ma'am." She goes off, but not too distant.

I notice, as she is walking away to the next bench, that she is in nursing shoes with white pants. How did I miss that? Her shirt, though, is a normal shirt, not like a nursing outfit. She is older, but nowhere as old as Mildred. She looks to be my mom's age, I guess.

"So chiiild." She looks at me with concern. "What brings you here?"

As usual, my legs begin to swing. She reaches over and touches my knee, and I know exactly what that means. I then cross my legs at the ankle, to be proper for her.

"What is wrong, chiiild?" she says, with a wavering voice.

"I'm going to college."

"Excellent, my chiiild!"

A reaction I was not expecting.

"But ..." I take a breath to prepare for the next words, " ... I need to move there." I whimper.

Deep down, I feel as if I am leaving a parent, and I am afraid to tell her.

"Oh, chiiild, I hope you do."

I can see the pleasure upon her face because I am going after my dream.

"It's okay that I'm leaving?"

I know I have not been spending as much time with her as I wish I could, but I was hoping she would be more upset that I was leaving.

"Why, yes, chiiild. Do you remember what I said?"

"Umm, I'm not sure."

She taught me so much that I'm not sure which part she is talking about.

"Your dash, chiiild. Your dash."

"Oh, yeah." I gaze off into the water, knowing exactly what she is talking about.

"Make your dash great!" She shoots her index finger off into the air like a rocket. "Find your dream. And make your life count."

Mildred reaches for her neckline and reveals her necklace that she showed me many years prior. I can't help but look. She begins to take off the locket that she held dear to her heart for so many years.

"Chiiild, help me with this."

I reach over and assist her with the latch that is the cement holding the locket close to her heart.

"Do you remember who gave this to me?" She raises the locket up in front of both of us.

"Yes. Your true love. Your husband."

"Yes, chiiild." Her fingers clench the locket once more.

I cannot help but feel the love emulating from the locket as we gaze upon the artistic design.

"Do you know why he gave this to ..." she looks down at the locket with great love, "to me?"

"Yes."

"Why?"

"To prove to you that he was coming back. That he was going to marry you when he came back. To prove his undying love to you."

"That's right, chiiild."

I sit there wondering where all of this is going, and why she took off the locket.

She reaches out and opens her fingers, almost in slow motion, one finger at a time, to reveal her precious gem.

"I want you to have it." She grabs my hand and places it into my palm.

"But why?"

"It's a promise that you will come back to me."

I could feel Mildred's love for me, and an overwhelming warmth within. I put my arms around her frail frame, and she does the same. I smell the lovely essence of her perfume that I have longed for so many times before. Sweet, but this felt bittersweet because I was leaving.

I whisper, "I promise," into her ear.

"You know," that all too familiar Southern charm comes out once more, with a bit of pep, "you are not only my friend. I think of you as my chiiild, too."

"Really?" What an honor.

"And this locket will keep you safe, chiiild." She rests her hand upon the hand that is holding the locket. "And when you are scared, chiiild, I am right there." She taps the hand that is holding the locket.

A smile with deep, endearing warmth, arises from my heart. I begin to put the locket on, but not before I inspect it with all its splendor. After fastening the clasp, I tuck it deep within my shirt, next to my heart.

"It is right where it belongs, next to my heart," I say.

"So, chiiild, go learn about art, and go make your special mark on this world."

It is hard to say goodbye, but I know I will be back someday.

"I will. I promise."

I get up and ask Antoinette to come back since I am leaving. She walks over and sits down next to Mildred.

"Please take care of my dear friend," I say to Antoinette.

"It is my pleasure to take care of her."

I turn to go back to my car. Halfway there, I realize that I forgot to show her my drawing. But when I reach for my newly acquired locket, it just doesn't seem to matter. I have something special. I have Mildred around my neck and next to my heart. I will never be alone in college. I suddenly feel strong enough to get through this move. Sure, I am still nervous, but I have a renewed strength within me.

⚜

College is going by quickly. I am studying marketing, with a minor in art. I listened not only to my mother with marketing, but also to Mildred with my desire to draw and make my mark on the world.

It is weird not hanging out with Sandy, but she ended up going to a school for music. She is well on her way to becoming a great pianist. I, on the other hand, am stuck studying math and marketing skills, but am still able to get a drawing class in here and there.

While sitting in my dorm room, I hear a frantic yell from my dorm mother.

"Mary!"

"What? I mean, yes, ma'am."

"I have a phone call for you on the house phone."

The house phone? Why aren't they calling my regular phone? I have it right here.

She hands me the phone that belongs to the dorm building.

"Mary?" A frantic voice is on the other end. "Mary?"

"Yes, this is Mary."

"It's Aunt Jackie. Oh, God! You have to come home."

Home? I'm in school. I can't leave. The semester isn't over. I'm going home after school is out.

"What?" I reply.

"Mary ... it's your mom." Her voice becomes hoarse.

"What? What is wrong with Mom?"

"Mary, I have a flight for you already."

"Why a flight? I have a car."

"No, Mary. You are too far away to drive. You have to fly here tonight."

I get upset and look at the dorm mother. I begin to pace with the phone in my hand. Not being accustomed to phones with a cord, I end up being pulled back against the wall where the phone was plugged in.

The dorm mother looks at me and mouths, *What?*

No words left her mouth, but her expression of sheer worrisome took me by surprise.

"Okay." I paused for a few seconds. "Okay, I will." I hang up.

I turned around with no regard as to who was next me and found myself almost knocking down my dorm mother.

"My mom! I have to go to the airport. I have a ticket. My mom needs me," I blurt, like a machine gun.

"I will drive you," says the dorm mother. "Go get your stuff."

Pushing me towards my room, she instructs me to go pack. I do so as fast as I can, unclear what to take with me.

The dorm mother comes to my dorm room, and she has the dean with her.

"Mary."

I hear his deep, raspy voice. You know, the ones that speak from the depth of the throat, like he smokes too many cigarettes, and with authority.

"Yes, sir," I say.

"Don't worry about a thing here at school. I will handle everything until you return."

Until I return. What does that mean? How long does he think I'm going to be? A day ... maybe two, at the most?

"Thank you, sir." I continue stuffing clothes into a bag. "I really don't know what is going on, but my Aunt Jackie said I had to be home tonight," I say, between each thrust of clothing into my obviously too-small bag. "I really don't know what to take."

The dean looks at the dorm mother. He holds his finger over his mouth to instruct her not to tell me what is going on. The dorm mother raises her eyebrows in concern, and the dean just shakes his head. She shakes her head to him in return.

"Mary, we need to go now!" She prods me to pack faster.

"Yes, ma'am." I zip my bag closed. "I'm ready"

After a swift drive, we get to the airport, and I find myself wanting to jump out of the car before she puts it in park. I sprint to the back door, grab the handle to open the door so I could grab my bag and run to the ticket counter.

The ticket counter is bustling with people all holding bags and their paperwork, trying to get flights to wherever they want to go. I couldn't help but interrupt the ticket taker while he was talking to another flyer.

"Hi, I'm Mary Parker," I blurt out.

The other people in line were obviously disturbed because they have been in line and I have not. I was just a rude college girl running to the counter, demanding service.

The airline agent already has my ticket punched up and printed for my arrival.

"Yes, ma'am." He tears the ticket off the printer and hands it to me, but not before he says, "ID, please?"

"Oh, yes." I reach in my purse and pull out my wallet with my ID and show it to the ticket agent.

My hand is shaking from all the stress. The people in the line are now voicing their displeasure. The agent gives a sweet, but stern look to instruct them to back off.

"Yes, Chicago," he says. "Here you go. Enjoy your flight."

I couldn't help but feel the pressure emulating off the people behind me.

"I'm sorry," I say. "Something has happened to mom, and I'm trying to get home from school." I'm holding back the tears. "I don't know what happened. They won't tell me."

How can I enjoy my flight? I don't know what is going on.

I grab my bag and ticket and head to the check in area.

My dorm mother is right by my side, ensuring that I get on my flight. She is holding my elbow to direct my movement and how fast I am walking. You know, the kind of instruction my mother gave me long ago in the park when she found me talking to The Bird Lady so many years ago.

"Got everything?" she says, her voice hurried, but also trying to reassure me with her calm demeanor.

"Umm, I guess so. Do you know what is going on?" I ask.

"No."

But I don't feel that she's telling the truth.

"Better get going through the gates," she says.

A quick hug, and I am off to the TSA inspection area. Once the TSA inspection is complete, I am then allowed to go to the gate to board my plane. It is all so quick, I don't have any time to think about it.

I find my seat on the plane and settle in for the flight. With all the uncertainty, the flight seems to last forever. I'm sure the time difference is nowhere as different as it feels.

When the plane lands, I find Aunt Jackie at the airport. I don't have any bags that were checked in, so we quickly leave the airport.

"Where are we going?" I say.

"They didn't tell you at school?"

"No, they didn't tell me anything."

"Your mom was in a car accident."

"A car accident?" My voice is an octave higher. "So, where is she?"

"She is in the hospital," Aunt Jackie says in a voice that is tense but calm at the same time.

I am afraid to ask questions as we drive wildly to the hospital.

We arrive at the hospital, and Aunt Jackie says I can leave my bag in the car. We hurry to the doors, and then run through hallway after hallway.

We arrive in the ICU. Aunt Jackie grabs my hands, and we both stop before we go inside.

"Are you ready for this?" she says.

Ready for what? I take a deep breath and am scared to respond. My hand is all sweaty, and I feel a bit embarrassed that Aunt Jackie is feeling it, too.

"Yes. I want to see my mom."

"Now, remember, she had a car accident, so it's not good."

"Umm, okay." I take a deep breath and shake my head.

Reality is about to strike.

Her clasp on my hand becomes even harder. We go through the doors to the ICU and meet a nurse. The nurse recognizes Jackie and takes us to her pod room.

The ICU is a large bright white unit with a bunch of sliding doors all around the perimeter. In the center is a huge circular desk with tons of computer monitors, nurses, paperwork, and charts. Everyone seems as if they have a specific job to do, but it still looks chaotic to me. Some nurses are yelling codes back and forth, and others are running into rooms, tending to their patients. All the while, they are keeping calm on the outside.

The nurse leads us to one of the sliding glass doors that is a pod-like room full of emergency equipment, all of which is in use. As I turn the corner to enter the room, there are a couple of nurses tending to my mom, getting her ready for my arrival. As they part, all I see are a bunch of wires, tubes, and bloody gauze that is wrapped around her head. I'm not sure if my mom is really under there.

The nurses all have a strange gaze upon their faces, as if they don't want to make eye contact with me. They all leave the room, and it is just me, Aunt Jackie, and Travis.

Travis? He was called home from school as well. We go to different schools, but he is closer than I was, so his flight was shorter.

"You can talk to her, honey," Aunt Jackie says.

Even though the commotion is wild out in the ICU, and the warning bells are going off in other pods, the pod we are in seems like a dream. I don't feel as if I am really standing here because things happened so fast, and I can't tell that this body laying before me is really my mother. That is, until I look up at all the wires, emergency equipment, and placard on the wall with instructions. There it is, my mother's name. Right beside it, written in bold letters: WAIT FOR DAUGHTER TO ARRIVE.

Wait for me? Why? Wait to do what? The importance hit me like a freight train hitting a car stalled on the tracks.

Coming back to the room from my out of body experience, I look at Aunt Jackie with tears forming.

"Can she hear me?" I whisper.

"Honey, she has been waiting for you."

Travis bursts into tears. Aunt Jackie puts her arms around him and escorts him out of the room.

"Talk to her," she says. "Tell her that you're here."

I feel around the bed for her hand, and I find her fingers. I interlace my fingers with hers. I look down at our hands embracing. I notice her fingers are pale, but still polished, as they always were. She has her rings on her fingers that she usually wears, that my father must have given her.

I take a slow deep breath and begin to speak. Afraid of what to say, I know that I have to say something.

"Mom ... Mom, it's Mary." I grab her hand and hold it close. "I'm here, Mom."

Buzzers go off, and the nurses rush into the room. Her heart rate spikes on the monitor.

"Honey, it's okay," says one of the nurses. "She knows that you are here."

They tend to her needs, and then leave the pod once more. They stay close by, just in case.

Then Aunt Jackie comes back into the pod, but Travis is not with her.

"She needs to hear your voice, Mary. Talk to her."

"Mom, I'm here."

I don't know what to say, and I look to Aunt Jackie for help.

She moves over to Mom's bedside and attempts to rub her arm.

"Mary is finally here." She rubs my mom's lifeless arm.

"What do I say?" I ask Aunt Jackie.

I'm at a loss. I feel numb. I guess I feel stupid, in a way. I am trying to talk to a person in a hospital bed, all covered in wires and bandaging, with no resemblance of the person being my mom.

"Anything, Aunt Jackie replies. "Tell her about school."

"Mom, I'm doing really well in school. I'm getting really good grades, and my dean says everything is going to be fine while I'm gone."

Suddenly, I realize the reality of this. I am going to be away from school for a while. How am I going to get my schoolwork done for the semester?

"I love you, Mom. I know I haven't said it in a long time, but I love you, Mom." I lean over and kiss her hand.

I want to kiss her cheek, but it is far beneath the wrappings that are now drenched with seeping blood.

Buzzers go off, and the nurses rush into the room once more. Expecting them to just turn things off and then leave, I stand there waiting.

"You have to leave the pod, please!" yells one of the nurses.

"But—"

"Please let us stabilize your mom."

Aunt Jackie and I leave the pod, but we stand just outside the sliding doorway. The nurse works on my mom for what seems an eternity, but it is really only a few minutes. The buzzers are turned off and carts come in and go out of the room with different surgical equipment. More towels full of blood are carted out of the pod, while bags of blood are carted in. I start to feel nauseous, seeing all the bloodstained gauze and towels.

Then a chaplain comes. He puts his arms around me without even asking. A welcomed gesture, though. I think he washed his clothes in starch. When he hugged me close, I could have sworn I heard his shirt crinkle.

I reach for the locket around my neck and pull it out. I caress the front of the locket, as to talk to Mildred, asking her to help me get through this. Then the nurses come out of the pod.

One of the nurses comes over to talk to us.

"You can go say goodbye to her."

What! Goodbye? Is she serious?

Aunt Jackie whimpers while she grabs my hand. She musters up the energy to reply to the attending nurse.

"Thank you."

We go into the pod, to my mother's bedside once more. The monitors are turned off, so as not to not disturb our final visit. We are escorted in to stand beside her bedside. They instruct us not to be boisterous. But how can you tell a grieving family that? When my own mother is on her deathbed!

I listen to the nurse and do what I am told. I do not want to be escorted out again. I want to stay with my mother for every minute that I can. With sobs, and fears of the future, we all say goodbye to my mother.

She dies quickly after my arrival. She really was waiting for me.

We are escorted into a room outside the ICU unit. A counselor is there to greet us and to take care of us in our time of need.

I am numb. Travis is sobbing in the chair, and Aunt Jackie is just standing there in shock. You can see her trying to plan what to do next. But what is next?

One by one, the nurses come in to check on us, as well as the hospital staff. I see their mouths move, but no words ever come to me. I just stare off beyond their eyes and shake my head when I notice they were waiting for confirmation that I hear something. I don't hear anything. My mind is in a fog.

Hours go by, and it is well into the morning. We gather ourselves, and we all go back to Aunt Jackie's. It is weird leaving a hospital in the early morning. It feels like a dream. Oh, how I wish this was a dream, and I could wake up and talk to my mom once more. I feel an odd pull that I need to get home because my mom is expecting me. But this is just an illusion. The memories of rushing home are just that—memories. I have to go to Aunt Jackie's house instead of home.

Back at Aunt Jackie's, friends of the family are calling and stopping over to try to comfort us. I am not sure how they all know what is going on. With each passing phone call, and my Aunt Jackie telling them, "Not today," was more of an aggravation than a comfort. I just want to scream for them to go away and leave us alone. I try so hard to go to sleep to see if this is indeed a dream. But it is not.

Aunt Jackie tells me to go into the kitchen so she can talk to me. I follow her and sit at the kitchen table. She is standing at the counter, making some coffee.

"Do you want coffee?" She turns to me, then gets a puzzled look on her face. "Do you even drink coffee?"

"It has been a while, huh?"

"You have been away for two years at school, and I'm not sure if you drink coffee with all your late-night cram sessions for tests."

"Yes, I do. But no, I don't want any today." I pick at my nails. "I don't know what I want right now."

"I know. I'm in shock, too." She pours the coffee and begins to put in the creamer.

"You know, on second thought ..." I start to get out of my chair.

"Oh, honey, I will get it for you." She reaches for another cup out of the dish strainer and begins to dry it for me to have a cup of coffee. She then pours it for me and turns. "Creamer?"

"Yes, please," I mutter.

She puts the bottle on the table and allows me to add the creamer. I find myself pouring it in and notice that it is hazelnut. I see the creamer swirl around in the cup of coffee, and I begin to fall off into a trance. I watch the slow swirl dancing around in the cup, and visualize romantic dancers, arm in arm. I think I am so tired that I may have fallen asleep for a second.

"Sugar?" she says.

"Yes, please."

Aunt Jackie puts the sugar on the table, along with a spoon. She slowly sits in the chair beside me and begins to fix her own cup of coffee with the sugar.

"You know, honey ..." She seems to be lost for words.

"Hmm." I think I'm delirious from lack of sleep.

"Your mom really loved you."

Does she not think I know this? Is she trying to convince me, or herself, that my own mother loved me?

I thought about all the times that I just wanted a hug or some praise about my drawings. But deep down, I did know that she loved me. I was her one and only since Dad was gone.

I arise and grab for my phone. "I need to call school."

I proceed to dial. The phone at school rings a few times, and then the operator answers.

"I would like to speak to the dean, please. This is Mary Parker."

I hear the secretary rustle through some papers, and then she pauses.

"Yes, dear, I see a note about you right here, that says you would be calling. Let me connect you."

I hear the phone transfer.

"Mary?" that familiar, cigarette-rattled voice answers.

"Yes, sir."

"How are you doing?" the dean says.

"Umm, not so good, sir. My mother died last night. Well, a couple hours ago."

"I'm sorry. I could not tell you how bad it was."

"So, you knew?"

"Yes, I did. I did not want you to worry on your trip."

Our dean is one of great authority, and a force not to be messed with. But this phone call makes him sound different, almost caring. But I dare not think of him as being weak.

"What do I do now?" I say, a hint of fear in my voice.

"I have already spoken to your professors, and you have very high grades. You do not have to take the finals in your classes, and you will have your grades processed for this semester. Now, you can take next semester off if you like, or need."

"Thank you, sir." I whimper.

"Again, I am truly sorry," he says.

The phone goes dead on the other end. I look at the phone in shock because I never heard him say goodbye.

I hang the phone up and stare off into space.

"Is everything okay at school?" Aunt Jackie says.

To my relief, she is able to snap me back to reality.

"Yes. I don't have to take my finals."

"Great! Well, that is one good thing that has happened."

"Yeah, I guess so," I mutter, and begin to bite my nails once again.

Aunt Jackie gets up and comes over to where I'm sitting on the other side of the table.

"You know, everything will be okay eventually. It is going to take some time."

"Yeah, I know."

"You can't quit school. Your mother would be very upset if you did—"

"But—"

"No buts! You are going back to school. Maybe not right away, but you will."

"Yes, ma'am."

I pick up my phone and begin to dial once more.

"Who are you calling now?" Aunt Jackie says.

"I have to call my dorm mother to make arrangements to get my things."

"Okay, but you are going back to school? If not next semester, then the one after that."

"Yeah, I know. But I need to take care of Mother's apartment here, and then there is the ..." The tears begin to flow.

"What?" Aunt Jackie says.

"The funeral thing."

"Yeah, I know. But your mother has already arranged everything. Not only for her, but for you as well."

"What do you mean, for me as well?"

"Honey, you will be taken care of. You are her only child, and she is leaving everything to you."

"Umm, okay."

"Your mom told me everything many years ago, of how she wanted things to be taken care of. And exactly how she wanted you taken care of. And ..."

"And what?"

"You also have your father's money now." She looks me in the eyes.

"What do you mean, my father's money?"

I am so confused. I had no idea that my mother was getting money from my father.

"The money is from your father's ..."

"My father's what?"

"From your father's life insurance, honey."

I suddenly realize that this is how my mother was paying for our apartment, along with her job. She made sure that I was taken care of, and that we lived in a safe neighborhood by the park.

"So honey, this is what I mean that you are going to be taken care of, and that you don't have to worry about anything. It's not a ton of money, but you will not have to worry anymore."

Aunt Jackie tries to put my mind at ease, but nothing is getting through to me.

"Uh-huh," I say, between tears.

"Just let me handle everything, and don't you worry," she says. "My sister was very organized, and I know where all the paperwork is to take care of things."

"Okay." I wipe my runny nose.

We hear a key turn the lock and see Travis as he enters the house. We both get up from the kitchen table to see if he is okay.

I turn to her and say, "Aunt Jackie, I really want to go for a walk. Is it okay if I leave for a while?"

"Yes, dear, go get some fresh air."

Off I go out the backdoor, leaving my hot cup of coffee behind. I want to go to the park to see if Mildred is there. I need to see her.

The walk is long, but welcome. It's weird not having my car.

I arrive at the park to see Mildred and her nurse there. I can't get to them fast enough.

Nearing at the park bench, where my long-lost friend is sitting, I find myself walking faster and faster. When I reach Mildred and Antoinette, I wrap my arms around Mildred and begin to cry so hard that it is difficult to speak.

"Oh, chiiild," Mildred says, with that loving Southern voice, weak, but caressing.

I can't help it. I keep crying, and I cannot speak. I look like a blubbering child.

"Chiiild, why are you here?" She pushes me away to arm's length so she can see into my eyes. "Chiiild, why are you home from school?"

All I can do is muster one word.

"Mom."

And then the sobbing starts once more. It is a few minutes before I can actually speak.

"My mother died last night." I hold her tight once more.

"Oh, chiiild, I am so sorry." Her grasp becomes tighter to keep me safe.

"I was in the hospital, and I held onto the locket, and I needed you so bad. I couldn't stop my mom from dying." I pull the locket out of my shirt neckline. "I am here." I begin to unclasp the locket that has been my protector for the time I have been gone.

"What are you doing, chiiild?" She reaches for the locket.

"Stop."

"But I have returned." I begin to work the locket once more.

"I meant for you to keep it and return to me."

Confused, I stop trying to work the clasp, and just leave well-enough alone.

Antoinette is still sitting next to us on the bench. I almost forgot she was there.

"We really must go, Miss Mildred." She pulls herself up off the bench and grabs her medical bag. "We need to get your afternoon medicine." She extends her hand out to Mildred.

"Yes, ma'am, you are right, I guess," Mildred says. "Would you like to come with us, Mary?"

"Where?"

"To my home, dear. I need to take my medicine."

"Umm ..." I was so accustomed to asking my mother that I am in unfamiliar territory. "Yes, ma'am. It would be an honor." I grab onto her hand. "But I do not have my car here. It's still at school. I flew here, and my Aunt Jackie picked me up at the airport."

"That's okay. You can ride with us," Antoinette says.

"Thank you."

We all get up, and Antoinette assists Mildred. I am not used to Mildred being so frail and needing so much help, but I have been gone for a long time at school.

We walk to Antoinette's car, which is parked in the handicapped parking lot. She helps Mildred with her arm to walk.

"You know, Mildred, we should have brought your walker today."

"You know I hate that thing!" Mildred pushes the imaginary walker away from her.

"Yes, ma'am, but it is for your safety,"

"You need a walker?" I say.

What have I missed? Why would Mildred need a walker? Is she really that frail?

I find myself watching her every move, and I come to realize that she does need assistance.

"Oh, chiiild." She pauses to catch her breath. "It has been a long time, hasn't it?" She tries to catch her breath once again.

"Yeah, I guess it has been," I say, with sorrow.

"Oh, chiiild, it is okay. Now, come along."

We get to Antoinette's midsized car, and I sit in the back to allow Mildred to sit in comfort up front. Once she is all buckled in, we set off for her home.

I am excited to see Mildred's house for the first time. My troubles seem so far away when I am with her.

We pull away from the curb and go down the street for what seems to be a short drive. We turn on the first street, which is at the end of the park. The car slows as we drive up to the big iron gates that I have always admired from a distance. We saw it from the window of our bus as we came to the park for our field trips.

I try to see what is in front of us to explain our slow drive, but nothing is there to see. No car, no one. Just us in Antoinette's car, and this big iron gate.

"So where do you live, Mildred?"

She just turns around with a smile, as if she doesn't hear me. Antoinette reaches above her visor, and it happens. The big iron gates begin to move.

"Are we going in there?" I says.

See, I have always been told that a mean old woman lives behind these big iron gates, and to never bother her. As kids, we always wanted to know who lived here, and some even played games with the gates.

When it was Halloween and all the kids were going door to door for candy, some of the kids would throw rolls of toilet paper over the gates and make sure that the paper got stuck on them. They would make it look like the gate was covered in a white curtains of toilet paper. Other kids would throw eggs. I thought all of it was mean. My mother always told me to never bother whoever lived behind the gates.

Once again, a smile, but no answer comes from Mildred, as the gates begin to part and open to an entirely different world.

All this time, I have lived just a few streets away from Mildred, and I never even knew it. I am surprised to find that she lives around the corner from the park. It is just too far for her to walk now, and Antoinette has to drive her here daily to feed the birds.

The gate opens up to a great estate. Trees as far as my eyes can see. I have never even seen behind these gates. As we turn into the street—or I guess, drive—the gates begin to close slowly. I am so fixated on the movement of the gates that I am not paying attention to what is happening in front of the car.

And then it comes into view. The house is so big; I had no idea a home like this was behind the gate.

The house is all white, with black shutters on every window. It looks much like the White House, with two stories and porches. The porch goes completely around the house, with big columns that are decorated with hanging baskets of flowers. There are gardeners working the flower beds and tending to the landscape. I feel like I'm in another world.

We enter the area where the workers are hard at work, and each of them stops to give their welcome to Mildred.

"Antoinette, I think I would like to enter the front today." Mildred smiles. "You know, for Mary." She beams with a glow, as to impress me.

Little does she know; I am already in awe just of the front gate. But I am much too embarrassed to let it show.

"Yes, ma'am." Antoinette turns the car and goes towards the entrance leading to two huge French doors with beautifully etched glass. The car comes to a halt; a man who is working on the front porch, watering the flowers, comes to assist Mildred inside, along with Antoinette.

I'm not certain, but I think he is a light-skinned black man. He is wearing clothing that does not look like he should be working in the dirt. He is a polite gentleman in his mid-fifties, I'm guessing. His salt-and-pepper hair glistens in the sunlight, and his smile is inviting.

He opens the door with great tenderness. He extends his hand to meet Mildred's with utter admiration. Such a pure gentleman, but much too old for me. He pulls his hands back and brushes them off on his pant legs to remove the dirt.

"Oh, goodness, Miss Mildred. Where are my manners?" He finishes cleaning his hands to assist Mildred.

It is unclear if he is a butler or a gardener, but he is obviously someone who cares very deeply for Mildred.

"Come on, Miss Mildred," says Antoinette. "Let's go inside now and get you some tea and your medications."

"Yes, Deary. I am moving as fast as this here old body can move."

The gardener is still tending to her every need to get her out of the car, while Antoinette reaches for her purse and empty bag of birdseed.

It is surreal, witnessing the type of treatment Mildred is receiving. In the park, most see her as a tired, old homeless woman with a life consisting only of feeding the birds while sitting on a park bench with no one there to talk to her, care for her, or even acknowledge her presence. Most make fun of her and avoid confrontation with someone who could possibly be contagious or hurtful. So many see her and acknowledge her as The Bird Lady because of what they choose to see.

On the contrary, here people go out of their way to ensure her safety, well-being, and speak to her with the gentleness and kindness a human being should be recognized with. I am so honored to be one that was able to look beyond the dirt on her clothing and the tears, on that first day we met. I could only dream that she feels the same about me.

"You live here?" I say, stupidly, my jaw scraping the driveway, and my eyes wide with amazement.

I'm sure I must have looked like that stupid four-year-old she met in the park so many years ago.

I quickly regain my composure and impress upon her that I am grown.

"Yes, chiiild. I told you many times, I was not homeless."

I feel so stupid. I had no idea that when she said she wasn't homeless, she lived in this mansion just a couple blocks from where I used to live in the apartment with my mom.

Oh, my mom. I remember again that my mom is no longer at the apartment, and I start to become somber once again.

"Why did you ask if this is where I lived?"

Afraid to tell her the truth, I say, "Umm, I just wondered," but I am not convincing.

I bite my lip to stop myself from saying anything else.

As we get to the grand porch, I see oversized rocking chairs that looked smaller than they really were, just because the porch was so large.

"Now, chiiild, why don't you sit here a while." Mildred instructs me to sit on the porch, in the large white rocking chair, right alongside her.

You can see that she has a favorite rocking chair because it has a cushion on it, and a small table on the left side of it to put her afternoon tea.

I sit and begin to rock back and forth. I feel so out of place in this house, and I am not even inside the house yet.

I take great care in my posture, keeping my head up as much as I can muster. My legs are not crossed at the knee, but they are crossed at the ankles, if only for a few moments, because I find it difficult to rock in the chair with my legs in that position. My hands are folded on my lap, just as she instructed me. My eyes are ever moving, trying to catch all the details of the moment, but not get caught by Mildred herself.

The porch is beautifully adorned with flowers of all colors. The bright white columns are accented with oversized white rocking chairs and baskets, just as if it was a grand Southern home. I can't help but notice the ceiling is painted sky blue. I wonder why.

I find myself staring off into the landscape and losing myself in all the splendor. The gardens that align the drive are unbelievably beautiful and hide the city, which is held back behind the walls and the grand iron gate in the distance. The huge trees are being held down by the flowers they have. A gentle breeze enables the trees to sway back and forth.

My eyes grow weary, even though the sights are majestic.

"I can't believe she's gone," I say.

Mildred slowly sits in the rocking chair and moves the pillow that she is accustomed to using to a different location to support her back. I then notice that Antoinette is adjusting the pillow for her. I am so caught up with the sheer magnitude that I momentarily forget Antoinette is there.

"Is that better, Miss Mildred?" Antoinette says.

"Yes, Deary." Mildred lets out a great sigh.

Moments later, Antoinette places a tray down on a table next to Mildred. It has two cups of tea, and a small cup of her pills.

"Would you like some tea, too, Mary?" she says.

"Yes, ma'am, I would." I reach for the cup of tea. "Thank you so much."

The teacups are quaint and hand-painted with pale-pink flowers adorned by the painted greens on the stems and leaves. I think the top ring on the cup has to be gold. I'm not sure if it is real, but it almost has to be. Must have been expensive. I am nervous holding it, careful not to drop it.

Antoinette turns to Mildred and ensures she is seated.

"Do you need anything else, Miss Mildred?"

Mildred looks about her and makes sure everything is here—creamer, sugar, spoons.

"No, Deary, I am fine. Thank you for asking."

"Okay. I am going to be in my room if you need me," Antoinette says.

Her room? Does she live here?

Antoinette goes inside and leaves the front wooded door open but closes the screen door, so no bugs get inside. I wait for her to disappear.

"Does she live here, too?" I say.

"Why, chiiild, I can't take care of this place all my myself." She takes a breath. "Antoinette takes care of me and my home.

I hired her some time ago." Mildred reaches for the sugar to put into her afternoon tea. "She takes care of all day-to-day needs." She glances at the workers to ensure everything is as it should be.

I look around, and I am still in awe of how big this porch is.

"I am glad she is taking care of you," I say, even though I am jealous.

I realize a part me always thought I might be the one to take care of her someday. I had no idea how bad off her health really was.

"So chiiild, talk to me." She sits up and readjusts herself on her rocker. "How did your mother die?"

I fumble with my cup of warm tea. "I am not real sure. I heard it was a car accident, but I have no details like whose fault was it, or where did it happen? I think Aunt Jackie is afraid to talk to me about it."

"Seems to me ..." she pauses as if to search the memories in her mind ... "I heard something about a car accident the other night."

"They haven't told me anything." I put my cup of tea back onto the saucer on the table. "I am sure Aunt Jackie will tell me more. I just got here last night, and I went straight to the hospital from the airport. After we left the hospital, we went to Aunt Jackie's house. I came on a walk to see you in the park."

I feel like I am explaining my day to my mother. But this is different. I *want* to explain my day to her. I don't feel like I'm being interrogated, like I did with my mom.

"Would you like to come inside, chiiild?" She begins to ready herself for the task of getting up.

Oh, would I? This house is so incredibly beautiful. I want to see it.

"Yes, please. That would be nice."

I regain my manners and attempt not to look so childlike. But on the inside, my heart is pounding, and I want to jump around like a little puppy.

Mildred attempts to get out of the rocker, and she reaches for me.

"Help me up, chiiild."

I reach for her hand that is extended to me. I put my hand under her arm to assist her. She is so skinny and frail; I am afraid of hurting her.

"Oh, chiiild, you won't hurt me. I'm a tough old bird." She stands to her feet and clenches her fist like she is a prize fighter.

"I see that."

We make it to the screen door as Antoinette is just about to open the door for us.

"Here, Miss Mildred. Allow me to help you." She takes Mildred by the hand and escorts her inside.

I follow so I am not in the way.

I find us to be entering a large foyer with white marble tiles. There is a beautiful stairway leading up to the second floor that is so big it splits into two directions midway up. The walls seem to go up forever, and the wallpaper is loud and gaudy but goes well with the décor. There are many rooms in all directions. The ceiling is framed with crown molding that features a glistening chandelier that looks as big as my car.

While I am too busy taking notice of all the character in the foyer, I see that Mildred and Antoinette are headed off to the doorway on the right. Antoinette reaches for the door handle, with Mildred still in tow.

"Here, chiiild. Come this way." Mildred turns to the doorway.

We leave the foyer and enter a brightly lit room that is on the other side of oversized doors. It looks like a sunroom. The room is bright due to the sheer size of the windows, where the early afternoon sunshine is beaming. A stone fireplace is constructed on one wall that seems to be so big I could walk inside. The mantel is just above my head. There is a seating area with white wicker furniture, and I also notice many potted plants that bask in the sunlight.

After taking in the beauty of the greenery and the warmth of the sun, I can't help but notice a shiny black grand piano in the corner. It catches my attention right off, so I gradually walk toward it. The piano makes me think of a friend in high school—Sandy.

Antoinette is getting Mildred situated into her seat, along with another cup of tea. The piano, as well as many shelves that line the walls, are adorned with photos. I pick up one of the frames, and then another. They are all children in ballerina dresses. There are even some young boys in dance outfits as well. The children range from all ages.

I turn to her. "Who are these children?"

"Oh, chiiild ..." Mildred says, with a chuckle in her voice.

Her teacup clangs as she misjudges the distance of her saucer.

I move closer to the photos to get a better look.

"They are kind of my children, when I was a teacher long, long ago."

She slowly gets up to join me near the piano, then reaches out and picks up one of the photo frames and tilts it for me to see.

"She is really pretty," I say.

"Yes, she was back then. Her name is Kathy. She was a star of ... hmm, now," she touches her forehead as to grasp the distant memory, "what was the name," she moves her finger against her temple, as if to reach deep inside her brain, "of that show? Hmm. It has been an awful long time ago."

I pick up another photo frame and turn it toward her.

"And, what about her?"

"Her name is Victoria," she says, with a big smile. "She had the longest legs I have ever taught."

She takes the frame from me and puts it back into its place. Then she points at yet another photo, and tells me about that child, and then that child. I think she could have talked about those kids all afternoon long. Sure, I am interested to know about the children, but my question is not about the kids, but her.

"So, you were a teacher?" I say.

"Why, yes, chiiild." She grins from ear to ear. "I danced when I was young and quit not long after I got married. I was," her demeanor turns to a proud lady, "a child star." She had a glimmer in her eye.

"You were a star?"

How could that be? I have never met a star before.

"Yes, chiiild. I would perform on Broadway." She chuckled. "Well, on Broadway Street in North Carolina." Her chin elongates, and I can see the beauty radiate from within. "I did travel some with the shows, performing here and there."

"Now, don't you believe her!" says Antoinette. "She really was a star."

"Really?" I reply.

"Yes, she was. She would dance with the best."

"Oh, Antoinette, I was. I guess so," Mildred says, with a hint of embarrassment.

"How awesome!" I say.

"Now do you understand?" Mildred says.

I'm not sure what she is asking, and what I need to understand, so I give her a puzzled look.

"Find your passion. Find what makes you happy. Pursue your dreams. Mine was the art of dance. That's why I have this school of dance. I am now passing on my dream to those," she turns her attention to the photos, "who have the same dream, too. I remember speaking about your dash. The dash of life. You now the one?" She waits for my response.

"Yes," I say.

"The dash between your birthdate and the date on your tombstone. The dash is what we do with our lives. Our purpose in life. Our hopes, dreams, goals. The everlasting mark we leave in this world."

"You have a gift." She turns to look me right in my eyes.

"My drawings?"

"Why, yes, chiiild! This is why I said to make your dash count. Nurture your dreams. Become the artist that you dream of being." Her voice is tired, but inspirational.

I am sitting in deep thought. My dreams ... what are my true dreams? I am in college, studying business, but my true dreams are drawing the details in life.

Mildred knows my true dreams from all of the afternoon

talks in the park. After all, she helped me choose the college that I am attending, because of the art department.

"So chiiild, have you figured out your dash in life?"

"Yes, ma'am. I believe I have." But I am not convinced.

My art is only mine. I keep it hidden deep within my heart. It is like the sketchbook I had in school, and the kids used to pick it up and make fun of me because of what I was drawing. Like the picture of the birds, or even The Bird Lady. They all laughed at me.

She says, "And ..."

Antoinette is intrigued with the answer as well. She lifts her gaze toward mine, hoping for satisfaction of her questions.

"I dream of ..." I am fearful of revealing my real heart ... "having my art for everyone to see. Maybe even sell some to make money to support my dream." My face drops.

"What, chiiild?"

"My mother always said that my art would not be a way to support myself. That I needed a real job. She called it doodling."

"Okay, so what else do *you* see?"

"I would like to see myself known for my art. Or at least be able to assist those with the same dreams as my own. But I can't teach someone to feel something when they draw."

"But you can teach them how you feel when you draw, and how it inspires you to draw different things."

I feel a renewed drive for my drawings. I have been so caught up with schoolwork that I wasn't drawing enough. I now want to draw again.

"Oh, Mary, now you are sounding like Mildred!" Antoinette says.

"Yea, I guess I do. But right now, I am just in college, and dealing with things with my mom."

A sad calm descended on the room.

"Do you want to see pictures of me, chiiild?"

"Oh, please, may I?"

She turns and goes toward the fireplace, where there are even more photos in frames. I notice that there is one large portrait. It is in an ornate frame that hangs high above the mantle. Mildred raises her frail arm and points her wrinkly finger to the painting.

"There you go. That was me during a show. My mother took a picture of me." She paused to catch the memory. "And the local artist painted it for her." Her face raises to the painting with pride.

As I gaze at the painting above, I notice a beautiful, pale picturesque woman in a ballerina dress, with ballerina shoes, standing on her tiptoes. Her legs are stretched, one to the floor, and one to the ceiling. Her arms are open to hold herself steady, with her chin stretched to the sky with grace, confidence, and poise. Her face is painted with blush and bright lip color.

I realize Mildred is looking at my facial expressions as I gaze upon the picture. Those eyes are deeper than the ocean. I turn to Mildred and meet those same eyes, now tired and much older. Nonetheless, same by every feature, and I could tell that it was Mildred.

Oh, how I wish I could have watched her dance when she was young. I would have drawn her so differently in my eye. Not in color, but in pencil.

"I won an award that evening for the show," she says, with shortness of breath. "Oh, I need to sit down for a moment." She proceeds to go back to the chair that Antoinette has ready for her. "All this excitement today."

"You really should lie down for a while," Antoinette says.

"Oh, if I must."

I can hear just how tired Mildred really is.

"I really should get going back to Aunt Jackie's. I'm sure she's going to be worried about me. Besides, I need to help her with Mother's things."

Mildred grabs my hand and holds it to her chest.

"Please do come back, chiiild. Now, you know where I live. And if I am not in the park, you know where to find me. You are always welcome here, my love."

"Yes, ma'am." I smile right back. "Get some rest."

I head toward the door to leave Mildred in the care of

Antoinette. I am no longer jealous of her. She is comforting not only to Mildred, but to me as well. I know that Mildred needs her. However, I do wish I could be here with her all the time. I feel a strange warmth, like I'm finally home.

I hear some whispering as I am turning to leave. The whispering is between Antoinette and Mildred.

Then Antoinette says, "Would you like to see one of Mildred's classes?"

I turn around with excitement. I am being asked to join them. An invitation. I can't help but fix my gaze on Mildred.

"Are you still teaching?"

A great chuckle comes up from her depths.

"Oh, heavens no, chiiild. But my classes are still going on."

"Miss Mildred still has her classes, and the children are so delightful," Antoinette says, with a beam in her eyes. "She likes to watch the children as they dance in class."

Both ladies are awaiting my response, and the invitation is so unexpected that I forget to answer.

"Would you like for me to pick you up since you do not have your car here?" Antoinette says.

"Oh, yes!" I place my hand against my chest in a gesture of admiration. "Please, I would love to come. But when?"

I have so much to do with my mother's passing, but I am just not sure what exactly I need to do, and when. But I really need this break from reality. School has been really hard, and now my mother ...

"Yes, please," I reply.

"Chiiild, give Antoinette your Aunt Jackie's address, and she will come get you." Mildred is straightening her dress from just getting up from the chair.

"Great!" I begin to turn to leave once more. "Oh, wait!" I stop. "When? And where?"

"I have classes going almost daily. Tomorrow afternoon?"

"Yes, that should be fine. I have some things to do with Aunt Jackie, for my mom. You know, funeral stuff. But I am sure afternoon will be just fine."

"Oh, yes, chiiild ..."

"Here." Antoinette hands me a pad of paper and a pen. "Write your Aunt Jackie's address, and I will come get you tomorrow, unless you cannot make it."

I grasp the pad, careful not to drop the pen that is placed on it. I write the address down, along with my phone number, and then hand it back to her. Antoinette glances at the address and smiles.

"Oh my, you are close by, aren't you? It's just about a mile away. Not too far at all." She folds the paper to keep it safe. "I will call you in the morning to make sure you can come."

"Thank you so very much for inviting me." Again, my hand goes up to touch my heart. "It means a lot to me."

I am now inside Mildred's world. All these years that have passed, and I have now been accepted into her private world. I feel such joy and warmth and love in a time of great loss and sorrow.

I turn for the last time to exit the room that leads out to the great foyer, and out the grand entrance, onto the white elongated porch filled with welcoming colors.

"Leaving so soon, missy?" says the gardener who helped Mildred out of the car when I first arrived.

"Yes, sir."

"Shall I call you a car?"

Call me a car? Hmm. I am not sure what that means.

"No, thank you. I live close by, and I would like to walk home." I begin my trek.

"Will we be seeing you again, missy?" His smile still inviting and warm.

I can't help but give the home that Mildred lives in another once-over and beam a big smile.

"Yes, sir."

He turns again to tend to his planter beds to ensure they are perfect. I turn as well and begin my walk and reflection of what a horrible and oddly comforting day this has been.

CHAPTER 7

My walk back to Aunt Jackie's is uneventful. The late afternoon sun is giving way to shadows and shapes upon the sidewalks. It is a walk that I used to take many years ago. It wasn't far from my mom's apartment, but close enough for me to walk now. I want to go back to my apartment, just to see if my mom is there. I know she isn't, but I can't help it. I find myself talking to God, even though we aren't churchgoing. My mom found it to be a waste of time, and she needed to be working to provide for us.

I find myself asking God questions like, *Why?* and anxiously awaiting an answer to drop out of the sky. Nothing appears, and I'm not sure if God really hears me anyway. I wait for signs. You know, like the ones they show on TV. But again, nothing. I can only hold on to the warmth that Mildred has for me. Sure, Aunt Jackie is family. Travis, too. But Mildred and I have a special bond.

Getting closer to Aunt Jackie's house, my one-sided conversation with God ends. As I walk through the door, I hear a familiar voice.

"Hey, there. You're back?" It's Travis. He's still here with his mom.

"Yeah, I went for a walk."

"Where did you go?" he says.

"I went down to the park to see Mildred."

Travis looks puzzled.

"Do you mean The Bird Lady?" he says, with the same childlike chuckle.

"Umm, no." Anger is beginning to boil within me. "She feeds the birds, but she isn't a bird lady." I pause to gather my thoughts, so I don't say anything wrong. "She is my friend."

"The Bird Lady is your friend? I didn't know you talked to her. How could she possibly have anything to say that interests you?"

Travis is enlightening me on his lack of intellect.

"As a matter of fact, I went to her house today."

"She has a house? Is it a shack on the top of one of those tall apartment buildings?" The laughing commences. "You know, the ones that house all the birds on top of the buildings."

"No, it's the big man—"

It's none of his business.

"So it is a real house?" he says.

"I sat and drank tea with her. She was a famous dancer, and I saw her dance pictures and all of her students, too."

"Yeah, right," Travis says, with sarcasm.

Aunt Jackie walks into the room. "What students?"

"She met someone famous, and saw photos of her and her students," Travis says.

"Who?" Aunt Jackie says.

"Mildred, the lady who feeds the birds in the park," I say. "She was a famous dancer, and I saw her pictures, along with her students that she taught ballet to." I shoot a smug look toward Travis.

It was like we were kids again, trying to get each other into trouble.

"But I always thought she was homeless and lived in the park," Aunt Jackie says.

I can't help but laugh. "No, Aunt Jackie. She isn't homeless at all. She lives in the mansion by the park, behind the iron gates."

"No way!" Aunt Jackie says.

Travis spills his drink from disbelief.

"Uh-huh," I say, with my lips closed.

"I would have never known," Aunt Jackie says.

She would have never known, because to her, Mildred was

invisible, as she was to most people. No one ever took the time to talk to her, or even say hi. This was sad to me, but I took the chance and made a wonderful friend. A friend for life!

"Honey," Aunt Jackie says, "we need to sit down and talk for a minute."

"Okay." I sit once again at the kitchen table.

"We need to go to your mom's apartment and pick out a dress," she says.

"A dress? For what?"

"Honey, for her showing,"

"Showing?"

See, I never went to my dad's funeral, so I don't understand what she means. It sounds like a horse show, or a showing for a new house on the market.

"It's for her showing, and her funeral."

Then it clicks.

"Oh, okay." My face goes long, and I know what I have to do.

"We can do it tomorrow, all right?" She reaches for my hand, which I put on the tabletop. "Right now, we all need to get some sleep." She begins to get up.

It is nowhere near bedtime, but we all are exhausted from not sleeping for the past day.

"You can sleep in here." She motions to the next room on the left. "Travis can sleep in his old room."

Or he can just go back to his cave, I thought, but didn't dare say it.

"And I will sleep in my room," as she motions behind her, "down the hall," like she forgot I used to come play here.

I know what every room is, and every hiding place, where Travis and I used to play.

"Okay, thanks." I retreat off to the room where I am to sleep.

They are fast asleep, but my mind is racing. Thoughts of the hospital, my mother, the funeral, and the dance class all take turns being the spotlight in my mind, each memory fighting for the forefront. I am so exhausted and excited at the same time. I end up rolling over and convincing myself that I need to sleep, and so I do.

Daybreak comes quickly. I think I'm dead to the world because I can't stay awake for anything.

After breakfast, Aunt Jackie and I go over to my mom's apartment. That is the hardest thing for me. All of my old stuff is still there, as if I still lived there. But I live at school.

We go back to my mom's bedroom to look for a dress for her. I remember all the times I looked for a dress in Mom's closet, for me, like for Homecoming and Sandy's recital. She pulls a dress out, and wouldn't you know it, it was the one that I wore to Homecoming with Jake. Oh, that damn haunting dress!

"Nah, she didn't like that one." I take the dress from Aunt Jackie.

Mom actually loved the dress, but I didn't.

Then I pull out another dress.

"Oh, I like that one," Aunt Jackie says.

"Yeah, she liked it, too."

And we settle on that dress for Mom to wear for the showing. It is plain black and has sleeves with a V-neck. Since it has a V-neck, I must find a necklace for her to wear, and I suddenly remember Mom's pearls. I go over to the jewelry box and find them tucked down deep, as if she were keeping them hidden. Hidden for a special day. A special day like this one, I imagine.

"Oh, that will look really nice together," Aunt Jackie says.

"What about these shoes?" I pull out a pair of heels that would look perfect with that dress.

"Umm, honey, she doesn't need shoes for this."

"Hmm." I'm so interested in the shoes that I'm not really listening to her.

"Honey, you don't put shoes on in a-a ..." Aunt Jackie bursts into tears and falls on the bed.

"Oh, crap. I forgot." I try to console her.

Sobbing, she regains her composure and says, "It's okay. You have never done this before. I had to prepare your father, too."

"Huh?"

"Yeah, I had to dress your father at his funeral, too."

"Umm ..."

"Your mom never told you?" Aunt Jackie sits up on the bed.

"Umm, no," I say.

"Your father did come home, but you were too young to even remember."

"Hmm."

"But your mom was afraid it would upset you, so she said that he never came home."

"But ..." I am so confused now.

"Your dad died on the way home from the service. Yes, he was in the service, but he died while coming home. He got drunk with his friends, celebrating their tour of duty being done, and well ... they never made it home alive."

What the hell does that mean?

"Your daddy was killed in a drunk driving accident."

"My dad was an alcoholic?"

"Well, I don't know about that. But he died with a car full of his friends from the service."

Well, that makes sense now. My mother always told me that he died in the service, and that he just didn't come home. She was kind of right, but she forgot to mention the part about the alcohol and the car crash. Now I understand.

"She never told me," I say.

"Oh, honey, I thought she would have by now. You are old enough to know the truth."

"Nah, she didn't." I ponder why she never told me.

I am digging through her jewelry box and come upon her wedding band. I put it on my finger to see if it fits, and it is a perfect fit.

"Can I wear this tomorrow?" I say, as if we are in her house.

I forgot that all of this jewelry was my mothers, not hers.

"Yeah, I guess so," she replies. "I actually think it was your mom's wedding band from your father."

I begin to finger the wedding band and examine every nook and cranny for details, hoping it will reveal something about my dad. But it doesn't. It is just a plain wedding band with a small chip on it, which is probably not even a diamond. I'm not sure why she even has it. My mom said they never got married. I guess he gave her the ring, hoping that someday, when he did get home, they would make it official.

"I like it." I turn it around and around my finger.

"Well, keep it safe." She gathers up the dress and pearl necklace for Mom to wear to her showing.

I still don't feel like she's gone, but she is. Gone, never to be seen or heard from again. I know I'm still in shock.

After we gather all the items needed for the service, I can't help but just stand there and look about the apartment that was once home. It feels surreal because I live in a small dorm room with a bunch of crazy girls just trying to pass their classes and party. I feel connected to my mom's apartment but disconnected at the same time. Everything looks the same as it always, but without her, it all feels different. It feels kind of dirty or dingy in a peculiar way. It feels empty.

I stroll over to what was my room. Standing in the doorway that enters the world I once knew, I feel odd. I feel like I'm not allowed to be in my mom's apartment without her.

"Is there anything else I need to do?" I say, trying to cover all the bases.

"No. Unless you want to do something else." Aunt Jackie grabs the final garment bag in one hand, and her purse in the other. "Ready to go?"

"Yeah."

I turn toward the doorway, then turn the knob to open the door, and there it is. That familiar squeak of the door as my mother was entering the apartment. It is then that I am sure I need to see Mildred.

"Are you okay, honey?" Aunt Jackie says.

"Would you be upset if I went to a dance class? We have nothing else to prepare, and I really need to do something."

"Sure, honey." Aunt Jackie says, as we exit the apartment. "I understand. And I have everything under control for today ..."

I don't think she really wants me to go, but I *have to*.

"I have someone coming to get me from your place because I

don't have my car, if that's okay," I say.

"Sure."

We drive back to Aunt Jackie's in silence.

Arriving back at her house, I notice I have plenty of time before Antoinette's arrival. I begin to get ready, but I am not sure what I'm getting ready for. I know it's a class. A dance class, actually. But I have never been to a dance class to understand what I'm expected to wear.

The phone rings, and it's Antoinette. She instructs me to just dress normal, and that she is going to be on her way soon. So I brush my hair and put some makeup on.

As I'm gazing out the window at Aunt Jackie's, I notice Antoinette's car pull up.

"Aunt Jackie, she is here!" I say.

"She? Oh, *she*." You could hear the relief in her voice, as she must have thought I was going on a date with a guy. "Who is she?"

"Antoinette is picking me up to go see Mildred and her dance class."

She doesn't recognize anyone who I mentioned, so she is just as confused as if I said nothing at all.

"Antoinette will probably bring me back, too." I grab a jacket.

"Okay, have fun."

It is weird. It's as if I were telling my mom what I was doing and who I was going to be with. Aunt Jackie has assumed the role of my mom; it is somewhat comforting, but strange at the same time. I am used to being on my own at school. No one to report to or ask permission from.

Out the door I go.

Antoinette drives me to the art gallery. I remember being here when I was in school, on field trips for art class. I had no idea that dance classes were held here as well.

We enter the gallery from the front door, but Mildred is nowhere to be seen.

"Where is—"

"Miss Mildred will be along shortly," Antoinette says.

While I'm waiting for Mildred, I find myself lost in the confines of the Art Museum. So much to see, and so much to take in. Wings in all directions for exploration, just as it was when I was in school visiting. I find a directory and decide to head toward the Isle of Dance. I figure this is where I am supposed to be, anyway.

As I approach the Isle of Dance hallway, I notice Mildred waiting for me, alongside Antoinette. I should have known that Antoinette would be close beside her. Children from all directions are pouring into the doorway. All ages are represented. Each child is eager to see Mildred, as if she were their mother. I stand there and watch in complete admiration.

Mildred bends down slightly to greet each child with a beaming smile, accompanied by a loving hug. Some children are so excited that they would tell her about their day. Some children are just happy to get their hug. I did notice that there are an equal number of black children as there are white. I find this pleasing. There are, however, more girls than boys. Dance is more for the girls, anyway. Or so I thought.

Mildred did not care where the children lived or how they got here. I can see that all she cares about is that they want to learn the art of dance. She speaks of sharing her gift and teaching others. I now understand her message.

"Come now, children." The teacher attempts to gather the students into the room with some sort of direction.

Each is still so excited with Mildred's presence that it is difficult to round them all up.

"Children, listen to your teacher," Mildred says, her voice tired.

With a roar of the voices, they all turn to go into the classroom, putting their minds in tune with the teacher. After the students are all in the room, Mildred, Antoinette, and I enter the room and sit in the chairs placed against the wall for us. The room is bright, with mirrors along the walls. The back wall has a bar about waist-high for the children to hold on to. The children are stretching their muscles and tightening their special dance shoes. Some are whispering, while looking in our direction. We are the only adults here, other than their teacher.

This is a real class. A private dance recital, just for us!

The teacher speaks quietly to the students to give directions. Each child finds their place on the floor and stands quietly to be instructed when to begin. The teacher then raises her arm toward the piano. The piano player strikes the first note, and the dance begins.

As each child races across the floor, dancing with their fullest efforts possible, I notice that Mildred's face is beaming with joy. It is as if she herself is dancing on the floor right along with them.

The young boys try so desperately to be perfect gentlemen, while holding their female partners with tenderness and grace. The young ladies are poised with elegance, while holding their chins high, elongating their torsos, and pointing their toes. I would not have known they were kids up there. They are so incredibly good. Each act follows without a hitch.

I realize that I am in a totally different world. Mildred is loved here by all. But how can this be? Out in the real world, no one talks to the lady feeding the birds.

The show is a success! A real Broadway production, in my book.

When the production is over, each child glistens with sweat from their endless efforts. Their breath is deep and labored from the strength it took to dance their hearts out for Mildred.

"Bravo! Bravo!" Mildred says, between each clap of her hands.

She tries to get to her feet to give them a standing ovation, and the effort is matched by Antoinette, reaching for her arm to steady her. She does eventually make it to her feet, and then continues to clap with admiration for each child's efforts.

I am in awe of the performance I just witnessed. I'm reminded of Sandy's piano recital and the excitement I felt then, too. I almost feel my body trying to emulate the dancers as they twirled and jumped. I could never dance as they did, but it is nice to feel the dance within me.

"Bravo, my children!" Mildred lightens up again. "I am so

proud of each and every one of you!"

The smile upon her face is unlike any I have ever seen. The true meaning of what she said about her dash is so clear now, more than ever. She lived her dream as a dancer. Now she is helping others live their dream in becoming a dancer, too.

Mildred sits back down upon the chair and takes a deep breath.

"Miss Mildred," says Antoinette, "shall I go get the car for you?"

"Yes, dear," Mildred says, with a tired, but cheerful smile.

"Honey, you stay with Miss Mildred, and I will get the car, okay?"

"Yeah, sure. Anything you need."

Antoinette gets the car, and I wait for her by the door with Mildred, who walks outside of the Art Museum with me to steady her every step. This frail lady sits in the car with the assistance of Antoinette. You can see that coming out like this takes a lot out of her. But she would not have missed it for the world.

Antoinette pulls away from the curb and around to the other side of the museum. I did not realize it, but the gates to Mildred's home are just next door. It is a short drive, but I didn't understand how it is all connected. I did not dare ask, but I sure want to. I am just pleased that she allowed me into her world, and to see the dancer she once was. I feel important.

Antoinette assists Mildred into her home and then takes me back to Aunt Jackie's. I thank Antoinette for driving me and for suggesting that I go.

I notice Aunt Jackie is on the phone, so I don't bother her. I just go into where I am going to sleep and get ready for bed. It is an early night, but it is a night I am not going to forget. It took the pain away from losing my mother. If only for a while, it is welcoming.

I decide to go to sleep with the dancers still dancing in my mind, and the music in my heart. What a wonderful night.

The next few days seem to drag on like an eternity. Most of the plans were already in place, per my mother being such a worry wort. She controlled everything. But this time I am okay with it.

I find myself sitting alone a lot, not in the mood to talk to Aunt Jackie, and surely not Travis. He is so busy goofing around with his girlfriend, it makes me sick. I decide to go to the park to get some peace.

Arriving at the park, I notice that Mildred is not sitting at her normal bench. So I choose to sit at a picnic table instead. I brought my sketch pad and my trusty pencil, which surely will not let me down. But I have no idea what to draw. My mind is as blank as the page.

Then I reach up and realize I am still wearing the necklace that Mildred gave to me so many years ago. My fingers caress the chain that holds it close to my heart. The details catch my attention, and I decide to take it off. I haven't taken this necklace off in years. But this time is different. It is my focal point, my inspiration.

I put the necklace down on the worn wooden picnic table, examining it to ensure the lighting would do it justice. Moving it around a bit, I find the perfect angle, and then it hits me. This necklace will be my subject for today.

Placing my pencil upon the paper, I begin to draw. Each stoke of the lead is a defining etch of the endearing love from Mildred's husband. The large M on the necklace is worn a bit, but still stands with great presence. The edges of the necklace are ornate and designed with perfection. Trying to catch the very essence of the age, I draw each line with sheer determination to tell the story in great detail. The chain that holds the locket is also worn and slightly out of shape. Each loop of the chain is different than the last because of the years of wear, not only upon my neck, but Mildred's as well.

Time goes by quickly, but for me and my subject, time stands still. The light of the day is giving way to the afternoon setting sun. Ah, perfection at last. But wait, it isn't finished. My mark ... I must leave my mark.

I etch my name on the drawing, ensuring that if someone were to see this, it is known that it was I who drew this work of art. This is the way Mildred would have wanted it. She taught me to always make my mark on all of my artwork, and so I have.

It's getting late, and I must begin to head back to Aunt Jackie's. After placing my notebook under my arm and my pencil in hand, I start to walk. I glance at the bench where my dear friend usually sits, only to see an emptiness, much like my heart. Knowing that it is far too late for her to come to the park, I turn to leave, dreading tomorrow.

Morning comes far too early. People are already gathering downstairs. Oh, to face the people is just too much to bear. I could hear dishes and smell cooking. Today is the day for us to say goodbye to my mother. I gather my thoughts and get dressed to head out into the world.

People are coming and going, crying and hugging me. Oh, I am so tired of people hugging me. I just want to be left alone.

The service for my mom is nice and short. People who I have never seen before come out to pay their respects. I know that most of them re from her work. I also meet distant relatives I have never seen before. I don't even know how they are related to me. Travis spends most of his time buried in his phone, talking to his girlfriend, who, by the way, wasn't allowed to come. Aunt Jackie said she didn't belong here yet.

The service ends, and people slowly go home. The last one left Aunt Jackie's house, and we are finally able to take off our dress clothes and slip into something more comfortable. Mom wasn't into dressy clothes much. She was more into jeans and old shoes to go for a walk.

As I'm changing into my sweatpants, it hits me. My mom is gone. I have to learn how to live without her. What do I do now?

I curl up on the bed and cry silently so no one will hear me. Tears come faster and faster, and I bury my head in my pillow, so no one comes. I want to go home. But where is home now?

The morning comes quickly. I must have cried myself to sleep. I decide to go back to school and get my car and belongings. I ask Aunt Jackie for my plane ticket back, and we book the flight. I leave that day to go back to school, but I intend to drive back to Chicago. It is going to be a long drive back, but I needed to take care of Mom's apartment. I'm not sure where I am going to live after this, but I need to take care of things first.

I contact my dorm mother, and she meets me at the airport. Once she sees me, she bursts into tears and wraps her arms around me.

"I am so sorry that I couldn't tell you," she says.

"Tell me?"

"I knew that your mom was dying, but I couldn't tell you."

"Yeah, the dean knew, too," I say.

We drive back to the campus and don't speak much. We aren't friends. I just respect her because she takes care of all of us girls.

I go up the stairway and into my room with a cordial thank you. I close the door behind me and begin to cry.

The school is empty now because they are between semesters. The dorms are still full of things, but the students are all on break. I have to pack my belongings and leave my room the next day. It is nice that the dean and the dorm mother kept my room safe for me. Everything is just as I left it—a mess. It's going to be a big job getting all this stuff home.

It is late, and I need to sleep. I fall back on my bed and stare at the ceiling, contemplating my next steps. Oh, I need to call Aunt Jackie to tell her I made it back to school, and so I do.

After all the small talk about the flight, my Aunt Jackie asks me to stay at school to finish. I tell her I need to come back to Chicago to take care of my mother's apartment. She convinces me to stay at school and finish. She says my mother would have wanted me to finish. I tell her I will talk to the dean in the morning. I am soon fast asleep from the exhaustion.

Morning comes, and I go to the dean's office. Even though the campus is quiet, there are a handful of students still hanging around. It's a short break, but most of the students went home for it. They will soon return to the hustle and bustle of campus life.

The conversation is short and to the point. The dean asks simple questions to keep my thoughts on track. He renews my dorm, and I suspect he really thinks I'm going to stay in school, because all of my next semester classes are still in place.

Here at school, it is like nothing happened. It's all so surreal, like I'm living a double life.

Before I know it, graduation is right around the corner. I want so badly to call my mom and invite her to my graduation, but I can't. I am graduating with marketing as my major and art as a minor. I try to call Antoinette to see if Mildred could come to my graduation, but she thinks it would be too hard on her. She will mention it to her, though.

Mildred never comes. I understand.

After graduation, I take a job close to Chicago, on the outskirts. Still a big city, but I continually heard my mom's voice resonate in my head about doodling not paying the bills. For the most part, she was right.

And that's where we are today, sitting in this stupid cubical, alongside Lilly, making calls, trying to earn a living. The days pass quickly, and soon they turn into months. Before I know it, years have gone by since my mother's passing.

Travis got some girl pregnant and had to get married. He quit school and began working in a factory. Aunt Jackie still lives in the same place, probably doing the same thing, except babysitting all the time. And I am stuck here with my best friend, Lilly. My sketchbook lies dormant most days. I guess I lost my dream—the dream that Mildred tried so hard to foster within me.

And then the phone rings.

"This is Mary. May I help you?"

You know, the usual greeting from my dull job at my desk.

"Umm, hello?" says a faint voice.

"This is Mary. May I help you?"

Telemarketing is an unforgiving job. No one wants to hear

me try to sell them insurance.

"Mary?" A pause. "Oh, dear God! I finally found you."

I am confused by the voice on the line. This is not a sales call. The voice sounds faintly familiar, but I still cannot place it.

"May I help you?"

"Miss Mary."

And it hits me. That voice on the other end is a voice from a life I left behind. I was so afraid of the next words.

"This is Antoinette."

My past flies through my thoughts like it was yesterday.

"Antoinette?"

Great concern comes over me. Why would she be contacting me?

"Mary, I have been looking for you for quite some time now." Her voice becomes clearer and more distinct.

"Yes, ma'am."

"You need to come see Mildred, quick! She needs you. She's calling for you."

Panic reaches deep within my bones.

"Uh-huh," I reply.

Visions of the conversation that I had at school were resonating in my mind.

"Child!"

That command only came from Mildred, but now it is coming from Antoinette.

"Did you hear me?"

"Yes, ma'am."

"Please come see Miss Mildred. She needs you."

"Yes, ma'am! I will be on my way."

I hang up the phone and look at Lilly with a blank stare.

"Well, girl, what's the problem?" she says, with her sassy tone, pulling back her thin braids from her glasses.

"Do you remember the lady I told you about from my childhood? The one who fed the birds?"

"Yeah, the lady ... The Bird Lady?" She looks up, reaching for answers.

"Yes." I start to get up and gather my things.

"Well ..." She starts to stir as she pushes her glasses up on her nose.

"I need to go to her now!" I put the day's end paperwork away and finish gathering my things. "But—"

"Mary, it is Friday," Lilly says. "Go!"

I look toward the boss's office. "But—"

"But nothing. You need to go!" She begins to push me towards the door.

I gather my purse and bag. My bag has my sketchbook in it, and I'm not sure why I grab it, but I think it's because of Mildred.

I run to my car, which is parked in our building's lot, and begin to drive. The journey feels long, but it really isn't. It is just to the next town over from where I have been living the past year.

Guilt wrenches my gut. I haven't been in contact with Mildred for so long. How could I have let time get so far away from me?

I arrive at her big iron-gated mansion. The workers are hard at work, and the man that I met so many years ago meets me at the gate.

"Well, hello, Miss Mary." His voice is deep and inviting.

How did he remember me after all these years?

"It is nice to see you again," he says, as the gate opens to allow me to drive in. "Miss Mildred is expecting you."

He raises his arm toward the house, and I drive in.

"Thank you," I say, in a somber voice.

I reach the grand wraparound front porch, which is still filled with ornate flowers of every color in the rainbow. Antoinette is sitting on the swing.

She rises to meet me. "Thank you for coming so quickly!"

And there she is.

I turn to the right to see who is sitting in the chair with the heavy quilt on their lap, and it is Mildred. She is paler and skinnier than the last time I saw her. Her eyes are tired and droopy, but the same soulful spirit still illuminates her face as she lifts her eyes to meet mine.

"Oh, Mildred," I say, in a soft voice, as I drop to my knees in front of her to hold her tight.

My head is in her lap, and I feel her frail and feeble attempt to hold my head, while stroking my noticeably darker red hair.

And then I hear a faint voice emit from within.

"Oh, chiiild, I knew you would come."

Each word took such effort that she had to take breaks between them. But that Southern charm is still present. She strokes my once curly red hair back from my face to reveal my pain.

I lift my head up. "I am so sorry. I have been gone far too long." I reach within my shirt to pull out the locket that Mildred gave me. "I made you a promise," I lift the necklace up, "and I have not kept it. I have been gone too long." My head falls once more upon her lap.

"Oh, chiiild." She reassures me with her gentle touch. "You kept your promise." She takes a shallow breath to speak again. "You are here now."

I lift my tearful face, questioning her judgment. She puts her boney finger under my chin to lift my head up even higher.

"You came back to me." Mildred acts as if a pain overtook her for a moment.

Antoinette reaches for me to stand out of the way.

"I'm going to take her inside now." Antoinette begins to pull her away from the wall.

I didn't realize it because of the quilt, but the chair Mildred is sitting in is actually a wheelchair.

"You stay here, and I will be right back," Antoinette says.

A few moments pass, and Antoinette soon reappears on the grand front porch. She heads over to the rocking chair and plops down in it hard. You could tell she, too, is tired, and age is taking a toll on her as well.

"So how are you, Deary?" She smiles.

"I've been so busy trying to make ends meet with my job and all."

I know it's not a good excuse, but I have no other to offer.

"I have been searching for you for quite a while." Antoinette reaches for her cup of tea. "Would you like some tea?" She reaches for the tea pot that is sitting on the side table.

"Umm, yes please."

I feel like I did the first day I came to Mildred's home. The mere essence of this home somehow keeps taking my breath from me.

Antoinette pours another cup of tea and hands me the cup. I set it down upon the glass tabletop next to my rocking chair.

"Miss Mildred has been very sick for quite some time," Antoinette says. "She was even sick the first time you came to this here home." She waves her hands around, as if she is showing me the sights for the first time.

"Okay." I reply, unsure how to respond.

"You see ..." Antoinette was noticeably afraid to tell me, " ... it's her heart. She's given so much of her heart away that it just can't take anymore. It's failing." She takes a slow sip of her tea. "Miss Mildred hired me many years ago to take care of her here, and to make sure her home is well-cared for since her husband died."

I reach for the cup and begin to sip the piping-hot tea. Being in the presence of Mildred's home, I know to be on my best behavior, with my ankles crossed and my pinky finger upright when drinking from her fine china. But I am confused as to why Antoinette is explaining all of this to me.

"Even though I live here and all," Antoinette puts her teacup back on its saucer, "I just take care of her." She looks at me.

"Okay," I say, utterly confused.

"Oh, Deary ... she thinks of you as her own child. Like the daughter she lost so many years ago."

"Her what?" I begin to cough from the thought. "How can she think of me as her child? I met her when I was just a young girl—"

"As a young girl in the park. I've heard the story, time and time again, about you and your red ball."

I sit back in my chair to catch my thoughts.

"Why do you believe she thinks of me as her child?"

"I think you need to sit down tomorrow and really talk to her, honey. Miss Mildred needs to tell you this, Not me. Do you have to work tomorrow?"

"No, I have all weekend off. But I should call Lilly and tell her." I begin to reach for my purse to get my phone.

Antoinette goes inside to check on Mildred while I am on the phone with Lilly.

The phone rings a few times before Lilly picks it up.

"Hello?" Lilly's voice is pleasant.

"Lilly? It's Mary."

"So what's going on?"

"I need to stay here for the weekend. Can you please take care of my cat while I'm gone?"

"Yeah, sure. Is everything okay?"

"Yeah, so far. I just need to stay. I will call you later."

"Okay, then. Call me when you can."

The phone goes dead. My comforting friend is no longer on the phone.

Antoinette comes out of the door with a dishrag in her hand.

"Is everything okay for you to stay in town a couple of days?"

"Yes. Lilly is going to feed my cat."

"Oh, you have a cat?" Antoinette's voice is higher, almost childlike.

"Well, he spends as much time with Lilly as he does with me. But yeah, he's mine." I giggle.

"You can stay here, if you like." She opens the door for me to enter.

Feeling like I am intruding, I say, "I'm going to stay with my Aunt Jackie, if that's okay." I put my purse back on my shoulder. "I haven't seen her in quite some time as well."

"Okay, well ... please come tomorrow to sit down and talk with Miss Mildred."

"Yes, ma'am." I reach for the top of the railing to head down the stairway, toward my car. "Besides, Mildred is too tired tonight, and it is getting late for her."

"Tomorrow, then?" Antoinette says.

"Yes, tomorrow."

I turn to my car and reach for the door handle when a hand reaches out from behind me and pulls the door for me.

Startled, I turn to see the gardener that I met so many years prior, being a complete gentleman and opening the car door for me.

"Will you be coming back in the morning, Mary?"

"Yes, sir, I will. Mildred needs me." I sit inside my car. "But it's too late to stay tonight."

I put my ignition key in, and the car starts without effort. My car is old, but reliable.

"Drive safely." He closes the door to wave me off.

I can't help but roll down my window. He is still standing beside my car.

"Thank you for taking such good care of Mildred," I say.

"Oh, Miss Mildred? She is a special lady." He chuckles. "I knew her husband, too." He stands upright, beaming. "I have worked for them since I was a young boy."

"Well, thank you." I begin to drive off.

I arrive at Aunt Jackie's house and am met by screaming children. Two, to be exact. And one exhausted aunt. I can't help but look around the room for Travis and the mother of these children, but they are nowhere to be found.

"Where is Travis?" I say, trying not to upset the children.

A grunt comes from Aunt Jackie as she picks up the youngest one and perches him upon her hip. Her eyes tell the very story that I do not want to hear.

A pent-up wail comes from the child, who is obviously missing his parents.

"I'll be back." She turns to take the youngest into a bedroom to go to bed.

It is, after all, way after everyone's bedtime.

"It's okay. I'll stay here and watch the other one," I say.

I really don't want anything to do with Travis's kids. They are absent parents in my book.

Aunt Jackie is gone for a few minutes, and the older child is busy watching TV. Ah, the ultimate babysitter. Mine was books. I guess, nowadays, TV wins.

Aunt Jackie returns and sits next to Alex, the oldest, so I don't have to feel responsible for him.

"Where is Travis?" I whisper.

Aunt Jackie just shrugs. Her mouth is pursed, as if she was disgusted with the entire situation she has found herself in.

"Does he do this a lot?" I point to Alex. "What about—"

"Hmm, yeah, she is a real piece of work, too."

Aunt Jackie has become the grandmother and the mother all in the same breath. She used to have the best relationship with Travis when we were kids. Travis is a year older than me, and he was in college before me. But ever since he dropped out to get married, things have not been the same for Aunt Jackie. I would have never thought of doing this to my mom.

"I'm sorry," I say. "It's not my place to be judging."

"That's okay, honey," Aunt Jackie says, as if she wants to be angry herself, but just doesn't have the energy to be. "So I know you called because you had some kind of an emergency you had to come home for?"

"Yeah, I got a call about Mildred." I take off my jacket.

"Mildred? Do you mean The Bird Lady, Mildred?" She puts a cover on Alex, hoping he will go to sleep soon.

"Yeah." I get comfortable in the chair. "I got a call from her nurse, saying that Mildred wanted me to come see her. That it is an emergency."

"Is she okay? Did you go see her?" Aunt Jackie seems genuinely concerned.

"Yeah, I did." I gaze down at the floor.

"Well ..."

"She is really sick." I'm still looking at the floor.

"So why does she need to see you? Is she in the hospital?"

"No, but she has a live-in nurse, Antoinette. Mildred asked her to find me."

"Did she say what she needs to talk to you about?" She checks on Alex once more.

"No, I have to sit down with her tomorrow," I whisper.

We notice Alex is going to sleep, so Aunt Jackie picks him up and takes him to his room.

Travis bursts in the door with a thunderous jolt, his wife in tow. Both are loud and obnoxiously drunk, making lots of noise that would wake the dead. And it does. Both children begin to cry, and the whole house is in an uproar once more.

"Well, damn it, Travis!" Aunt Jackie yells.

"What!" Travis chuckles and stumbles into the wall.

Aunt Jackie is still holding Alex. The tired, cranky boy does not hold still while grandma is holding him, that's for sure.

"Hey, buddy." Travis goes to reach for him.

"Oh, no." Aunt Jackie pulls Alex away from his father. "You are too drunk to hold this child." She bounces up and down, trying to calm the youngster.

"Hey, there, Mary." Travis just notices I am standing there.

"Like I said, worthless," I mumble. "Hey, Travis."

"Honey, you can sleep in my room." Aunt Jackie says to me.

I turn, gather my things, and go to Aunt Jackie's room to find solace. Oh my God, I wish I would have stayed with Mildred, in her beautiful, quiet home.

I get to the room and close the door to shut out the commotion. Aunt Jackie is still arguing with Travis. I will never understand why they brought children into this world if they weren't going to take care of them.

The night begins to calm down. I guess they both passed out by now. I am tired from all the commotion of the day. Hard to believe that I was actually at work earlier, then drove all the way here and spent some time with Mildred and Antoinette before coming here to this zoo. My exhaustion overtakes me, and I am fast asleep, even with the voices out in the hallway.

The night is short-lived, and morning comes quickly. I must have slept like a rock all night. Pushing back the covers, I sneak into the hallway. Aunt Jackie is already up, and she has Alex in the highchair, eating. She has the baby with a bottle, slowly pacing the floor. Well, that is a way to keep the children quiet—just put food in their mouths.

"Good morning," she whispers. "Coffee?" She motions to it.

"Yes, please." I sit at the kitchen table.

Looking at the two children, they really aren't that bad. They were just tired and became restless when Travis showed up, obviously too drunk to take care of them.

"Cream? Sugar?" she says.

"Do you have any creamer? You know, the one that tastes like hazelnut?"

"Oh, yeah, I almost forgot." Aunt Jackie puts the baby in her other arm and reaches for the refrigerator door.

"Oh, wait, I'll get it." I jump to my feet.

Funny, but Aunt Jackie looks confused because she seems used to waiting on everyone.

Aunt Jackie is my aunt, not my servant.

"Wow, honey, thank you."

I grab the creamer out of the refrigerator and put it next to my cup of coffee. Sitting in the chair, I begin the dance I learned to love all these years. It has become a ritual. One that I would miss if not able to do.

I pour the creamer into my rich dark coffee, and the dance begins. Two lovers, arm in arm, dancing to the silent love song that only plays inside my head. Then it is abruptly ended by none other than Travis.

"Oh, you still here, Mary?" he mutters.

He obviously has a splitting headache because he is talking softly and rubbing his eyes. I don't feel one bit sorry for him.

"Why ya here?" he says.

"I needed somewhere to stay while I was in town."

"In town for what?"

"She is here to see Mildred," Aunt Jackie says.

"Hahaha. You mean that bird lady?" Travis bursts into laughter.

"Travis! Quiet down!" says Aunt Jackie. "The children are being quiet right now."

Travis puts his finger over his lips, and he looks like a stupid man still drunk from the night before. Oh, I am not going to put up with this crap. I just don't understand why Aunt Jackie is putting up with it either.

I hear the bathroom door open, and I don't want to be around to explain why I'm in town. If Travis is still visibly drunk, then she should be, too. I don't need this.

"Aunt Jackie, I'm going to head out, if that's okay with you."

"Will you tell me what's going on with Mildred later?"

"Yes. I'll call you." I get my things together to head out the door.

The TV turns on to the Saturday morning cartoons; the laughter and chaos has begun for the day. Yeah, it's time for me to leave. Travis is getting a fresh pack of cigarettes to go outside to smoke, but I make sure I'm well ahead of him, so I do not have to talk to him.

I drive straight to Mildred's house. The big iron gates are open and waiting for me to arrive. I enter and notice that they are closing behind me. I feel safe behind the gates. The driveway is wet from the morning dew. The flowers are all beginning the day with their petals touched by the morning dampness.

As I reach the front porch, the gardener—well, I think he's the gardener—instructs me to pull my car around the side of the mansion. Every time I come here, he is always working. But it's Saturday, and he is still here.

My car comes to a stop, and he approaches the side of my car to grab the door handle and assists me out.

"Welcome back, Mary," he says, with a bright smile and an upbeat tone.

"Well, thank you." I look puzzled at him because I don't know how to address him.

"Oh, goodness, where are my manners?" He steps back and extends his right hand, offering for me to shake his, while pulling off his hat with his left hand, and placing it behind his back. "My name is Alfred."

We shake hands.

"Weird, I know, because we have seen each other many times," he says. "But now you know my name, and we can be friendly."

We are still shaking hands.

"Yeah, I was wondering what your name is," I reply.

"Miss Mildred would shoot me if she knew I wasn't polite enough to you to tell you my name." He pulls his hand back and puts his hat back on.

"You are always here," I say.

"Yes, ma'am. I live in that part of the house, near the garden. I take care of all of this for Miss Mildred." He motions to all the beds of flowers. "I also take care of any maintenance for her. I used to take care of this here house for her and her husband, but now it's just Miss Mildred."

"Yes, I remember." I shut my car door.

"She is expecting you." He motions to the house.

"Thank you. I hope I'm not too early."

"Oh, not at all," Alfred says. "Breakfast is being prepared as we speak."

He doesn't need to tell me that breakfast is being cooked. The smells permeating through the air are of bacon and sweets. Oh, I am hungry.

"Please follow me." He turns to take me inside.

I follow him, and we arrive at the side door. He quickens his step to reach the door before I do. I am so used to just grabbing the door for myself that I am not accustomed to being treated like a lady.

"Please allow me to get that." He grabs the door to open it.

We enter the side door that goes into a kitchen area. There are many people cooking, baking, and preparing the day's feast. I am confused. All of this for one lady? Mildred?

The kitchen is adorned with white, country cabinets that go all the way to the ceiling. The stove is not really a stove, but a rare gas range that is much larger than any I have ever seen. The refrigerator is monstrous, with two stainless doors, fit to be in the finest restaurant. There are women huddled around an oversized, elongated center island, preparing and cutting fresh fruit. Then there are others putting together flower arrangements to go on the tables. It is like a hotel kitchen getting ready for their guests. All dressed in what would be the finest hotel staff attire.

I just don't understand why they are cooking so much.

"They are in the side garden," Alfred says. "Would you like to join them?"

"Yes, please," I reply.

"Please follow me." He turns to leave the kitchen area.

He takes me out a door that leads into a garden with paths and seating areas. The garden is a beautiful courtyard full of statues of people and animals. I hear the trickle of fountains, and I find Mildred and Antoinette seated in a section that is next to a statue of a woman in a dancing pose. The dancer is in a seated position, with one leg stretched outward, and the other leg bent up towards her head. She has her head resting on her knee, as if she were so tired of dancing that she needed to rest. It appears that the dancer, while seated, is holding her foot with her other hand. I'm assuming she is exhausted.

The sculpture is made of marble, and it is sheer perfection. It looks lifelike, realistic. The dress appears to be flowing in the wind when actually it is molded in marble. It is the mind that makes it appear to be blowing gently in the wind.

The table that Mildred and Antoinette are sitting at is already prepared for another person—me.

"Please, chiiild, come eat with us," Mildred says, with a struggled voice.

"Thank you." I sit in the chair, minding my manners and crossing my legs at the ankle, just as instructed so many years ago.

A lady comes around my side and places a cup on the table. She begins to pour a piping-hot cup of coffee. She then places my favorite creamer in front of me—hazelnut. I can't help but smile because she remembered. I lift my eyes to meet Mildred's, and the message is clear of how delighted I am to be there.

After the lady with the coffee pot is gone, another lady comes to serve a breakfast made for a queen. Or in this case, three queens. Platter after platter arrives with fresh fruit, pastries, eggs and bacon. Food in such abundance; I keep wondering where the rest of the people are who are going to eat. I am used to eating a small bowl of cereal in the morning. Here, we eat breakfast with small talk about the gardens and how beautiful the day is.

Antoinette rises from her seat and puts her hand on Mildred's shoulder. Our breakfast is finished, and the server is clearing the dishes to be taken into the house. I feel like I'm in a fairy land, unclear of how I came to be in such a wonderful place.

"Would you like to be alone with Mary?" Antoinette says.

"Yes, dear." Mildred places her hand on Antoinette's hand that is still on her shoulder and pats it a few times in a gesture of love.

"I will be just inside when you need me." Antoinette leaves toward the house.

I am still unclear as to why Mildred wants to see me, other than she misses me, and I was away, way too long.

I sit there quietly, waiting for what is to come. I sip my coffee, remembering to keep my pinky finger up.

"Mary, chiiild,"

This makes me nervous. I turn my body to face her to show she has my full attention.

"Yes, ma'am," I say.

"You have no idea how long I have ..." Mildred lifts her eyes after she closed them to gather her thoughts, " ... I have been looking for you," she says, with a twinge of disappointment.

I feel ashamed. "I'm sorry."

My voice is that of a young child. I feel myself falling into that childish stature, as if I were going to be scolded by my mother.

"No, chiiild. I'm not upset at you." She places her hand on my hand, which is sitting on the table.

She gathers her thoughts, and I just wait quietly.

"Chiiild, I want you to know something very important."

Mildred is grabbing for words, and I wish she could have just said what she's looking for. I can't help her find her thoughts. I feel helpless.

"Yes, ma'am, I'm listening."

My heart begins to pound with anticipation, and I feel myself pushing back the nervous swing of my legs that bothers Mildred to no end. Instead, I just sit waiting. Waiting for my friend to talk.

"You remember the first day we met?"

Her eyes are tired, and facial features aged. Her words are chosen carefully, as if she has been anticipating this very day, this very conversation.

"Yes, ma'am, I do," I reply, with a perk of energy.

"You, chiiild, spoke to me. You were how old?"

"If I remember right ..." I gaze up in the sky for answers, " ... I was four. It was in the park, and I was with my mom. Boy, was she mad at me." I chuckle.

"Whew. Well, you were just a child, and she was to protect you."

"But protect me from you?" I lift my hand toward her, with a sadness in my voice.

"Yes, chiiild. From me," Mildred says, with a matched sadness in her voice.

"I didn't understand why. I think I cried the whole way back to the blanket."

"Yes, you did, chiiild. I think the whole park heard you bawling." She giggles once again.

I can't help but giggle after she shows me how funny the situation must have looked. It didn't feel funny at the time, though.

"Anyway, it was then that I knew ..." she touches her heart, " ... that I knew you were different." She purses her lips to hold back the tears.

I sit there and smile. I must admit, the lapse in time is awkward, but I still wait patiently.

She pulls her hand down from her heart and holds it up in the air, as if she is grasping for a thought.

"You met me on the worst day of my life." She points up in the air. "He took the love of my life away, and ... I had to bury him that day."

Another moment passes, and then she regains her thoughts.

"I knelt down at his graveside, begging for him to come back." She begins to rub her knees. "And I was so dirty from the rain."

My thoughts went back to that day, and I recall how dirty she was. But she was beautifully dressed, wearing her huge hat.

"I had my husband's overcoat on over my dress. And it was quite dirty as well." Mildred rubs her arms like she is trying to clean the dirty overcoat from years past. "I also had on my hat that he loved so very much." She raises her hand up to her head, as if she were fixing her hat once more.

"I have not seen you in that hat in a long time. What happened to it?"

"I have it safe. I wear it from time to time. I wore it a few years afterwards, but not much anymore."

She regains her thoughts once more.

"Oh, chiiild, I went to see the birds, and asked God for ... an angel." Her gaze focuses on me. "I was taking care of my dear husband's birds ... and," her painful eyes look into my soul, and our eyes meet, "you came."

"Me?"

I am stunned that she thinks of me as an angel, but then I remember she has mentioned this once before.

"When you looked at me with your bright red curly hair, hiding those big eyes, I knew, chiiild, that it was you." She wears a soft smile. "God sent you."

I am not sure what I am supposed to do.

"When your mom took you away ... I felt your pain." She reaches up to her heart again. "You, chiiild tried, to talk to me so many times." She looks up to the heavens, as if she were grasping for words. "Your mom forbade you to talk to me." Her voice becomes hoarse in an attempt to fight back the emotions. "Parents would pull their children far away from me, much like your mother did with you. Other kids called me names, but you never did."

I hear all the voices echoing in my head, of the kids mocking her and making fun of her as I tried to talk to her on field trips when I was in school. I knew they were hurting her, but she never admitted it.

"Other kids treated you badly because you talked to me. They chirped and squawked like birds when they saw me."

"Umm, yeah, I know. I didn't think you could hear them. They called you names, and I am sorry."

"They called me homeless ... and other names like, Bird Lady." Her eyes go heavy and her gaze falls down to the ground.

"I'm sorry."

I felt an odd responsibility for the behavior of the other kids.

"You have apologized before, chiiild, because they were being so mean." She lifts her gaze to meet mine once more. "So many people passed me by as I fed my husband's birds." Tears form in her weary eyes. "So many people were afraid to even talk to me. Parents kept their children away from me." Her gaze drifts off to the flowers that are nearby. "But you spoke to me with kindness when I needed it the most." The warm smile is back once more. "Sure, I taught many children how to dance. And the children loved me. But in public, their parents turned away from me. I don't even think they knew I was the same person."

I can't help but fight back the tears.

"I was so alone, on the inside."

"I wanted to talk to you. You are special to me. I tried so hard to talk to you every time I could."

"I know." Her smile is as deep as the ocean.

"Over time, you taught me all about life. Do you remember Jake? The guy from school? The one who raped me?"

It's weird saying the word *rape* because it was so long ago, and I have not admitted to many people what happened.

"Oh, yes, chiiild, I do. I called the school and reported him. I demanded he was expelled." She sits upright.

"You called? I was told someone from the school board called the police on him." I look up at her. "You were on the school board?"

"Yes, chiiild, I was."

"Thank you. I didn't realize it was you."

"I have always tried to protect you, and you didn't know it."

"Protect me? Why? How?"

"I have always thought of you as my daughter. I needed to protect you."

"You taught me so much about life and the proper way to be treated by people."

"Oh, chiiild," Mildred says, with a smirk of joy. "And you ... taught me how to live again." She puts her head down, almost in shame to admit. "Taught me how to love again."

"And the dash in my life! You taught me to find my dream and nurture it. To make my dash count."

"Yes, chiiild. You do remember."

"My artwork—or doodling, as my mother called it—is my passion, my dash."

"I am sorry that your mother did not see your artwork like I see it."

"It's okay. I have a degree in marketing now to make a living, but I also have some drawing classes, too."

"You remember the Art Museum?"

"Yes, I do,"

"That was my late husband's dash," she says, with a beam of sunlight in her eyes.

She picks up her cup and takes a sip before setting it back down.

"The school of dance, where we went to see the class, was in a special wing for me." Her face beams with joy. "I was able to teach all my children to dance since I could no longer dance on stage."

Her head is now held high, and her back elongated, just as she was on stage once more. But her posture is tired.

"He founded the museum for me, but he loved all different types of art. That's why it is so big, with so many wings."

"I remember going there as a little girl in school, for art class. I would be mesmerized by the artwork on the walls, and the structure of the building. The building is a piece of art all by itself."

"That's what he said." Mildred giggles with a childlike laugh.

A few moments go by, and then Mildred looks at me with a puzzled expression. She is contemplating what to ask and how to ask it. Once she forms the question in her mind, I see it come to light.

"Do you remember the first day you came here?" She leans forward, while waving her arm around the property like she is showing me the grounds.

"Yes, ma'am, I do."

"What did you mean when ... what did you mean when you asked if I lived here?"

"Hmm ..." I lift my gaze and meet hers.

"It is okay, chiiild." She leans back into her chair once more.

"When I was little," I take a deep breath, "all the kids would make fun of you. You know, like they did in the park."

"Yes, chiiild."

"They would do mean things, like throw eggs and toilet paper on Halloween. They also said you were a mean old lady." My voice is filled with angst.

I didn't want to tell her anymore, but it just kept coming out, like a pressure cooker boiling over from the heat.

"Alfred told me."

"My mom said you were a mean old woman, but ... how could she know you were a mean old woman if she didn't even know you?"

"I don't know," she whispers.

"She never even knew you. Did she?"

"No, chiiild. I guess it's the gates that everyone is afraid of."

Just as she becomes full of life, she sits back into her chair, exhausted, and the life is soon gone. I glance up and notice Antoinette striding toward us. Once she reaches us, she touches Mildred's shoulder.

"Miss Mildred, is it time for your afternoon nap?" Antoinette says, with a loving voice.

"Oh, I suppose it is."

Mildred becomes that helpless old lady once again. She attempts to rise from her seat, and Antoinette has to assist her. Once upright, Mildred presses her hand down her dress to primp herself, as she has always done.

"Oh, it is an awful thing, this getting old." She winks at me.

"Miss Mildred will be taking a well-deserved nap, Miss Mary."

"Oh, chiiild." Mildred stops and turns around. "Please stay. You don't need to leave on my account. Please enjoy the gardens. Besides, I am sure you will find some inspiration out here."

"Yes, ma'am."

Mildred and Antoinette head off to the house and leave me in the garden, along with my cup of tea. I can't help but notice just how beautiful the garden is. It is so well-maintained and orderly. It is like a completely different world within these gates.

I reach down inside my oversized purse and pull out my sketch pad. I haven't drawn in so long, I'm almost afraid to.

Gazing at my sketchbook, I feel a familiar presence over my shoulder.

"What are you going to draw?"

I can't help but look up and am blinded by the sun's beam.

"Oh, I am sorry, Miss Mary." He moves over to block the sunlight from my eyes.

His face is revealed to me afterwards. It's Alfred.

"I'm not sure yet," I reply.

"With all this beauty back here, I am sure you will find something, that's for sure."

And Alfred is gone as fast as he appeared.

He's right. There is so much beauty here that I would be crazy not to find something.

And then an image comes to mind. It is a memory. Not an object that I can study to draw.

Mildred sitting at this table, talking to me. I know her every line, her every wrinkle, her skin texture, even the moisture of her eyes. My pencil takes control and begins to etch out her very essence from just a few moments ago. But this one is different. With each stroke of the pencil, a feeling of sorrow is growing in her eyes, and an eerie tiredness is deep within her visage. Even though the tiredness is etched within her skin, her glow of solitude and accomplishment radiates. A slight smile hinges upon the edges of her lips, which are in deep contradiction to her eyes. Mildred is my greatest subject.

When my drawing is complete, I have to put my special mark upon it. This makes it especially mine, and mine alone.

I find the evening approaching. The workers, including Alfred, keep a safe distance from me because they understand all too well the importance of creating art. Living in such a wonderfully enchanted world of beauty, they allow me to delve deep within my soul to draw my most cherished subject.

While I'm gazing at the completed artwork, the voice comes once again.

"Magnificent. Simply beautiful!" Alfred's voice is welcoming and warm. "You capture her like no other."

His words are affirmation that I have created a masterpiece.

After sizing up my own work, I reply, "Thank you. She is my best subject. Well, she's basically my only subject."

"Will you be staying for dinner, Miss Mary?"

Dinner? I haven't thought about dinner. I don't want to sit and listen to the arguing of Travis and his clan about who is going to watch what TV show when. I want this moment to last forever. But wait, I can make my own decision. I am not bound to Aunt Jackie. If anything, I am more of a burden being there.

"Yes, please. If it is okay with Mildred."

"Why, yes. She is the one who asked me to invite you." Alfred chuckles as he turns to head back into the house.

I make a quick phone call to Aunt Jackie to tell her of my intentions. I know that I made the perfect decision, because all the commotion on the phone is more than enough for me to decide not to go to Aunt Jackie's. Saturday night is in full swing there, and I do not want anything to do with it.

I am instructed to go into a grand dining room. There are several place settings, and I am not clear where I am to be seated. Antoinette comes around the corner with Mildred in tow and instructs me to sit next to Mildred. I am happy to do so.

The dining room is long, with vases of flowers from the gardens. The windows are adorned with the finest drapery. The walls are boxed with molding that encases formal wallpaper designs behind huge portraits of landscapes from all over the world. I notice that there are two crystal chandeliers just over the dinner table.

The staff is waiting on us, hand and foot. I am not accustomed to this type of treatment. I knew that Mildred had people working for her, but this feels unreal.

The food was prepared by Mildred's chef. Each person has more plates and silverware than I have ever imagined. I am not sure which fork goes with which plate. I try to follow along with Antoinette and Mildred as best I can.

Alfred glances over at me and points to each fork and mouths when to use which one. I just smile back like I am a schoolgirl too embarrassed to ask.

The dinner is to die for. It comes in several platters. Each person is carrying a different part of the dinner. This is a feast that no one will believe. Especially Travis. He is still sure Mildred is homeless.

After dinner, the plates are removed, and coffee is served. People go their own ways and leave Mildred and Antoinette, along with me, at the table for privacy, I guess.

"Would you please stay with us tonight?" Antoinette blots her lips with her napkin.

Mildred is too busy sipping on her nighttime coffee and cutting her pastry for dessert.

"Are you sure it's okay?" I ask Mildred. "Honestly, I don't want to go back to Aunt Jackie's house with all the noise and commotion."

"Nonsense. Please stay with me tonight."

I have not heard her speak like this. It's as if she were

protecting me once more. Protection from those unruly kids is welcomed.

"You can sleep down the hall," Antoinette says. "I will show you where."

Mildred rises from her chair, which is at the head of table, and says she is going to go to bed early and read. But before leaving the room, she asks if I found inspiration out in the garden.

"Well, sort of," I reply.

"Beautiful. Maybe you can show me tomorrow." She turns to leave the room.

Antoinette is close at hand to assist her.

"Yes, ma'am," I say.

Alfred comes back into the room. "Would you like to take your coffee on the front porch, Miss Mary?"

"That would be nice. Thank you." I rise from my chair and follow Alfred out to the front porch.

He sits beside me in a rocking chair, just as Antoinette did.

"You are a beautiful artist, Mary." His voice deep and sultry.

"Thank you," I say.

"Miss Mildred thinks the world of you." He turns to give me full attention. "I am very happy that you are here with her."

Sipping my coffee and listening to the night, I feel a sense of peace and love that I have not felt in quite some time. Sure, Lilly and I are best friends, but nothing like this. I am sitting on a porch with a man, the gardener, whom I barely know, and I feel a weird warmth from him. It's almost as if I have known him for years. I completely understand why Mildred feels the way she does toward him.

With both of us rocking back and forth, taking in the night air, listening to the crickets and the occasional car horn, time slips away.

Antoinette comes out to greet Alfred and me.

"Well, Miss Mary," Alfred slowly gets up from the comfortable chair, "it is getting to be that time, and I have a lot of work to do tomorrow." He reaches down to shake my hand.

Feeling strange, I reach for his as well, and shake it. He then turns to Antoinette.

"Antoinette, do you have our fine guest all taken care of for the night?"

With a smile and a wink, she says "Why, yes, sir, I believe we are all taken care of." She turns to me once more. "You have a nice night, Alfred."

Alfred turns and disappears into the night.

"Where did he go?" I say.

"Who, Alfred?"

"Yes."

"Alfred has his room back by the garden, along with his family."

I vaguely remember someone telling me that.

"Oh, I forgot," I say.

"Are you ready to see your room?" She reaches for the grand doors.

"Yes, ma'am." I reach for my cup while getting up from the chair.

"Oh, honey, you can leave your cup here. They will get it in a bit."

"Umm, okay."

Feeling strange about leaving a cup on the front porch, I set it back down for someone else to pick up after me.

We head into the house, through the grand entrance and down past the sunroom. We come to a magnificent staircase and ascend to the second floor. The wood on the staircase is hand-carved and smooth with years of loving hands going up and down the railing. Once we hit the second floor, we find several doors that lead to different rooms. Antoinette shows me her room, which is adjacent to Mildred's. Then she shows me the one I am going to be in for the night. I grab the handle to open the door and am taken aback by what is inside.

There is a small light on the nightstand, next to a canopy bed draped in white linens. Antoinette goes over to the window and opens the shutters that let in the night air.

"If you get cold, you can close these." She begins to leave the room.

Stunned by the magnitude of the house, I find it hard to speak.

"Thank you," is all I can muster.

Antoinette turns around. "Bathroom is down on the left."

And off she goes, into her room for the night.

I stroll over to the window with the shutters. The night air is cool, but not too cold to close the shutters. So I stand a while and watch the night. The crickets are talking to each other.

All I can do is wonder how I got here. I mean, how did I get to be in such a wonderful place, with such wonderful people?

I decide to head over to the bed, which isn't too far away from the window. I can't help but turn around with my back to the bed and jump up high enough to land with both arms extended like I was falling into a cloud. A deep breath overcomes me.

Not being accustomed to turning in for bed so early, I find myself laying on the bed, staring at the canopy, in reflection of my day. Mildred thinks of me as her daughter! I feel a deep warmth emit within my heart. So warm that I fall fast asleep, even with the shutters open.

Morning comes, and the house is full of life. Unlike Aunt Jackie's house, this full-of-life is welcoming. I pull myself together and proceed down the hallway to the bathroom and then downstairs to greet the day.

After heading down the grand stairway, I come upon the kitchen, where people are laughing, and dishes are clanging. Service trays are being loaded, and coffee is permeating the morning air.

"Well, hello, Mary."

I turn to see a man wearing white clothing, like a chef.

"It is Mary, right?" he says.

"Umm, yes, it is. How do you know who I am?"

"You are our special guest, Mary."

"Special?"

"Why, yes, Mary. My name is Nelson. I work here with

Antoinette and everyone else taking care of Miss Mildred."

Nelson appears to be head chef in the kitchen. He wears the usual white apron, much like Charlie, but his demeanor is that of authority. He is always looking off in all directions, ensuring everything is as it should be.

"I also make sure the museum café is well-taken care of, but I do all the cooking from here and take it over."

A voice comes from inside the kitchen area.

"Nelson, we need four napkins."

A voice comes from around the corner.

"Oh, hi, Mary." The lady puts her tray down and wipes her hand on her apron before holding it out to shake mine. "Hi, I'm Theresa."

I extend my hand to hers, and we shake as she speaks.

"Oh, honey, I usually like to hug." She pulls me into her arms and gives me a hug.

"Yeah, me too." I hug her as well.

It is a welcomed hug, unlike the hugs I would get from someone at work, or even Aunt Jackie. It is genuine, loving. There is no awkwardness.

I turn to look at the others in the kitchen, and they are all smiles and talking to each other. I notice two of the girls are standing by a countertop full of pastries, whispering to each other, as if they're sizing me up. But I may be imagining things.

"Are you hungry this morning, Mary?" Nelson says.

"We have fresh squeezed orange juice," Theresa says.

"Oh, yes, I would love some."

I am excited to be accepted into this home and accepted by all the workers ... well, I'm not sure what they all are. Everyone seems so happy to take care of Mildred. So how can they be workers?

Antoinette comes around the corner. "Ah, Mary, good morning." Her face is beaming and appears well-rested.

"Morning," I reply.

"Nelson, we will be eating in the sunroom again, if that won't be too much trouble. Mildred would like to be near her children again."

"Yes, ma'am. That is no trouble at all." Nelson turns is attention to the kitchen staff. "You heard the orders, guys. The sunroom."

"Children?" I say.

"Yes, dear. The photos?" Antoinette says.

"Oh, yes, I understand."

I don't fully understand, but I'm just happy to be here.

We all retreat from the kitchen and walk down to the sunroom. As we are leaving the kitchen area, I hear voices coming from the kitchen. I'm not sure who it is speaking, but they say, "Is that her?"

When Antoinette hears this, she turns to me and tells me to proceed down to the sunroom, and that she will be there soon.

I keep going down the hallway toward the sunroom, but Antoinette turns to enter the kitchen once more. The kitchen door closes, and then I hear it.

"What do you mean, is that her?" the voice, although muffled, belongs to Antoinette.

"Is that the girl that is after Mildred's—"

"Mildred's what?" Alfred says, his voice stern and deep with authority.

"Her money." The girl giggles.

I hear the whole room gasp. I then hear a lot of yelling back and forth, and I think it is best if I am nowhere near the commotion, since it is all about me. I turn to go to the sunroom as instructed.

Right after my arrival at the sunroom, a tray of fruit is being wheeled in, along with a pitcher of orange juice. The tray has a press on it, with a basket of oranges ready to be pressed. This really is fresh-prepared orange juice. They sure aren't kidding, are they?

The place where Mildred was sitting yesterday is dressed with the finest china and linens. Nelson is cleaning the silverware with another napkin to polish watermarks that were not there.

He wants the place setting to be perfect for Mildred when she arrives.

And then she enters.

Antoinette reaches for Mildred's arm to assist her to her chair. She sits with great effort. She attempts to be graceful, but grace tends to leave at this age.

After getting Mildred settled, Nelson begins his service to Mildred.

"Good morning, Nelson." Mildred's face beams with joy.

"Good morning, Miss Mildred." He hands her a glass of freshly squeezed juice. "Beautiful day!"

"Why, yes, it is, indeed." She lifts her head and smiles. "It is, indeed." She takes a sip of her orange juice and turns to me. "Mary, juice for you, chiiild?"

"Yes, please," I reply.

Nelson finishes squeezing the oranges for my juice, and hands me a glass. I take a sip, and the juice is heaven.

"I have never had fresh-squeezed before." I take another sip. "It is so sweet and full of ..." I can't find the word.

"Pulp, Mary. It is pulp," Nelson says.

"Hmm. They don't sell orange juice like this in the store," I say.

"Nelson loves to impress people with his fresh-squeezed juice." Antoinette chuckles.

"Yes, Nelson loves to impress us. Huhhh, Nelson?" Mildred gives him a loving smirk.

"When it comes to pleasing you, Miss Mildred," he says. "I will do anything."

"Oh, Nelson, come on," Theresa says. "Let's get things going in the kitchen."

"Oh, my." He looks down at me and winks, then turns to head back to the kitchen. "I'm on my way." And he is gone.

Antoinette places her hand on my shoulder and whispers in my ear how sorry she is about what happened in the kitchen. I can't help but feel out of place and that I don't belong here.

Antoinette also tells me that she took care of it. Whatever that means.

"Mary," Mildred places her glass down on the table, "did you sleep well, my chiiild?"

"Oh, yes!"

It was so perfect that I slept the entire night, and before I realized it, the deep dark night turned into a bright sunny day.

"Were you comfortable enough?"

"The bed was perfect. I even kept the shutters open all night."

"How long can you stay this morning?" Antoinette says.

"Umm, not long after breakfast. I have to drive back and take care of my cat. Lilly has my cat. And then I have to get ready for work tomorrow. However, I would like to see some old friends before I go."

"Old friends?" Mildred says, knowing the answer.

"Why, yes." I smirk.

"Are they the old friends that maybe can fly?"

I can't help it, but a laugh comes out right at the table.

"Yes, the birds!" I reply.

"Oh, I wish I could come with you, but I have things I need to do."

"It's okay. I will tell them."

"Please do so." Mildred takes another sip of her orange juice.

A cart with chafing dishes comes around the corner, with Nelson pushing it. He wheels the cart next to the piano, and begins opening each lid carefully, not to get burned by the steam. He explains what is in each dish, and then asks if Mildred would like to be served. She does. I think it's because she doesn't want to get up from her comfortable chair.

Nelson serves her food, and then asks me if I want to be served. Feeling weird, I decline.

"I am able to get my plate. Thank you." I proceed to get up.

I notice that Antoinette is getting her food as well.

The tray is filled with scrambled eggs, pastries, fruit, and different types of toast. The food is much like the other day. I can't image this type of meal being served every day.

I am able to put a little of everything on my plate, with room to spare.

Breakfast is wonderful, and I feel like royalty. I can't get used to this. This is not my world. This is Mildred's life. I feel a twinge in my stomach, like I still don't belong here. What if other people feel this way about me?

"Mary, my chiiild, I want you to know the room that you were in last night will be there for you anytime you like." Mildred puts her hand on mine, which is resting on the table next to my plate.

"Really? Why?"

"Why, chiiild, I told you yesterday." Her face lights up with a smile.

"You did?"

"I think of you as my own child, Mary." She pats my hand once again.

I can't help but look over at Antoinette. She is minding her own business, eating her breakfast.

"But I only spent the night here."

"Yes, chiiild, I know. But from now on, you are welcome here any time. And I mean, anytime." She pulls her hand back and begins to eat once more.

"Thank you so very much."

"I know losing your mother has kept you away from here. And I want you to be able to come anytime."

"Yes, ma'am. Well, anyway, I do need to get back to my apartment fairly early. So I am going to see the birds before. Would you like to see them?"

"Chiiild, I really can't. Maybe next time you are in town."

The dishes are being cleared, and the morning breakfast is over. It is time for me to go see my friends. I proceed upstairs to my newly designated room to gather my things. I can't help but to ensure my bed is made and that the room is just as I found it.

As I'm leaving, I notice my car is already pulled up to the front, at the bottom of the grand staircase, which is connected to the grand porch.

"Leaving so soon, Mary?" The soothing voice echoed from behind a bush.

"Yes, I am. I have to get back to work."

"Please don't be gone so long this time, okay?" He flings his arms around me and gives me a loving hug.

"Thank you, Alfred. I promise I will be back." I hug him in return.

"Well, let me at least get the door for you." He reaches down for the door handle and hands me a brown paper bag. "Here. Miss Mildred wants me to give this to you."

It's a bag of birdseed.

"You *are* going to see the birds?"

"Yes, I am."

"That's nice. Miss Mildred would go see them every day."

"Thank you. You are so kind." I put my bag into the car.

"Just doing my job, Mary." He closes the door when I am inside my car. "Just doing my job."

CHAPTER 8

THE DRIVE TO THE PARK IS SHORT but exhilarating. I feel like a breath of fresh air. I had a restful sleep and a beautiful breakfast. Since it's Sunday, parking is easy. I am able to walk quickly to the park bench where Mildred was usually feeding the birds. Oh, wait. I need seed for the birds.

I turn around to head back to the car to get the bag of seed. Once the bag is in hand, I go back to the park bench and call for my old friends.

Birds come from every direction. I don't even have to say anything. They just know I'm there. I sit on the park bench, and the birds land and settle down, all waiting for their seed. The sun is bright and beginning to warm the air that surrounds me. The bag makes a rustling noise as I open it. The birds become restless and eager.

I reach inside the bag to pull out a handful of birdseed and fling the first of many seeds onto the pavement. I watch the birds all fight for position and eat their fill. Of course, we all know that birds never really stop eating.

I begin to gaze out over the water.

"So how are you guys? I'm sorry I haven't been here in a long time," I say to the birds, as they flock to the seed.

Glancing down periodically to see if I recognize any birds, I notice one in particular. He looks familiar.

He looks me in the eye, and I see his soul. He gets up, and there it is. It is the bird with the broken leg. Could it be him? He watches my every move as I reach for more seed. I throw the seed in his direction because I have some feeling that he cannot eat like other birds. I am so wrong. He isn't disabled at all. He moves freely.

"I'm sorry I have been gone so long."

He just keeps looking up at me, like he is understanding my every word. He stretches his wings and yawns.

"Mildred wants me to tell you she misses you," I say to all the birds.

Then I realize I am waiting for them to talk back to me. Oh, boy.

"Oh, what am I doing?" I look around to see if anyone is looking at me, and suddenly feel stupid talking to the birds. "I must be going crazy," I say, under my breath.

I grab the paper bag and begin to crumple it up because the birdseed is all gone. I know I have to be going, so I sit up. The birds fly in unison, high into the air. All except one. The one with a broken leg. He cocks his head, as if to get a better look at me, and I just know it is him.

"I knew it was you. I have missed you. I'm sorry can't stay long."

My phone rings, and I am forced back into reality.

Oh, my phone. I forgot I have it with me. It has been such a nice weekend, even though it was scary how I got here. I was afraid of Mildred being hurt or something.

And then the phone rings again.

"Hello?" I answer.

"Hey, girl! It's Lilly," says the cheerful voice on the other end.

"Lilly, oh my gosh." My voice is odd, like a stuttering car trying to run. "I'm actually leaving now. I was visiting some friends first."

"Friends?" She giggles.

"Yeah, you know, the ones that I talk about, next to the water. That eat birdseed."

"Oh, yeah, the birds."

"Sorry, I am really on my way. I'm going to my car now." I get up and head toward my car.

"Drive safe, and see ya soon, babe." Lilly hangs up.

I couldn't resist turning around once more.

"Bye. See you next time," I say to my long-lost friend, gazing up at me with his beautiful eyes that I drew so many years ago.

I crumple up the empty bag of birdseed as I turn away for the last time. I head back to my car to drive home to Lilly and my cat, but not without a glance back at the empty park bench. I think I secretly want Mildred to be sitting here. I know she is safe and sound at her home, but I still long for her in our special place.

My head is filled with thoughts to keep me occupied on the drive home. Pulling into the apartment complex, I see Lilly standing at my door, holding my cat, Joey. She puts him down and wraps her arms around me like she hasn't seen me in weeks.

"Your cat was so lonely. He wouldn't eat the whole time you were gone. I was afraid to tell you because I thought you would come back home." Lilly picks Joey back up.

"Is he okay?" I bend down to check out my little buddy.

Lilly hands him to me, and the purring begins.

"See, your mommy is home." Lilly steps back. "Thank God. I was starting to think I was becoming that lonely cat lady who stays home on the weekends." She whispers in Joey's ear, "You know, like your mom."

"Lilly, come on." I set Joey down. "That's not fair!"

"So how was your weekend?" Lilly bounces over to the big rocking chair and plops down.

Her braids dance in the air from all the action but are soon tamed by a swoop of Lilly's hand across her face.

I walk over to the sofa and sit. Lilly is rocking next to me. She already has a cup of coffee ready for me, waiting on the coffee table in front of us. I find myself sitting upright, as if I am still being judged by Mildred for my posture and demeanor.

"Oh, girl, relax. You're home now." Lilly pulls her legs under her like a child all curled up in her parents oversized chair, but still attempting to rock.

"Oh, I'm sorry." I relax and take a big breath, which turns into a sigh.

"So tell me about it." Lilly gets more comfortable.

I take a deep sip of my coffee, and my heart fills with joy. "Mildred is sick and all, but I wasn't asked to go there because she is dying."

"Okay. So what was the big emergency?"

"Mildred has been looking for me for a long time, I guess. And ..."

"What?" Lilly leans forward and stops rocking.

"I don't know. I think she is preparing for things, and she really needed to talk to me. You know?" I turn to get a better view of Lilly's body language.

"Umm, okay?"

"She lives in pure luxury and has a staff that takes care of her and the grounds."

I was afraid to go into detail because I felt like I was betraying Mildred's privacy.

"Grounds?"

"Yeah, grounds. Gardens full of, like, flowers, trees, and bushes in all beautiful colors when they are in bloom." I say, with stars in my eyes. "And the sunroom and the gardens for afternoon tea. We actually ate breakfast in the garden."

"Breakfast in the garden?" Lilly smirks and flings her hand into her hair, brushing it back like royalty. "And did you ask for the Grey Poupon, too?"

"Oh, stop. It was beautiful, and ..."

"And?" Lilly prods again, with a silly look of snobbery.

"She said I ..." I feel emotional.

Lilly is acting stupid, and I didn't want her to make fun of this as well. I don't understand why Lilly is acting like all the other kids in the park.

"What?" Lilly says, with a softer tone, because she realizes I'm getting upset.

"She said I was like ... her daughter."

"Daughter? But your mom ... you already have a mom."

"I know she isn't my real mom. But she thinks of me like a daughter because of watching me grow up for so many years. I even have my own room in her huge house that I can go anytime to stay." I smirk.

Joey jumps up on my lap and begins purring while headbutting my arm. I begin to pet him.

"Hmm. Like royalty."

And the jokes begin.

"No, not like that." I look into the kitchen.

"Well," Lilly gets up and begins to head to the door, "we have to work tomorrow. You know, what all of us normal people do? So," Lilly grabs for the door to leave," we should eat lunch in that café that you like so much."

"Café?"

Oh, I almost forgot about Charlie.

"You know, you should ask him." Lilly says.

I pull Joey close to me to listen to him purr against my cheek.

"Nah. Besides, I have my boyfriend right here." I hold Joey closer. "Charlie and I are just fine."

"Umm, what?" Lilly stops in her tracks, her eyes wide open, and her mouth matching. "What did you say?"

I stop petting Joey and look up at Lilly.

"What?"

"Did you hear what you said?" she says, with a cute little smirk.

"Umm, yeah. Me and Joey are just fine."

"That's not what you said!" She giggles.

"Yes, it is," I say, with a stupid look.

"You said," she gets this really funny look on her face as she flips her braids back like she's Cher, "Charlie."

"Umm, what?" I become unsure of what I really did say.

"You said, Charlie! Charlie! Charlie!" Each time she says his name, she gets even more giddy.

"I did?" I whisper, in shock.

"Uh-huh. See, you *do* like him." She turns back to the door.

"Go home, Lilly! Thank you for taking care of Joey for me." I giggle.

"Yeah, I will see you tomorrow morning. Back to the grind.

Back to the real world. How exciting." She turns for the door. "Not!"

<hr>

The day at work seems to be dragging on and on. Calls are slow, but there are enough to get through the day.

And then lunch.

Lilly does her usual peeking around the wall of our cubicles. "Café?" she says.

"Sure. Be ready in a minute." I grab my purse and finish up a few last-minute things.

We walk to Charlie's Café. The usual door chime rings with our arrival, and Charlie is close by.

"Hello, Mary. You guys can sit over there." Charlie is running around because it's very busy today.

He has menus in hand and is trying to take care of several customers at the same time.

"Thank you, Charlie." I sit where he wants us to sit.

The tables are just as they usually are, and the place settings are the same as well. I glance up and notice that his mother is in her normal location, against the wall, with her usual oversized dress on and her big Southern belle hat.

Looking at the menu, I feel a presence over my shoulder, and the smell of powdered sugar, mixed with a manly cologne. Not too overpowering, but just to my liking.

"The specials are on this page." Charlie's arm goes over mine, touching me softly.

I feel that schoolgirl surface again. I want so badly to turn my head and kiss his sweet lips to see if they, too, are made of powdered sugar. But I don't dare. I am too bashful to do anything so brash. Now Lilly would have. But I think she understands that Charlie and I are meant to be together someday.

The room begins to get restless and Charlie has to tend to another table.

"I will be right back, ladies." He rushes away.

Shortly, he takes our order, and our food comes just as quickly.

"Ask him, stupid," Lilly says.

"Ask him what?" I take one last bite of my sandwich.

"You know you like him. So ask."

"Ask me what?" Charlie is beside us, gathering up the empty dishes from our scrumptious lunch.

"Are you single?" Lilly says.

"Lilly!"

Oh, how I wanted to ask myself. Leave it to Lilly to do the dirty work. Sometimes her antics embarrass me. But I, too, wanted to know. I guess I'm happy she asked, but I wouldn't dare tell her that.

I try to hide in my napkin as I wipe my mouth.

"Why, yes, Lilly, I am." He turns to me. "And no, I'm not dating anyone, either." He is still looking at me. "Why didn't you ask me, Mary?"

His eyes are dreamy, and his curly black hair is tousled by the day.

"Umm ..."

Let's see, I'm too embarrassed to ask you? I'm shy? Oh, yeah, I can't talk in front of you!

"Umm, I wanted to, but Lilly asked."

Charlie turns to look at her. "Besides, Lilly, I have my eye on someone."

And without Lilly knowing it, Charlie winks at me.

Oh my God, if Lilly could have seen that!

We finish eating and really need to get back to work. As I am reaching for the bill, I see a note on it that says, *On the House*, and his phone number is below it. I look for Charlie, but he is fast at work, trying to get all the customers taken care of so they, too, can get back to work.

I tuck the phone number in my pocket, and we head out the door, but not before a glance back to see if Charlie is looking. He is.

I mouth, *Thank you*, to him, and he smiles as he quickly turns to help another customer.

"You know, you should go for him," Lilly says, with a bounce in her step, her braids swaying in the wind.

"Charlie?" As if I don't know who she is talking about.

"Duh, girl. You know, the guy that really has *it* for you, Charlie," Lilly says, as we get to the building.

We run to the elevator to get to our desks before our boss knows just how late we are. We giggle about being like school kids talking about a childhood crush behind the teacher's back.

"I don't know. Maybe," I say, even though I really want to see him.

I begin to think about Mildred and all that she has taught me. I want to make my life count, and to find the love of my life, as she did with her husband. Maybe Charlie is the one. But right now, I need to get these damn phones! Back to work.

⁓⋙⋐⁓

Back at home, I open the freezer to see what I have, and I pull out a TV dinner. I didn't have time to shop because I got home yesterday from Mildred's and I had to work today. So TV dinner it is.

I find myself sitting in front of the TV with Joey. While eating my dinner that tastes like the paper tray it came in, it hit me like a Mack truck. Lilly is right. Oh, how I hate to admit that! Here I am, sitting in my apartment with my cat, eating a TV dinner with globs of supposed food on it, watching a TV program that I'm not interested in, when I should be living life. Mildred would not approve of this dash in my life. I get an idea and look over at my phone.

Suddenly, the phone becomes this scary thing that I'm afraid to touch. Oh, I have to be an adult here and just do it.

After pulling the number out of pocket, I begin to dial.

"Hello?" says the sultry voice on the other end.

"Charlie?"

"Yes, speaking." He sounds so professional.

"It's ... Mary." I pray he doesn't hang up.

A great sigh of relief comes from the other end.

"Mary, I am so glad you called. I have been hoping you would call me."

"Well ... I was afraid to call."

"Can I interest you in dinner?" Charlie says.

"Umm, yeah, sure. I would love that."

"Friday?"

"Yes, Friday will be great. I get off work at five. Oh, wait, what about the café? Don't you have to work?"

"It'll be fine. I have employees who will take it. I may be the owner, but I don't have to be there all the time. I am just there all the time because I love it."

I hear him pull the phone away from himself and yell to someone in the background.

"I'm coming. One moment!"

"Is everything okay?" I say.

"Yes. It's my mother. She lives with me, and she needs me to get something for her."

He lives with his disabled mother and is taking care of her. She even comes to work with him. It takes a special person to take such good care of his mother, and I kind of like this.

"I will let you go," I say. "I'll see you on Friday. Unless we eat lunch there this week."

"Well, I hope to see you before Friday," he says, with his sultry voice. "Until then."

"Yes, until then."

The phone goes dead on the other end. He didn't say goodbye. He said, *Until then*. That's different, moving, mysterious. And what did I do? I said it, too.

The work week goes unbearably slow. But it isn't until Lilly and I go to lunch on Friday that the excitement is heightened. As we walk into the familiar café door, even though the café is the same, it seems different today.

Lilly and I are sitting at the table, waiting for our order to be taken, and my sultry Charlie comes up to us. He has his usual white apron on and his all too hypnotic aromas. He takes my hand off the menu and pulls it close to his face. His cheeks are rose-colored and warm. His eyes are bright and sparkly. Lilly is a total blur to me because I have melted. It feels like my heart stops. Or at least skips a beat or two. His lips purse, and he kisses the back of my hand, as if a prince has met his queen. The room stops; time stands still. Oh, how I wish I could stop time forever.

"Umm, Mary?" Lilly's voice brings me back to reality.

"Oh." I pull my hand back, as if I were just caught by my mother. "I'm sorry."

The giddy schoolgirl is now in the forefront once again.

"Uh-huh, I knew it." Lilly smirks.

With my heart still skipping, and my face flushed with excitement, I find that Lilly was right. I will never admit to her that I really do have it bad for Charlie.

Charlie takes our order—you know, the usual. It comes quickly. I try so hard to stop this conversation from happening, but Lilly just has to start it.

"Would you like to explain that?" she says.

"What?"

"Uhh, girl, the passionate-kiss-on-your-hand thang?"

"Umm. Oh, yeah. We have a date," I say, under my breath.

"You? A date? Like, a real date?"

She said it so loud that it felt like CNN was announcing it on the local news.

"Lilly, stop!"

"When?" She leans toward me. "How?"

"I called him. He asked. That's it." I keep on eating, trying to get her to understand that I really don't want to talk about it.

Lilly is one to talk about all her loves and sexcapades. But I am not. I don't usually date. I haven't had a date since college.

"Pick you up after work?" Charlie says, as he is passing by the table.

"Yes, see you tonight," I say.

And he does it again.

"Until then." He kisses the back of my hand.

I feel my face flush with embarrassment.

Lilly and I go back to work, and we don't talk about my date again. Since it was Friday, the phones are ringing like crazy. It is a welcomed busy, though.

I hear a tap from a pen on my desk. It's Lilly.

"I want details! See ya Monday." She is gone in a flash.

I choose a generic black dress, along with black high heels, for my first date with Charlie. Wearing my hair? Down? Up? I fluff up my auburn curls. Down it is.

I glance down at my jewelry box. Joey is sitting beside me and trying to help with my every decision, because I seem to be nervous.

I look up into the mirror at my dress. The black dress I chose has a V-neck, which frames out the necklace that I already have on. I am wearing Mildred's locket. After all these years, the locket is still illuminating with life.

No, I will continue to wear the locket. It is so beautiful with this dress.

"Joey, do I look okay?" I smile down at my buddy.

With my makeup on just right, I turn to Joey for his final approval. I stand in the mirror's reflection in the bathroom, and Joey is pacing on the countertop.

Deep breath. I think I'm ready. Oh, who am I kidding? This date is a real live date. I'll never be ready.

"Here we go, bud." I take one last glance in the mirror.

The nervousness takes over, just in time for the doorbell to ring. I look down at Joey.

"Well, Joey, here he is. Wish me luck."

Yep, I am talking to my cat, like he is a human helping me get ready for my date. I guess I actually talk to Joey a lot more than I realize.

I head to the door, but not before saying a little prayer. Reaching for the door handle I close my eyes in hopes that it is, indeed, Charlie. I think I need affirmation that this date thing is real.

The first thing I see is a beautiful bouquet of mixed flowers. It isn't the Charlie who I see every day at the café, but a true knight. He is not in his usual white apron. He is wearing a pressed suit with a tie. He still smells sweet and inviting.

Charlie reaches for my hand and kisses the back of it as he did at the cafe. He holds out the bouquet, and I reach for it with my other hand.

"Shall we go?" he says.

"Yes, but please allow me to put the flowers in a vase." I turn to put them in water.

Charlie follows me into the kitchen, and he sees Joey.

"Aww, what a pretty kitty," he says, with a childish voice.

"That is Joey." I finish putting the flowers in water. "Joey will take care of the flowers while I am gone." I give him a pat on the head. "Won't 'cha, Joey?"

His purr is loud because I think he knows he is in competition with Charlie.

"Well, shall we go?" Charlie says again.

"Umm ..." I look back at my apartment to ensure all is okay to leave, " ... yes."

When we arrive at his car, he stops me.

"Allow me." He grabs the door handle.

Wait! Charlie is opening the car door for me.

The door opens to allow me to sit inside his beautiful car. I pull my legs in, and he closes the door. He drives to a quaint French restaurant. No, wait. We have reservations?

The maître d' must know Charlie because they speak fondly.

We are seated by the window, a place where I feel comfortable because I can watch the people passing by. But this evening is much different. My attention is not what's on the other side of the window, but on the man who sits before me.

Charlie orders our dinner in French. I don't care because I know he will get something good. After all, he owns his own restaurant. Dinner arrives, along with the perfect wine. I can't help but notice that he keeps staring at me.

"That is a beautiful locket." He sips his glass of wine.

His statement forces me to reach up and finger the chain

that it is attached to. My fingers caress its intricacies.

"It belongs to a very dear friend of mine," I say.

"Well, it is beautiful. And so are you," Charlie says, his eyes sparkling from the candlelight on the table.

The music begins. We are finished with our dinner, and the waiter takes our plates away without us even realizing it. Neither of us want to leave. We have not finished with the evening.

Charlie extends his hand to me as he stands by his chair.

"Shall we dance?"

Taken back, I am not sure how to dance with a man. I mean, I used to dance in college, but it was all modern music. Nothing like this.

"Yes, I would love to." I arise from my seat with hesitation, but excitement.

Ensuring my dress is just right, I reach back for his hand. Oh, my heart is warm with something that I am not sure of. But I am enjoying it.

We arrive on the dance floor, and another couple is there. I'm not worried about them making fun of me, but what about everyone else in the restaurant?

Charlie pulls me close, and I feel his breath on my neck. I'm lost in his scent.

"I can't really dance that well," I whisper in his ear.

He begins to gaze into my eyes to comfort me.

"Just follow me." He takes the lead. "My mother taught me well in her days. She taught me that a true gentleman knows how to dance and how treat a woman."

He twirls me around the dance floor and holds onto me, never letting me go. I look like a pro, but in actuality, he is flipping me around the floor, and I am holding on with all my might. I have no idea what I'm doing. I'm just following him.

With each passing song, I begin to get the hang of things. The romantic evening could not get any better than this!

We go back to the table to cool down and drink our drinks. It's getting late, and he motions to the waiter that we need our check.

"Shall we go?" His gaze meets mine.

I steal a glance at his eyes; they are much more relaxed than they usually are at the café. I can see that he is enjoying the evening as well.

I take the final sip from my drink and blot my lips.

"Yes, that would be nice," I reply.

The night air has a coolness. Charlie takes off his suit jacket and puts it around my shoulders to keep me warm. I was so worried about looking stunning for him that I forgot to dress for the weather. But that doesn't matter. I am well-taken care of.

"Shall we walk for a bit?" Charlie extends his arm to the sidewalk.

"Sure."

We walk for a short bit, arm in arm. I feel a warmth that I have not felt in so very long. A romantic dinner, dancing, and now a walk. How could I resist?

After we walk for a few blocks, we stop by a streetlight and sit on the bench.

"You know the locket that you mentioned at dinner?" I hold my locket.

"Yes." He looks deep within my eyes.

"It belongs to a lady that I have known since I was a child," I say, with a somber tone.

"Well, that's nice."

"Your mom reminds me so much of her."

"My mother?"

"Yes. Her name is Mildred, and she wears a large Southern belle hat, just like your mother does. Your mother brings back some fond memories of her."

The street corner is quiet because of the hour. It is late, and there is not much traffic on the streets.

"How does she remind you of her?" he says.

"Mildred is a very special lady. I met her when I was four years old, in a park in the inner city. It's a long story, but the kids all called her Bird Lady."

"Bird Lady?" Charlie chuckles. "Well, that's not very nice."

"No, it wasn't. But she was always feeding the birds, and that's how she got her nickname. But it wasn't really a nickname. It was like a name they called her out of anger ..."

"Did she live in the park?"

Why do people think that if someone is in the park feeding the birds, that they are homeless? I get mad, but only for a split second. I'm hoping deep down that he really is different than everyone else who makes fun of her.

"No, she was just there every day." I reply. "My mother did not allow me to talk to her for many years. But ..."

"But what?"

"Something drew me to her. I wanted to get to know her. Everyone made fun of her." I pause. "I felt sorry for her. That's why I wanted to talk to her so bad."

"And you did," he says.

"Yes, she became my best friend. I told her everything as the years went by." I find myself trying to sit properly.

"Someone very special, then?" he says.

"Yes." I wear a gentle smile. "She has a special way about her. She talks like she's from the deep south. You know, with a drawl, and she pauses between each spoken word."

"Hmm," Charlie says, as if he is trying to hear Mildred in his mind.

"Yes. And someday, I would like you to meet her." I gaze into his eyes again.

What am I thinking? This is our first date. But it's like we have been dating for a lifetime. It is so natural to be with him. All the giddy school-girl childishness is replaced by a fondness, a tender admiration. Charlie is a pure gentleman. A real keeper. I feel it.

"I would like that." He puts his arms around me and holds me tight.

"Well, I don't mean to cut this date short," he says, "but it is after midnight. And I have to open in the morning."

Charlie drives me back home, and the gentlemanly charm is not an act. He is perfect. I am in love.

He walks me up to my door. Standing face to face, Charlie uses his finger to push back a lone curl that found its place over my nose.

"May I?"

I lean in, and our lips meet for the first time. He raises his hand to gently meet my cheek. His hand then moves behind my head to hold me tenderly. I melt. A deep sense of warmth wells up inside me. I suddenly don't need that suit jacket.

"See you tomorrow?"

"Yes," I reply, without even opening my eyes.

I am lost in his heart already.

I take his suit jacket off my shoulders and give it back to him. He takes my hand and kisses it once more.

"Until next time." He turns to leave.

I have found that he never says goodbye. It is an inviting gesture, endearing.

"See you, umm, later today." I wave. It's after midnight, so it's technically the next day.

I can't even get my words to come out right.

I close the door, only to find Joey sitting there, just sneering at me like a parent. I saunter right past him, as if I were still dancing with Charlie. Joey doesn't move until I make it back to my bedroom. He runs and jumps on my bed, like he is begging for the information.

"What?"

I lie back on the bed, and Joey comforts my every move, purring and kneading the blanket next to me.

"Oh, Joey." I let out a deep sigh. "I think I'm in love. What do you think? Do you like him?"

Oh, how I wish he could speak to me. But purrs of approval will have to do.

"I know, first date, but ..."

I get up to get undressed. I crawl into bed, with Joey purring so loud alongside me. He settles in for the night.

I find that my night is filled with wonderful dreams of what awaits me when I see him again.

CHAPTER 9

SATURDAY IS JUST BEGGING ME TO GO to the café. I know it may be forward to go there, but I have to see him, and I know that he's working.

I decide to take my sketch pad and do some drawing. I sit by the usual window and watch the usual anonymous people walking by. They are gazing into the mysterious mirror again, but this time, I am not focused on them. My focus is on trying to find Charlie. He isn't out in the front this morning. There is another guy in a white apron waiting on tables. I know Charlie is here because he told me he had to open the café. I figure he is in back, cooking or baking.

I order and proceed to pull out my pad and pencil.

While searching for a fresh sheet of paper, I am simultaneously looking around the café for my subject to draw. And there she is. Charlie's mother is sitting in her usual corner. Her hat catches my attention. I can't take my eyes off her. I told Charlie why I was drawn to her presence, and now I have to draw her.

After examining her features, I begin to put my pencil on the paper. Her facial features are close to Mildred's, but different. She has a lost characteristic in her eyes. It looks like she is trying to remember the woman that she was at one time but cannot find her. I do not see a smile in her eyes, but a distant worrisome stare. Perhaps the stare is an attempt to see into her past, to find her identity.

The hat on her head is dirty from the years of life. Some of the lace is torn, and the edges are frayed. The stories this hat could tell would be extraordinary.

Tiny whips of hair are peeking out from under the bottom of the hat. Her hair color is unclear to me because the gray has overtaken her once full head of hair. Even though it is thinned greatly, she still has beautiful hair that is somewhat wavy.

She sits in a quietness only she can hear. With her distant stare comes a peacefulness deep within her heart. Her posture is tired, but like an aged debutant. All of her poise and posture are hard to keep in the forefront, but her training will never fall short. I glance down to see her legs crossed at her ankles and think of the training that Mildred has put me through.

Her nails are long and unpolished but kept with care. I wonder if Charlie files and paints her nails. Her fingers are frail, just as Mildred's, and wrinkled with age and wisdom. A ring on her finger reveals a past love. Her fingers meet the sleeves of her dress, many sizes too large for her frail frame that once could have filled it out. Her dress is much like the hat, torn and frail, but still to her, it is adorned with elegance and splendor of days past.

I don't realize it, but I have been sitting here for hours. I am consumed by Charlie's mother. Undisturbed by the people coming and going from the café, I find myself sitting back and checking the detail of my drawing.

"Isn't she beautiful?"

I hear a whisper over my shoulder and glance up to see Charlie almost in tears as he examines the picture. I look back at my drawing, not realizing that I have just drawn a masterpiece.

"You really have a spectacular talent." His voice cracks.

"Thank you." I run my fingers over the freshly drawn portrait. "This is how I see her." I glance back up at him.

He has his apron on, and his hair is messy with his curls adrift over his eyes and nose. He pushes his hand over his forehead, forcing his hair back over, out of his face. I'm not sure, but I think he pushes back a tear or two.

"I hope you like it." I smile.

"Like it? I love it!" He smiles in return and reaches for my sketch pad. "May I?"

"Sure."

He takes the sketch pad over to his mother.

"Look, Mama." He places the drawing in front of her.

"Oh, Charlie." Her eyes are filled with some sense of familiarity, but confusion quickly takes over.

"Look, Mama." He points down at the sketchbook.

"Pretty," she says.

Charlie was hoping for another reaction, but he is quickly reminded of her illness.

"Who is this?" she says.

Charlie looks as if he was hit by a bus.

"It's you, Mama."

"Who?" And she just stares off in the café, looking for answers.

"It's okay, Mama." Charlie takes back the sketch pad and brings it over to my table. "She doesn't recognize herself, but ..." his voice cracks, " ... but, I love it. Thank you for taking the time to see my mother as the beautiful woman she is."

He sets the sketch pad down and turns around to go back to work. I want to hug him and tell him everything will be okay, but I know that it is only going to get worse. Someday, his mother is going to be gone, just like mine.

I wait a short while for him to return, but the restaurant becomes busy. He may be in the back cooking again. I will call him later and leave him be for now.

I let Charlie have his space, and the weekend goes by quickly.

Monday came too quick. Back at work, Lilly is incorrigible. I try hard to keep to myself, but I can't.

"Well ..." I hear Lilly say, as she is bending her head around the wall to talk to me.

"Well, what?"

"Umm, Charlie?" She smirks, her arms crossed.

She rolls her chair all the way into my area and is determined to get the scoop.

"Do you really want to know what happened?" I say.

"Yeah," she says, with a teenage attitude.

I can't help it. I begin to blush, and then I begin to giggle.

"He was a perfect gentleman. We danced, talked, walked for a while. He gave me his suit coat to stay warm," I say, as if I were reading a romance novel.

I feel her attitude turn into envy.

"Wow," she says.

"Uh-huh." Now I am the one with the teenage attitude.

But I keep it in check.

"Are you going to see him again?"

I think, deep down inside, she wants to take him on a date. But that is not happening.

"I saw him on Saturday. I drew his mother." I pull my sketch pad out. "Want to see?" I thumb through the pages to reveal the portrait of her. "Oh, there it is." I give her the pad.

Lilly gasps and looks at it with admiration.

"Oh, Mary, this is so good!"

"Thank you."

"Did Charlie see it?"

"Yes, and he was almost in tears."

"When are you going to see him again?"

"I'm not sure. Soon, I hope." I turn to go back to work.

I hide in my work and try not to daydream about the past weekend.

The week drags by slowly, and it is killing me not calling Charlie. Lilly and I go to eat lunch at the café on Friday, but Charlie and his mother are not there. I want to ask where they were, but I don't want to pry.

I decide to go see Mildred and call Antoinette.

"Antoinette, can I come see you and Mildred?"

"Yes, dear. She would love to see you."

"I will come after work today. Can I still stay there?"

"Why, yes, dear. I will make sure your room is ready for you."

Friday ends, and I am on my way to see Mildred. I was gone for two weeks, and I am excited to see them.

Pulling up to the gates is an inviting feeling. Memories of yesteryear are pushed back with newly formed memories of fresh linens and garden aromas.

Driving down the long drive, I notice that the house is lit with fresh lighting all along the drive. How inviting against the setting sun.

Pulling up to the house and the grand staircase, I see Alfred coming toward me with a beaming smile.

"Awe, lookie who came back to see me!" He wraps his arms around me and kisses me upon my cheek.

"Oh, hello, Alfred!"

What a welcoming feeling to be received like this.

"She is waiting for you in the sunroom, dear. Allow me to park your car and take your bags to your room."

"Really? I'm able to."

Before I know it, my bags re in his care.

"Yes, dear," he says. "Now, go get inside to see Miss Mildred."

I run toward the stairway and enter the grand entrance as if I lived there and I was coming home from college or something.

The entrance is much as it was when I left. The only difference is that the flowers in the vases are different.

I turn to enter the sunroom. She is sitting in her chair, with her usual cup of tea.

"Oh, chiiild, you have come back." Her face lights up. "Please come over to me. I cannot get up."

Mildred's arms open up to greet me, and I come over to her. My arms open up as I bend over to hold her tight. Oh, the love that radiates from her.

After our embrace, I sit in the chair next to her. Even though the drive isn't that long, I worked all day and then made the drive. I am tired, and it shows.

"Would you like some tea, chiiild?"

"Sure."

She motions for someone to get me some tea.

"So, chiiild, how are you?"
Her voice is tired, but I expected it.
"I'm actually really good. Work is going well, and ..."
"Chiiild, and what?"
Before I can answer, a lady enters the room, holding a tray with my tea on it. She also b some sort of cake with it.
"Oh, thank you so very much," I say to her, as she leaves the room.
I do not know her. I didn't meet her last time I was here. She may be new. I'm not sure.
"Where is Antoinette?" I say.
"Oh, she is taking care of her family." Mildred takes a sip of tea. "You did not answer me."
"Hmm?"
"You didn't finish your sentence, chiiild."
"Oh, yeah. I went on a date!"
"A date?"
"Yes. And he is a true gentleman, just as you taught me."
"How so?"
"He opens doors. He brought flowers. He has a mother that is a lot like you." I turn my body to be more in line with her.
"Reminds you of me, how?"
"She wears a Southern belle hat, with a gown."
"A gown?"
"Well, she has dementia, but that is not what reminds me of you. It is the way she looks and carries herself. She has the appearance of elegance, but confusion of years past." I take another sip of my tea.
"Hmm," she says.
"Her son, Charlie, takes care of her, and it's the way he takes care of her that is so wonderful. Charlie idolizes his mother."
"Hmm."
"He owns a café and works very hard."
"Oh, a café." Approval brightens her eyes.
"He is special." I feel my cheeks blush.
"Special? I see."

"See what?"
"I see it." She smirks.
"See what?" Curiosity is killing me.
"You are in love, chiiild."
"Umm, me? No. How could I be?"
"Sure, you are, chiiild."
"I-I think I am ... I ... think I am ... in love. But how do you know?"
"You look like I did when I met my true love. I married him, by the way." She giggles. "When God puts the right person in your life, your soul knows it."
"I remember you married him." I take another sip of my tea.
"I see it all over your face, chiiild."

I eat the rest of my cake and drink my tea. I sit in my seat with my back against the chair. This is something I rarely do here. Mildred probably never sits back in a chair, other than to rest from a hard day.

"Oh, chiiild, go get some rest. I'm going to go to bed myself." She begins to get up.

Without Antoinette's help, she struggles, so I reach over to assist her. Finally in the upright position, she takes a deep breath and begins to move, with her walker, toward the door.

"Good night, chiiild." She turns around the corner and is gone for the night.

I find my room fit for a queen, once again. Even though it is early in the evening, I still need to sleep from the hard day at work. And so I lie down. The fresh linens are crisp and delightful. Oh, nightfall engulfs me.

I awake to a ton of commotion, people scrambling in all directions. It seems to be a chaotic situation, much unlike what this household is used to.

I manage to make my way downstairs. Two women are holding each other hurrying along, too quick for me to stop them. They seem upset. I notice Alfred in the distance.

"Alfred! Alfred!" I have to yell for him to hear me.

"Oh, Deary, I forgot you were here."

He seems upset as well. Fear strikes me.

"What happened? What is going on?"

"Oh, Miss Mildred fell this morning, and she is on the way to the hospital."

"The hospital?" I feel like he punched me in my stomach. "What happened?"

"She was in the bathroom taking her bath, and she wanted to get up without Antoinette there to help her."

"Is she okay?"

"Yeah, she will be fine, dear." He sounds more like he is trying to convince himself than me.

"Should we go be with her?" I feel panic setting in.

"No, Deary. Antoinette is with her. Allow her to do her job. This is why Miss Mildred hired her. The hospital will take good care of her, like last time."

"Last time?"

What? This happened before? How have I been missing so much with her? Guilt overcomes me.

"Yes, Mary. She fell in the garden and twisted her ankle." He starts to leave the room.

"You just wait here with the rest of us, and Antoinette will provide us with information as she gets it."

I feel helpless.

"Just go into the sunroom," he says, "and I will have someone bring you your breakfast."

⁂

Alone in the sunroom, I force myself to eat because I am more worried than hungry. Alfred comes in with the phone.

He keeps saying, "Uh-huh. Okay. Uh-huh."

I wait patiently for him to finish, when I really want to scream for him to talk.

Then he finally hangs up and sits down beside me. He puts the phone down on the table.

"That was Antoinette. She wants me to talk to you."

I take a deep breath in preparation for the worst.

"Okay," I reply.

"Miss Mildred broke her hip this time," he says, with a deep, soothing voice.

"How bad?" I say.

"She is in surgery and will be in the hospital for a few days." Alfred smiles.

"So, nothing permanent?"

"No, Deary, she will be fine." He hugs me.

"So I guess I should be going home, then," I say.

"Nonsense! You are part of the family. Stay with us. Whatever you need, just ask, and it will be served."

"Umm, okay, thank you," I say, feeling uncomfortable with the privilege they're affording me.

Alfred is gone again.

This is strange. Part of the family? If I need anything, just ask? Be delivered to me? I know Mildred has people waiting on her hand and foot, but why me?

A couple hours pass, and Alfred finds me once more in the garden.

"Hello, Alfred. Any news?"

"She did fine. She is in recovery."

I am able to settle down, but I still feel helpless. Mildred has always been there for me. I feel like I need to be there for her. I can't just sit here.

I decide to drive to the hospital to see her. Once I get there, I am able to locate the room she is in. I see Antoinette there, and she asks me how I was able to get in. I just smirk as another nurse walks by.

A bed is being pushed into the room by a male nurse wearing scrubs with teddy bears on it. This is a sight to see. I see it is Mildred, hooked up to a lot of wires and hoses. I decide to sit in the corner and wait for her to wake up.

After a short time, Mildred begins to stir. He eyes begin to open, but surely not focused yet.

"Chiiild, is that you?" she says, with a raspy voice.

"Yes, it is." I get up from my chair and walk over to the bed. I grab her hand to comfort her. She moans from the pain. Again, I feel helpless.

"Chiiild, how did you get in here? How did you find me?"

"Umm, I told them I am your ... well, daughter."

"Smart thing, chiiild." Mildred giggles, and then a twinge of pain.

"I couldn't just sit there. I was worried." I squeeze her hand.

"Oh, chiiild, I'm a tough cookie," Mildred says, visibly fighting off the pain.

"Should I get the nurse?" Antoinette says.

"No, dear. I just need to get ..." Mildred takes a deep breath, " ... some rest." She closes her eyes.

"Why don't you get some coffee or rest, Antoinette?" I say. "You have been with her for a long time."

"Hmm." She yawns. "I suppose you're right. I need to get some coffee. Would you like some?"

"No, I think I am good for now. Maybe later." I sit on the edge of the chair.

Antoinette leaves the room to get her coffee and take a breather. I want to sit with Mildred for a while. Even though she is sleeping from all the meds, I know she is being well-taken care of. I sit back in the chair.

Mildred awakes for a moment.

"Oh, chiiild, you still here?"

"Yes, I'm here. Are you feeling okay?"

"Yes, I may need more pain meds soon, though."

I can hear the pain she is in.

Just then, a nurse comes in to take her vitals and give her another dose of pain killer. All is well again.

"Chiiild, you go home," she says to me. "I will be fine here."

"It's too late for me to drive all the way home now." I say.

"No, chiiild. I mean the manor. Go home to the manor."

Home? She is calling the manor my home now? Maybe she just means her home. She must be confused.

Antoinette comes back into the room.

"See, Antoinette is here with me," Mildred says.

"I will be with her at all times," Antoinette says.

Another nurse comes in for the next shift.

"Honey, visiting hours are over," she says. "You really should allow Mildred to get some sleep."

"Can Antoinette stay with me?" Mildred says.

"Now, Miss Mildred, you know Antoinette can stay with you anytime you need her to," the nurse says.

I leave to go back to the manor and drive through the big iron gates. This time, it feels different. I am usually coming to see Mildred, but I know she isn't here. The home suddenly feels like a big empty shell. I see Alfred, though, and the emptiness leaves me.

He comes to me and gives me a big hug.

"Oh, Alfred, she is in a lot of pain, but she is okay."

"Honey, I knew you couldn't stay away from her," he says.

"Are you mad because I left?"

"Mad? Why, dear, you did what I expected you to do. You care for Mildred, just as we all do. She cares for you a lot, you know." He steps back to look into my eyes.

"Yeah, I know she does."

"Now, go get inside, and I will park your car for you." He holds his hand out for my keys.

I put them in his hands and turn to enter the grand stairway.

"Go get some rest."

"Yes, sir." I smile as I leave.

I decide to go right up to my room because I need to get some sleep after all the excitement today. I need to drive back home on Sunday morning to work on Monday. Oh, how I wish I could just stay here.

I decide to make that phone call to Charlie. The phone rings and rings. There's no answer, but I leave a message.

"Charlie? I am at Mildred's. I'm coming back on Sunday. Hope everything is okay. I haven't heard from you, so thought I'd give you a call."

I hang up with disappointment, and soon fall asleep.

CHAPTER 10

I GO TO THE CAFÉ Monday for lunch. As I enter, I look around for Charlie but don't see him. Lilly and I are seated close to the window, as usual. We order, and still no Charlie.
"Where is Charlie?" I ask the waiter, as he passes by.
"He isn't here today." He hurries around the table.
I wait till he passes by again.
"Is he sick?"
"What's going on, Mary?" Lilly says.
"I haven't seen or heard from Charlie in a while," I reply, "and I'm worried."
The waiter must have overheard me.
"You're Mary?"
"Yes, I am."
"Charlie has spoken about you. He said that if you came in, to tell you," he looks around the room to see who is listening, "that his mother is really ill. He doesn't know when he will be back to work."
"Sick?"
"Yeah. He's looking for a home for her to go into. While you were gone, his mother left the café one day and walked away. He was so worried. She was found by the police and taken to the hospital." The waiter pours more water in our glasses. "He will call you when he gets back into town."
The waiter goes off to another table.
"Lilly, I'm worried about Charlie."
"Charlie will be fine. You had to go through things with your mom, remember?"

"Yea, I did."

"Call him after work." She takes a long drink from her straw.

"I will." I take a bite of my sandwich.

We finish eating and go back to work. Eager to be done, I keep looking at the clock.

I know it's late, but I call Charlie anyway, and he answers. His somber voice penetrates my ears.

"Hi, Charlie."

"Hey, Mary." He tries to sound like his usual cheery self, but I hear right though the facade.

"I went to the café for lunch. The waiter said that you were out for a while, and that your mom isn't doing well."

"Well, my mother, as you know, has dementia. She walked away and got lost. I couldn't find her. I'm so busy with the café, and I got sidetracked, and she just ..." his voice cracks, " ... she walked away. I couldn't find her!"

"I'm so sorry. Can I come see you?"

I actually say it! I don't want to seem to forward, but I want to be the person he can count on.

"Sure," he replies. "How about if we meet down at the cafe? I need to get out of here for a while."

"Umm, it isn't open."

"Have you forgotten I'm the owner?" He chuckles. "I have a key."

"Oh, yeah." I laugh along with him.

"See you in a half-hour?"

"Sure."

We hang up, and I leave, but not before giving Joey a quick pet. When I arrive at the café, the lights are already on. It is surreal because the lighting outside is different than the inside. It gives a totally different feel, not only to the building outside, but to the ambiance inside.

I open the door, and the usual chime rings, but it is different as well. Charlie yells from behind the wall that he wants me to come back. I hear pots and pans clanking. It is unfamiliar territory behind the wall of the café, a place that no one other than employees are allowed to venture.

"Oh, hi," Charlie says, wearing his usual white apron.

He's cooking. Why is he cooking? He is supposed to be upset, drinking coffee.

"I hope you're hungry." He turns to the grill, flipping chicken or something, and then stirring his concoctions on the stovetop.

"What are you cooking?" I try to look over his shoulder, but he is so efficient in the kitchen that he moves at the speed of light.

With arms flailing, pots and pans clanging, I am not about to interrupt him.

"I feel best when I cook. I told you I would cook for you. It's a surprise. Now, just sit over there." He points to a chair by the freezers, out of the way.

He comes over and kisses me on the forehead, while keeping his hands far away from me. Then he flicks my nose, putting flour all over my face. We can't help but laugh.

"Allow me to cook something special for you."

"Yes, sir." I perch myself up on the chair and watch the show.

Here is a man dressed in blue jeans with holes in the knees, a worn T-shirt and loafers, and his hair is tossed, yet he is oh-so-sexy.

He turns around in front of me, bending over to get something out of the oven. Oh, I can't help but look at his sexy features and that fine rear-end.

"Umm, missy? Do you see something you like?" He catches me looking.

"You have no idea."

"Dinner will be in ten minutes," he says, as he is stirring things and plating.

"I'll go wash my hands." I head to the restroom to gain my composure.

While washing my hands, I can't help but look at myself in the mirror. I find myself talking to myself, just as I do with Joey.

"Oh, Mary, Mary, Mary." I turn off the water and grab a paper towel. "Pull yourself together."

Once I feel more composed, I go back to the kitchen.
"Can you set a table for us?" he says.
Sounds funny. He's telling me what to do, like I work here.
"Yes, but ..." I have no idea where anything is.
I scan the kitchen for where the dishes are.
"The settings are behind the wall," he says.
I grab napkins, silverware, glasses, and place them just as he would want.
Charlie comes out of the kitchen with plates of food. He glances down at the table, and I can see that he is pleasantly surprised.
"Oh, I almost forgot." He goes back behind the wall, only to appear once again with a bottle of wine and two wine glasses.
He stands beside the table and begins to open the bottle. I am already sitting, and he takes my glass.
"May I?"
"Yes, you may." I giggle.
Then he plops down in his chair, which almost falls over. We laugh once more.
He begins to pour his glass. He lifts it up and waits for me to lift mine as well. Our eyes meet.
"To a beautiful caring woman that ..." his face lights up with a deep warmth, " ... that I could fall in love with."
I am in shock. I am feeling the same warmth. I'm not sure what I should say back, and I just sit there.
Finally, I say, "I could fall in love with you, too."
Oh my God! What did I just say?
Charlie arises from his seat and leaves for a moment. Then I notice the lights dimming. He brings out his cell phone, turns on some romantic music, and sets it down next to the table. He has to turn it all the way up for us to hear it.
"The music here isn't for this kind of evening, so this is the best I can do."
Charlie extends his hand and asks me to dance. I raise my hand to meet his, and he kisses the back of my hand.
"May I have this dance?" he says.

"Yes, you may."

We slow dance in the café, on our pretend dance floor, cheek to cheek. We begin staring into each other's eyes. He puts his hand on my cheek, holding me close, and then puts his lips meet mine. I close my eyes and try to drink in the moment. Time stands still. We are all alone. He is so incredibly romantic, charming, and ... and I'm so lost in his presence. Our lips separate. I am so immersed in the moment that I bite my lip.

We decide to sit back down and eat our delicious dinner that has just come out of the oven. I lift the lid on my plate, and there it is—a beautiful fillet cooked to perfection, with bacon wrapped around it, baby carrots with an orange glaze, sautéed mushrooms, onions and peppers, and a pile of white grains.

"What is this?" I point my plate.

"It's risotto. You haven't had this before?" He dives his fork into it to show me the texture.

"No, I haven't," I'm embarrassed to say.

"This is going to be fun. I can teach you so much. Finally, I have someone to cook for who will appreciate what I cook!" He wears a loving smile.

We eat our dinner with light conversation and make googly eyes at each other.

Charlie suddenly becomes quiet and looks at his plate, and then at the corner where his mother's usual table is.

"Are you okay?" I say.

"Yeah. It's just hard. I used to cook for my mother. She taught me so much about cooking." He looks up at me. "She said a good man knows how to cook and clean. Household chores are not just for the woman, but also the man. She would put me on a stool next to the stove when she was cooking and teach me all the ingredients and how to cook with them. She even taught me how to cook with wine way before I was in middle school. Can you imagine being a young boy wanting to buy wine for a special dish?" He giggles. "It's just hard seeing my mother being taken away with such a horrible disease. Now, she doesn't know the difference between scrambled eggs or cereal."

"I'm sorry." I put my hand over his, on the table, to comfort him.

"We used to spend hours in the kitchen, and the kids at school would tease me for being a mama's boy," he says, with a half-witted smile.

I smile in return. "Hmm."

"We used to go shopping for cookbooks and talk about life. She told me to find my passion." He gathers the empty plates.

"What? What did you say?"

"Mama told me to find my passion and ... well," he extends his arms out to show the café, "here it is."

"I completely understand. Mildred told me the same thing!"

"I love cooking fine dishes, but I have found the general public is so hurried. They yearn for a good cup of coffee and a quick sandwich or a warm pastry. So I made a menu to best suit them."

He goes off to the kitchen, with dishes in hand. Soon, he returns to finish his thought. "But you ... you make me want to cook again." He stops by my chair. "I mean, really cook." He uses his finger to start at my forehead and push back the auburn curls that frame my face. "I feel alive again when I'm with you."

"I haven't really dated anyone since college," I say. "And not really even then, because I was such a bookworm."

"But your passion is drawing. Why are you working in that tall building, hiding behind all that glass and carpeted cubicles?"

"I have to pay the bills. Working in the glass high-rise pays my bills."

"But you are not happy. Sure, you joke around with Lilly, but you really are not happy."

"Funny that you say that. Mildred keeps telling me about enjoying life, drawing, and again, finding my passion. Making my dash count."

"Dash?"

"Yes, we all have a birthdate, and then the date that we die. But it is the dash in the middle that actually means something about who we were, what we accomplished, our passion, values, character, and our dreams. You know, stuff like that."

"Hmm." He looks around the café. "And this is my dash?"

"Yes, this is your dash. But your dash just isn't all of this. It's much more also."

"How do you see more?" He kneels down next to me.

"Well, it's the way you take such good care of your mama. It's the way you treat your customers. It's the way you treat me. You are a good-hearted man with good values."

He smiles. "Thank you. That means a lot to me."

He kisses my lips once more, then my neck on one side, then the other side. My heart rate rises, and my body begins to radiate. He turns me to face him, as he is still kneeling before me. He begins to kiss me harder and harder. I feel his hand move slowly along my back, down to my waist. His fingers are caressing tenderly. I hold him close as well.

With dinner done, only our dishes are on the table. The next thing I know he is picking me up and sitting me on the table. The dishes go everywhere. Some even break. The eroticism is in full intensity. My body is begging for his next move, and his is yearning for mine. The next thing I know, we are making love right there in the middle of the café. With every touch, every kiss, every glance, my heart melts that much more.

Time goes by in a flash. Soon, it is daybreak, and the café needs to be opened. We need to clean up, so it looks like we weren't even there.

He cleans the kitchen to standards, and I clean the dining room. We finish just as the morning crew is beginning to arrive.

"Oh, no! Quick, follow me." He grabs my hand.

We whisk out the back into the kitchen, and then into another room off the kitchen that leads to a staircase.

"Where are we going?" I can't help but giggle, like we are school kids running from our parents.

"Shhh. I don't want them to see me. I am taking time off. If they see me, I will have to stay and work. I'm not ready for that yet." He takes me to the staircase. "Would you like some coffee?"

Our attention is taken from each other and directed toward

the employees coming in for the morning.

"Mmmm. It smells so good in here," says one of the chefs.

"It seems awfully late for Charlie to be cooking," a waitress says.

Charlie puts his hand over his mouth and holds back the laughter. I am forced to do the same, so we don't get caught.

"Umm, yes, I would," I reply. "I'm game for a cup of coffee."

"Wait here a minute and try to keep quiet," he whispers.

Charlie turns away from the stairway, and it looks like he sneaks back into the café kitchen for a moment. He returns with a bottle.

He holds it up. "Can't forget the hazelnut creamer!"

He thinks of everything. But where are we going?

As soon as we arrive at the top of the stairway, we come to a door. Charlie opens the old door that is missing paint and has lost all its splendor, and we arrive at another hallway. This one leads into what looks like an apartment over the café. Charlie goes in first and heads right to the kitchen. I follow slowly because I'm just not sure where we're.

"It's okay." He turns to go into the kitchen. "I live here."

I start to hear dishes clang as he begins to heat the water for coffee.

I decide to venture around and take a look at things, like the furniture, pictures on the wall, and knickknacks on the shelves. I notice a bed in the living room that looks like a hospital bed.

"Is that for ..."

"Yeah, that's for my mother. But she is not here anymore ..."

"I'm sorry to ask."

"Oh, no. She lives in a home for people with dementia and Alzheimer's. It's really okay. I can't take care of her the way I need to anymore. She needs closer care and I couldn't handle it if she were to get hurt."

He finishes the coffee cups and sits them down at the kitchen table, and I join him.

"I'm sorry, Charlie. My mother has already passed away, so I know it is really hard."

"I just feel like ... if I—"

"Wait. You couldn't do anything different. I couldn't either. I was at school when my mom had her car accident. I cried and cried because I should have been home. But I wasn't, and it happened. There wasn't anything I could have done differently. Same with you. You can't control her disease. You did not give it to her, either."

Charlie looks at me like he is finally understanding that the burden is not his to carry.

"But—"

"No buts. You are protecting her right now. And with her living where she is, that is the best protection she can get."

We talk for a little while longer, and then I decide to head home. After all, I am not used to pulling all-nighters, and this is the best all-nighter I could have had.

<hr />

After that night, Charlie and I are inseparable. We go everywhere together. Days turn into weeks and months. I feel like I've finally found my soulmate.

I need to take Charlie to meet Mildred.

Charlie is able to get coverage for the entire weekend. We arrive at Mildred's on Friday night, and Charlie stares in awe at the iron gates.

Oh, I remember that look of amazement. What a feeling.

I drive up to the huge white staircase that is met with white pillars. Alfred comes to meet us.

"Well, hello, Mary. Nice to see you again. And who is this?"

"This is Charlie," I say, with a big smile.

"Hi, I'm Charlie." He holds his hand out for Alfred to shake.

Alfred shakes his hand and gives me a smirk of approval.

"Miss Mildred is waiting for you in the gardens out back. I hope you are hungry, dear." He gives me a hug. "I will take your luggage to your room, as usual."

I give Alfred my car keys and grab Charlie's hand as we head up the staircase. When we get to the doorway, I open the grand entryway and we walk inside.

"Why is he getting our luggage?" Charlie says. "I could have carried it in."

"Alfred actually works here."

"What do you mean, *works here?*"

"Well, just watch this weekend."

We journey through the house to the sunroom, where Mildred is seated at her favorite table setting. The gardens outside are beautiful at half-light, and the sun is illuminating the flowers majestically. The table is already set for us.

I head over to Mildred and wrap my arms around her.

"Mildred!"

"Oh, chiiild, you came. And who is this fine fellow?" she says, even though she already knows all about him.

She knows the way he kisses me, the way he opens the door for me, the way he touches my heart.

"This is Charlie, Mildred." I move away to allow him to get closer to Mildred.

He reaches out for her.

"Now, sonny, come closer so I can see you."

He takes a few steps closer to Mildred, and she wraps her arms around him, like he is a long-lost son. Charlie kisses her on the cheek, and then the other, like the Europeans do.

A lady comes up with a tray, and dinner is to be served.

"Shall we eat?" Mildred says.

We all sit at the table.

"I'm sorry it's so late," I say, "but I had to work 'till five again. Traffic was heavy, but I'm glad I'm finally here."

"I just hope you don't mind eating so late, chiiild." Mildred puts some sugar into her tea. "It's a light, late-night dinner." She begins to squirm in her seat.

"Are you okay, Mildred?" Antoinette asks, as she approaches us from behind. "Is your hip hurting you again?"

"No, dear, I'm fine." Mildred seems unnerved that Antoinette is asking.

She doesn't like to seem weak.

"Well, hello again, Mary!" Antoinette puts her arms around my shoulders before I can properly get up.

Charlie is already up out of his chair, with his hand extended to Antoinette.

"I'm Charlie." He shakes her hand while kissing her cheeks, then sits back down.

He is family and doesn't even know it.

When I've come to see Mildred, Alfred, and Antoinette, I've told them all about him every chance I can. I am in love. They just play along with the game, like this is the first time they have ever seen or heard of him. It is fun, I must say.

We all sit and begin to eat the finger sandwiches that were prepared. Antoinette doesn't stay long at the table because she ate earlier. If Antoinette ate earlier, then so did Mildred. I guess she is eating just to be polite.

Charlie is looking around the room, and sees the grand piano adorned with photos of the children. He is intrigued. Mildred tells him of the children she taught in dance class. I just sit back and admire both of them.

I start daydreaming.

"Chiiild."

I am still not paying attention.

"Mary."

Oh, boy. She said my real name.

"Yes, ma'am."

"Would you mind going to see where Antoinette went?"

"Sure." I arise and I do as she asks.

"Besides, I would like to get to know Charlie."

Hmm. Should I be worried? I bet she is going to size him up to see if he is for real or not. I'm not worried about that. I know they both hold my heart close and will protect it at any cost.

I leave the sunroom, looking for Antoinette, and I run into Alfred.

"Well, how is it going in there?" he whispers.

"Why are you whispering?"

"You know how Miss Mildred is. She is probably drilling Mister Charlie right now to see if he is ... you know, the one."

"Yeah, that's what I'm sort of worried about. She sent me to find Antoinette."

"Uh-huh. Sure she did." He chuckles deep within his belly."

Alfred has a distinct laugh that is one of kind.

"She just wanted you out of the room. She is sly like that."

"But ..."

"It's okay. Just wait a few minutes, and then go in. We will see who won." He chuckles as he leaves.

Antoinette comes around the hallway. Ah, my job is done. Now I can go back into the room.

"Antoinette, Mildred asked me to come get you," I say.

We both go back into the room, and there they are. Charlie and Mildred are laughing hysterically.

Well, I guess no one got hurt. They both love each other.

Mildred plays it off when we enter the room and reaches for Antoinette so she can assist her to get up. Charlie jumps to the occasion and holds out his arm for Mildred to grab onto.

"Oh, what a perfect gentleman." She reaches for Charlie instead of Antoinette.

Charlie gracefully assists Mildred to her feet and to her walker.

"Are you stable?" he says.

"Why, yes, sonny. Whhhere—"

"My mom. I took care of my mom for many years." He sits back down in his chair. "She is in a nursing home now."

"Oh, sonny, I am so sorry to hear that." Mildred is getting situated to head out of the room and turns to me. "Chiiild, your room is still there, ready for you." Then she looks at Charlie "Sonny, you can follow Antoinette, and she will get you settled in for the night." She looks at me. "Is that okay?"

"I wouldn't have it any other way," Charlie says.

Mildred begins to leave. "Good, because that is the way it is until—"

"I know," I say. "We are not married. I wouldn't think of doing anything at all. Besides, Charlie is a perfect gentleman."

We all retire to our rooms. I go to my window and open the shutters, then sit and gaze out at the gardens, which are lit from the moonlight. My gaze is lifted up into the heavens, and I can feel my mother looking down at me.

"I know, Mom. I think he is the one, too."

I miss my mother.

The weekend goes by in a flash. Mildred and Charlie seem like old friends by the end. Even Alfred spent time with him.

Charlie spent a lot of time with the cooking and serving staff. He taught them a few dishes, and they taught him a few as well. He seems to have a renewed spirit for cooking.

I don't want to go home. I think Charlie feels the same. It was a welcomed mini vacation for him. He works incredibly hard.

It is Monday morning at work, and I just don't want to be there anymore. But life goes on, and I have to pay the bills, as my mother always said.

"So where did you go this weekend?" Lilly peeks around the corner of her office.

"Oh, nowhere."

"Did you go to Mildred's again?"

"Yep," I say, with a big smile.

"And what happened? Come on, Mary. My life is so boring. I need some excitement."

"Really? Since when is your life so boring that you need to hear about my exciting life?"

Here is Lilly, the life of the party, the beautiful one who can light up any room or catch everyone's eye on the dance floor. Now, she is trying to get excitement from my hum-drum life, which she says is going to turn me into that crazy cat lady. How ironic.

"Come on, enlighten me." She perches her head on her hand.

"Well ..."

"Mary!"

"I took Charlie to meet Mildred."

"You took Mister Wonderful to Mildred?" Her eyes are wide open. "And ..."

"They got along great. They love each other!" I can't contain myself any longer.

"Wow. This is like Charlie meeting your parents, kind of. Wow."

"Yeah, it was nice. It was like my two worlds have finally come together."

"Well, you guys have been dating for quite a while now, so it was fitting." She disappears around the corner to go to her own desk, then peeks around once more. "You know, your sista here approves." She laughs as she points to herself.

"Yeah, I know you're just jealous."

"Me, jealous? I have tons of men flocking all over me." She flings her braids around her shoulders like a diva, then goes back to her desk.

I am so eternally blessed to have Charlie in my life. And Mildred, who has stepped in as a mother figure for me. Life is good.

Charlie and I spend every day together that we can. With his mother in the nursing home, he spends a lot of him time between her and the café. But he still finds time for me, which I cherish so deeply.

Then I get that frantic phone call from him.

"Mary," he says, obviously sobbing.

"Charlie! What happened?"

All I hear are sobs coming from a grown man. This is not something I am accustomed to hearing. I didn't have a father around, and I only heard my mother cry like that when my father didn't come home.

"Charlie? You there?"

"Yes, I'm," *sniff, sniff,* "here," he says, trying to hold back the unmanly sounds.

"Charlie, what happened? Are you okay?"

"It's Mama." Then the tears come.
"Oh, no, Charlie. Where are you?"
"I'm at the nursing home."
"I'm on the way!" I hang up and jump into my car.

The drive isn't far to the nursing home. Charlie and I have been going there often, but he has been up there for the past few days. She hasn't been doing well, and I was kind of jealous, in a way. Charlie had a chance to talk to his mother and ... well, say his final goodbyes. My mother died after a car accident, and I didn't even know if she heard me. It's weird being jealous about that. But I am happy to know that he did have the opportunity.

As I pull into the nursing home, Charlie is standing outside the door, waiting for me. The nursing staff is doting over him and making sure he's going to be okay.

He runs out, wraps his arms around me, and cries and cries.

"Mama died," he says, between sobs.

I can't say or do anything but stand there and listen to him. With his arms still holding me tight, he pulls back so I can see into his swollen red eyes, just begging for me to love him. I now feel horrible for being jealous. How could I be so callous?

I am able to pull myself away enough to reach up to swish the tear-soaked hair out of his eyes. I try to wipe away the pain, but that is impossible

"Is there anything I can do?" I say.

"No." He shakes his head.

I look at the nurse. "Do we need to do anything?"

"No, we will handle everything here." She puts her hand on Charlie's shoulder. "You guys go home. But please be careful driving. Or you are more than welcome to sit in the chapel here, if you like."

Unsure of just how religious Charlie is, I wait for him to answer.

"No. I said my piece with God." He sounds upset with God.

I understand.

Charlie takes another look at the nursing home, knowing that this is the last time he is going to be spending long hours here. Then he turns to leave.

"I just want to go home," he says, disgusted.

As he is walking to his car, I start to get an uneasy feeling.

"Wait, you driving back?" I say.

"Yeah, I can't leave my car here."

"Hmm. Then you call me when you get home. Or I can follow you home."

"I will call you. I just need to go home."

I understand what Charlie is doing. He wants me. Needs me, too. But he also just wants to be alone to process all of this. I had to go through the same thing with my mom.

A few days have passed, and I know Charlie's mom's funeral is soon. I get a call from him.

"Mary." His voice is quiet, yet different.

"Hi, Charlie. How are you?"

"I'm okay. Just getting things ready for Mama's funeral, and I need a favor."

"Sure, Charlie. Anything you need."

"Do you remember the picture you drew of Mama in the café?"

"Ah, yes, I do."

"Can I have that, so I can frame it? I want to put it over the casket."

"Absolutely, Charlie. I'll frame it for you and bring it by today."

"Thank you, Mary. I love you."

Did I hear that right? He said *I love you*. Maybe he's just so delirious that he said it and didn't really mean to.

OMG! He said *I love you!*

Oh, stop it! Get ahold of yourself.

I frame the picture at the local gallery store and take the picture to Charlie's. He is going through old papers, and when he sees the framed sketch, he is both full of joy and heartache. I just sit back and allow him to go through whatever he needs to.

The funeral service is attended mostly by people from the café. Regulars who knew her, or knew of her, came to pay their respects. But not many people show up. Some neighbors, and the staff at the café come as well.

The flowers are overflowing. I even notice a bouquet from Mildred. That is very special.

⁂

The next two weeks are weird without Charlie. He is taking time off from ... well, everything and everybody. I allow him to mourn.

After the two weeks, Charlie asks me to go to Mildred's. Stunned by the thought, I am all for it. I know he has had a rough time and, and I think he needs to sit in the gardens. I want to see her, and I feel that Charlie needs the time away.

We arrive at Mildred's on the usual Friday after work. She is waiting for us, as always. Tea in the side garden, with some sort of finger food is the order. Laughter and cheer have been lacking and are welcomed. Things are getting back to normal again. Although, this time, Mildred is carrying something much more obvious now—an oxygen tank. The perfect makeup and hairstyles just don't do this oxygen tank, and hose running under her nose, any good. I don't mention it. I wouldn't dare to embarrass her.

With Charlie to my right, and Mildred to my left I, feel an awkwardness about the garden. I notice people standing behind me. Although it is normal, there seems to be a few more than usual.

"Mildred, there is something I would like to ask," Charlie says.

"Yes, sonny."

"Oh, Mildred, not to you." He turns to face me, as he still looks in Mildred's eyes. "I need to ask, Mary." He slides off his chair and down on one knee.

He reaches inside his coat pocket and pulls out a box. My heart races, and my hands begin to sweat.

"Oh, sonny, you want to speak to Mary." Mildred chuckles.

Charlie's eyes are beaming with love, and his hair is wild, as usual, as he kneels before me.

"Mary, you have made me the happiest man alive. You taught me that true love still exists. Your beauty is radiant."

I am beaming and trying so hard to listen to his every word, but it is hard.

"Since I met you, I found my passion in cooking once more. I love the beauty in your drawings. You are so talented. When I am away from you, my heart aches. I can't stand being away from you any longer."

He opens the box to reveal a beautiful diamond ring. My heart skips a beat. Charlie holds the box out to me, with the ring pointing in my direction. I can't contain my excitement any longer. My eyes begin to well, blurring my vision. I can't blink. If I blink, the tears will fall.

My gaze is fixed on him, making everything else disappear from the garden.

"Mary?"

"Uh-huh."

"Will you walk through life with me, beside me, and love me for the rest of our lives together?"

Will I? Really? He is asking, *Will I?*

My heart is in my throat, and I try to speak. Nothing comes out as I grab my chest, trying to breathe. How can I say yes when he didn't ask for permission first?

I look down at the ring, and then down at the gray stone pavers under the tabletop and chairs.

"I can't."

"You can't?"

"You didn't ask permission."

"Umm, chiiild," Mildred points her boney finger in the air like she is bidding on an antique at an auction, "he already did."

I feel restored.

From behind, I hear, "Mary."

It's Alfred.

"Charlie came here several times to speak to Mildred. He asked then. I was there!"

I look over at Mildred, with tears forming once more.

"He did?" I ask Mildred.

Her face is beaming with joy, and she also has tears forming in her eyes.

"Yes, chiiild. He most certainly did."

"Since your mother died," Charlie says, "I didn't know whose blessing to ask. But Mildred is next in line. "Well, what is your answer now?"

"Yes!"

The garden rings out in cheers. I jump because I have no idea just how many people are standing behind me. Alfred, Antoinette, as well as all the household staff, are there.

Charlie's arms, flailing in the night air, swing around me, and he picks me up and twirls me. Mildred sits in her chair, clapping in approval. The rest of the gang is all clapping and yelling congratulations. One by one, they all congratulate me, and then head back off to work.

When everything is somewhat calmed down, Mildred says, "Chiiild, I have one request."

"Anything," Charlie says for me.

"I would like for you two ..." her pauses were more prevalent due to her failing health, " ... to have the wedding here, in my gardens." She waves her hand around to indicate the gardens.

Charlie and I look into each other's eyes, and reply, "Yes!"

◈

That Monday comes too quickly, but I am eager to show off the new ring on my finger to Lilly. I am so excited, and Lilly is, too. She is going to be my maid of honor.

Charlie and I travel back and forth to Mildred's every moment that we can. Planning for the wedding is tiresome but exciting. From the gown to the color of the napkins, the details are staggering. Mildred is there for every step of the way, and she has staff waiting on me, hand and foot, throughout the process. She keeps saying to spare no expense and do this up right.

She has ice sculptures being made; flowers planted in newly dug gardens. Pergolas built next to the ponds, over the decks, are full of splendor. She even has new marble sculptures placed in the gardens, next to the pond where ducks swim. Her gardens are heavenly. I find myself hiding in them at times, with my sketchbook, drawing the newly decorated grounds.

It is hard to go to work during the week. And I know it's hard for Charlie as well.

The wedding is approaching quickly, but work is a task I must if I'm going to have some kind of normalcy. Besides, I do need to pay my bills. Oh yeah, I do have bills still, even though I have my parents' money.

While sitting at my desk, trying to keep my mind on work, my phone rings. The wedding is just two weeks away, and things still need to be put in place, so the phone call isn't a surprise. Mildred or Antoinette call daily.

"Mary?" It's Charlie, and his voice sounds different.

"Oh, hey, Charlie. I'm almost done for the day."

"Mary, stop a minute."

I focus on my ring. "Okay, Charlie, what's up?"

"Mary ... Mary, it is Mildred."

I feel like I just jumped off a huge cliff, and my body is falling into a deep fog bank far down a mountain range.

"What?" I say. "What is Mildred?"

"Mary, Mildred ..."

"Mary, what is going on?" Lilly says.

My face is as white as a ghost, and my breathing is basically nonexistent. I have the phone up to my ear, but I can't hear anything.

"Mary, what's wrong?" Lilly says.

I can't say or do anything. I have the phone in my hand, but it is moving away from my ear. My gaze is fixated on Lilly, and I'm in complete shock.

She grabs the phone away from me and puts it to her head. "This is Lilly. Can I help you?" She waits for a response. "Oh, hi, Charlie," she says, while looking at me.

There are a lot of, uh-huhs, yes's, and okays, before she hangs up. With each word spoken, her voice changes. I know something is terribly wrong. I am still in shock.

She looks at me. "Charlie is on his way."

Charlie comes to pick me up from work, and we head to Mildred's house in complete silence. The gates were already open. Everyone is running around frantically.

I bolt up the front steps so fast, I'm not even sure how many steps I actually touch. I rush out into the sunroom, where my flowers are all ready, as well as the place settings that are on display to instruct the workers on how the wedding is supposed to be set up. They have been busy, and it shows.

I walk around the manor in a daze. People are stopping me to ask if there is anything they can do for me, but I don't even hear them. I just see their mouths moving, and nothing, not even a squeak, is registering in my jumbled mind. I keep walking around, looking for Mildred to pop out from the corner, but she isn't there.

I find myself moving out through the kitchen area, and outside into the gardens. I go over by the docks, next to the pond, under the pergola. And then it happens.

I realize she is gone!

I fall to my knees and scream. I can't stop the frantic cries. I gasp for air, but the air is so heavy. My lungs are filled with the scents of jasmine, and all the other flowers in the air, but it doesn't matter. I may as well have been breathing hot asphalt.

The lady that I have come to love so dear—The Bird Lady—is gone. I knew from the moment I met her, at four years old, that we were meant to be a pair.

Our wedding is two weeks away, and she isn't going to be there. I need her there!

I feel the presence of the entire house weeping with me and for me in the shadows of the manor and gardens. My world has crumbled.

I feel a hand on my shoulder.

"We all loved her dearly," Antoinette says, between tears.

"She will be missed," Alfred says. "I can't stop crying."

"We are all family." Charlie touches my other shoulder with a sense of protection.

We all cry, laugh with happy memories, and try to console each other throughout the night. I get to know many of her staff, and they tell me their stories of how they met Mildred, and what she meant to them. I feel sorrow for every one of them. They all worked for Mildred. Some lived in the manor, like Alfred and his family, as well as Antoinette. Their stories bring back memories of the first time we met.

Then I feel a twinge of panic.

"What about the wedding?" I say, between sobs. "I'm going to cancel it."

"We have to have the wedding here!" Alfred says. "Miss Mildred would not want it any other way."

Each person gives their approval on continuing with the wedding at the manor. Mildred would have insisted it be at the manor, and I am going to honor that.

"We also have a memorial service to plan," I say.

"Miss Mildred already has all her arrangements in order," Antoinette says. "That was part of my job,"

Everyone is relieved that Antoinette has everything under control, but it doesn't take away the pain.

⁂

I take off the next couple weeks to not only plan my wedding, but to also grieve Mildred's passing. I just can't go back to work.

Mildred's memorial service is huge. She was family to everyone. It seems like the entire city was there, along with the art community, the school board, former students and their families, and the workers, all dressed in their finest attire. Who would have thought that a lonely woman who sat in a park and fed the birds had so many friends that loved her like family?

I can't stop thinking about all those years, when strangers would mock her and call her names.

The manor is decorated in its finest glory, not only because of the memorial service, but also the wedding coming next weekend. A wedding I am happy and grateful to have, but that makes me sad because my dearest friend won't be there.

d

The wedding comes and goes so quickly. It's hard to smile without Mildred there, but I feel her spirit right beside me.

All the staff attend the wedding, just as I want, and it makes me feel like my family is huge and warming. Charlie needs the extra support as well since his mother is gone, too.

Lilly is like a bright penny, with her dress that sways in the wind, and her braids pulled up in perfection. She smiles from ear to ear as Charlie and I say our vows.

Charlie's best man is his chef, who has taken a liking to Lilly. I think they are going to make a great couple. I just need to get Lilly to settle down long enough to look into his dreamy eyes.

❦

After the honeymoon, Charlie and I are sitting at Mildred's, in the sunroom, and Antoinette comes in.

"Miss Mary, you have a visitor."

"I do?"

"Yes, ma'am." And she leaves the room.

I go to the door to see a man in a suit, with a briefcase. He tells me he has documents for me to sign.

We go into the sunroom to sit and discuss what he wants me to sign. Charlie is right there beside me. Looking over the documents, I begin to understand the importance of my friendship with Mildred. I was her angel. She was mine.

I'm not even sure what all I am signing, but the man ends up leaving me with a mound of paperwork, along with a sealed white envelope. When he hands it to me, he gives me strict instructions not to open it unless I am alone. I look down at the envelope in confusion, and before he leaves, he tells me again, not to open it unless I am alone. They were strict instructions from Mildred.

I decide to go for a walk to clear my head.

It takes me a few days ... well, possibly weeks to open the envelope. I am afraid to. I feel like it makes Mildred's absence too real, too permanent.

I decide to go to my familiar friends at the park so they can give me strength to open the letter.

Dear Mary,

I am sorry that you are reading this letter, but I have been writing it for quite some time. No one knows of this letter except you and my lawyer. He has the only copy.

My Child, when I met you, you were such a little, naïve, beautiful girl. I sat upon the park bench in such terrible pain, talking to God, pleading for my husband to come back to me. He was my only friend. Sure, everyone at the manor is a friend, but I pay them to be. Alfred may be close to me, but you are so different. I asked God that if I could not have my dear husband back, then send me an angel. And then, you were there.

I have seen you grow up and develop the most extravagant qualities in a person who I honestly admire. When all was against you in school, I saw you persevere. So many classmates were against you talking to me. They mocked you and called me names. They did horrible things to you when you just tried to be a friend to me. You stood up to them. You stood your ground. You became brave.

Regarding your mother, when we first met, she saw me as many others saw me. I was a disheveled lady feeding the birds in the park. Therefore, I must have lived in the park, making me homeless. I never tried to correct your mother's thoughts of me. I saw you overcome someone else's thought and wrongdoings to find the truth. And this you did. For this, you gained the integrity for truth and justice.

I have seen you grow from being a small headstrong child to a beautiful young lady full of life. You learned from me things that I wanted to teach my own daughter. As time passed, I thought of you as my daughter. I gave you a locket necklace, just as my husband gave to me to ensure your return. Over time, you have returned, still with the locket placed securely around your neck for safekeeping. It is just as if you were guarding my heart. With this, you displayed honesty.

When your mother died, you didn't see me, but I was there with you. When you were hurt in school, you didn't see me, but I was there with you. When you walk down the aisle on your wedding day, you won't see me, but I am there for you. When you have your first child, you won't see me, but I will be there for you. All you need to do is hold the locket close to your heart, and I will be there, just as you were there when I buried my husband, and for many years afterward.

You taught me that life was still worth living. Dreams can still be achieved. My dash has been fulfilled. My Child, you were the last and final part of my dash. My dash has been completed.

I have seen your dash become ever more meaningful with each passing day.

Now, the meaning of this letter is two-fold. One, so you know just how much of an angel you have become to me over the years. And, two, to act as a letter of instruction, to be completed by my lawyer once you read this letter.

The manor has been turned over to you, my child. The staff comes with the manor, for its upkeep and maintenance. Their salaries have been covered for at least ten years. I know Antoinette is not really needed as a nurse. However, she is excellent at keeping the daily functions in order. Alfred is wonderful maintaining the land, as well as the manor. He understands what is needed for daily functions.

The Art Museum has been donated to the city. It is still under the control of the corporation, which the lawyer can assist you with. Classes must be maintained in categories. However, you have one entire wing that has been dedicated solely to your artwork. I expect your pictures to be displayed in frames under glass, to fulfill a dream of yours.

I do have one last request: I want the halls to be filled with the laughter of children. The children of our lives are the future of existence. Assist them in finding their dreams and achieving their passion in life. Maybe even one or two of those children may be yours. I entrust everything I have to you, my Child.

With love,

Mildred, The Bird Lady

The next day, I want to sit and talk to Mildred for a while, so I decide to go to her gravesite. I cut an arrangement from her gardens, which I know she would have loved.

It is hard to sit there all alone. The wind is blowing softly, and the treetops are dancing, as if for Mildred's spirit. After pushing back the leaves and debris off the bottom part of the headstone, I am able to open the flower door so I can put the vase into the headstone to display the beautiful colors. After the flowers are in place for all to see, I find myself touching the top of the headstone. My fingers caress the indentation of the lettering. I begin to trace her name with my finger.

I am not sure if I'm happy to be here with her, or sad because she isn't here for me to cry on her shoulder. I know that she is up in heaven watching me, and I don't want her to know just how sad I am.

And then it hits me—the dates on the headstone.

I brush my hand over Mildred's dates, and then her husband's dates, who died many years ago before her. The dates are insignificant, but the dash is the important part.

I reflect upon Mildred's dash—well, at least the short time that I have known her. She had lived such a wonderful life, even before I met her.

"Thank you for teaching me about my dash," I whisper.

A cool rush of air dances through the cemetery. I feel the chill upon my face. I think she hears me. The hairs on the back of my neck stand at attention and I feel goosebumps forming on my arms.

Feeling confident that she is here in spirit, I say, "I promise to make my dash count as well."

Our afternoon visit is complete. I want to go visit our other family. You know, the birds. So off to the park I go.

Some time has passed since I read Mildred's graciously written letter. I find myself sitting on the side of the park bench, which I had replaced by a new one with a plaque on the back of it. It states:

In Loving Memory,
Harold and Mildred (The Bird Lady)

CHAPTER 11

NOT QUITE A YEAR HAS PASSED. I find myself coming to the park often. I begin to look back on my life. This very park bench is the spot where I met Mildred. I was only four years old, but I was a feisty girl.

Charlie opened up a café next to the art studio, but he keeps his other one in his hometown. Lilly and Charlie's head chef started running it together after they got married. Lilly has a baby on the way.

I am the new owner of the manor, where Mildred has paid for the staff to stay on for life. Some of the staff actually work for Charlie at the new café called Mildred's Tea House.

My drawings are now featured in the Art Museum, in the wing called Mildred, A Lady and Her Birds. Mildred is the only subject of the drawings, with many portraits of her birds. Each sketch is placed under glass encasement and hung with precision. It is an honor to be featured. Oh, how I wish my teachers could see me now. I know my mother is looking down on me with a half-smile, pleased with what I have accomplished.

I no longer work in the outskirts of the city. Charlie and I live in the manor. No one lost their jobs. It is as if Mildred is still there.

I have found my passion. My dreams are fulfilled. I married the love of my life, my best friend. My art is featured in a gallery. And yep, I am still alive. My mother always said I would not have any art displayed, or become famous, until I die. Yeah, I got that one beat.

I glance down at my stomach, rubbing it, caressing it. See, I am pregnant, too. I'm going to go tell Charlie the great news. I know Mildred is happy. I feel it in my soul. If it is a girl, I know I'm going to name her Mildred. I can't help but cry tears of joy, which makes my mascara run all over my face.

A small girl comes up to me and wants to sit with me. I am feeding the birds, as I have been doing for the past several years. It's sprinkling, and my hair is wet. To top it off, the mascara adds a touch that even I can do without.

Although the weather is bad, the young girl doesn't seem to mind much. She just wants to sit and talk with me. She is intrigued by the birds. She is a cute little girl, maybe four or five. Her long blonde hair is obviously dirty from playing in the muddy park. Her clothes are mud-filled, as well.

"Are thems your birds?" she says, with a bright smile from ear to ear.

"No, they are my friends. I just take care of them now."

"Why?"

"My friend is no longer with us to take care of them. So I take care of them for her."

She points down at one. "He's cute!"

She giggles and starts to play with her hair. A childish gesture, but so cute, I can't help but smile.

"Get away from her!" A lady runs up to grab the unsuspecting youngster off the park bench.

"But, Mommy!"

"But nothing! She is a stranger," she yells, dragging the child away by her arm.

The child is wailing with tears of confusion.

"I mean the child no harm," I say to the mother.

"Stay away from that woman!" she yells once more.

They disappear into the park, never to be seen again by me.

All of a sudden, I realize the irony of the situation. I appeared to be some homeless lady in the park, feeding the birds, just as my mom saw.

She saw Mildred, The Bird Lady.
Oh, wait! She saw me. I am The Bird Lady!
A smile comes from the depths of my soul. My dash is full of wealth.

ABOUT THE AUTHOR

ROSE JONES, who was raised in snowy northern Ohio, has found her heart-home in the coastal life of Wilmington, North Carolina and her passion in writing.

With her husband Seby "Chip" Jones, Rose works to help people recover from addiction and serves as a mentor to teens and preteens regarding addiction.

She loves animals, including her cats Sadie, Joey, and Kelly; her Chinese Crested Powderpuff dogs Molly and Maddie; and her miniature Poodle Lilly.

Rose developed her interest in writing while in college at the Cape Fear Community College, where she completed an Associates in Arts and at the University of North Carolina of Pembroke with a degree in Sociology.

The author is currently working on her next book about enduring love on a 19th-century plantation.

Connect with Rose:
rosejones.author@gmail.com
Facebook: Author Rose Marie Jones
Instagram: Rosejones8681
Twitter: @authorRMJones1

YOU MIGHT ALSO ENJOY

The Particular Appeal of Gillian Pugsley
Susan Örnbratt

Family Weave
Lee Sowder